SAPPHIRE

Midnight Oasis - Book Two

JILL SHANNON

Published by Blushing Books
An Imprint of
ABCD Graphics and Design, Inc.
A Virginia Corporation
977 Seminole Trail #233
Charlottesville, VA 22901

Jill Shannon
Sapphire

EBook ISBN: 978-1-68259-949-5
Print ISBN: 978-1-64563-603-8
v2

Chapter 1

Madison stood holding the maid of honor dress she had agreed to wear for Sadie and Cameron's wedding. She couldn't believe how fast the time had passed. It seemed like yesterday they announced their engagement.

Isabella came into the dressing room carrying a similar looking dress, as they were both Sadie's maids of honor. However, Sadie didn't want them in the same dress, so they were here, trying to decide.

"I kind of like the one you're holding," Isabella said.

"Here you try it on." Madison handed her the dress. "Can you believe the wedding is a month away?" she shouted when Isabella closed the dressing room door.

"I know. They say time goes faster as you get older." Isabella came out with the dress on, laughing.

"Wow, that really looks good on you, it's a good color too." Madison turned her towards the mirror.

"It does look nice, if I do say so." Isabella turned to the left, the right, then all the way around, to see the back.

"They'll have to hem it a little, but if you don't mind I'd like this one?"

Madison looked over her shoulder in the mirror. "I think you should wear it; it really does look better on you." The gown was a satin sapphire blue, thick sash halter dress, leaving her shoulders exposed. It was gathered in the waist to one side, held by a silver clasp designed like angel wings. The bottom flowed to the floor with a small train in the back.

The dress hugged her curves in all the right places. "Sadie said to just buy what we liked, and Matthew from costume design will do the alterations we need. Cameron set up an account for us for anything we need."

"Shoes included?" Isabella asked with glee in her eyes.

"Yes, even shoes!" Madison confirmed.

"Do you think Cameron's brother will be at the wedding?" Isabella shouted from the dressing room.

Madison hoped he wouldn't, but wasn't too confident he wasn't coming. "I don't know. Sadie hasn't said whether or not he sent back the response card they sent with his invitation." Every day Madison prayed he wouldn't be there.

She and Dimitri had been together since the launch of the *Onyx*, but with the launch of the *Sapphire* a month away, she hadn't seen much of him and when she did, he just dragged himself into bed.

She was starting to think he was losing interest with her, they hardly played anymore, and when he wasn't working, he was catching up with his friends. She had been feeling very neglected lately, and with her past relationship with Xavier hanging in the balance, it was better if she didn't see him.

Isabella came out of the dressing room again, "Hey where'd you go, I was asking you if Dimitri has hinted about a collaring ceremony for you and him on the ship?"

Madison stared blankly at her. "Hey, what's the matter?" Isabella went to her, holding both her hands.

"I don't know, it's just that he's been so distant lately. I think instead of a collaring ceremony, he's going to end our contract." A single tear slid down her cheek.

Isabella wiped it away. "Madison, he's just really busy. Caleb comes home and does the same thing I'm sure."

"Okay, does Caleb fall asleep when you're talking to him in bed?"

"Well, we don't talk much in bed, but when we have, no, he's stayed awake." Isabella hesitated. "But I'm sure all that will change after the launch."

"You know if it wasn't for the wedding being planned for the ship, I would not go." Madison sounded so sad.

"You have to go. You can't let his work get in the way. You'll have his total attention when we're underway."

"Well, of course I'm going, I wouldn't miss Sadie's wedding. I just think I might book my own cabin with Melanie. Nothing like being prepared. Besides it's either do that or bunk with you, and I don't think Caleb would be on board with that."

"I think you're seeing something that's not there, but you do what you have to."

They left the store, bags full to the brim with what they would need for the wedding. Madison dropped Isabella at her apartment then headed home feeling a little better after talking to her.

When she got there, she carried her bags in and threw them on the couch. She called for Dimitri, but got no answer. She headed to the answering machine and pressed play.

The first message was from the dress shop, reminding her that they could do the alterations on the dress. Delete. The next message was from her sister telling her that her father was in town. "Big deal," Madison muttered under her breath. Delete.

The last message had her holding her breath, it was from

Xavier. "You refused to talk to me on the ship, and now you've blocked my number from your cell phone. We need to talk eventually. I've missed you Amber, please call me."

She stood and stared blankly at the answering machine. Then she thought, "What if Dimitri heard this message, and left?" She headed to the bedroom to look for his stuff. Thankfully it was all still there. She raced back into the other room to erase the message.

Madison was in the process of pushing delete when Dimitri walked in the apartment. "Who called?" he questioned as she pressed the delete button.

"Just some newspaper looking for an interview."

"Why did you delete it, we can use all the publicity we can get, and if it's free, that's the best kind." He smiled, giving her a kiss on the cheek.

"Oh, sorry. I thought Melanie had set up all your interviews for the launch."

"She did, but the more the merrier." He put his stuff down on the couch and headed back towards her, scooping her up in his arms. "We are just about a month away from the launch. I don't remember being this nervous with the last one."

"Maybe because last time, Cameron took some of the edge off by helping. Remember, he did all the ground work so he wouldn't run into Sadie."

"Oh, yeah that's right. I did forget that. He has helped, but not as much as the last time. He's too preoccupied with his bride-to-be."

"Can you blame him? It's exciting getting married, so I'm told."

"Well, they can keep it, I'm just fine being a Master to my sub. Don't you agree?" Dimitri questioned, placing her on the ground.

"I guess so." Madison's response was close to a whisper.

"No rings and collars for us, we know who we are, Right?"

With every question Dimitri asked, Madison retreated a little more within herself. "Yes, you are correct, Master." She reached for her bag and keys.

"Where are you going?"

"I have to meet Isabella to go over wedding stuff. I'll be home late so don't wait up. I'm sure you're tired." She stood were she was as he bent to kiss her goodbye.

"Say hello for me." Then turning on his heel, he waved over his shoulder as he walked down the hall to the bedroom.

Madison sat in her car, her phone in her hand looking at the *Sapphire*. It really was a beautiful ship, similar to the *Onyx*, but the colors were all in blues and grays.

She looked at her phone in her hand. If she didn't call him, he could call the apartment and leave another message, and she couldn't have that. She dialed Xavier's number.

"Hello, beautiful. I knew I'd be hearing from you. Still haven't said anything to Dimitri about me have you?"

"No, and I plan on keeping it that way. You have to stop this, there is nothing between us, and there never will be."

"That's where you're wrong, Amber. I would have never let you go if I had known what was happening. Where are you? I will meet you."

Madison knew he wasn't going to go away until he saw that she had moved on, and she was with Dimitri. "Fine, I'm at the docks by the *Sapphire*, and Xavier, it's Madison now."

"I'll be there in ten minutes, don't go anywhere." Then the phone went dead.

Madison looked around the area. Usually it was busy with activity, but it was a Sunday and everyone but security had the day off. That reminded her. "Stay away from the cameras."

Xavier pulled up next to Madison's car, and joined her in it. "You look the same, yet different. I mean, your hair is longer, and a different color, but there's a maturity in your face that wasn't there when we were together. It suits you."

"Xavier, we can't do this. We weren't right then, and I can't imagine us being good now. Why can't you just let me go?" As much as the words were coming out of her mouth, he knew there was no conviction behind them.

"Because deep down you know I'm right. We had a few bumps in our relationship, but nothing we couldn't have worked through. You just disappeared." There was a pleading look in his clear blue eyes.

Madison started to panic; she didn't know how to answer him. There were things in her past no one knew about and Madison wanted to keep it that way. Hearing the plea in his request pulled at her heart, though. The timbre of his voice vibrated through her, making her wet. She needed to concentrate or she'd be in deep shit. She couldn't hurt Dimitri.

She shook those thoughts off. "Things have been hectic with the launch of the new ship, then the planning for the wedding. No one has had time for anything," she lied with a straight face.

"There is always time for the person you love," Xavier said as he brushed some hair from her face, cradling her cheek in his palm.

She leaned into the warmth of his hand, remembering a time when she craved his touch all over her body.

"You still remember my touch; I can feel it." He captured her lips. Coaxing them open, he deepened the kiss.

She responded just like he knew she would. She was everything he had hoped to find in his perfect mate, but she had disappeared from his life in the blink of an eye, and he planned on getting her back. No matter what it took.

Dimitri had waited for Madison to leave the garage before he climbed into his black Mercedes SLK550. Then he followed her to the dock.

He watched as an Audi R8 Spyder pulled up. He saw Xavier Legend get out, then climb into the passenger seat of Madison's car. His anger grew with every lie he caught her in. He had heard Xavier's message but had left it to see what Madison or Amber would do with it. Amber, that was the name Ryan had called her.

From where he sat he couldn't see what was happening in her car, her tinted windows didn't help either. He sat there for almost thirty minutes before the passenger door opened and Xavier got out.

Dimitri liked Xavier, Cameron had introduced them on the launch of the *Onyx* and he had ended up going to lunch with them. The conversation had covered a wide range of topics, and then it hit on the upcoming launch, and with that the wedding.

"Dimitri is going to be my best man, but Sadie has asked both Madison and Isabella to be her maid of honors, so I guess I need two best men, you up for the job?"

"To walk down the aisle with Madison. Hell yeah!" The words were out of Xavier's mouth before he could stop them. "Sorry, dude, but she's hot," he said quickly to cover his admission.

"I get it. Don't think I don't know what I have!" Dimitri countered. He looked at Xavier as if seeing him for the first time. He had a military cut hairstyle, a chiseled jaw, with thick brown eyebrows that covered crystal blue eyes. His olive skin gave him a Mediterranean look.

His shoulders were wide, his arms bulged with muscles, and around both biceps he had tattoos wrapping around them. He imagined he had a six-pack under his shirt. His gaze had traveled further catching a look at the bulge in his pants, and as he raised his eyes he caught Xavier looking at him as well.

Dimitri had never been attracted to men before, but there was something about Cameron's brother that affected him. Dimitri hid his growing erection not knowing how to deal with the feelings he was having. He had had a similar feeling when they had met on the cruise. He had excused himself from lunch and had not seen Xavier since.

Now, he watched him adjust the bulge in his pants before closing the door and getting back into his own car. He wasn't sure if he was mad at Madison for meeting Xavier behind his back, or for Xavier having the same effect on him?

Dimitri knew there was something missing from his relationship with Madison. Things had changed after Xavier came into their life, but now sitting in the car, an idea was forming. He figured it could be a win for everyone. He just wasn't sure if he could really follow through on it. Sharing Madison would take a lot of getting used to, but if that's what it took to keep her, he would.

Dimitri watched until both cars had left before he started his car, and headed towards Cameron's penthouse. He knew if anyone could convince him this was right, it would be Cameron.

Chapter 2

Madison stood holding a bouquet of white roses and blue irises. The flowers matched the sapphire color of the strapless gown she wore. Her long brunette hair was piled high on her head. Her red highlights noticeable in her curls. Her smoky blue make-up accented her green eyes. Being tall to begin with, she chose a smaller heel for her dyed blue shoes. A string of pearls adorned her neck and a matching set of earrings completed her appearance.

She stood waiting for Isabella to turn and look at her, the signal that it was time to begin walking down the aisle into the *Sapphire's* dining room, the newest ship added to the Midnight Oasis Cruise Line. Marco and his crew had transformed it into a beautiful chapel for Sadie and Cameron.

The early morning wedding had been planned right down to the minute. The tables had all been removed. The chairs lined the center aisle ending at the lattice archway filled with blue and white flowers. The minister stood in the center waiting for the attendants to be in position before the bride made her way to it on the arm of her dad.

Madison smiled, looking towards the bride's side of the room. Sadie's parents, although open minded people, didn't know anything about the BDSM lifestyle, and she sure as hell didn't want them finding out about it at her wedding. That's why the Dungeon Arena which held all the equipment used during scenes was turned into a beautiful buffet area for the brunch that would follow the wedding.

After Sadie's family and relatives left the ship, the crew would have all of the equipment back in place before the passengers began arriving for the evening departure. The early hour of the wedding was planned to allow the crew to attend.

When Madison turned to the groom's side, she saw quite a few familiar faces. Many that had sailed on the *Onyx*. The *Onyx's* captain being one of them.

Gabriel the entertainment producer and his partner Logan were there. As well as Greyson, who was now part of security team on the *Sapphire* and a beautifully glowing Payton. Nicholas had that proud father look on his face as he smiled at her from his spot with the groomsmen. The captain of the *Sapphire*, Captain Russell, and a few of his crew members filled the back row.

Madison's eyes locked with Maximillian Greco. "Max" to his friends, he was seated with Raynor and Mason. Madison had hired Max to help her get the money her grandmother had left in trust for her.

While Madison had told Sadie and Isabella the version she always told people as to what happened with her mom, brother, and sister, she had told Maximillian the true story. But now was not the time to be thinking of the past. She needed to focus on the here and now.

In the front sat Cameron's grandmother Constance. Next to her was Harley, next to him sat Emmett Legend, Xavier's father. What a small world Constance lived in. Her life had gone full circle. Emmett had been her first real love, and a part of her secretive past. Who would have ever guessed that Xavier and Cameron were half-brothers? Only a few of those close to Sadie and Cameron knew of that secret.

Madison put a smile on her face and began her slow procession down the center aisle towards the altar. Stopping next to Isabella, she turned to see Sadie move into position. She looked stunning in her Allure bridal gown. The tight strapless champagne bodice was inlaid with sparkling diamonds, which led down to the textured ruffle ball gown. Her hair was wrapped with a diamond tiara and her veil fell to her waist with diamonds interwoven into the design. Around her neck she wore the angel wing collar Cameron had placed on her neck, at the ceremony that really mattered to them. The day he had become her Master, and hers alone.

———

Madison remembered the first time she had ever dreamed of her own wedding. She had been thirteen and her name had been Amber. One of the members of her church had gotten married right after service one Sunday. The congregation had been invited to stay.

Amber had looked across the aisle right into the eyes of Brian Boxwood. He was older than her by four years, closer to her brother's age, and every girl in school was in love with him. He was that all-American boy, went to church on Sunday, played baseball and was the quarterback on the school football team.

Amber had developed early for her age, and suddenly all the boys were interested in her, and all the girls hated her. Brian had been one of them. Amber had really thought that he had liked her. As she sat and listened to the bride and groom profess their love for each other, she pictured her and

Brian standing there. For two years Amber, ducked and dodged every roaming and groping hand, till Brian finally asked her to the Banquet Dance at school.

Her brother and father had been opposed to it, but her mother pointed out that she was growing up and it would be a good experience for her. After all, Brian had been from a very prominent family, and anything her mother could do to rub elbows with the wealthy families in the area she was all for it. Her sister just thought it was so romantic that the hottest boy in school was going out with her sister. All her friends had been so jealous of her.

Brian had picked her up in his Mustang convertible. She had worn a simple pink spaghetti strap sun dress. Brian had bought her a wristlet made of red roses and baby's breath. He had held the door for her to get in, and Amber thought the night was starting out how she had always dreamed it would.

She had been so nervous, but Brian had reached over and placed his hand on her knee and told her to just relax and enjoy herself for the night. On the drive she remembered that they had talked about different kids from school, where they had wanted to go to college, and by the time they reached the dance, Amber had felt relieved that they could talk so easily.

They had found a table and, little by little, it filled up with other teammates and their dates. Most of the guys had treated her like she was one of them. The girls however were harder. Amber tried to get into one of their conversations about different music, but when she interjected her opinion, they just looked at her, then continued on like she hadn't even spoken. She stopped trying after that.

Brian had brought her some punch, and then asked her to dance. They had danced to three straight up-beat songs, so when she got back to the table she had downed her punch.

She'd taken some time to go to the ladies' room. When she got back, the music had slowed down, and all the couples from the table were on the floor.

Brian extended his hand and she went willingly. All of her fantasies were happening. He held his arms open and she walked in reaching for his left hand, while placing her other hand tentatively on his shoulder. He rolled her wrist holding it to his chest, pulling her up against his body as his hand rested on the small of her back.

He gazed down into her adoring eyes. She thought for sure he was going to kiss her. His head began to descend towards her lips. But at the last second turned and brushed his lips over her ear. "Have I told you, you look beautiful tonight?"

He leaned back to look at her; the blush she felt in her face followed his eyes down her body. "You look beautiful too." Amber heard the words coming out of her mouth as her brain was screaming at her. He looks beautiful too. You should have said handsome, you're such an idiot. That's the best answer you can come up with? If you act like a kid, he's going to dump you.

"I meant handsome, you look very handsome tonight," Amber quickly corrected herself.

He smiled down at her, moving his hand up her back rubbing his fingers against the wide strap of her bra. "I have something special planned for later, I think you'll really like it."

"Are you going to give me any clues?" She leaned forward so she wouldn't have to shout, pushing her breasts against his chest.

She caught his intake of breath before he responded, "And ruin the surprise? No way. You'll just have to wait."

The next song was also a slow beat. Brain took both of Amber's hands and wrapped them around his neck. "Keep your hands wrapped around my neck and don't let go." It was the first command Amber had ever received and she answered with her full attention.

With her arms pulled up, it gave Brian free rein over her body. He gazed into her eyes as his thumbs brushed against the outside of her breast. Sliding them up and down, creating a yearning deep in Amber's stomach. He leaned back just enough for his thumbs to brush against her pebbled nipples. Never in her life had she ever felt the sensations her body was feeling. So far, this surpassed any fantasy she had ever had of him. She couldn't have ever imagined that he cared about her this much.

He was gyrating his hips into hers, to the slow rhythmic sound coming from the D.J.'s speakers. He moved both hands down, cupping each cheek of her ass in his hands, He squeezed, then pinched, slapped, and rubbed, soothing the sting she had felt. She wasn't sure what had just happened. At first it had hurt but then, as he rubbed the pain, it turned into a totally different feeling, one that made her panties wet.

She started to pull away, but he leaned into her ear. "Don't be nervous, Amber, I'll take care of you." He had kissed her down her exposed neck to the crook of her shoulder, smelling her perfume. "You smell so good it's driving me crazy."

He had sounded so sincere. Amber closed her eyes and leaned her head back, giving him more access. He moved in and began kissing along her jaw down her neck towards the top of her dress. She whipped her head up, losing her balance. If Brian had not been holding her, she would have fallen.

"Are you okay?" he asked, concern showing on his face.

"I'm a little dizzy; I think I need some air." She started walking towards the table to get her sweater. She'd bounced off of three people by the time she made it to the table.

Brian followed behind her. He helped her put her sweater on, as she quickly drank another cup of punch.

They walked out a set of French doors that led to a garden area lit by soft pathway lighting. They walked deeper into the garden area. Brian's arm wrapped around her from behind. Pulling her close to his side, his hand drifted up towards her breast. They followed a path to the center of the garden area. The fountain was surrounded with benches. The water changing colors to the music tempo. The fragrant flowers and bushes finished off the romantic area.

Brian and Amber sat on one of the benches, "Are you feeling better?"

"Yes, the air seems to be helping." Amber smiled at him.

"You know, Amber, there were a lot of girls who wanted me to ask them to this dance, but I chose you over all of them. Do you know why?" Brain asked her, rubbing his fingers along her cheek, looking into her dazed eyes.

"No, I was really surprised you asked me. We've hardly said two words to each other."

"So, tell me why did you say yes?"

Amber smiled at him. "Are you fishing for compliments?"

"Maybe; why did you say yes?"

"It made me feel special. I knew all those girls would hate me, but they all hate me anyway." Amber looked down at her hands in her lap. "I also thought it was because you might like me."

"I do like you, but I knew you would appreciate it more than the other girls." Brian had started kissing her on her neck.

Amber had never been kissed before, and the butterflies that were going off in her stomach made it easy for her to tilt her head allowing him better access.

"Do you like how that feels?" he asked as he moved further around her neck.

All Amber could do was groan, as he made his way to her mouth. He moved his lips across hers in a gentle nip. His tongue teased the seam of her lips. Amber opened her mouth allowing his tongue entrance. His arm wrapped around the back of her neck, locking her in place. His other hand began roaming over her hip, giving it a gentle squeeze, continuing its route across her stomach, and ended on her breast. Rubbing against her erect nipple. "Your body tells me you like what I'm doing, does your head say the same thing?"

Amber tried to answer him but when she spoke she wasn't making any sense. She moved her arm up to stop him from touching her, but her body would not follow her brain's direction.

Her arm finally moved to her head as she tried to press her finger to her temple. "My head feels strange. I think I'd like to go home. Would you please take me?" She had pulled back from Brian's kiss.

"In a little while your head will be feeling just fine, just relax back and enjoy the ride," Brian said as he kissed his way down towards her chest.

"What are you doing? You need to stop!" Amber started to panic, her body was now not moving.

"Relax." Brian moved to look in her eyes that were starting to tear up. "It will be okay." He began to move his hands up her thighs. "All the other girls were more willing than you. Why are you fighting it? You know you want me to be your first. All the girls want me."

"No, you need to stop. Now!" His hands had reached the top of her thighs and were prying her legs open.

"I believe she told you to stop. I suggest you do that and I mean, 'Right' now." Amber heard a voice but she couldn't see anyone.

Brian paused his hands where they were. "I don't know

who you are but this is none of your business. Just keep walking."

One minute Brian was in front of Amber, the next he was lying on the ground getting the shit kicked out of him. "I'm making it my business, you piece of shit. That's my sister and if you ever come near her again, I'll kill you." With that Matthew knocked Brian out. He stood up breathing heavy. "Are you okay, Amber?"

The tears streamed down her face. "I can't move. I can't believe, he was going to rape me, Matthew." She sobbed into his shirt. "I thought he was so nice."

Matthew gathered her in his arms. "I got you, I won't let anything happen to you. Come on, I'm going to get you out of here." He scooped her up in his arms. "I'm going to take you to the hospital. Who knows what he gave you or what could have happened to you?"

"No. You can't. Then Mom will find out, and we'll both be in trouble. Besides the feeling is starting to come back into my arms and legs."

"Amber, you can't always do what Mom wants you to do. She's only out for herself, haven't you realized that yet? It's like she had us kids just to use us as her pawns on her chess-board of fun."

Their parents had been together for over twenty years. When they had married, they had bought a rundown car dealership in town, turning it into a million-dollar business. There were no other dealerships within a seventy-five-mile radius, so they were the ones everyone went to. They also began buying up the property in the area, opening a real estate office as well.

"Come on I'll take you home, but if you start to lose feeling again. I'm taking you to the hospital. Screw what Mom will say."

"Thank you, Matthew, I love that you're my big brother."

Amber tucked her head under his chin as he walked them back to his car.

That was the last time Amber ever dreamt of getting married.

Madison's focus came back to the present, looking over towards the two men she knew she loved. Did they even know how much? Madison looked at the couple standing next to her thinking, I'll never be the one standing there as a bride. Who could ever love me that way, after all I've been through?

Madison was drawn back from her thoughts. She plastered a smile on her face, as she heard the minister pronounce them, "Husband and Wife, you may kiss your bride."

Chapter 3

Three Weeks Earlier

Dimitri watched the activity in the busy deli. Seated at a table in the back of the room, he waited for his guest to arrive. He reached into his jacket, touching the envelope resting in the pocket. Thinking to himself, it doesn't really matter if he signs it, as long as he's willing to help.

He was pulled from his thoughts as a path opened through the crowd as Xavier Legend walked into the room. He smiled when he made eye contact with Dimitri giving him a head nod of acknowledgment as he moved towards the counter to place his order.

Dimitri's hands began to sweat when Xavier made his way to the table. "I was very surprised to hear from you. I got the feeling the last time we saw each other that you weren't interested." Xavier winked at Dimitri.

"I'm not but I'm not too sure about Madison." Dimitri

had noticed the change in Madison ever since Xavier had come back into her life. "Don't get me wrong, you're a good looking guy. Hell, you're my best friend's half-brother."

Xavier was smiling at Dimitri's awkwardness. Dimitri swiped his hands through his sandy blond hair, which had started to grow out from his original military cut. Most women would be jealous of the length of his lashes, covering Dimitri's intense hazel eyes. Those eyes that locked onto Xavier's blue eyes.

The fact that he and Dimitri had similar features didn't escape his notice. "Has she talked to you about us yet?" Xavier asked. When she had been with Xavier, she had been contracted with an escort service in L.A. He had been trying to buy out her contract, when she had just disappeared. He had tried to find her, but every lead had been a dead end. Till the day he heard from her BFF Marco.

"No, that's part of the reason I called. We'll get to the other reason why I called later. I feel as her Master I should know her entire history, but I know she has kept her life with you completely to herself." Dimitri paused as the waitress brought Xavier's coffee to the table.

Sitting back in his chair, Xavier's smile widened as he thanked her, before she was on her way again. When she left, Dimitri continued. "I would like you to tell me what happened between the two of you. Will you do that?"

Xavier sipped the hot coffee. Placing it back on the table, he looked at Dimitri. "I can only tell you how it was from my side. Which I thought was going good, up until she left. When I saw her on the *Onyx*, I couldn't believe it was her. I did have my doubts with the name change. They say somewhere in the world there is someone who looks like you. I thought she was her double till I heard her voice." He paused picking the cup up again. "Good coffee."

Dimitri just nodded in agreement. "Just tell me what happened."

"I had been on a business trip and wanted some company. I was told that this particular escort company accommodated all appetites. I booked a girl for the evening and that's when I met Amber. Her hair had been shorter and red and those green eyes showed every emotion she felt." Xavier got a faraway look.

Dimitri knew what he meant, Madison's eyes were the windows to her soul. These last couple of weeks before the wedding, Dimitri had seen the lust for adventure go dull. "I know what you mean; since you've come back they haven't been as focused." His eyes met Xavier's. "What happened next?"

"I started booking her whenever I was in town, but it wasn't enough for me. As a Master I understand a subs need to please. I'm sure you understand what I mean?" Again Dimitri nodded in agreement.

Xavier continued. "She felt an obligation to her contract, and wouldn't break it. The night I told her I was buying her contract, she became subdued. I think she thought I meant I was buying her and that's not what I intended. Then one night I went to her apartment and it was cleaned out. Everything was gone, like she had never lived there."

Dimitri sat forward, placing his elbows on the table, leaning further. "What did the neighbors say when you asked where she went?"

"That's what the strangest thing was and why I couldn't find her. They had said no one had lived there in months. She had told me that she was part of a community playhouse and that she was learning to perform. I found where it was and again when I asked, no one knew her. It was like a giant conspiracy. She just disappeared."

"How is that possible? Everyone is traceable with the

technology we have today. Didn't you ever try to find her again? I would have never stopped trying to find her," Dimitri growled and sat back in his chair.

"You do when you're finally told she's dead." That got Dimitri's attention really quickly.

"What the hell are you talking about?" His question and tone drew looks from people at nearby tables.

"You know her as Madison MacIntyre. I knew her as Amber Sinclair. If you want answers she's not ready to give yet, you need to talk to Marco. He was a part of her life, even back when we were together."

"When you talked to him about her, what did he say?" Dimitri questioned.

"He was devastated, or he put on a good act. He even told me where I could find her grave. I never went, I couldn't face looking at her tombstone, knowing the vibrant woman she was."

"IS!" Dimitri stressed. "If they are the same woman, she is very much still alive, but I feel like a part of her is dying inside. I've noticed her withdrawing more and more. I can't lose her, Xavier, and I think you can help."

Xavier finished his coffee and put down the cup, giving Dimitri his full attention.

"What I'm proposing, I've only done with your brother and it was never with someone I was in love with. If Madison will agree I would like to propose a shared relationship with her."

"You, me and Amber?" Xavier asked.

"You, me and Madison," Dimitri corrected. "I want what is best for her. I think you still hold a part of her and if you being a part of our lives puts the light back into those beautiful green eyes, then that's what I'll do." Dimitri paused. Xavier felt the intensity coming from Dimitri and knew this wasn't easy for him.

"Like I said before, I've shared women before, but for a night. This is for life, so either you're all in or you're not. I want you to think about this real hard. Make sure of your decision. We will, of course, have to approach Madison with this, but if you're in and Madison isn't. Then you're out. Simple as that."

"Are you going to be able to handle a ménage?" Xavier leaned in closer to Dimitri, "And what would our relationship be in this?"

"I've never been how would you say it? Moved by another man. Especially another Master. However, I think because of the bond you have with Madison, I find myself curious about you." Dimitri quickly added, "I know I don't want your cock anywhere near my ass, but I can't lie, the thought of you sucking my dick, has led to a few wet dreams."

Xavier's cock twitched at the image Dimitri had laid out. "You've been a part of a few of mine. What are you truly proposing?"

Dimitri withdrew the envelope from his pocket, sliding it across the table towards Xavier. "Are you really trying to proposition me? You can't buy me out!" Xavier started to rise from his seat.

"Sit down!" Dimitri practically shouted, gaining a few more head turns from the other patrons.

Xavier sat slowly back into his chair. "It's not a bribe, idiot, it's a contract. I know nothing about you other than what I've read. I can't even ask your brother. He's only known you as long as I have." He paused to finish his coffee and let Xavier take in what he had said.

"I have been doing a lot of thinking about this and I've come to the conclusion that if Madison is going to be truly happy with me, you're going to have to be a part of our life. The contract lays out a plan in which to make that happen.

Read it over. You have until the wedding. But, if you're the man I think you are, I'll have it back before that and we can begin." Dimitri rose from his chair, extending his hand. "I'll wait to hear from you."

Xavier rose and took his extended hand, shaking it in agreement.

Dimitri squeezed it a little harder pulling Xavier in close, so only he heard him. "And, don't ever call Madison behind my back again."

Leaning in towards Dimitri, Xavier whispered in his ear, "I don't think that will be a problem." He kissed him on both cheeks. "I'll talk to you tomorrow." With that he started towards the door, saying over his shoulder, "I'll set up an appointment with Melanie your assistant, keep a spot open."

Dimitri watched Xavier walk out of the deli. He dropped a hundred on the table for the waitress and then followed him. When he was out the door, he watched Xavier get into the waiting car, waving the envelope as he disappeared behind the dark glass windows of the Mercedes, saying to himself, "This has to work."

Xavier's ass hadn't hit the seat in the car, before he had the envelope ripped open, and the contract in his hands. Scanning it for anything that kept him from Amber. No. He shook his head. Madison. Madison. Madison. He laughed out loud, saying to his driver, "I bet somewhere in these papers it states I have to call her Madison."

Curtis was the driver behind the wheel. New to the position, he seemed to get Xavier. He looked at him in the mirror. Xavier had a tendency of annoying every driver he had ever had. But so far Curtis seemed to understand him. "If this is about Amber, sir…"

Xavier cut him off mid-sentence, his face darkening in an angry scowl. "Her name is Madison and you will remember that. If I cannot call her by her name, you will not either."

Curtis nodded, and kept on going like nothing had just happened, "You got it, boss. Does this have to do with Madison?" His sarcastic tone was not lost on Xavier, but he also couldn't let him get away with it either.

"Watch the tone, Curtis, or you'll be skateboarding deliveries around the city instead of driving this incredible car for a living, understand?"

"Totally, boss. Is Miss Madison okay, sir?"

Xavier had no clue why he could talk to Curtis about her, but it just seemed to ooze out when he asked. "Yes." He smiled looking up at the dark eyes reflecting back at him. "He wants a ménage, but knowing him, I'm sure these are the rules." He waved the document in his hand.

"Will you agree to them?" Curtis was pulling to a stop in front of Xavier's office building. Parking the car, he came to open Xavier's door.

"I'll let you know later. I have to do some reading. I'll call when I need you later. Go take your mother to lunch." Curtis had complained his mother had been, "getting on his crap!" the other day. "Go to Enrique's on 49th, they have the best guacamole." Xavier passed a hundred in the handshake he gave Curtis. "It's small, but good food. Still can't believe your mother loves Mexican food."

"What? Asian people can't eat Mexican food? Who says we have to eat rice every day?" Curtis teased with Xavier. It was the same comment and the same response every time Xavier suggested Enrique's. "See you tonight, boss, I'll tell mom you said hi." Curtis had moved back to the driver's side, as Xavier waved his acknowledgement.

Chapter 4

As the reception was winding down, some of the guests began departing the ship. Madison and Isabella stood with Sadie as she kissed her parents goodbye. Dimitri's eyes were fixed on Madison, when Xavier came up on his side. "You ready for this?"

Madison chose that moment to look their way. "The question is, is she ready for this?"

For the past three weeks they had met at different functions. Dimitri had events for the launch, and Xavier had business receptions. They had also used their personal time, bars, sporting events, and a few private dinners to get to know each other.

Dimitri had escorted Madison to the events pertaining to the *Sapphire*. Xavier had extended invitations to Madison, but she had refused every one of them. Smiling at Madison, Dimitri said, "She will be, once she sees the lengths we have gone to make this happen. I need to get changed before the press arrives." He grabbed Xavier's arm, moving him to the railing. "She has booked her own room. I told Melanie to make the arrangements. She will be in the adjoining room to yours. I have also made sure that maintenance has disabled the lock to the door."

Dimitri had also commissioned a set of spiral stairs to be put on Madison's balcony, up to his penthouse suite. It had cost a small fortune. But he needed to know he still had access to her, if she really wanted to stay in her own cabin.

"I also need to check in with Captain Russell. After that, Wyatt and Cooper down in security. We need to make sure we have no stowaways on this trip. I couldn't imagine Ryan Arcola living through being shot, and then falling over the railing. For everything he put Sadie and Cameron through on the *Onyx*, he deserves to rot in hell. But you know what they say about rats and cockroaches. They'll still roam this earth long after we're gone."

"You haven't heard what happened to him?" Xavier asked.

"No. The three of them; Tia, Dwayne, and Ryan vanished without a trace. But I have to keep an open mind that he made it and we have to be prepared for any retaliation. His psycho of an uncle can also still pull strings from behind bars. So at no time is Madison to be alone. Understand?"

"I will have Jasmine shadow her when we can't be there." Jasmine was Xavier's personal assistant. He had hired her seven years ago, when as a temp, he put her to the test. His father had always taught him to trust no one unless they passed a test they didn't know they were taking.

Being Richard Arcola's biological child, his father Emmett Legend had put security measures in place to protect him. Among themselves, Xavier and his dad had designed a test for anyone who came into close contact with him on a daily basis.

Xavier would say he didn't want to be disturbed for say

the next hour. His father then would call every five minutes, with his temper climbing with each phone call.

Finally, he would show up at the office irate and obnoxious, demanding to see Xavier, and if you knew anything about Emmett he was ruthless when he wanted something. Jasmine was the only one who stood her ground. She had said that unless he could prove someone was either dying or dead, there was no way in hell he was getting in that office until Xavier said he could.

Xavier smiled at the thought. When Jasmine had found out about the test, she had almost quit. She agreed to stay when Xavier agreed to pay for her yearly membership at his dungeon, *Black and Blue*. He caught Jasmine's attention, waving her over.

Jasmine excused herself from the conversation she had been involved with and made her way over to Xavier. "I need you to keep an eye on Madison; we have some planning to do for this evening." When Jasmine had just stared at them, Dimitri continued.

"There was an incident on the launch of the *Onyx*. Some bad people from Madison's past came back into her life and we just want her to feel secure. Got it?" he emphasized.

"You don't have to be so rude. I like to know why I'm doing something, that way I can do it right. Got it?" Jasmine snapped back.

"Jasmine, we are under a lot of pressure right now. Couldn't you tone it back a little?" Xavier gave a pleading look.

"Fine," she huffed out, "I thought this was supposed to be a vacation." She started walking backwards away from them. "This is going to cost you big, Sir!" She smiled like a Cheshire cat.

"It will be worth every penny," Xavier shot back. Jasmine straightened, and her face turned from surprise to recognition. "I'll take care of it, Xavier, let me know if you need anything else." She then turned and Dimitri watched as she made it appear like she was working the room. When the whole time, she had a bead on Madison.

"What the hell just happened?" Dimitri asked in disbelief.

"It was the phrase. I told her if she ever heard that phrase leave my mouth, to not question it, just do as I asked. She has never failed me."

"All right, now that I know Madison won't be alone. I need to get ready. We'll meet in my cabin before dinner and finalize our plans for our obstinate little sub. No more running and hiding. Between us, we should be able to get her to tell her story."

"How are you going to get her to join us?"

"She'll be there, she may have her own room, but she'd never want to disappoint her Master. See you later." Dimitri smirked, his beautiful straight white teeth gleaming as he turned and headed towards the elevator.

Xavier watched till Dimitri was enclosed in the elevator, and then swung his gaze to where Madison was standing. "Tonight, my pretty, will be the first night of the rest of our lives. You'll never be alone again, no matter what your real story may be." Xavier headed to the sports bar; he needed a drink.

Madison had watched the exchange between Dimitri and Xavier under hooded eyes. She had an uncanny ability to sense when she was being watched. Ever since her incident with Brian, the hair on her arms would stand as if static was running across her body.

She knew something was up with the two of them, she

just wasn't sure how or if she fit into it. Dimitri had been very attentive and caring the past three weeks, like he was dating her. But he hadn't touched her. Prompting her to arrange for her own cabin.

Being a guest on this cruise, Madison intended to enjoy her time off. First on her list was soaking in a whirlpool after getting a much needed massage. Then she was off to the salon to have her make-up and hair done for dinner. Dimitri would be there at 6:00 pm, to escort her to the dinner. The only problem was dinner wasn't till 8:00 pm. Her stomach did a little flip flop at the thoughts that entered her mind.

Madison felt as if she had been on a roller coaster lately. Dimitri had rented her a house in the San Diego area. He had told her he wanted her close while they were finalizing and doing check runs with the *Sapphire*. He had also told her that he had been thinking about how they had come together. Since the night of the auction on the *Onyx*, they had been together.

One night while they were at one of her favorite restaurants, he had laid out his plans building up to the launch of the *Sapphire*.

"Madison, I have rented a house for you, in San Diego until the launch. I was thinking that with you and Isabella planning the wedding of the century, you might want to be close by."

"Will you be staying there too?" She could tell from the way he hesitated she had her answer. She figured it was finally happening. He was moving on, and not with Madison. Her face showed the disappointment she was feeling.

"Madison, look at me." Dimitri's voice had deepened to his Master voice. Madison's eyes, locked with his. "I have done this for you and me to get to know each other. I don't even know your favorite flower. What your hobbies are, your go-to movie." She smiled when he said that.

"How do you know I have a go-to movie?"

"Every woman has a go-to movie. There's one for every emotion." He caught the napkin she had thrown at him. He reached for her hand resting on the table. "Believe me, it will be a long three weeks for me as well. I need you to do some thinking. I feel there is a lot from your past that you have withheld from me, and as your Master I cannot allow it to go on."

Her eyes never wavered as she gazed into Dimitri's. She was now thankful she had time to figure out how to explain her past. Or, for the second time in her life, she could run and disappear.

Dimitri continued, "I will expect you to attend every function Melanie schedules. I know you will be busy with wedding plans, but these events will be about promoting Midnight Oasis Cruise Line both here and on the East Coast." He paused, and Madison could see as he clenched his jaw.

"Madison, there is something I need to tell you about my family. Something I've never even told Cameron." Dimitri tightened the hand holding hers as if expecting her to pull away when he told her a snippet of his life. He had to be as honest with her, as he wanted her to be with him.

Madison remembered a feeling of dread sweeping through her. If he had to bring her here to tell her, it couldn't be good.

"If I am going to demand full disclosure from you, I feel I should also disclose something about myself." Dimitri hesitated, "This is the only time I will speak of this."

Madison had squeezed his hand in understanding. Her attention focused on what Dimitri was trying to say.

"Madison, my father is the 'Sovietnik,'" he paused to gauge her reaction. When she just sat there with no understanding of what he had said, he continued. "He is the right hand man to the most powerful Russian mafia crime boss." Dimitri let his statement sink in.

If Madison had to be honest, she was glad he hadn't said his father "was" the crime boss. "What does that mean?" She knew just about every nationality had a mafia, and each had their own way of dispensing punishment. If what he was going to tell her would put his life in danger, she didn't want to know. "Will you be putting yourself in any danger telling me what you're about to tell me?"

Dimitri glanced down at the table; he knew she was going to try and stop him from telling her. He looked back into those beautiful green eyes. "I will not be in any danger telling you."

"Why didn't you ever tell Cameron?" Madison asked knowing how close the two were.

"I was sworn to secrecy. I had to swear I would tell no one who my father was, or what he did. They would have killed him." Dimitri reached for his wine glass his hand visibly shaking. "Cameron was the only person who didn't look at me different, like everyone else. My English was a little rough then. As much as I wanted to, I knew it would have put a strain on our friendship. Then after what happened with his parents, I didn't want to tell him I had a father, but I chose not to have anything to do with him. I didn't think he would have understood that."

"When was the last time you spoke with your father?" Madison was rubbing her thumb along the back of his hand.

"The day I left for college. I told him I wanted to go to school in America. He thought it was a good idea, so I could learn the American way of business. I knew he wanted one of his sons to follow in his path, but that wasn't going to be me." Pulling his hand away from Madison, he sat back in his chair. "My mom had died the year before, and after that happened, he was never home. It was like Sabastian and me were orphans. The man ate, drank and slept for the 'Pakhan.' He had no idea I was leaving until that day. I also told him I was doing this for me and not him. That if he wanted to know the 'American way' he could learn it himself. I thought he was going to disinherit me, but I think he understood I wanted to be my own man."

"So you have a brother?" Madison asked, trying to lighten the mood.

Madison's smile lifted the heavy feeling on Dimitri's chest. He grinned as he replied, "Yes, I have a brother. I haven't spoken to him since that day as well. I think that was my punishment for leaving. I tried to call him when I landed on U.S. soil, but his phone number had been disconnected. He probably thinks I abandoned him. Knowing my father, he did that to make Sabastian dependent on him."

"How old is he?"

"He's three years younger than me. We used to do everything together." The tightness of Dimitri's face softened as he spoke about his brother. "We used to pull pranks on all the staff, like putting frogs in the pool. It took the pool man two days to get them all out. When he had gotten the last one out, we put more in. He never figured it out that we kept adding them." Dimitri's smile brightened when another thought hit. "One day when our tutor came, we glued him to his chair, locked him in the room, and went and played ice hockey all day. That's where I got this scar." He pointed to the puckered area by his right eye.

"Sabastian always loved hockey. The last I heard he was playing for the Russian Men's National Hockey Team. In 2014, they took fifth place at the Olympics and the gold at the World Championship." The expression on Dimitri's face showed he was proud of his brother's accomplishments. But his expression quickly changed as he sat forward leaning his elbows on the table telling her, "Then nothing, he disappeared off the grid. I tried calling my father, but he refused my calls. I haven't heard anything about him since May, 2014."

"You don't think your father had something to do with his disappearance do you?"

Dimitri sat back running his hands through his hair. "I don't know what to think. I just hope wherever he is he's all right." Dimitri sat forward gathering her hands in his. "Now, to answer your question, no I won't be staying at the house with you. However, I will be close if you need me. I'm serious about us getting to know each other."

Madison's thoughts were interrupted when Sadie threw her arms around her. "Thank you so much for being here today with us. I never knew a person could be this happy." Sadie pulled back from Madison moving her fingers to her cheek. "I can't stop smiling, my cheeks hurt."

"I know you and Cameron are going to be very happy together. I hope I get what you have one day. You look very relaxed. I take it your family has departed?" Madison questioned. "So now go enjoy married life. I have a massage to get to. I plan to enjoy this vacation to the fullest." Under her breath she said, "because after I reveal my real life to Dimitri I might not enjoy anything again." Sadie was so preoccupied with well-wishers she didn't hear what Madison said.

Sadie's attention was back to Madison. "I'll see you there. Cameron has to meet with Dimitri and the media for the launch, so I have some time to kill before the honeymoon begins. It will give us some girl time. We haven't had much of that lately with all the wedding planning."

"That would be nice. Is Isabella going to join us? Last I saw she was being led away by Caleb. I saw Dimitri leave. I think he is changing his clothes as we speak." Madison paused and watched the crew of the *Sapphire* as they prepared the ship for the guests that would begin arriving, as well as the media. "By the time we are done with our massages they should have everything back in place for us to leave port." When Sadie looked confused, Madison pointed to the activity going on behind them. Sadie's eyes followed Madison's line of sight to the crew, and nodded in agreement. "How did you tell your parents they couldn't be guests on the cruise?"

"Just that it was a special cruise for investors. This way they would think that it was all business. They understood, but they did want to know when they would be able to sail on their new son-in-law's ship. To that I told them that the cruises had been booked months in advance, so it could be a while." Sadie giggled like a little girl. "I don't know how long I'll be able to keep them in the dark."

"Don't you think they could have already tried to find out about booking a cruise?" Madison questioned.

"No, because I asked Caleb to hack into their computers. He made it so that if they went to the web-site for Midnight Oasis Cruise Line they would be redirected to a fake web-site that Caleb set up. That man is a genius when it comes to computers."

"I'll keep that in mind. Well, I'm going to my cabin. I need to change before I go to the salon. I'll see you there." Madison hugged Sadie again. "I really am very happy for you."

"You never know. By the end of this cruise, it could be

you who's collared and engaged," Sadie said as she hugged Madison back.

"From your mouth to God's ears," Madison said over her shoulder as she walked away. But we'll see how Dimitri feels about that. She could only pray that he would be able to handle everything she had to tell him about her life. If he couldn't, there would be no engagement, and definitely no collar.

Chapter 5

Dimitri put his cabin key in, pulling it out when he heard the familiar release sound of the lock. Walking through the now open door, he stood in stunned silence. Lying across his bed, flipping through the ship's catalog was a very large man. His feet dangled from the side of the bed. His head that had been resting on his hand snapped up when he heard the door close. Moving to the edge of the bed standing his athletic framed body up. He spread his arms wide, his grin widened as he spoke in perfect English. "Hello, brother, it's been awhile."

Dimitri couldn't believe what he was seeing. His feet started moving forward. Still trying to wrap his mind around the fact that the brother he hadn't seen in years was standing in his private cabin. When Dimitri was standing right in front of him, looking eye to eye with him he asked, "Sabastian, why are you here? Is our father dead?" Dimitri figured that was the only reason he would be here.

Sabastian wrapped his arms around his brother saying, "What? I can't just come and visit my long lost brother?

Congratulate him on his success, and in the interim take a well-deserved vacation?"

Dimitri hugged Sabastian back. "You didn't answer my question? Is he dead?" He pulled back from Sabastian to look in his eyes.

"No, he is not dead. Yet. He's not as healthy as you remember him, but he's not dead. However, Yakov is and with his son Viktor taking over, father thought it was time for me to leave." Sabastian walked over to pour himself a drink. Holding a glass up to Dimitri, he asked, "Care to join me?"

"No, I need to change and get back up on deck to meet the media. You are also going to have to get off. As much as I would like to get caught up, your timing is really shitty. I don't know how you got on board to begin with, but you can't stay. This is the maiden voyage for the *Sapphire* and our guest list has been set for months. All the paperwork has been filed for our exclusive passenger list. I have an idea, I rented a house here in San Diego, maybe you could go there for the week? When I get back, we'll get together and reminisce. How does that sound?" Dimitri began moving about the cabin getting his clothes to change into.

"It sounds like you don't want me here, and after all the trouble I went through to surprise you." Sabastian stuck his bottom lip out as if he were pouting.

"Oh, you surprised me all right." Dimitri threw his jacket on the couch, and began undressing as he spoke. "Where have you been? I was following your hockey career and then after the World Cup, nothing?"

Sabastian took his drink, and stretched his six foot four frame across the king size bed. "Well, that story will have to wait till you have more time. It's a doozy. I'll tell you about it after your ship has had her launch. You see, we will have all week to get to know each other again. A lot has changed, and you need to know what's happening so you can be prepared."

"What do you mean we have all week?" Dimitri asked as a knock sounded at his door. "Go in the bathroom, I don't want anyone to see you."

Sabastian smiled, but did as he was asked.

Dimitri opened the door to find Cameron on the other side. Walking in the cabin, he asked, "So, how did you like your surprise?" Looking around the empty room, he turned a questioning look on his face. "You did see your surprise didn't you?"

"Oh, he saw me." Sabastian said as he exited the bathroom, walking over to greet Cameron with a handshake. "He's just trying to hide me from everyone. Nice to finally put a face to the voice."

Dimitri watched the exchange between his friend and brother. "I take it you two know each other?"

"We've only spoken on the phone, but I assumed who he was by his question. Now, why don't you two run along to your meeting? I'm going to my cabin, put on my swim trunks and head to the pool. I need to work on my tan. Then I'm going to enjoy some leisurely time by the dungeon arena. Scope out the crewmembers for the auction tonight."

Dimitri stood looking from his brother to Cameron. "What is he talking about? How does my brother have a cabin on this cruise without me knowing anything about it? For that matter, how did you know I had a brother?"

Cameron closed the distance between them. "I've known about your family for some time. I figured when you were ready you would tell me about them." When Dimitri still didn't say anything, Cameron continued, "You used to yell his name while you slept. I did some research and found out about your father, as well as your brother. I never said anything because you never said anything. A few weeks ago, I intercepted an email that came to the company email. It was from Sabastian wanting to come and see you. I told Sadie about it, and she suggested we set everything up so you could get to know your brother again. We had Melanie reserve the Jr. Suite on the Emerald Deck, he has filled out all the paperwork, and has been cleared by Doc. We did this all under an alias first so you wouldn't know. Second, so your brother could still be off the grid."

While Cameron talked, Dimitri changed into a black suit that hugged his muscular frame. His sandy-blonde hair hung to his rugged jaw. A sapphire blue shirt pulled the blue forward in his hazel eyes. As he tucked the black, silver, and blue swirled designed tie into his jacket he turned to Sabastian. "I need to know," pausing he looked at Cameron. "We need to know, is trouble following you, brother?"

Sabastian exchanged a look with Cameron who gave a slight head nod. "I will explain everything tonight. Right now you have business to attend to." He tried to herd them towards the door. Dimitri sidestepped his out stretched arm.

"This is my cabin and I'll leave when I want. Are you in trouble?" Dimitri demanded.

Sabastian hung his head, then gathering his courage he looked Dimitri in the eyes. "I may be trying to avoid this 'guy.' He wanted me to do something, and I agreed. But then I changed my mind because it didn't feel right. So, he's not really happy with me right now. Like five million reasons not to be happy."

"Who's the 'guy?'" Dimitri had a bad feeling he was not going to like the answer.

"Oleg Kozloff." When Dimitri showed no sign of understanding, Sabastian explained. "He is now the leader of the 'AP-13.'" When he still didn't acknowledge any recognition, Sabastian clarified, "'Armenian Power'. They were always trying to hone in on Yakov's territory. They finally gave up and expanded their chapter right here in California. Trust me, Dimitri, only Cameron, Sadie, Doc and now you know that I'm here. You just have to call me Kristoff, that's the alias Cameron and Sadie came up with, Kristoff Markovich."

Once Sabastian explained who Oleg was, Dimitri now understood how serious the situation really was. He didn't let on because apparently Sabastian hadn't told Cameron the real reason he needed an alias. For five million reasons, Dimitri was sure there was a hit ordered on his brother. "Until we are at sea you are to stay out of sight." Sabastian started to interrupt, but Dimitri cut him off. "You have a lounge chair on your deck. Catch some rays there. I will have Caleb check the ship's manifest to make sure no unwanted or unexpected guests slipped in under the radar. You just came back into my life. I don't want to take a chance of you disappearing before you tell me everything that has happened since I left."

Sabastian grabbed the duffle bag lying on the floor. "Okay, I get it. I'm not back in your life for ten minutes, and you're acting like a big brother again."

Dimitri grabbed Sabastian in a bear hug. "That's right, I've missed you, little brother. I couldn't have asked for a better surprise. Now, head to your cabin and we will talk when I'm done. Remember stay there." Dimitri opened the door and the three men filed out.

Walking on the sapphire blue rug towards the elevators, they passed through cream colored walls scattered with paintings and lighting fixtures. The hall opened to a wide landing leading to the stairs as well as the elevators. Dimitri pushed the button for the glass elevator, as Cameron handed Sabastian what looked like a credit card. "This is your room key. I have opened an on-board spending account for you.

You will need this card to access it. Don't forget to answer to Kristoff as it's written on the card."

Sabastian turned the card over in his hand looking it over. "Is there a limit?" he asked grinning.

"No, but if you start to get out of control, I will put a limit on." Cameron grinned back at Sabastian. Dimitri stood watching them interact.

"How long have the two of you been planning this?"

The two looked at each other smiling. "Long enough," they said at the same time.

"I'll find out all the details later, right now we need to go. The media circus should be arriving." Dimitri looked at his brother as the doors opened for the elevator. "You are a welcome surprise, brother. I'm glad you're here, but please, stay out of sight till we depart. I will see you at dinner, all passengers are required to attend tonight."

"Go down one flight of stairs to the Sapphire Deck. Your cabin is at the end of the hall." Cameron held his hand out to Sabastian. "I'm glad you're here too. I know he's been worried, even if he never said anything."

"I'll see you at dinner. Do I get to sit at the captain's table with you guys or are you going to put me in a corner some-where?" Sabastian teased.

"You will sit with us. I will let Monty know. Try not to be late and, in the meantime, really read the rules of the ship. I can't have my brother being detained for something he should already know."

"Have no fear, I won't embarrass you. I've had my share of submissives." The doors began to close as Sabastian shouted, "Something about being a hockey player really turns them on." With that, the doors closed on anything else he said.

Dimitri looked at Cameron. "He is a great surprise, but why didn't you ever say anything? Do you know how many times I tried to tell you about them? I just knew if I did and something happened to you. I wouldn't be able to live with myself. You're my best friend and I couldn't take the chance."

"Don't beat yourself up too hard. I understood. I didn't tell you everything that was happening with Arcola until after the girls were taken. Remember? Each of us have had our share of skeletons in our closets. But we move on. Who would have thought we would come this far? Partners in Midnight Oasis Cruise Line and now I'm married to a beautiful, giving submissive. I predict you will be next."

"Madison and I have been getting to know each other. On a different level. I know what she likes in the bedroom, I just didn't know anything else. By the way, I've been meaning to talk to you about your brother. We've also been spending time together." Dimitri looked at Cameron to gauge his reaction.

"It's still weird hearing I have a brother. So, what's up with that?"

"I'll give you the abbreviated version. I know Madison and Xavier have a past and I think that Xavier will be the key to me cementing my relationship with Madison," Dimitri stated.

"How was Xavier's reaction when you told him?" Cameron asked with raised eyebrows.

"He was all for it. Signed the contract I had drawn up, and returned it the next day. We have also been learning about each other. Tonight we plan on telling her on how our new relationship will work. As well as getting Madison to tell us about herself. There are things she's hidden from both of us." The doors opened and Dimitri followed Cameron out.

"I'm glad that's all over for me. Sadie and I are still learning things about each other. But I know when I come home at night she'll be waiting for me. Standing in the middle of the living room in her perfect submissive position. Sometimes wearing an outfit for our play time in the dungeon, other times nothing at all. I can't help the rush that I get. When I roll over in the middle of the night and wrap her up in my arms, I'm home. There's nothing like that feeling. It doesn't matter where we are, as long as we are together, that's home. I think once you work out the kinks with Xavier and Madison, you'll understand what I mean."

"That's what I'm hoping for too." Dimitri punched Cameron in the arm. "You've inspired me."

"Hey, easy there," Cameron rubbed his arm. "I have a honeymoon I need to start after this. I don't want to explain to Sadie how you abused me and I won't be able to consummate our wedding," Cameron teased.

He turned to Cameron with a smile on his face. "Let's go greet the media, and get this cruise started. I have plans of my own."

They walked up to the group of people waiting for them. "Good afternoon, ladies and gentlemen. We would like to thank you all for coming here today for the launch of our second ship the *Sapphire*. With the success we are having on the East Coast, we hope to build that same reputation here on the West Coast. We are relying on all of you to help us in that endeavor. The articles you write will go a long way in how the public will perceive us. Now, if you will follow us, we will begin on the Diamond Deck and work our way down."

The ship was set up similar to the *Onyx,* however they had changed the deck names. Thinking that having the names of gem stones fit better with the title of this ship. When they reached the Diamond Deck, Cameron pointed out the gym and the spa. Dimitri showed them the Master's Lounge, as well as the pool, hot tub and sundeck area. They had added a virtual golf simulator as well. Which was a suggestion from most of the male passengers on the *Onyx*.

While most of the women suggested a desert shop be added offering cakes, pies, cookies, ice cream and most of all chocolate.

None of the passengers had arrived, so the photographers were snapping pictures as they went. They followed the owners down to the Sapphire Deck. On this deck was the sport's bar, security, as well as the main feature on both their ships, the Dungeon Arena. The area that just a few hours earlier had been a buffet brunch area, was now back to being a dungeon. The St. Andrew's crosses, the spanking benches, the bondage chairs, and the inversion tables had been put back into place. Racks of crops, floggers, cat o' nine tails and other spanking and whipping implements were placed around the arena area. Blindfolds, handcuffs, ropes, spreaders and chains were also spread around the area. More personal items such as ball gags, nipple clamps and bondage hoods would also be supplied by the ship, but passengers would need to stop at Kink Haven on the Ruby Deck to acquire them.

On the Emerald Deck was guest relations, the casino and the piano bar. The final deck was the Ruby Deck. Here you would find the dining room, Kink Haven, Erotic Jewels, the new desert store Cakes, Chocolate, and Caresses and finally the Sapphire Theater.

"Mr. Zilkin, Mr. Alexander can you tell us, since the launch of the *Onyx* have things changed in how business associates treat you?" The question was called out from the back of the crowd.

Dimitri couldn't see who had asked the question, so he answered in general to them all. "As far as business dealings go, I can say that we haven't lost any business and new opportunities are popping up every day."

"Are you planning to add more ships to your fleet?"

Cameron handled this question. "As we speak, plans are

being drawn up for our third ship. This one will be an international BDSM cruise ship. We haven't finalized any of the plans for it yet. When we return from this voyage, we will be able to focus all our attention on it."

"Why do you think you have been so successful with your cruise line?" Again, the question came from an unknown face.

"First, we are extremely aware of the safety factors related to the BDSM lifestyle. Both Cameron and myself hold Master titles. Along with those titles come responsibilities which we have integrated into the contracts that are signed by both crewmembers as well as passengers. Second, there has to be a trust factor. Most of the passengers booked on our cruises have been a part of the BDSM lifestyle for some time. They understand what is expected from them and from us. Trust makes that possible. The third and final thing is privacy. We are protective of our clienteles' identities. If a passenger was to lose their anonymity, there is no telling what the ramifications could be."

"Aren't you worried that with people knowing about your preferred lifestyle they will treat you differently?" Cameron saw the news woman who asked this question.

Looking at her, he replied, "That's something we have had to deal with. How do I say this nicely? There are some very closed minded people! We have also had to deal with protesters as well. But through it all we have stood together as a community. That's part of what being involved with the BDSM lifestyle is about. Trusting others with your private life goes a long way when you start dealing with your public life."

"I hope that has answered all of your questions, but our time is running short. Our passengers will begin arriving shortly, so if I can have you all follow us. We will do the christening and get this ship on its way." Dimitri said as he headed towards the elevators with the media following. Traveling down to the second deck where all passengers and crewmembers were checked in. They departed the ship. Cameron and Dimitri climbed the scaffolding to christen the ship, while the media turned in their temporary passes.

"Both Cameron and myself would like to thank you all for coming. When we started talking about going into business together, we always knew it would be successful. We just didn't know how successful. Your kind words have gone a long way in promoting that success. Now, without further ado, I christen thee *Sapphire*, Jewel of Midnight Oasis Cruise Line and of the sea." Dimitri swung the champagne bottle at the side of the ship, shattering the glass and wine to the ground.

A cheer went up from the crowd on the ground, as well as the crewmembers by the railing. Photos were snapped, as confetti floated to the ground. Cameron and Dimitri began making their way back to the entrance to the ship, shaking hands, receiving congratulations and pats on the backs as they went.

Just before the last photo was taken of them waving goodbye, one of the reporters yelled out a final question. "How do you screen your passengers? Is it just medical history, or do you look at criminal backgrounds as well?"

Dimitri looked in the direction were the voice had come from, trying to find the person it went with. When no one stood out, he answered. "Both crewmembers and passengers are given confidentiality contacts and yes medical and criminal screening is also done. It's like I said in the beginning, safety is one of our highest priorities. We again thank you for your time and we look forward to your reviews." Dimitri waved and started walking backwards onto the ship. When they were out of sight from the media, he looked at Cameron. "What the hell was that? I thought after the champagne, question and answer time was over. And what a question!"

"You handled it just fine. You didn't avoid it, but neither did you offer too much. I wouldn't worry about it. Now, I'm off to find my wife and begin our honeymoon. After tonight do not expect to see me or Sadie for the rest of the cruise. We may make an appearance every now and then, but for the most part we will be otherwise engaged."

"Go have fun. I'm going to go have a chat with my wayward brother. Seriously, how long have you been talking with him?"

"A few weeks. Give him a chance to explain. You'll understand once you hear everything. He's not a bad guy, Dimitri."

"So, he grew up okay? I wish you would have told me you knew. It would have been nice to talk about him with someone."

"But if we did, and the wrong person heard, it could have done more damage than good. Our guests will be arriving within the hour and I plan to use my time wisely. See you at dinner."

"Cameron, if I didn't say it before, thank you. Knowing where Sabastian is, definitely helps with some of the anxiety. The rest should be worked out later. I'll let you know how that goes."

Cameron was getting into the elevator. "You better. I know Sadie will want all the details. I'm trying to curb my sub's obsession with helping her friends find what she has. However, its near impossible right now with the wedding and all."

"Well, if I have my way, we will also be unavailable for most of this cruise. We will attend the necessary functions. But every free minute I have I will be making sure Madison knows how important she is to me."

"Care to tell me how Xavier fits into all of this?"

"I will when I know. See you later." Dimitri watched as the elevator doors closed. He then went back to the check in desk.

"Vincent, make sure no unwanted guests get past you. We've had it happen once, and I do not want a repeat of it."

"Don't worry, Mr. Zilkin, I will make sure everyone is signed in before we leave. No one, will get past me. By the way, I wanted to say thank you for this opportunity. I'm looking forward to working with Wyatt and Cooper. I've heard good things about them."

"They are the best. Otherwise they wouldn't be working for me. I trust their judgment for the choices they made with the security on the *Sapphire*. You included. I'm leaving now. I'm sure we will meet up during our voyage." Dimitri headed for the elevators again. Now to go deal with Sabastian.

Chapter 6

Madison had gone to the spa and met both Isabella and Sadie there. They had spent the afternoon getting pampered for their Masters. Now, she stood before the full view mirror in her cabin wearing a floor length sapphire blue lace high neck gown with a small train. Her four-inch Jimmy Cho ankle strap heels added to her five foot nine-inch height. She thought back to another time in her life when she had worn a similar dress though the color had been white. The night had changed her life. Madison's thoughts drifted back to that night.

Her mother, Lisa, had been chosen that year to head the fund raising committee for the local hospital. Lisa had been waiting for this moment all her life. Finally, she would get the recognition that she had craved ever since she and her husband Walter started making money from their investments. They were still waiting to be accepted by the high society she so wanted to be a part of.

Lisa had chosen a casino themed gala. She felt this would bring in some big spenders. She also knew it would draw

Pamela Boxwood away from whatever social event she had planned. Lisa had found out through the grapevine that Pamela had a weakness for blackjack. She wouldn't miss an opportunity to sit her fat ass at a table and try to outwit the cards.

The evening began with a bang for Amber, when her mother chose the dress she would wear that night. Not one to create waves with her mother, knowing it would get her nowhere, Amber just wore the dress. Her sister Sarah was so excited, this was the first time she was attending a fancy function, and she planned to have fun. She had spun her way into Amber's room, wearing a green satin knee length dress, that flared out as she was spinning. Amber looked at her sister. She was growing up to be a beauty. Her green eyes were shining brightly, enhanced with the makeup that drew the color out. Her long brown hair had been curled artfully down her back making her look older than she was. She wore a pair of low heels, dyed the color of her dress. "Mother wants to know if you're ready to go?" Sarah was smelling the different perfumes Amber had on her dresser. Choosing one and using it she said, "Mother wants everything to be perfect tonight. I think if something goes wrong, she just might do something stupid."

"What are you talking about?" Amber had just stood up from putting her shoes on.

"Wow, you look like a bride. All you need are the flowers and the vail," Sarah had exclaimed, but when she saw Ambers face she added," You do look really pretty, Amber."

Amber looked at herself in the full view mirror, and had the same thought her sister had. The long lacey white gown hugged all of her curves. The bodice was a heart shaped strapless neckline that sunk to display her well-developed chest. Her long brown hair hung down, with large curls adding a bounce and curling just under her chest. She always chose a low heeled shoe, because she was usually taller than most of the boys at school. But tonight she was going to wear her first real pair of high heels. Her mother had bought her a pair of Louboutin four-inch heels. They were white lace with flowers and butterflies over the peep toe, with sequins on the heels and platforms. She really did feel like a bride.

When she had asked her mother about the gown, she had just said. "Well, consider it a coming out party. When this gala proves to everyone that I belong as part of their society, you will then have a second chance with Brian."

It had been two years since she had heard that name, and it still sent chills through her. "I'm sure he's found some new girl at college, Mom. I wouldn't get my hopes up." Amber had said trying to steer her mom away from that subject.

"Oh no, he hasn't. I've been keeping tabs on him. You'll see, he will be at the gala. You should be able to get reacquainted." Amber could hear the excitement in her mother's words.

She felt sick the minute those words left her mother's mouth. After that Amber didn't have any desire to go, but it was too late to back out. Besides there was nothing she could say that would be more important to her mother. Even if she came up with an excuse.

The family had climbed into the waiting limousine. Amber had wished her brother could have been there, she would have felt better. But with Matthew away at school, he wasn't able to be there. They made their way to the banquet hall, arriving before the other guests. Lisa wanted to be there to greet every guest, so they would know who to give the credit to when the event was a success. Or until Pamela got there. As Amber stood in the receiving line with her mother and sister, she knew the moment when Pamela and her family arrived. This woman could make or break her mother's event. A chill ran through Amber as she had to stand

there and greet the one person she never wanted to see again
—Brian Boxwood.

Amber felt the temperature in the room drop twenty
degrees. Amber's back stiffened, as she came eye to eye with
Brian. She raised her hand slowly to greet him as she had
others before him. When he flipped her hand to kiss her
palm, she shuddered with disgust. "It's been too long,
Amber," Brian said, his eyes moving from her eyes to her
chest. "You've grown up even more since the last time I saw
you." Brian's smooth voice grated on her ears.

Amber turned slightly towards her mother to see if she
was watching. Seeing her mother's attention distracted by her
father who was collecting another scotch from the waiter, she
started to yank her hand from his, remembering his mother
to her left. She gently pulled her hand from his. "We're
happy you could attend," Amber had said with the sweetest,
most sarcastic sound she could muster after plastering a fake
smile on her face.

Her mother's attention now focused on her interaction
with Brian. "I look forward to our dance later." Not giving
her a chance to answer he moved on to greet her sister.
"Who is this tasty morsel?" Brian crooned. "What lovely
brown hair you have." Reaching forward he wrapped a
strand around his finger twirling it.

An almost shy, yet seductive look came over Sarah's face
as she answered. "Thank you, I'm Amber's sister Sarah."
She shook his hand.

Brian's eyes zeroed in on her chest as well. "I can see the
resemblance."

Amber tried to stay focused on their conversation when
Pamela Boxwood stood in front of her. Pamela drew Amber's
attention back to her when she said, "I see now what the
fascination is with you." The short woman's eyes were level
with Amber's chest. Lifting her head, she looked Amber in

the eye. "I, however, only see a small town girl, looking to be something she is not." By the time she finished her sentence, Pamela's head had turned to look at her mother.

Amber ignored her comment and just said. "We're happy you could attend." Extending the same greeting she had given all night.

"I think this should be an amusing night for us all." Pamela smiled the same sarcastic smile Amber had on her face. Then moved down the receiving line towards her mother. Totally bypassing her sister.

"So, Mrs. Sinclair. Should we expect honest tables tonight or have they been rigged for the house?" Pamela continued. "This is a charity event, not a way to fatten your pockets correct?"

"Pamela, I'm glad you could attend tonight." Her mother drooled. Amber could not understand her mother's need to be a part of this woman's group. Her mother continued. "I only hired a company to set up the tables. I have no idea if they are rigged. You'll have to play to find out. I don't usually gamble, so I wouldn't know. I am, however, looking forward to trying it though. The money is for a very good cause." Pamela nodded and headed for the entrance. "Anything you want is yours, just let me know. Enjoy your evening, Pamela, I'm very happy you could attend."

"I'm sure you have nothing I want," Pamela said over her shoulder as she walked into the ball room.

The final member of the family trailed behind, Stanley Boxwood. The man was clueless to what happened around him. He had been put in his place years ago by his wife, not to say he didn't have his own secrets. He now stood before her mother. He placed a kiss on the back of Lisa's hand. "It's hard to tell who the mother in this family is." He smiled smugly at her. Now, Amber knew where Brian got it from.

Amber had been greeting Stanley when she had caught

the tail end of what her mother had said to Pamela. She grabbed Sarah before she could leave. "What was Mom saying to Mrs. Boxwood?"

"I don't know, something about, 'anything she wants it's hers.' Something like that. I wasn't paying much attention I was watching Brian. I wish I was another year older, then I could be with him. I just know I could make him happy."

Amber couldn't believe what she was hearing. "You stay very far away from Brian. He's not for you."

"Why? Cause you're still hung up on him. You had your chance and you blew it. Don't ruin this for me. I know he'll wait for me if he knows I want him," Sarah sighed.

"Stay away from him, Sarah. He's not what you think he is." Before she could say anything further, their mother stood in front of them blocking them from moving.

"Do not do anything to embarrass me tonight," she growled through clenched teeth. She then released her jaw and continued. "Now, let's go and show everyone in that room that we belong here." Nothing else was said as the girls followed their mother and father into the room.

They entered the ball room as a family standing at the top of the stairs. Down the bottom of the staircase a floral designed carpet surrounded the room, and dance floor. To the left of the stairs tables were elegantly set with china, crystal stem wine glasses, and silver flatware. To the right of the stairs were the gaming tables for tonight's entertainment. The walls stretched high to the cathedral ceiling. Columns were placed in front of the walls, with sheer cloth curtains around the perimeter. The lighting rising from the floor mixed with the chandelier over the dance floor, giving the room a party atmosphere. Along the back was a wall of glass looking out onto the outside patio, with stairs leading down to the garden area. From the top step you had a clear view of the manicured lawn and gardens. As darkness descended outside, the lighting lit the path, while white lights flickered to life in the trees.

Amber had done a good job of watching her sister, yet avoiding Brian every chance she got. She had a half hour to go, and then she would be able to leave. Her mother was approaching the podium to announce how much money they had raised for the hospital.

"Excuse me, everyone. Everyone, can I please have your attention for a few minutes." She waited till all eyes were on her. "I would like to thank everyone for coming tonight. The turnout for this charity event was a rousing success. I would like to personally thank the Marshalls, the Saxons, and especially the Boxwood's for their generous donations. Putting us at our goal of five hundred thousand dollars. This money will put a substantial dent in what is needed to expand the trauma center. As we come to the end of our evening, the dancing will continue as well as the tables for another fifteen minutes or so. Everything you win from here on out goes into your pockets. So, good luck. I hope you all had a fun time and get home safely." She moved away from the podium accepting the congratulations from those standing near her.

Amber looked for her sister and couldn't immediately see her. When she spotted her, she was standing by the garden doors talking to Brian. She headed in that direction barely noticing anything around her. When she was standing in front of them, she said to Brian, "Stay away from my sister. She's too young for you. I don't think you want a repeat of what happened the last time we were together!"

His attention now centered on Amber as if Sarah wasn't even standing there. "Amber my dear, you remembered our dance. I thought you had forgotten." He grabbed for her hand pulling her in so only she could hear him. "Your brother is not here tonight. I have nothing to fear."

She grabbed it back. "Don't touch me and stay away

from my sister. Matthew might not be here, but I know how to take care of myself now." She grabbed Sarah's arm and pulled her behind her to find their parents. Only to find her father still sitting at the table with yet another scotch in his hand and her mother sitting at a blackjack table with Pamela Boxwood. This could not be good. She dragged Sarah with her to the table just in time to see Brian lean into his mother and whisper something in her ear. He then stood looking right at her, his mother's gaze followed.

Pamela then looked at her mother saying, "Okay, Lisa, let's put all our cards on the table. One hand. If you win I will allow you to join our society group. However, if I win, your daughter Amber spends the rest of the night with my son."

Most of the guests had already left, but the few who had remained made an audible sound of disbelief. Amber herself stopped dead in her tracks. She knew exactly what her mother would do, and it terrified her. Her mother was going to make her part of a bet she couldn't win. Could she? Without even thinking before she answered her mother said, "It's a bet."

Amber couldn't believe what she had just heard, but then again there was only ten more minutes left in the evening. She could endure his presence for that much time.

Two cards were dealt face down to each player. Both players looked at their cards, Lisa asking for another card. Pamela holding. Lisa asked for yet another card. She held with that last card. She then laid her cards face up on the table with a smug smile. They totaled twenty. Pamela paused for a minute adding the cards in her head, and then she smiled wickedly. Turning her two cards showing the King and Ace of spades, twenty-one.

Pamela then stood from her chair, quietly saying in Lisa's ear, "I guess you did have something I wanted. I can't promise you anything, but and it's a very big but, I will consider your membership, if she makes my son happy. So, I would stress the importance to her." Pamela then put a hundred-dollar bill on the table for the dealer. Saying her goodbyes, she grabbed her winnings and her husband. Before she left the ball room she stopped by her son and whispered in his ear. His smile said everything he was thinking. He gave his mother a kiss on the cheek and then she was gone.

Amber stood in stunned disbelief. Her mother gained her undivided attention. "Amber, I know you think what I did was wrong, but it worked out perfectly. Now, you get to be with Brian, and you will make him so happy I'll be able to become a member."

"Mom, I don't want to be with Brian. I've been trying to tell you that but you just won't listen," Amber pleaded.

Lisa stood and changed her tone. "You will make that boy so happy he will be farting bubbles. If you don't do that, don't come home." She turned on her heels and sent Sarah to collect her father. "Don't disappoint me, Amber." Amber watched as her mother joined the rest of her family. Her mother gave her one last look, then helped Sarah get her husband to the car. Amber knew this would be the last time she saw her family.

She started to follow them when Brian stepped in her path. "Going somewhere? The final song is playing. You owe me a dance." He took her hand, guiding her to the dance floor. Joining the remaining couples, swaying to the music, he said, "I've waited two years for you, Amber. I know you will not disappoint me."

She awoke from the haze she was in realizing the implications behind his words. "No, the evening is over with this dance. That was the bet," she spoke with confidence.

"No, sweetheart, the bet was for the rest of the night.

After this dance you will accompany me to my room. There you will give me what was taken away two years ago. You also have a broken nose to make up for." He pulled her stiff body in close to his. "I suggest you loosen up so it will be more enjoyable. Or you can stay straight like a board. Either way it doesn't matter to me. Your choice!"

Amber had gone with Brian. She had made him so happy her mother received a call from Pamela the next day. Explaining that she was still keeping him happy and would be staying with them for a few days. At which time she had told Lisa her membership was approved on a six-month trial basis.

Amber had woken up in the hotel room the next day. She could hardly breathe with the broken ribs in her chest. Brian had only hit her in the face once, and that was to repay the broken nose he had received. Other than that he used her as a punching bag, after repeatedly raping her. He would have said she was willing, but nothing she had done that night had been done willingly. Rolling onto her side, she found a handful of hundreds. She knew if she went anywhere for help they would document what happened. So she stayed in the room. She paid the maid to bring her clothes. After which she had her burn Amber's bloody stained gown. The maid also brought her food. When Amber was strong enough, she bought a bus ticket to California. Her mother had sold her for a chance with a society that didn't really want her. Amber left a huge tip for the maid and never looked back. From that night on, she didn't have a family anymore.

Madison shook her head, clearing the memory. She had finally found a place she felt safe. She knew the first time she saw Dimitri he would be the Master who would make her nightmares go away. She had thought Xavier was that person. Things had taken a turn for the better for a while when she had been seeing Xavier. Then another devastating night, took that from her.

She had done a lot of thinking, and tonight would be the night she told Dimitri anything he asked. She prayed he could accept her with her sorted and complicated past.

Chapter 7

Dimitri had an hour in between the launch and picking up Madison. An hour to get changed and talk to his brother. Dimitri had left Cameron to do the greetings with the arriving guests. Grabbing his tuxedo and the specially designed room key, he left for Sabastian's cabin.

Knowing Madison's room was a few doors down from Sabastian's gave him more time to talk to his brother. He knocked on the door. Sabastian opened it wearing a pair of black sweat pants. "You did bring a suit with you correct?" Dimitri asked as he walked into the room. "I need to change while we talk."

"Yes, I have several suits with me. I came prepared."

"That brings me to my next question. Why are you here? Not that I'm not glad you're here. It was just a surprise."

"Then it worked. It was supposed to be a surprise. I needed to leave Russia and I hadn't seen you. I figured I could kill two birds." Sabastian picked up the weights he had put down to answer the door, putting them out of the way.

Dimitri was stripping out of his clothes. "Where did the weights come from?"

"I asked Harley if I could bring them here, since you didn't want me out in public till we spoke."

"No, I wanted you in your cabin till we launched. That way no one could snap any pictures of you. You did mention you were hiding from an organization you stole money from."

"I gave it back, but by that time they had lost so much they wanted blood." Sabastian moved back to the couch he had been sitting on, flopping down. He looked at Dimitri to gauge his feelings on what Sabastian had just said. "I owed money from another bet. I figured this was easy money. I'd pay off my debt and pocket the rest." He shifted his body to the edge of the couch, pushing his hands through his hair. "Problem was, as soon as I hit the ice I knew I had made a really big mistake."

Dimitri stopped buttoning his shirt. "What did you promise them to do?" He had a clue as to what Sabastian was edging around, but he needed to hear him say it.

"I was supposed to make sure Russia didn't win. I really didn't think it would be that hard. Problem was, when I stepped out on the ice, feeling the energy running thru the arena, everything became clear to me why I was really there. I was supposed to be a role model. How could I go out there and lose on purpose?" Sabastian looked up at his brother. "I've been hiding out since then. Dad set me up with some old contacts in the beginning. I thought I had finally out run them. I was holed up in a hostel in Germany. I started to get comfortable. I let my guard down. I started going to a dungeon seeing a sub on a regular basis."

Sabastian paused. Dimitri could see his brother cared for this woman. "I was picking her up for dinner. I arrived at her apartment but when I knocked on the door, it swung open. I closed it behind me as I walked into an apartment turned upside down. I picked my way through the debris to the bedroom. I found her bloody abused body chained spread eagle to her bed. A note stapled to her chest. 'Next time, they'll have nothing to bury'. I haven't been with another woman since. That was over a year ago. I started moving so much they lost track of me." Sabastian stood up grabbing his t-shirt and putting it on.

"Then I saw that you had finally achieved your American dream. The launch of your first ship gave me the idea to leave Europe. Dad helped me with credentials. Cameron helped with a private jet, then he sent a car. All done under another alias Kristoff Markovich. You have a good friend and business partner, Dimitri."

"You don't have to tell me." Dimitri was putting his jacket on as Sabastian finished his story. "I have to go get Madison. Dinner is at eight. Monty has set a place at the captain's table." He grabbed Sabastian with both hands around his neck area giving him a slight shake. "You did the right thing. You wouldn't have been able to live with yourself if you had gone through with it." He then hugged him. "I'm glad you're here. I've missed you. We will have more time to talk tomorrow. You were an unexpected surprise." Dimitri checked his appearance in the mirror one last time. His sandy-blonde hair curled to his shoulders. The blue in his hazel eyes sparkled with anticipation for the upcoming night. Walking to the door, he opened it. "You are now free to do as you please." Pointing his finger at him. "Make sure you're at dinner as it's mandatory for all guests. Until then, don't get into any trouble. Try to have some fun."

"Don't worry, brother, I will behave myself. But it has been a while since I've been with a woman. I plan on indulging in every pleasure your ship has to offer. See you at dinner."

Dimitri heard the last sentence as the door closed. Straightening his navy blue tuxedo, he headed towards Madison's door. He didn't know how the night was going to progress, but he knew by the end of this night his future would be cemented.

The knock came at exactly 6:00 pm. Madison invited Dimitri in. He took three steps in the room and had her in his arms before the door closed. "You continually astound me with your beauty." He pressed a gentle kiss on her cheek. His eyes took in the dress hiding her beautiful body.

"You're not too bad yourself. You've let your hair get out of control," she said, wrapping a short curl around her finger. "I like it though. You'd be surprised at how a little hair pulling can get your senses feeling." She gently tugged.

"I have a few surprises for you tonight. I will tell you one of them now, the rest will come throughout the night. I have anticipated this night since our dinner." Dimitri kissed her again on the other cheek. "Bringing me back to your first surprise. Mine as well. My brother Sabastian is on the ship with us. Cameron and Sadie smuggled him in under my radar. I will introduce you at dinner. However, you must call him Kristoff. I will explain everything later. Right now, I want to take you somewhere. Do you trust me?"

"Always, Master."

"Let's get going; I don't want to be late." Dimitri waited for Madison to collect her bag. Opening the door, he followed her out. Placing his hand on the small of her back, he guided her down the emerald colored carpet. When they reached the landing for the elevators, he turned her towards the stairs. Climbing the stairs up one level, they arrived by the spa/ salon. He escorted her to another set of stairs leading to the Sun Deck. Dimitri kept her tucked up close to him till they reached their destination.

They were the only ones on the deck. He settled her in front of him, wrapping her in his arms. He leaned his chin on her shoulder. "Isn't it beautiful?" Stretched out before them on the horizon was a giant orange flaming ball. The sun had just begun its decent.

Madison pulled forward, and smiled at Dimitri. "I've watched the sun come up, many mornings. But I've never watched it go down. It looks like it's dropping into the water. Thank you, Dimitri." She leaned her head back against his shoulder. "It's so peaceful."

"Am I late? Have I missed the sunset? You look beautiful, Madison." He placed a kiss lovingly on her cheek.

Madison's entire body went ramrod straight at the question presented to them. Xavier walked up next to Madison and Dimitri bumping her in the hip.

"No, you're just in time," Dimitri said to him. To Madison he said, "Remember you said you would trust me correct?"

Madison tried to move from Dimitri's arms, but he held her there. Moving her so she now stood in between their two bodies. Dimitri wrapped his left arm around her hip, while Xavier wrapped his right around her other one. Holding her quietly watching the sun set.

She shifted her head back and forth between these two beautiful men. The blackness of the night was pushing down the pink and orange colors of the day on the horizon. One sandy blonde, the other brown. Hazel eyes to blue eyes. Both with strong chiseled jaws, similar in height. Their features close enough to make them look like brothers. Both of them wearing tuxedos.

Madison could feel the butterflies beginning to grow in her stomach. Being with Dimitri had always had that effect on her. Add Xavier, and that just doubled the sensation she was feeling. Her nipples grew hard and the wetness between her legs was starting to saturate her panties.

"Do you remember the night I told you about my father?" She nodded her head in agreement. "I had had a conversation with Xavier earlier that day. We talked a lot about you." Again she tried to pull away, but they held fast to her. "We also talked about he and I. By the end of the conversation we had come to an agreement. A contract was signed. But you will have final say in how our relationship progresses."

He could feel her starting to tense up again. "Madison, please listen to me." He kept her between them, turning his body so he could see her face. "I explained at our dinner how I wanted you to fill in the blank years you never talk about. I know Xavier was a part of those years. A very important part."

Xavier shifted his body, so it appeared like they were blocking her in. "I have never stopped loving you. I grieved for you until the day I saw you on the *Onyx*. Even then I didn't think it was you."

They all stood quiet, watching the sun. Each one taking in the moment, and the implications of this moment.

Madison wasn't sure she was totally understanding what was happening. As soon as the sun had finally dropped out of sight, Madison calmly asked, "What was in the contract you signed?" She knew it involved how her life was about to change. Again.

Dimitri disentangled himself. He took Madison's hand and guided her to a deck chair, making her sit down. Xavier sat in the chair next to her. "We have gotten to know each other. We found out that besides you, we actually have a lot in common. I went to Xavier first as a Master wanting to help his sub. I could feel how a piece of you was missing.

After meeting him, and learning of your history with him. I felt he was that missing part. I'm sure this is not how you envisioned your evening going." Dimitri crouched down in front of Madison taking both hands in his. "Part of the contract we signed stated neither one of us would touch you while we got to know each other. That changes tonight. While you are at dinner tonight, I want you to think about the new contract I have in my jacket."

Xavier jumped in to continue explaining to Madison the new contract. "If you agree, we will both become your Masters. If you don't, nothing changes. I will go back to my life in New York and that will be the end of it."

"So in the past three weeks that you two have been getting to know each other, I was left in the dark about a major change in my life, and neither one of you thought I would need more than what, three hours to make a decision?" Madison tried to stand up, but Dimitri kept her in the chair.

"Answer me honestly, Madison. If we had told you about this, after I had already told you that I wanted answers about your life. Would you have run?"

A light shade of pink rose up on Madison's skin. "Exactly. I had a feeling you might run after what I had already requested from you. We didn't want to add more pressure. Now that your decision has been made to tell me, and now Xavier about your life. This decision should be much easier."

"After dinner tonight, Madison, you will unload the baggage that has kept you from being completely honest with me," Dimitri explained as he stood.

Xavier stood as well. "Madison, if this helps make your decision easier, we are both in agreement. We both want you in our lives, we also think this will work."

Dimitri removed the contract from his jacket placing it

on the table. Xavier placed a pen next to it. Dimitri then told her. "Read the contract, we can amend just about anything except the first paragraph." He leaned down. Wrapping his hand behind her head and gently pulling her hair so her head tilted up, he captured her lips. Dimitri deepened the kiss, sliding his tongue across the seam, sinking it in when she responded. Her body heated instantly, leaning up out of her chair as he began ending their kiss. He placed a gentle kiss under her ear saying. "We will be back to get you for dinner." Then he stepped back out of the way as Xavier approached her.

Xavier took her hand gently in his leading it to his lips, kissing her palm. Feathering kisses up her arm, around her neck, and across her cheek taking her mouth in a hungry kiss. He brought both hands up to hold her face in place. "You taste delicious. Read the contract." He kissed her palm again. "After dinner we will discuss it." Both men turned and headed towards the stairs. Neither one of them looking back.

Madison watched them leave. She hoped they were feeling as frustrated as she was. Looking at the contract sitting on the table, she adjusted herself in the chair flipping to the first paragraph.

'This contract is a binding agreement between, Madison MacIntyre (Submissive), Dimitri Zilkin (Master), and Xavier Legend (Master). This contract lays out the terms for which all parties will agree to. Both Master's commit to providing their submissive with trust, open communication, and laughter. They further commit to her financial stability. As well as taking care of their submissive's health, living arrangements, and transportation. They will be responsible for all of the submissive's orgasms. The 'Submissive' agrees to full disclosure of both her past and present life for the duration of this contract. Under no circumstance will this contract be broken by one party. All parties must agree, before the contact can be found null and void. If the submissive does not agree to

the contract, things remain the same between Master Dimitri and the submissive.'

Madison flipped to the last page, seeing that both Dimitri and Xavier had already signed the document. She looked away from the contract sighing. They were offering her the stability she had craved all her life. They were willing to sign this contract before knowing what mysteries she was keeping. Could they really do this? Could she really do this? She plopped her head in her hand, her elbow resting on the table as she held the contract in her other hand.

Dimitri had gone to such lengths for her, for them. He had never indicated he would entertain a ménage. She knew when she was with Xavier she had held a part of herself back from him, always cautious. But not with Dimitri, she had jumped and Dimitri had caught her. She had freaked, and he had comforted her.

She picked her head up, and flipped thru the five-page contract. Searching them, she found the hard and soft limit page totally blank. A frown appeared on Madison's face. Why was it blank? With both men she had had a list of limits. Even if she agreed to the contract, she couldn't sign it without that page being filled in. The rest of the contract was pretty standard. No urination, animals, and blood play were among those standard things. However, the length of how long the contract would be, was also mysteriously missing. She placed the contract on the table and walked to the railing. Would they end the contract when she told them? Would they act differently towards her? Would they try and coddle her or treat her with kid gloves? She didn't know if she could handle them changing for her.

Dimitri and Xavier stood at the bottom of the stairs, watching Madison. "She looks confused. Do you think we are doing the right thing?" Xavier questioned Dimitri.

"At any time when we were drawing up this contract did you have any doubts?"

"No."

Dimitri faced Xavier. "Then why are you doubting it now? We both know this is the right thing for all of us. We all need this. I've gotten to know you pretty well." Dimitri grabbed a napkin off the table closest to him, handing it to Xavier. "I've seen you handle multimillion-dollar business deals better than this. Relax." Xavier used the napkin to wipe his sweaty brow.

"You can relax, if she doesn't sign she's still your sub. I, however, am out of the picture." Xavier looked back up at Madison. "To be really honest, I don't know what I'll do if she doesn't sign. I have never felt like this with another woman. I love her."

"Then how can you doubt her?"

"Because of the total disclosure thing. She has always been private about certain aspects of her life. Like you, I could tell she was holding back," Xavier huffed out.

"If this is going to work, we need that clause. She's ready to tell someone. Otherwise she wouldn't have come on the cruise."

"Yes, but she could have very easily have gotten off too." Xavier was now looking at Dimitri.

"Exactly my point. She could have gotten off, but she stayed. I think she's stronger with the two of us. Besides, there's nothing she will tell us that will change how I feel about her." Dimitri had known that was an option, but when she hadn't gotten off, he knew they had a chance. "While we wait I'd like to tell you about my brother." Xavier had a look of disbelief on his face. "I know, I told you I wouldn't talk about my family with you, but that changes tonight. I have thought about it for a while, but I didn't think you needed to know." Dimitri looked Xavier in the eyes. "What I'm going to tell you could put your life in danger. So, it's your call whether I tell you or not?"

"Continue," was all Xavier said.

As Dimitri spoke, his vision was focused back up on Madison. "Cameron and Sadie surprised me. They got my brother on this ship without me knowing. He will be sailing with us. I talked briefly with him before coming here. The shit he just told me that he's going through could bring some very bad people to our door. Still want to know?"

"If it involves you and Madison, of course I want to know. Like you said, we are stronger together. Wow, he's really on the ship? I did a little web search after I signed the contract." Xavier shrugged his shoulder. "I was curious. So I know he's an awesome hockey player. They didn't say that much more about him. Just so you know."

"It's because of hockey that he's in trouble. He got in with the wrong people gambling. He took a lot of money, but didn't follow through on what they wanted to happen. Now, they want blood."

"Okay, but he's here with you now. We should be able to figure something out together to get them off his back." Dimitri looked back at Xavier. "What, I'm in this for the long haul. If you're in danger because of your brother, that puts both me and Madison in danger. We're a team now, correct? If I can help in any way, you just need to let me know."

"It's been awhile since I have felt the need to rely on anyone but myself. I think between the two of us we just might be able to help him." Dimitri smiled with the thought of them working together.

"So, what are the two of you doing?" Cameron asked as he came up behind the two men. Sadie by his side.

"We are giving Madison some time to read the new contract we proposed."

"We?" Sadie questioned. Looking between Dimitri and Xavier.

"Yes. We!" Xavier exclaimed.

"Why have I heard nothing about this?" Looking up at Cameron.

Holding his hands in front of him Cameron pleaded. "I knew nothing about this either."

"We didn't say anything because we didn't want anything to sway her decision. The only people who needed to know were the three of us," Dimitri answered for Cameron. "We both agree that this is what's best for Madison."

Sadie moved from Cameron's side to hug both men. Then moving back to Cameron, she slid her hand into his knotting their fingers together. "I couldn't agree more. While planning the wedding there were times I could feel her withdrawing. Like she was battling a big decision, but then she'd snap out of it, and be her normal self. Now it makes sense, she had to be thinking about this." Sadie smiled to herself, as if she had just solved a mystery.

"No, that would have been her deciding whether to tell her Master all about herself. As every good sub should. Don't you agree, Master Xavier?"

"Absolutely, Master Dimitri, all subs should be truthful with their Masters. Don't you think, Sadie?"

Sadie's eyes got as round as saucers. Glaring at the two of them.

"Am I missing something here?"

"No, no nothing that can't wait till later," Sadie spoke up quickly. Still glaring at Dimitri and Xavier. "Now, if you will excuse me. I'd like to go talk to Madison. I'm sure right about now she could use a friend." Sadie kissed Cameron on the cheek. "I'll be right back."

When Sadie had made it half way up the stairs Cameron asked, "Okay, what's going on? What is she up too?"

"We were sworn to secrecy. You'll just have to wait and find out." Dimitri smiled, knowing how much Cameron hated to wait for anything. "Don't look so worried. It will be all right."

His smug smile scared Cameron. "So, the two of you and Madison. How did you come to this conclusion?"

"Dimitri came to me. He came up with the idea, and it made sense. I was making peace with the fact she was with Dimitri. Then one day I get a phone call to meet him for coffee. At the end of the conversation I would have agreed to any demands he had just to have her in my life again. But what he came up with was even better. The three of us with Madison at the center of everything."

"And you're good with this? I've only just met my brother. How can you be sure it will work?" Cameron looked at Dimitri.

"I really think it what's best for Madison. Not to worry; we've been getting to know each other. That was part of our agreement. We've spent the better part of the past three weeks leading up to the cruise meeting at different events. Hanging out, and spending time together. Your brother's not so bad."

"Okay, I'm good with this. My best friend and brother happy with the same woman, puts a whole new spin on the word family." Cameron punched him in the shoulder.

⸱

"Madison, are you all right?" Sadie questioned as she reached Madison's side by the railing.

"I guess so. Do you know what they are proposing?" Before Sadie could respond, Madison quickly said, "A ménage! Do you believe that? I have a rough enough time pleasing one Master. How am I supposed to please two? Then on top of everything they wait until we are at sea to bring up this new tidbit."

"If it makes you feel any better, I just saw them. They weren't standing there with smiles on their faces. They are concerned too. They know this is a big decision, and they won't put pressure on you."

"No, that's where you are wrong. I have to tell them after dinner. They've had three weeks to get used to this. I have three hours."

"Madison, do you really need three hours? You and I both know this is exactly what you need. You've been struggling with your feelings for Xavier ever since you saw him on the *Onyx*. Now you don't have to."

"I understand that, but what if my feelings for Xavier overpower what I feel for Dimitri?"

"They won't and you know it. You have more than enough love for the both of them. I think each one of them already has a piece of your heart. Plus, you'll never know unless you try. What's the harm? If it doesn't work out, at least you tried. You do love them both don't you?"

Madison turned her head looking at Sadie. "I do, but will that be enough after I tell them?"

"Tell them what?"

Madison looked back at the water. "After I tell them about myself. There is a lot of shit that they have no clue about. I just don't know how they are going to react when I tell them the whole story."

"Is this about your family? You told Isabella and I. I'm sure they will understand what happened with your mother."

Madison pushed off the railing moving to the table. She picked up the contract handing it to Sadie. "Read the first paragraph, which according to the both of them is the only paragraph not to be amended." She waited for Sadie to read it. When she lowered the document, she saw Sadie smiling. "Why are you smiling. I have to tell them everything."

"Don't you get it? They aren't looking to break the contract. They are looking to see if you can handle it. Everything relies on you."

"But what if I can't do this, Sadie? Will Xavier understand?"

"According to the contract he will. I really don't think you have a decision to make. I think the three of you together will be a good thing. Try and open up to the idea during dinner. Now that you know what they want, think about what you want. Then go for it. That's my advice."

Madison hugged Sadie. "Thanks for the advice. I am going to think about it. I'll see you at dinner. How are your plans progressing?"

"Dimitri and Xavier almost made me spill my guts right before I came up here. I'm going to tell him tonight." Sadie smiled. Just as she got to the stairs she yelled back to Madison, "If it's any consolation, they're pretty nervous too." Sadie smiled and waved as she descended the stairs.

When she was at the bottom, Cameron reached out and took her hand. "I think it's time we start heading to the dining room and let these two get back to Madison. We'll see you there."

"Hey, Cameron, would you take the lead tonight at dinner? I have a feeling my mind will be preoccupied with other things," Dimitri asked.

"No problem. You take care of Madison. I'll take care of business."

Cameron and Sadie headed off to the dining room. Dimitri turned to Xavier. "Should we go and get our sub?"

Xavier smiled. "I think that is an excellent idea. Do you have the room key?"

Dimitri tapped his jacket pocket. "Right here. I think she will be blown away by what we have planned for her."

They both began climbing the stairs. Reaching the top step, their eyes locked on Madison. "If she gives this a chance," Xavier said, looking at her solemn face.

"Think positive. Things will be fine. Are you ready for dinner?" he asked, approaching her.

"I don't know if I'll be able to eat much. But I'm ready to go," Madison replied to Dimitri. She handed him the contract and the pen. "Will you hold this until after dinner?"

"It will be my pleasure and don't think I missed that comment. Eating is very important. You will need every ounce of energy you can gather." Tucking it back in his jacket pocket, Dimitri asked her, "Have you decided to sign it?"

"We will discuss it after dinner as you said earlier." She was going to leave them waiting, as they had already had more time to come to terms with this new relationship. "Shall we go?" she asked, holding both arms out for them to tuck into theirs and escort her.

Xavier took one of her hands in his bringing it to his lips again. "The pleasure is all mine. By the way I don't think I've told you how lovely that dress hugs all of you. I can't wait to help remove it." With that he kissed her palm, then tucked her arm through his.

Dimitri followed suit taking her other hand. "Now, let's go to dinner. The sooner we get there, the sooner it will be over."

———

They were the last three passengers to arrive at dinner. Walking confidently to the table, Dimitri greeted people as he passed. They made their way to the Captain's table.

Three seats were vacant to the right of Cameron who sat at the head of the table. They helped Madison into her seat as Cameron rose to make the announcement. "We would like to take this opportunity to say welcome aboard the maiden voyage of the *Sapphire*. The second ship in the Midnight Oasis Cruise Line. As we cruise, tonight plans are underway for our third ship. This one will be an international cruise ship. We are still working on the details, but we hope you will all be able to join us when we are ready to set sail."

Cameron introduced the captain and certain members of the security staff then went on to explain the ships computer system, games and contests. As on the *Onyx*, they included the fantasy experience at the end of the staged show. He introduced Rachel the beautiful red-head, full-figured, blue eyed actress who would be their muse for the fantasy. Cameron also explain that after the staged shows each night there would be a themed after party. He explained about the use of the red wrist band and the three drink limit per day. Then he introduced Master Chef Raymond, an abnormally large man as head chef. He stood six foot five and had muscles on top of muscles. Not the kind of guy you pictured as a chef. The chef then gave the order to begin serving dinner.

While Madison tried to sit and listen to Cameron, the two men beside her were making that very hard. Each of them had been slowly and methodically moving their hands up her thighs, pulling her legs open in the process. She was straddling the chair when they were done. As each began sliding their fingers through her slick slit, she couldn't help the moan that escaped.

Dimitri leaned in to her. "I know it's been too long, but we can't have you announcing it here at the table. If you are quiet like a mouse, we will allow you to climax at dinner. Another moan like that one and we stop." He kissed her cheek and turned back to the table. Everyone at the table were all in mixed conversations, even Kristoff. Dimitri got his attention from where he was sitting next to Sadie. "Kristoff, I'd like to introduce you to Madison and Xavier. He's a close family friend. When I heard he was visiting from Russia, I had to ask him to join us." That was the story they had come up with to explain his appearance. Dimitri again couldn't thank Cameron enough for his handling of the situation.

Xavier was first to respond. "It's a pleasure to meet you. Will you be in the States for a while, or is this a short visit?"

"It really all depends on my Visa. If I find reliable work, they may extend my stay. I'm kind of hoping that happens. So far, I'm having the time of my life. This is the first vacation I've taken in a long time. I plan on experiencing everything this beautiful ship has to offer." His eyes began scanning the room.

Madison was on the verge of exploding in her chair and knew if she opened her mouth no words would be uttered. She decided to push the envelope. She began to lean forward to put both elbows on the table to hold her head. When her body shifted, it pushed the four fingers probing her entrance, shooting them straight to her core, erupting her orgasm. In the position she was in, she made not one sound. But the euphoric look on her face, eyes closed, mouth slightly ajar, told everyone at the table what had just happened. With her breath panting, she looked Kristoff in the eye. "It's truly a pleasure to meet you."

She grinned as she sat back in her chair feeling very pleased with herself. When she looked at both of her Masters, she realized how easy it was to call them both her Masters. They did not look happy. The euphoric look was replaced with a lip biting face. She whispered, "What did I do wrong?"

Xavier answered for them. "It states right in the first

paragraph we will be responsible for all orgasms. You just broke that."

Dimitri chimed in, "By you taking control, it was not us who controlled your body." He leaned close to her. "Your punishment will be determined later. Now finish eating. You've hardly touched anything."

Madison began picking at her dinner. She had a small knowing smile on her face as she did. She had gotten away with having the best orgasm she had in three weeks. Now she had a punishment to look forward too. Which meant more orgasms. Where was the down side? Then the thought hit her. What if the punishment was no more orgasms? That would really suck she thought to herself, the smile fading from her face.

The waiters and waitress began removing the dinner plates. Everyone was anticipating what Chef Raymond had planned for dessert. Throughout dinner there had been a panel next to the band. Chef Raymond got the attention of the band and made his entrance. "I hope you have enjoyed your meal. I have heard of the masterpiece Chef Isaac presented on the *Onyx*. I also wanted to do something special to commemorate the launch of the *Sapphire*. Would you please remove the panel?"

Two waiters grabbed each side of the panel sliding it out of the way, revealing what looked like a picture of the *Sapphire* floating on the sea. Jewels such as rubies, diamonds, emeralds, and sapphires floating in the water. However, when you examined it closely, you saw people layered on top of each other creating the look of the ship. They had been placed on pedestals then body painted to match the ship. The gems floating on the sea cake, were white chocolates, as well as grapes, strawberries, and blueberries. The display was about five feet long and about four people in height. From a distance it actually looked like the *Sapphire* floating in the water. It was absolutely stunning.

"Everything you see is edible, even the paint on the models. I have also prepared a table of other desserts, not as fancy, but just as good. Master Cameron, Master Dimitri, please join me in cutting the cake. Bon appétit everyone."

Dimitri's hand slid from Madison's leg as he rose from his chair. Kissing her on the forehead, he asked, "Do you remember the last dessert I ate on the *Onyx*? I imagined it was your nipple I was sucking into my mouth. I will bring you some dessert." Dimitri turned and walked to join the other two men by the dessert ship. On closer approach, Dimitri could see where the bodies began and ended. "A spectacular display. It's fascinating, it looks so real. Even the gems look like the real stones. Thank you, Chef Raymond. This will be another memorable event for the dining room." He shook the man's hand.

Cameron followed suit with his complements as well. Then all three men picked up knives slicing down thru the five layered cake. Cameron took this opportunity to announce the crewmember auction. "Excuse me, everyone." He waited for the room to quiet. "For those of you unaware, tonight after the stage performance we will be holding the crewmember auction. Certain members of the crew have volunteered to be actioned off to the highest bidder. The crewmember has the option of staying with the purchaser for the entire cruise if that is requested. But is only required to stay with said purchaser for twenty-four hours. For donating their time and bodies, the money spent on them is given to a charity of the crew member's choice." Looking to where Sadie was seated he smiled. "You never know what will happen. Thank you again for joining us on the maiden voyage of the *Sapphire*. Cameron and Dimitri both shook Chef Raymond's hand again then returned to their seats.

While Dimitri had been at the front of the room pulling everyone's attention to him. Xavier had taken the opportunity to slide his chair closer to Madison's, as if they sat on the same chair. His hands began roaming over her body slowly and seductively. He took his knuckle on his middle finger and stroked it down her arm, creating goose bumps. He then glided his palm over her tightened nipple, grazing the underside of her breast as he moved his hand down to her stomach. He stopped to circle her navel tickling her, making her jump. Pushing her closer to him, his chest was now resting on her back. Further down her body he went till he had reached the destination she craved. Finding her wet, he slid through her folds, sliding and squeezing his fingers along her clitoris as he continued his trek to their final resting place. Deep within her, he could feel her muscles clamp down. As he began to move them in and out in rapid succession, her breathing became erratic again and he whispered in her ear. "Same rules apply, Madison, not a sound."

They were trying to kill her. She just knew it. How in the world was she not to make a sound with what he was doing to her body? Her only consolation this time was Xavier was driving her to her orgasm quickly. So quickly, that by the time Dimitri was in his chair again, Xavier was working Madison down from another mind blowing orgasm.

The band began playing again. Conversations resumed and guests began making their departure from the dining room. Dimitri looked to Xavier with a shake of his head. Giving the signal he was ready to leave. Rising from his chair, he turned to Kristoff. "I have plans tonight, but tomorrow you and I will have some time to catch up. Enjoy your night, and don't put me in the poor house at tonight's auction."

He walked over to Cameron extending his hand. "Congratulations again, my friend. You two belong together. I'm hoping that by the end of this cruise, Madison will be planning our wedding," he added quietly.

Cameron shook his hand. "Good luck tonight. I look forward to being your best man."

Dimitri went back to help Madison from her chair. Collecting her and Xavier, they walked to the exit of the dining room. "By the end of this cruise, all secrets will be put in the past. We want you to know, we will be there no matter what."

Madison really hoped they could handle what she needed to unload. Because she didn't know what she'd do if they couldn't. Now that she could have both of them, she intended to be selfish for the first time in her life and go after what she really wanted.

Chapter 8

Dimitri lead Madison and Xavier to the Sapphire Deck. He stopped in front of a door retrieving the room key from his pocket. Handing it to Madison he said. "I had this suite specially designed with you in mind. For the rest of this cruise you will have access whenever you want. But when you do, one or both of us will be with you."

She looked confused as she accepted the room key inserting it and opening the door. What she walked into could literally be considered paradise. The cabin had been widened with a wall of windows in front of her. The balcony outside the window showed no joints in the railing. Making the view out the window extend without anything to impede your vision. The carpet was the exact color of the ocean. Lighting from the floor moved on the walls, giving off a wave effect. The walls were painted to match the time of day. As the sun rose in the morning, the walls would change color to match. As the sun set in the evening. The walls changed to match. When night was upon them as it was now, the walls matched again.

The furniture in the room was placed facing the view out

the windows. The bed was to the right of the room. It had a canopy with silk curtains at the corners and was big enough for the three of them. The couch was to the center of the room. To the far left was an open plan bathroom with a clear brick wall separating it. Behind the wall was a shower big enough for all of them. With shower heads all around. There was a double sink vanity, with a large mirror above the sinks. In the corner of the room closest to the wall of windows was an oversized bathtub, with water jets and cushioned headrests.

Facing the bathroom, Madison turned her head. She saw a bar with a kitchen area behind it set next to the bathroom area. Just to the left of the walkway it opened into a walk-in closet. Filled with clothes for her as well as Xavier and Dimitri. She walked around the bed on the right side of the doorway finding another glass brick wall. Behind this wall was a complete dungeon. A St. Andrew's Cross by the wall. An inversion table in the middle of the area as well as a spanking bench. Crops, floggers and other implements lined the far wall. A ledge ran around the wall holding blindfolds, handcuffs and nipple clamps.

Imitation candle light gave the room a soft glow. She turned around and looked at Dimitri and Xavier a smile on her face. "This is the most beautiful room I've ever seen." A single tear slid from her eye. "You made me a safe room. A place where I can tell you anything and it never leaves the room. Is that right? That's why you don't want me here by myself?"

"Yes, that's exactly what it is. You will still have your room down the hall. Xavier is in the room next to you, and I have had stairs installed on your balcony. If at any time you need us, you can get to us. However, we would prefer you stay with us." He looked at Xavier then back at Madison.

"My cabin has been redesigned to accommodate all our needs."

They both began walking towards her. Taking the key from her hand, Dimitri placed it on the table near the door. Xavier took her bag and placed it with the key. Dimitri withdrew the contract and pen from his jacket. Xavier guided Madison to sit on the couch. Putting the contract on the table, he threw his jacket onto one of the chairs on either side of the couch. She watched as Dimitri's fingers slowly glided down his shirt popping buttons as he went. Removing his shirt, tossing it aside with his jacket, exposing his beautifully sculptured chest.

Xavier followed suit. Kicking off their shoes they stood before her in their slacks. "Your turn. Stand up. We are going to help get you comfortable. Then we will begin. In this room you will call us Master Dimitri and Master Xavier. Do you understand?" Xavier asked her.

They could see her tense up. "Madison, relax. Nothing has changed. These things we are requesting of you are normal commands." He began unzipping her gown.

Xavier brought his hands up sweeping the material from her shoulders. Letting the dress puddle in a pile at her feet. Stepping out of it, she stood before them in her sapphire colored corset and a string thong. She started to step out of her shoes, but they both stopped her.

"Before the talking begins. We are going to remedy a situation that has been neglected for three weeks." Dimitri pulled Madison into his arms, kissing her as if his life depended on it.

Xavier came up behind her, wrapping his arms around her. He began loosening the ties on her corset. Removing it, he threw it off to the side. His hands then encased both of her breasts. Squeezing down to her erect nipples, he pinched with just enough sting, making Madison gasp. With Dimitri's mouth free from Madison's lips, he leaned down taking her breast in his mouth. His tongue lashed her nipple, easing the sting before sucking it to a hard point again.

The minute her mouth was free, Xavier moved to take control of it. Possessing her. Still holding one breast in his hand. He moved his other further down. Pulling on the string of her thong, Dimitri grabbed the other side. Ripping it from her body. Then they both moved their free hands down sliding their fingers through her slick folds. Madison was so wet the moisture was sliding down her leg. One playing with her clit, the other pushing towards her core. Her legs began to buckle.

Dimitri stepped back as Xavier gathered her in his arms carrying her to the bed. Settling her in the middle, he moved to the end of the bed, removing the rest of his clothes as he went. Madison turned her head, watching as Dimitri tugged on his belt. Sliding it deliberately through each loop. He heard the hitch in Madison's breath. "Not tonight, lovely. Tonight there will be no bindings." His pants hit the floor, his erection springing free. "Tonight we learn about each other."

Dimitri climbed onto the bed from the side. While Xavier crawled straight up the middle to the apex between her legs. Swiping his tongue up her pussy as he settled in to devour her.

Dimitri was again kissing her, tweaking her breasts at the same time. Madison reached out, wrapping her fingers around Dimitri's huge cock. She started rocking her hand up and down. Loving the smooth feeling in her hand. Madison spread the pre-cum around the tip of his dick. She pulled back from the kiss. "May I have your cock, Master?"

"I've waited what seems like forever to hear that." Dimitri moved his body up on his knees next to Madison's head. Madison guided his cock into her mouth. Her moan vibrated straight up Dimitri's spine as he pushed to the back of her throat. Madison had the beautiful gift of no gag reflex. It was Dimitri's turn to groan. He could tell Madison was close to coming, by the way she was sucking his cock. "Madison you are free to come at will. Our first time all together will have no restrictions."

Xavier began crawling up her body. Nipping and sucking as he went along. When he reached her chest, he lapped up one nipple while pinching the other. His hand glided down her thigh lifting her leg as he settled between them. He began his kissing trek once again. Up her neck to her ear. "You are so beautiful," he whispered in her ear, as he pushed his cock smoothly into her. Feeling her tightness gripping him, had him almost spilling right there. "Let yourself go, Madison, we will catch you." Xavier reared back pulling almost out of her, then slammed forward. Madison wrapped her legs around Xavier as he hit home. Madison exploded around him.

Dimitri could feel her scream around his cock. Pulling out of her mouth, he allowed her to show Master Xavier what he had done to her. Looking at Dimitri with those sub-space eyes made his cock twitch. Easing it back into her mouth, he began pumping. Hitting the back of her throat, he wrapped his hands in her hair holding her in place as he came harder than he had ever come in his life. Madison lapped up every drop, loving his cock as he removed it again from her mouth.

Xavier flopped to one side of Madison, while Dimitri stretched out on the other. Neither one of them could stop touching her. None of them spoke, each of them taking in the moment.

Madison lay in between them, her body cooling. Feeling the heat from their bodies kept any chill from her. The scent of sex was heavy in the air. "Masters, as much as I don't want to move, I need to go to the bathroom." She looked back and forth between the two of them with a pleading look on her face. Dimitri was the first to move. Placing a kiss on her forehead, he moved so she could slip off the side of the bed. He smacked her ass as she made her way past him. Rubbing her hand on her cheek. "What was that for, Master?"

"I couldn't resist. You have a beautiful ass, but I prefer it a deeper shade of red. Go, we will remedy that another night."

Madison bounced off to the bathroom with the biggest smile on her face. "I think our sub is very pleased with herself," Xavier said from the bed. Arms pillowing his head, he stretched his long frame on the bed.

"Our objective is to keep her that way. The next part of our evening is going to determine the rest of our lives. So, get up. Throw on some pants and I'll grab her robe." Dimitri picked up the lacy robe, and headed towards the couch. Xavier following him.

They met Madison in the living area, as she was returning from the bathroom. Dimitri held the robe open for her to wrap herself in. Looking at the serious faces of her Masters made Madison's stomach drop as well as her smile. Guiding her to the couch, Dimitri sat, pulling her onto his lap. Xavier sat next to them, pulling her legs across his lap. Taking her feet in his hands he began rubbing them.

"How are you feeling?" Dimitri asked, settling her more comfortably on his lap.

"Incredible," she said, stretching her arms out, raising them over her head, then lowing them to her lap. "I've never done that." Her cheeks gathered color in them, and she bowed her head in embarrassment.

"What do you mean? You've never done this?" Xavier asked her curiously.

"I've never been with two men at the same time. I've

come close, but it never happened. Now, I'm very thankful it never did. It made our first time together so much more special," Madison explained, snuggling her head to Dimitri's chest.

"We are also happy to hear that." Xavier laid her feet on the couch, as he rose. "I'm going to start the water." He leaned over her pressing a kiss to her temple. "Don't get too comfortable. You'll be following me as soon as it's ready."

Madison tilted her head up to look at Dimitri. "You really are all right with the three of us being together?"

He smiled down at her. "Madison, I would do just about anything to have you. If adding Xavier makes you happy, it makes me happy." He squeezed her in a hug. "Now, let's get you cleaned up. We have a long night ahead of us." He stood up, placing her feet on the floor. Madison started walking towards the bathroom area, but Dimitri stopped her. Capturing her lips in a promising kiss and removing her robe, letting it slide to the floor. Tossing her over his shoulder, he carried her into the shower, were an already wet Xavier awaited.

Opening the door, Xavier guided her in, Dimitri following. Xavier had turned all the spray jets on. So, when Madison stepped in the warm water, it began massaging her body. She let the water cascade over her, allowing her body to adjust. She raised her face, her hair soaking up the water and pulling it down her back. Lowering her head, water glistened on her long eye lashes. Blinking the wetness away, she focused her attention on the man in front of her. Water was slipping down her nose. Dimitri lowered his head taking her lips in a possessive kiss. Madison opened to him, knowing exactly what he needed.

Dimitri pulled back from the kiss, looking into her eyes. His hands creating suds from the bath gel, he lifted them to her shoulders, and he started lathering her arms. Xavier began lathering her back. Their hands moving in tandem with each other as if they were one person. Madison's whole body relaxed into the feeling these two men were generating. Everywhere they touched was responsive. Dimitri's hands lathered their way down to her breasts, watching as the suds made a slow trek down to her erect nipples. Using the palms of his hands he massaged the suds around her breasts. His hands traveled down her stomach, circling his index finger around her naval. His palms continued their journey till they reached the patch of hair between her legs. Sliding his fingers through her wet folds, he swirled the lather around.

Xavier followed the same downward path, gently lathering her body with more lavender scented gel. Separating her ass cheeks, his fingers slid over her puckered hole. Circling, and teasing. His fingers continued on meeting Dimitri's. Both of them working her pussy into a frenzy. Xavier's fingers plunged into her, while Dimitri pinched and stimulated her tight clit.

Xavier caught Dimitri's attention. Giving him a head nod Dimitri pulled back from Madison. At the same time, Xavier shifted away from her back. Madison who had been on the verge of coming, wavered with their loss. Water hit her from all angles rinsing the soap from her body. Before she realized what was happening, Dimitri had her in his arms. Her body positioned over his already hard erection. "My turn to feel your tight walls around my cock when I make you come." Madison wrapped her legs around him locking her ankles together. Dimitri lowered her ever so slowly, savoring the feel of her sliding down his cock as he entered her. Xavier helped guide Dimitri back towards the wall. Giving him more control over Madison.

Xavier positioned himself so Madison could lean her upper body back on him. Leaving her breasts exposed for him to tease. Dimitri grabbed her hips, helping her raise off of him. Then pulled her back down, grinding her clit. Between Xavier pinching her nipples and Dimitri's long, hard cock slamming into her, it didn't take long for Madison to go over the edge. When she let loose, her body stiffened, pulsing around Dimitri. He continued pumping into her till he erupted. He never wanted to move from this position. Xavier kissed first one nipple then the other, as he helped Madison lean forward back onto Dimitri. Hugging herself to him, she released her ankles, and let her legs slide down his. Still clinging to Dimitri, her feet hit the floor. With a dreamy look on her face, she looked up at Dimitri. "I don't think showering will ever be the same again." Putting a huge smile on her face, she said, "We just might have to do this, every day! Thank you Masters." Madison felt energized.

"It could be arranged." Dimitri smiled, saying, "Come, we need to get you cleaned up again." Lathering his hands again he started moving towards her.

Madison put her hands up to stop him. "Wait, wait, wait." Looking between the two of them. "If you do it, we'll never get out of here." Teasing them while she grabbed the bottle of gel. When neither of them moved, she raised her eyebrows in a questioning look.

"We may not be able to help, but we can most certainly watch," Xavier said as he raised his eyebrows right back at her.

A shiver of anticipation ran through her as their eyes never left her. She began working the gel into a lather, washing her body, then grabbing the shampoo. Dimitri and Xavier had taken care of business on their end, so they decided to help with her hair. Once Madison had rubbed the shampoo in, Xavier took over massaging her scalp. Leaning back, she rinsed the bubbles away. Dimitri poured the conditioner on and took over the process of spreading it over her hair.

Exiting the shower, Xavier tossed a towel at Dimitri while wrapping one around his own waist. Xavier held a towel open for Madison to step into, wrapping it around her body. Dimitri held a smaller towel for her hair. Xavier rubbed down her body, getting all the moisture off her body. Dimitri held her robe open for her to step into.

They escorted her back into the living area. Xavier went to the couch with Madison, making her sit. Then he went to the bar to retrieve a bottle of champagne and three glasses. While Dimitri went to a panel by the wall of windows. Flipping a switch, the windows turned into frosted glass, then mirrors. Dimitri flipped another switch, and a section of the floor dropped out. In its place rose an entertainment unit. A huge television screen, above a smaller screen. Dimitri walked over to the coffee table picking up a remote. Pressing a few buttons, the room came alive with soft music, the lighting dimmed, and a fire appeared on the lower screen.

Xavier popped the cork on the bottle, making Madison jump. Dimitri joined her on the couch. Accepting the glass Xavier held out to him, as did Madison. "I think we need a toast!" Xavier said, placing the bottle in the ice bucket, next to some fruit and chocolate. Holding his glass high, he said, "To life, love and truth. May they only bring us closer." Holding his glass out and touching it with Madison and Dimitri's, he then joined them on the couch. Settling his sculptured body close to Madison, he took Madison's hand in his. "Remember, nothing you tell us will leave here. We will not judge you and we will hold nothing against you. Who you are today is all that matters to us."

"Then why do I need to tell you? You may say you won't judge, but people always do. That's from my experience." Madison downed the rest of her champagne.

Dimitri set his glass down then reached for Madison's. "We need to know because you are important to us." He repositioned Madison on the couch so she was resting between Xavier legs. Then he sat back down dragging her legs across his lap. Extending his to the coffee table. "Now, we are all settled in." Looking at Madison, his tone deepened as he said, "When you are ready. Begin as early in your life as you think we need to know. But from that point forward do not leave anything out."

Madison knew this was the moment she had tried to avoid her entire life. Looking between the two men she could love for the rest of her life, but still fearing their rejection. She closed her eyes letting the memories filter forward, blocking out their existence. Madison started sharing her memories. "My name was Amber Sinclair."

Chapter 9

The words started flowing from Madison's mouth. She told them her dream to wed Brian. She told them how her brother had protected her the first time from him. Her entire body tightened up as she told them how her mother had sold her for a place in society. Both Dimitri and Xavier kept touching her in some way, rubbing her tense muscles trying to keep her relaxed. She told them how she had survived and traveled to the West Coast. Where she met Richard Arcola and her life took another turn.

"I had taken a bus. Being seventeen it made it easier to travel alone. However, being seventeen, also left me open to any leech on the street. I'm sure you've seen the news reports about teenagers on the streets. That was me. I was a little more cautious after what happened in the hotel room, but I was still young and naïve. I had some money in my pocket and I was going to become an actress. The perfect mark for anyone watching young girls getting off a bus in L.A." Madison paused, picking up her champagne flute. "Master

Dimitri, may I have some more?" Giving him an impish smile.

Grabbing the bottle's neck, he said, "Last one, after this it's juice or water." Filling her glass, he served her the plate of fruit, encouraging her to help herself.

Madison ate a few pieces then settled back against Xavier's chest. She closed her eyes, going back to where she left off. The memory playing out as a movie in her head.

Amber knew she needed to look confident when she exited the bus. She just couldn't help herself. As soon as her feet hit the ground, she turned in a circle, taking in her surroundings. She was standing on the curb in front of a brick building. Walking inside, wondering where she should start. To the left, two workers were fielding questions behind a Plexiglas counter. Metal seating filled the room, restrooms were on the opposite wall. Straight in front of her was a wall of lockers. Some beat up, others working properly.

After using the restroom, Amber noticed a board on the wall by the exit. Sheets of paper hung on it advertising room rentals. Others selling cars and things. Underneath it where racks holding real estate newspapers. A map of the area was hung next to the board. She made her way over to the board and began perusing the notices. She pulled a slip of paper off and was trying to find its location on the map when someone bumped into her. Catching her balance, she glared at the idiot who almost knocked her over.

"I'm so sorry. I wasn't paying attention to where I was going." Hands reached to help steady Amber.

An uneasy feeling ran through her. "It's okay. No harm done," she said, her attention going back to the wall.

"Um, I know you're going to think this is just a line, but are you here to be an actress?"

Amber looked over her shoulder at him. "If I were, why would I tell you?"

He reached in his pocket, removing a business card. She took it from his hand reading it. Alluring, Rocking, Captivating, Offering, Loyalty, and Acceptance. TOP TALENT AGENT—Ryan Romano 888-555-9890 Modeling Specialist. "If you need any help, you could give me a call. I have to catch a bus, but think about it. You believe in fate?" She shook her head no. "Well I do and I think I was supposed to run into you. Hope you call." He quickly walked away tossing his bag over his shoulder.

Amber flipped the card forward and back. Staring at the guy who had just given it to her. She went back to the map again. Finding the location for the ad in her hand, and seeing that wasn't too far from where she was, she opted to walk the few blocks. She was very grateful she had arrived in the afternoon. It gave her a chance to take in the area she was walking thru. It wasn't too run down, but it wasn't Beverly Hills either. She arrived at the dingy motel. Going to the front desk, she requested a room for the week. The guy behind the counter gave her a double take. Her voice was young compared to the mature body it was coming from.

"Payment up front, ID, and no stay overs. That will cost you more." Amber produced a fake ID the maid at the hotel had gotten for her.

Counting out the cash, she signed the registry with the information on the fake license. The clerk slid a key attached to a diamond shape key ring. "Don't start no trouble, mind your own business, and you'll do fine. We are not responsible for missing items. Make sure you lock your door." He finished recounting the money she just handed him.

Amber looked around confused as to which way her

room was. "Out the door, thru the walkway, up the stairs, your room is at the end." Following his directions, she made her way to the room. Opening the door, the stench of cigarette smoke assailed her nose. Flipping the light switch, she walked into the room. Closing and setting the bolt to the door, Amber tossed her stuff on the bed. She walked into the bathroom, turning on the light, saying a thank you to God that no bugs went scrambling when she flicked the light on. She ran the water checking that it worked. Going back to the bed, she opened her bag and the business card fell out. Looking it over again, she placed it on the night stand. She was going to try this acting thing on her own. If she didn't get anywhere, then she'd call. Going back to the bag, she took most of her money and hid it around the room.

Amber decided right then that she couldn't wait to find a job. She grabbed her room key and some money. She made her way back to the street. She thought about asking the desk clerk, then changed her mind. Nothing about that guy gave her a good feeling. When she hit the side walk, she headed to the left, walking till she reached the local shopping area. A little diner sat on the corner, a clothing, hardware and liquor store stretched out on one side. On the other side was a school, and a church. Amber headed to the diner. Getting something to eat and scoping out if they might need some help, killed two birds.

The older woman behind the counter had a kind face and a soft voice. She explained that they were a family business and didn't need any help right then, but she'd keep her in mind. She did offer up the grocery store at the other end of town. After eating a burger and some fries, she was on her way again. Finding the grocery store, she filled out an application. She did some shopping and headed back to the hotel to get comfortable for the night.

Making it back to her room, she changed and got

comfortable in bed to watch some television. She must have dozed off, because she woke up to pounding on the door next to her. A man was shouting and cussing at the person behind the door. Then everything stopped. Amber, however, could not fall back to sleep. Turning the television up, she dozed off again watching infomercials.

Amber was on day five of her new life. She still hadn't found a job, and her nerves were pretty frayed from lack of sleep. The yelling man came every night at the same time. After taking a quick shower, she was planning on spreading her search for a job out further today. Glancing at the business card still on the night stand, she decided that if she didn't find a job, she'd call today.

Amber had been gone all day, but to no avail as still no job was to be found. As she approached her door, she saw that someone had pried the door open. She pushed the door open to see her room totally ransacked. She stood in the doorway surveying the damage. She knew right away the money was gone. She moved forward in the room, gathering her belongings as she went. This was her breaking point. Tossing the key at the clerk, she left the motel.

Within a half hour Ryan was picking Amber up and moving her into a room with all the rest of the models they employed. They pulled into a long tree covered driveway. A huge white colonial house came into view. He pulled up and around the back of the house, parking the car in the garage. Closing the door behind them, Ryan looked over to Amber. "Welcome to your new home. You are free to wander about. Get to know some of the other girls. If you're hungry, we can stop in the kitchen. You'll love Mildred. She's like a mom to all the other girls. Now, let's get you settled. You'll meet my uncle tomorrow. He meets all the girls before they start working. He'll also tell you what he wants you to do." Ryan opened his door, with Amber following suit.

"How many girls live here?" she asked, walking around the car.

"Right now I think there are fifteen. The number changes daily."

"Why is that?"

"Sometimes one of the girls will land a job out of the country. Normally when that happens, we cut them loose so they can pursue their career." Ryan's eyes ran across Amber's chest. "I would think with your looks, you won't be here too long." His eyes flipped back to her face. The grin on his face said he knew something she didn't. "Come on. Let's get you something to eat, then I'll show you to your room." Ryan made it a point to visit with her whenever he brought another girl to the house. She started looking forward to his visits.

For the next week, Amber posed in bathing suits, lingerie, and evening wear. Her schedule was pretty regimented, breakfast, pose, lunch, pose, dinner, pose. She had been told at her meeting with Richard Arcola what would be expected of her. Follow directions, don't make any trouble, and they would make sure she got a job.

Her first day there she was introduced to Mildred. Mildred was like the house mom, and you could always find her in the kitchen. She was a tall older woman, with greying hair. Amber could tell that at one time this woman had been a beauty. All the girls felt comfortable with Mildred and would just go and hang out in the kitchen with her. That's where she met Lucy and Tia. Amber took an instant liking to Lucy. Tia, however, was the total opposite.

Tia was Vietnamese, with olive skin. Long straight brown hair with blonde streaks, and deep brown cat shaped eyes. Her slim five-foot-eight frame carried a chest you would have thought would have made her topple over. She also had one hell of a chip on her shoulder. She gave off the attitude that she hated everyone and everyone was out to get her. She had been at the house the longest, and the only place she let down her guard was with Mildred. Otherwise, she just snipped comments at all the girls to make them keep their distance.

Lucy, on the other hand, had short brown hair and light brown eyes. She was about five-foot-seven. Her hips were wider, but they supported her ample chest. When she walked into a room, she lit it up with her smile. She got along with everyone, except Tia.

Amber had been at the house for two weeks, when one day she overheard Tia talking to Mildred. "Mr. Arcola wants me to meet him in his room tonight. Mildred, what am I going to do? He's going to find out. What if he makes me leave? Where would I go?"

"Calm down, sweetheart. This could be a good thing." Mildred got Tia's attention. "He hasn't been with any of the other girls. Why does he want you? Hmmm? Maybe it's because you're different and he might want you for himself. Did you ever think of that? Would it be so bad to stay? So many girls come and go through this house, it would be nice for one to stay," Mildred confessed to her.

"When you put it that way, it makes me sound special." Amber heard the change in Tia's voice. It was a mix of happy and planning. "I've always wanted a powerful man. To be spoiled and taken care of." She stopped pacing and looked at Mildred. "You're right; this could be a good thing." Then the doubt entered her tone again. "Unless, I'm just too different for him. Then he could just toss me to the curb. What am I going to do, Mildred?"

She was hugging the woman when Amber pushed through the kitchen door. "What's for lunch?" Amber's voice trailed off when she saw tears in Tia's eye. "Is everything okay?"

"Even if there was something wrong, what would make you think I would tell you?" Tia wiped the last tear away, then turned on Amber. "You're just another wannabe with no talent. You'll be lucky if they don't sell you off to the first bidder." Tia threw those words at her as she left the kitchen.

Amber looked back and forth between Tia and Mildred. "What was that all about? I just came in to get some lunch. That girl's got one bad attitude." Amber walked casually over to the refrigerator, opening the door. Then she stood there as if she was looking for something. "Mildred, what did Tia mean when she said they would sell me to the first bidder?"

"Well, the way it works is, they take your picture, then they post it on this thing called the web. Then they have a party and people come and bid on whether they want you to work for them. If they are the highest bidder, you go home with them. That's why so many girls come and go from this house." Mildred gestured her away from the refrigerator. She reached in and took out some cold cuts to make sandwiches. "That's how Mr. Arcola recoups the money he lays out for taking you girls in."

"But isn't that like selling people?" Amber asked, a pit forming in her stomach.

"No, like I said. It costs money to clothe and feed you. It also takes money to keep this roof over your head, plus heat and water. Did you think all this was free?"

"I never really thought about it." Amber sat down in front of the sandwich Mildred put on the table.

"Well, now you know so I wouldn't get too comfortable. Eventually you all go," Mildred said as she walked out the door leaving Amber to her thoughts.

The next time Ryan came to visit she asked him about what Mildred had said. "Well, yeah. That's how my uncle makes money. We all get our cut, but you girls also get a career. You understand, right?"

"I guess so. It's just… I kind of like being here. What are the places like that the girls go to? Are they like this?"

"Some are, but then some aren't. You'll just have to wait and see. I think you'll be just fine." Ryan had said.

The next week, Lucy and I were told to pack our bags and to wear what was laid out on the bed. We walked to the car together holding hands. In the car was a bottle of champagne and two glasses with a note. 'Good evening, ladies, as you have guested it is now time for you to leave our little house. Time for you to spread your wings and fly. Please sit back, enjoy the ride, and the champagne. I will see you at the party. Try not to be nervous. Everyone at the party has already seen photos of you, and want you to join their company. Your job is to charm them into wanting you the most. Enjoy. R.A.'

By the time the car stopped, the two of them had finished the bottle, and were feeling its effects.

They were both giggling when Ryan walked up to them. He reached for Amber's hand guiding it to rest on his. He began to escort her into the party whispering to her. "If I had the money, I would bid on you. Just smile and be yourself. They are going to love you."

That statement caught Amber's attention. She was feeling very light headed when she walked into the dimly lit room. There were tables all around with a bar at the far end of the room, and a magnificent view of the water out the glass windows to the right. The lights shining on the water from other homes as well as boats gave it an elegant appearance. Music played in the background and a podium was set up in the left corner of the room.

Ryan escorted her to a table and sat her down. Lucy

followed behind them and sat with Amber. "What are we supposed to do? Just sit here?"

"Sit here till you feel comfortable to start mingling. Then grab a drink from a waiter and make an impression. One of the people in this room will be your, shall we say 'employer' for the next few years. Have fun." Ryan strutted away, leaving the two of them at the table.

"This is probably the last time we'll be together. I just wanted to say you are a good friend. The only friend I've ever had. I hope you get everything you ever wanted. I'm going to miss you." Lucy had tears in her eyes as she leaned over to hug Amber.

"Don't say we'll never see each other. It's not like we're going to be held hostage or anything. How about in one year we meet somewhere? I don't know too many places here in California, but I know the Greyhound Bus Station where I got off." Amber took a pen from her purse, and wrote the address on a napkin. "One year from today, we will meet there. Say five o'clock, we'll get some dinner." Amber held her at arms-length. "Thank you, Lucy, you've been my only friend too." Amber took another napkin from the table, catching the tear as it left her eye. "Now, let's stop this blubbering, and go have some fun."

Lucy grabbed two more glasses of champagne from the passing tray. She handed one to Amber raising her glass. "I will never forget you. And I promise if I can get there, I will see you one year from now. If not, we'll try for the year after that, then the year after that. Till one year we will be reunited again." She tapped her glass to Amber's. Then they both downed the glasses of champagne.

"Now, let's get this party started," Amber said, dragging Lucy with her to the DJ. "Can you play something a little more, you know something like this. But where you can dance to it.

You know what I mean? Like Diana Ross, or the Temptations, maybe some Stevie Wonder? You know, dance music?" The DJ smiled at their request and nodded his head. He held his finger up, and made eye contact with someone on the far side of the room. Amber assumed it was his boss. When the man came over, the DJ leaned over to talk to him. When the DJ moved back, the man turned questioning eyes on Amber and Lucy. Then without looking at the DJ he nodded his head. And with that the music instantly changed to Diana Ross *I'm Coming Out.*

Amber grabbed Lucy's hand and led her to the dance floor, where they danced like they were the only ones there. After the second song played, more people joined them; by the third dance, they had been separated and were now dancing with other people. Eventually, the music changed back to a slower pace. By then people were partnering up and they just continued dancing. A very tall man, wearing a cowboy hat came up behind Amber. Leaning his large frame against her, he asked, "Would you like to dance, missy?"

Amber knew the point of tonight was for her to hopefully find someone she wouldn't mind working for. So, when he asked, she agreed. He led her to the dance floor then pulled her in tight to his body. He held her from behind with his hand just above her ass cheeks. Taking her other hand in his, he started moving them around the dance floor. "I've seen your pictures, and they don't do you justice. You are very beautiful. I could use someone like you in my stable."

When he said the word stable, Amber tripped. If he hadn't been holding her so tight, she would have fallen. "Did you say stable? Like in a barn?" Figuring him being a cowboy and all, Amber thought that made sense.

"Yeah, something like that." He grinned back at her.

When the music ended, Amber heard someone tapping on a mic trying to get everyone's attention. "Ahem, excuse me. Can I have everyone's attention? We will begin the bidding in the next five minutes, so can we all take our seats?"

Lucy had come to where Amber was standing. Ryan joined them. "Don't be nervous; you'll do just fine. Now come with me."

As they approached the podium, the Master of Ceremonies began announcing their information from a card he held. When he was finished introducing Lucy, he started the bidding. It went pretty fast and the next thing they knew Lucy was walking out the door with some stuffy lawyer type guy. Then he introduced Amber. The paddles were being raised up all around the room, and the price kept climbing. It finally came down to two bidders. "Do I hear one point two?" The paddle in the front of the room went up. It was the cowboy. Do I have one point three?" The paddle in the back of the room went up. Amber couldn't see who was bidding, but she got the feeling they weren't going to give up. "I now have one point three. Going once, going twice." The cowboy in the front raised his paddle again. "One point four. Do I hear five?" Things were quiet for what felt like forever to Amber. Then the muffled voice in the back said. "Two point five." There were gasps all around the room. Even the MC blew out a pent up breath. "I think that is a new record people. I have two point five. Going once, going twice." He paused given ample time for someone else to bid, and then he said those final words, "Sold to the bidder with paddle number sixty-nine for two point five million dollars. Enjoy your purchase."

Amber started to weave like she was going to pass out. Ryan caught her arm and led her to a chair to sit. He had her drink some water, and put her head down. In that position she saw a pair of very pointy, very high heels come into view. "What's wrong with her? If I just spent two point five million on a sick girl, your uncle will be hearing from me."

"No, no it's just the excitement. Right, Amber?" Ryan cut in.

"I'm fine. It's like Ryan said, it's just the excitement." She raised her head to look at the woman speaking to her. Her eyes kept going up and up. The women before her stood tall at six-foot-two, in her bare feet, with her heels on she was six-foot-six. "It's a pleasure to meet you." Amber rose from the chair extending her hand.

"I'm Madam Mia, but you can call me Mistress or Mia. Now, say your goodbyes. We have a plane to catch. I'll meet you by the door. You have five minutes."

Amber turned to Ryan. "Where is she taking me? Do you know?"

"No Madam Mia has many different places. You'll be fine, she's one of the best. You'll see. You better go now. You don't want to anger her. Take care, Amber. I'm sure we'll meet again." He hugged her and sent her on her way.

Amber made her way to the door. "Where are your belongings?"

"In the trunk of the car I came in."

"Reggie, go get the bags, and meet us at the car." Madam Mia led the way and Amber followed. Within minutes they were on the road. They reached the airport and the car drove to a private jet. Amber stood in awe looking at the plane. "Well, don't just stand there. Let's get going." Mistress Mia, nudged her as she passed her climbing the stairs.

When they were boarded and belted in, Madam Mia kicked off her shoes. Wiggling her toes, she said. "I love my heels, but they don't love me." She looked to where Amber was seated. "Now, let's get the rules out of the way. Break my rules and there will punishments. Understand?"

"Yes," Amber whispered.

"Tell me about yourself. How did you end up with Arcola?"

"Well, I grew up in Florida. I got beat up and when I woke up, I had enough money to get out of town. I came to California. Ryan bumped into me at the bus station and he gave me his business card. When I couldn't find a job and my motel room was ransacked, I called Ryan and he picked me up."

"Did they explain what you would be doing?"

"No, I figured I would be doing what I was doing. Modeling?"

"Do you have any skills? How far did you go in school?"

"I left school before I graduated. So, no I don't have any skills. Although, I thought I was a pretty good model," Amber confessed.

"Well, while you are working for me you're going to learn some new languages. You will also be schooled in what pleases a man. Be it cooking, sports, or drinking games. You will learn them all. I have a distinctive clientele and their tastes vary. You will need to be able to please them. You will also read. All types of reading material, auto mechanics, computers, astrology, even golf. You will need to be able to hold a conversation. These will be some of the things you will learn. You will go to the ballet, opera, and Broadway plays. Once I feel you are ready I will then put you into the rotation. I figure about a year."

"What does it mean 'put into the rotation?'"

"You will start going out with the clients and do whatever is asked of you. Understand?"

"So, I'm to be a prostitute?"

"No, you will be a high class escort. That's why you need to learn. My clients pay for discretion as well as intelligence. Eventually, you will develop your own following. Regulars if you will. Some will just want a beautiful woman on their arm for the evening. Others will want more. You will also learn how to please a man sexually. Do you understand?"

"Yes."

"Yes, what?"

"Yes, Mistress?" Amber said hesitantly.

"Much better. Now, you are still young. As much as some of my clientele like the young ones. I will not allow any of my girls to start working till they are twenty-one. So what are you nineteen, twenty?"

"I'll be eighteen in October."

"What? You're only seventeen?" Amber just nodded her head. "Well, at least you're old enough for your tattoo."

"Yes, Mistress." Amber answered her. When it registered what the Mistress had told her. She asked clarifying, "What do you mean tattoo?"

"All my girls wear my logo. A four-leaf clover on the right breast. Don't worry, it's tasteful. I'll have Alan meet us at the penthouse. Besides that, we'll still be able to work with your age. You'll just be in the learning stage longer than I thought. You will begin training when we get back from this trip. Until then, keep your mouth shut and your ears open. Become a sponge and start sucking up as much as you can. The more you know, the better things will be. I will give you the same opportunity I give all my girls. If you can earn the funds I paid for you, you can buy out your contract. If you can't, you will be working for me for the next ten years; that is the length of all contracts. Now get some rest, we should be landing in New York in a few hours. There is a bed in the back if you want to lay down."

"Thank you, Mistress. I think I will." Amber made her way to the bedroom. She took her gown off and got comfortable in bed. She grabbed the pillow and stuffed her face in it as the tears flowed freely.

Madison felt Xavier wiping the tears from her face as her focus came back to where she was and who she was with.

"The night of the auction on the *Onyx*, you remembered what you just told us, and you were reliving it weren't you? That's why you had the panic attack. It brought all those memories back, didn't it?" Madison just nodded her head yes. "Were you afraid I would do the same thing?" Dimitri asked, his finger sliding over the clover tattoo.

"No. I knew in my heart that's not what that auction was about. But my mind went into overdrive and it just overwhelmed me. I have been seeing a therapist, but there is a lot to sort out. She said it could take years before I can live with what happened to me."

"I know there is more for you to tell us, but that is enough for tonight. Seeing you in tears hurts my chest." Dimitri put his hand over his heart. "I don't like it. You are too beautiful to be crying. Now, let's get you into bed. It's been a long day." Looking at his watch he saw it was just past midnight. "Tomorrow night we will continue." He gathered her in his arms, tucking her head under his chin. "The rest of tonight will be for us." He started walking towards the bed. "Unless you would like to go back to your cabin?"

"No, Master I would like to stay with you and Master Xavier. I feel safest with the two of you."

"That's what I want to hear," Xavier said as he moved the hair from her forehead, and placed a kiss there."

Dimitri got to the side of the bed and waited for Xavier to pull the covers down. Dimitri stood Madison on her feet, and removed her robe. Picking her up again, he placed her on the clean cool sheets. He climbed in next to her as Xavier climbed in on the other side. Tucking her in between them, Xavier framed her face with his hands. He lowered his mouth to hers, gently kissing her. Then feeling her desperation in the kiss, he slid his tongue in, possessing her mouth.

His hand glided down to her chest, molding his hand over her erect nipple. He brought it to a peak, then squeezed it between his fingers, as a moan escaped from Madison's throat. "Your nipples have always been so responsive when I've played with your breasts." He moved, taking her nipple into his mouth, sucking it to a hard nub. "When we play, I will be using a new set of nipple clamps. I had them commissioned just for you." He again lowered his head taking as much of her as he could fit in his mouth. "I don't think I will ever get enough of you."

Dimitri took over where Xavier had left off. He lowered his head to her. Taking her lips in a gentle kiss, showing her how much her story affected him. The thought that she had been sold by that bastard Arcola only made Dimitri hate him more. That man had ruined the lives of so many people Dimitri cared about.

Then there was Xavier, a product of this man's cruelty. Dimitri gave a silent thanks to God that Xavier was nothing like his biological father. In fact, he was the total opposite. Xavier, Dimitri had found was a standup guy. His business dealings were all legal. The relationships he had previously were all consensual. He would have stepped aside had Madison not been able to be with the two of them. These were just a few of the things that Dimitri had seen for himself. The attraction he had thought he felt for Xavier was really an extension of his feelings for Madison. He loved her, and now he could say he loved Xavier as well. He deepened the kiss with that realization.

They began working Madison's body into a frenzy. Xavier focused on her breasts, Dimitri working his way down her body. Kissing and nipping as he went, he slid his big frame between her legs and placed her legs over his shoulders. Swiping his tongue up her clit, he savored her aroma and addicting taste. Dimitri licked his lips with appreciation.

"No finer taste in all the world." Then he dove back in, lapping her juices, igniting Madison, bringing her to the brink then backing off. He thrust two fingers into her, seducing her as he moved them in and out. Stroking her, pushing her, he slid his thumb across her clit. Her head rolled back on the pillows, her body bowing as her orgasm shattered through her.

Xavier continued teasing and sucking on her nipples, helping Dimitri drive her to the edge. Her hips were rising off the bed to meet Dimitri's lashing tongue. Xavier brought her nipple to a peak. Taking it between his fingers he began to twist it back and forth. Heat from the friction raced to Madison's core. Lowering his head, he licked the very tip of her nipple, then blew cold air on it. It was so gentle Madison was unprepared when he bit her. Madison screamed as another orgasm ripped thru her. Her body stiffened as the orgasm flowed through her. Dimitri and Xavier, smiled at each other. Knowing how responsive she could be, they intended to broaden their exploration of her body. And when they played, they were going to push her limits.

Exhausted from the pleasure she had just received, she looked at both men with a satisfied smile on her face. "I needed that. How did you know?" Madison asked, a yawn escaping.

"We know your body better than you. Soon, we will know how that mind of yours works. Once we have that information, we will be able to better care for you," Dimitri said as he placed a kiss on her forehead. "Now, close those eyes and get some sleep. We have a busy day ahead of us."

Madison closed her eyes, snuggling down in the blankets. Xavier spooned her from behind, while Dimitri wrapped her in his arms, her head resting on his chest. Madison fell asleep, safe in their cocoon.

Chapter 10

Madison was having the most delicious dream. She was bound spread eagle on the bed. The great things about dreams were, you could do everything you normally wouldn't do. If Madison were awake, there was no way she would be this relaxed being bound. That was always at the top of Madison's hard limit list.

This was one dream Madison hoped she wouldn't forget. Having Dimitri sucking one nipple to a hard point while Xavier worked on the other made it easy for Madison to relax and enjoy submitting to her Masters. Their bodies laid along each side of her. Their timing with their movements manipulated her body as if they were the same person. When Dimitri's hand trailed down Madison stomach straight to her entrance, pushing two fingers in her drenched opening, her body clamped down. Xavier's fingers followed Dimitri's, only to stop and latch onto her clit, again working in tandem.

Madison bound, knew she would need to ask permission. Even if it was just a dream, she wanted to please her

Masters. Wishing she were awake and free of so many hard limits; to have the freedom to relax and make this fantastic dream go on forever.

"Masters may I come?" Madison whispered in her dream.

Both men raised their heads looking at each other, pleased grins on their faces. Then at Madison, with grateful smiles. "Keep your eyes open on us. I love watching how they dilate with your desire," Xavier commanded as he growled.

Madison had never had such a real dream, she just prayed she didn't wake up. It had been so long since Madison had been able to submit the way her Master had needed her to submit to him. This moment felt like the first time she had given her submission to a Dom when she could trust someone would watch over her and catch her if she fell. With that thought, Madison's body stiffened and came off the bed. Holding nothing back she erupted. This orgasm was unlike any before it. Her walls convulsing, they worked her body. This was the submissive she wanted to be, giving them total control of her body. Madison began to float back on the bed.

Lowering her head back on the pillows, she caught her breath. Her eyes fixed on the mirror above the bed. She could see everything they were doing to her. The view was one she hoped to carve in her memory. Madison looked at her position, bound to the bed. Two heads were at her breasts while their fingers continued their assault. Switching positions, Dimitri worked her clit as Xavier proceeded to hit her g-spot making her squirt. Madison didn't think she would ever stop coming. She had never felt anything like these two men made her feel. She felt the tears slide from her eyes. Partly because it had been so long since she had felt loved and partly because she knew when she woke up, she wouldn't be that sub. She was too damaged.

She felt them kiss the tears away as they moved up her body. "Why the tears beautiful?" Dimitri asked with concern.

"I don't want to wake up. What just happened was so freeing, I don't ever want it to go away."

"Madison, look at me," Dimitri's voice commanded. She turned her attention on Dimitri. "You have been awake this whole time. Well, maybe not in the beginning. But definitely when we latched onto your soaking wet pussy."

Madison started taking shallow breaths. Glancing up over her head at her bound hands. "Madison! eyes on us." Madison tilted her head so she could look at them. "Do you know why we left your hard and soft limits list blank?"

"I just thought you wanted me to confirm them first."

"That's part of it. The other part is, we are writing a contract for 'Our' future." Dimitri waved his hand at the three of them. "Not a contract of our pasts. We think a lot of the things on your hard limit list are because you can't trust the Dom or Master you may be with. That is not the case with us." They started to unbind her from the bed. "As you can see, with us, binding is a pleasurable experience. Would you deny your Masters their pleasure?" She shook her head. "We would never do anything you didn't want. We just think rewriting your limits more accurately will suit all of us. It is something we will try. We just need to be sure."

They started rubbing the feeling back into her arms and legs. "The next time we bind you, you will be awake right from the beginning," Xavier said, kissing her shoulder. "That way you will see with us it will be something you will crave."

Madison didn't understand. Any other time she had been bound in any way, she had had a panic attack, but not with them. Could they be right? Could they really rewrite her limits? "The one I will not bend on is the ball gag," Madison announced.

"Then we will write it on the sheet if you feel that

strongly about it. As your Masters we are here for you. To find out what pleases you as well as us. We will not disregard your feelings, but you have things on your hard limit list that we both desire from our sub. It would be remiss of us to not make sure they absolutely need to be on the list. Are you willing to trust your Masters to know what is best for you?"

"Yes, Masters. Now, if it would be all right with you both, I would like to go take a shower." She put her hands up stopping them from moving. "Alone. Then, I'd like to go relax in the sun. This is still a lot for me to take in, and I'd like some girl time." She looked at them with pleading eyes. "I'm sure you must have some business you need to take care of?" She tilted her head towards Dimitri.

"That will work. First, you will have breakfast. We can order it in, or you could come and get to know my brother? Xavier, what are your plans?" Dimitri's attention going to Xavier.

"I really hadn't thought about it. My mind was so wrapped up in making last night happen. I never thought any further. Breakfast does sound good. Then, I think I'll go workout. How about we all meet for lunch?"

Dimitri rolled off the bed, dragging Madison with him. Xavier smacked her ass, as it slid past him. Standing next to the bed rubbing her ass, Madison watched as Dimitri changed the mirrors back to windows. The view was beautiful. The sun had risen, and you could see water for miles.

Madison walked to the windows, where Dimitri wrapped her up in his arms. "I created this room with this exact position in mind. Now that it's here, it's so much better then I imagined." He snuggled his chin in her neck.

Xavier joined them. "Was I part of that vision?" Wrapping Madison's arms around his waist, he pressed his back to her front, leaning his head on her other shoulder.

"Not at first, but after we met and talked, I began to envision how Madison would melt into the both of us. I'll be honest when I did think of it, I walked around semi-erect. However," snuggling closer to her. "Nothing compares to reality."

They stood taking in the moment. Dimitri was the first to move. Smacking Madison in the ass, he asked, "Breakfast in or out?"

Rubbing her cheek again, she said, "Out. I'd like to get to know your brother."

"I was hoping you'd say that. I'll call him and arrange it while you are in the shower. Xavier, help her get clean. We want our girl sparkling when she greets the world. I'll jump in after I lay out her clothes."

Dimitri joined them as Xavier was rinsing the conditioner out. "As much as I would like to prolong this shower, we need to speed this up. Kristoff will meet us at the buffet in a half hour."

"No problem, we're finished. We'll be ready." They exited the shower, and left Dimitri to his. Laid out on the bed was a dark green string bikini with a green floral sarong. A four-inch pair of wedge sandals rested on the floor. "When you're dressed, I'll dry your hair for you."

"If it's all right, Master, I was going to let it dry on its own?" Madison was tying her bikini bottoms on. She bent to pick up the top, or what she assumed was the top. Holding it up to Dimitri as he came up shaking the towel over his head, she said, "Master, I don't think it's the right size top for me?"

"No, my pet. It's the right size. Let me help you." Dimitri had her turn around. He tied the strings behind her back then reached up to take the strings she was holding. She pulled her hair up when Dimitri began tying the strings.

Madison tried to adjust the small pieces of material to cover her nipples. "If I didn't know better, I would think that you are putting me on display."

Dimitri walked over to her wearing a pair of jeans and a black t-shirt that fit tight across his chest. "Exhibition is another thing on your soft limit list. And before you start to panic, we will not be doing scenes in the arena. You're a beautiful woman. Why wouldn't we want to show off our special sub?" Dimitri said, kissing her shoulder. "Now let's get going. I can't wait for you both to really meet my brother." He stopped by the sofa table, holding out a key to Madison. "Put this with your cabin key. We would like it if you would stay in this cabin. If you choose not to, you will need a very good reason for why you are not staying with us. But we will listen with an open mind when you explain why you need your space."

"Thank you, Master. I enjoyed our night together. If this is what I have to look forward to, I don't think I will need my other cabin." She leaned over and kissed his cheek.

Pulling her close and kissing her, Dimitri said, "I knew I would love these shoes when I bought them. I look forward to you wearing them tonight."

Xavier wearing jeans, and a muscle shirt, was holding the door open his gym bag in hand. "After you." He wound his arm around, his hand pointing towards the hallway.

They walked to the elevators in a comfortable silence, taking it down to the third deck. They turned towards the dining room. During the hours of six and ten in the morning, the dining room was transformed into a breakfast buffet. Instead of the elaborate elegant look the dining room had for dinner, the breakfast dining room was a very simple design, with tables placed by the windows for guests to enjoy the view. Food stations lined the opposite wall. After filling their plates, they found Kristoff quick enough. He was seated at a table next to the window, and he wasn't alone.

"Good morning, Jasmine, how was your first night at sea?" Xavier asked, holding the chair for Madison.

Kristoff had stood up, as his manners demanded, introducing himself. Shaking hands with Xavier, then Dimitri, he cut in. "I had the best night. While on my way to the crewmember auction, I literally ran into Jasmine. No bodily injury, but I couldn't wound her pride further by walking away. So, I invited her for a drink and let's just say we got to know each other." His smile grew with his cryptic description.

Madison reached across the table to Jasmine. "Hi, I'm Madison."

Jasmine reciprocated. "Jasmine. I'm Xavier's assistant. I've spoken with you on the phone."

"Oh, it's a pleasure to finally meet you." The smile fell from Madison's face, remembering some of the conversations she had had with Jasmine. "I'm so sorry for my poor behavior towards you. You were only doing your job."

"No worries. I told him he should have made the calls himself. But, no, Master Xavier always knows best. Right, Sir?" Jasmine gave him her most sarcastic face.

"You were right as usual. Now, can we move on to any other subject."

The women laughed at how uncomfortable Xavier became.

"All right, what are everyone's plans for today? I will be working till lunch. After that, a little mingling. Madison?"

"Well, I'll be up on the Sun Deck for about an hour. I'm hoping to run into Sadie. I can't wait to hear how Cameron reacted? Then lunch."

Jasmine chimed in. "The Sun Deck sounds good to me. Mind if I join you?" Although Xavier hadn't asked her too. Jasmine had the feeling she was still needed to keep an eye on Madison.

"Sure. If you're anything like Melanie, you're the one who can tell me all of Xavier's secrets. Right?"

"The will be no secret telling. I will answer any question you have. Just ask," Xavier growled.

"Thank you, Xavier. I will keep that in mind." Changing the subject, she turned her attention to Kristoff. She knew his identity needed to stay a secret. "So Kristoff, how do you know Dimitri?" Once she knew that answer she would know how to proceed.

"Our families lived near each other. You could say we were as close as brothers." He smiled at Dimitri. "We did everything together. Right, Dimitri?"

Dimitri's sarcastic smile at Kristoff told him he wasn't happy with his play on words. "Yes, I would describe you as an annoying little brother."

Kristoff put a shocked look on his face. "Me! I would have been the perfect little brother and you know it."

Nodding his head yes. "Yes, as I remember you were a good substitute for a little brother."

Madison cut into their bantering. "So, Kristoff, how long has it been since you two have seen each other?"

"Too long. So much has changed. For starters, I made this trip. I've never been to the states. I haven't seen much of them either. I got right on the ship after arriving. I do, however, plan on doing some exploring when we get back to port. I hear Las Vegas is a den of iniquity. Sounds like fun! I'd also like to see New York too. That's the city that never sleeps. Right?"

"New York is where we live. You'll have to visit when you're in town," Jasmine chimed in, smiling at Kristoff.

"Yes, I will. I would like to see where Dimitri's offices are. I hear you have an incredible view of the city. That's what Sadie told me."

"I think coming to New York is a much better idea then Vegas. I remember you were never very good at betting,"

Dimitri added with an edge to his voice. "How is the old country? Things pretty much the same?"

"It's old. Nothing ever changes there except the seasons. We'll speak of the old country another time. Right now I want to enjoy hearing about you and the two people who make you happy. Hum?" He leaned his chin on his bridged fingers, elbows on the table.

"That sounds like my cue to leave. You ready, Jasmine?" Madison asked, standing up. To her Masters she said, "I will see you at lunch. The Master's Lounge? When both men agreed, she turned her attention to Jasmine.

"I agree. Too much testosterone at this table." Jasmine rose from her chair. Kristoff stood as well as Dimitri and Xavier.

"Would you like to join me in my cabin for dinner tonight?" Kristoff asked Jasmine, taking her hands in his and raising them to his lips.

"That sounds like an offer I can't refuse." Jasmine smiled looking up at Kristoff's face.

"See you at six?" He released her hands when her head gave a nod of approval. "Till then." He bowed at the waist, his eyes glued to hers.

"Till then." She smiled down at his gesture. Jasmine joined Madison and they headed to the Sun Deck.

All three of them watched as the women walked away from them. Kristoff said to Dimitri and Xavier, "Your Madison is very beautiful. However, Jasmine is sex personified."

The men all sat back down at the table. "Jasmine is not to be played with. Do you understand, Kristoff?" Xavier's focus zeroed in on Kristoff.

Not realizing that Xavier was voicing a warning, Kristoff said off handedly. "But that is what subs are for aren't they?"

Dimitri put a hand on a rising Xavier, quietly saying,

"Don't fall for his childishness. He knows full well how a sub is to be treated. He was just being Sabastian."

Both men turned and looked at Dimitri. Stunned looks on their faces. "What? Is there something on my face?" Dimitri questioned. Wiping the napkin across his face.

"Dude. You just called him Sabastian!" Xavier whispered.

All three men swiveled in their chairs with heads turning in all directions making sure no one had heard his comment. "I think we're good." Kristoff looked at Xavier. "No worries, Xavier, I really was just playing. She's special, I knew it the minute I looked in her eyes. We really did connect. No worries, I'll take care of her."

Xavier released his clinched fists, relaxing back in his chair. "As long as we're on the same page. She hasn't had a steady Dom in some time. I have been told it's my fault. I think I just might have to get my assistant an assistant." He gave a chuckle at that thought. "I am very fond of her and I tend to be overly protective of her. She doesn't play games, so don't play games with her. That's my advice if you really think something can happen with the two of you?" He turned a surprised face to Dimitri. "Look at me, I sound like my father."

"My advice would be stay away from her till your problem is solved. But I know you won't. So, make sure you are honest with her. You know that if you're not it will be a sure way of her getting hurt. Both physically and emotionally. If that happens, 'brother,' I will unleash Xavier on you."

"I got it! No hurting Jasmine. Moving on."

"Yes, moving on. What are your plans?" Dimitri asked drinking his coffee.

"I plan on enjoying myself for the next five days, and then worry about it. How does that sound?"

Dimitri and Xavier exchanged looks. Both men being

business minded. They knew having a plan in place before playing was always the way to go. "I think your time would be better spent working on how you're going to get out of the mess you are in. Don't you?"

"But I just got here, can't you give me a day to enjoy myself. Then I'll work on a plan," Kristoff pleaded with them, putting his hands together as if he was praying.

"Fine, little brother, you have until tomorrow at dinner. Then either you come up with a plan or we will."

"We will?" Xavier questioned.

"Of course. He's part of your family now. You should be involved with the decision making. Don't you think?"

Xavier's body seemed to relax. He didn't realize until just then how tense he had been. Initially he thought it was because he was meeting Dimitri's brother. Now he knew that hadn't been it at all. Xavier had been worried about how Dimitri would be with him after last night. Now he knew things would change, but he would be a part of them. "Of course he is. When do I get to hear this fantastic story that has now put us all in danger?"

"I'm going to tell Jasmine tonight. No game playing. She'll need to know what she's getting into with me. Then we can meet tomorrow and we'll talk. How does that sound?"

The men exchanged looks, both nodding in agreement. Xavier picked up his gym bag and rose from the table. "I'm off to the gym if you'd like to join me?" Looking at Kristoff.

"If it's okay with Dimitri, I'd like to follow him around. See what an American business man does? Get to know my brother again."

"I think I would like that," Dimitri replied.

"Okay then I'm going to head out. I will see you for lunch." Xavier looked at Dimitri. He offered his hand to Kristoff. "Welcome to the family. I'm sure whatever your problem is we'll find a solution for it. Dimitri can be very resourceful."

"So I've heard." Kristoff held onto Xavier's hand applying pressure and pulling him in so only Xavier heard him. "Same as your Jasmine, don't hurt my brother."

"You have my word on that," Xavier said with confidence. "Later."

They watched as Xavier left the room. "You trust him?" Kristoff asked, his eyes still following Xavier.

"With my life." Dimitri looked Kristoff in the eyes. "I've gotten to know him these past months. Don't let his appearance fool you. He is a very intelligent man. We've even done some business deals together. All of them successful."

"He just comes off as a real douche. You know what I mean?"

"Yeah, I know what you mean. The first time we met I almost walked out. I'm glad I stayed. If last night is an example of how things are going to be, I'm really glad I stayed. He's a bit to take in, but once you get to know him, you'll love him just like the rest of us. Now, let's go. I need to meet with Captain Russell. Then Cooper and Wyatt and get a security update. After that paperwork. Still want to follow me around?" Dimitri asked with a big smile on his face.

"Yes, I really do. I can't tell you how much I missed you. When you weren't there anymore, well, let's just say, it really sucked."

"I'm sorry, Sabastian." The words were barely whispered. "I couldn't stay anymore. I needed to move away, you know that."

"In my mind I always thought you would come back. But in my heart I knew you wouldn't. I'm just glad I'm here now."

"All right then, let's get this day started." Dimitri got up from his chair. "I'm happy you're here as well. We have a lot to catch up on."

Kristoff followed Dimitri to the elevators. The doors opened and inside stood Cameron. The smile that spread across his face to his eyes transformed his face. "Good morning, gentlemen, going up?"

The two brothers looked at each other, grins on their faces. Dimitri spoke first stepping into the elevator. "By the look on your face, I'd say it was a satisfying evening? So is married life all it's cracked up to be?"

"It's not what happened. Although, putting our wedding night into a scene is something I could do over and over again." Cameron shook the thoughts from his glazed over eyes. "No, it's what Sadie gave me." He smirked at them as the doors closed.

Madison and Jasmine settled into the lounge chairs, drinks in one hand, e-readers in the other. "So, Jasmine, how was your first night on the cruise. No sea sickness?"

"No. I grew up on boats. This is my first erotica cruise though. I am looking forward to observing the dungeon arena later. I never made it last night, after bumping into Kristoff on my way to the auction. Not that I'm complaining. I've heard good things about the arena. It's been awhile since I've had time to even go to my club. I plan on sucking up, all pun intended, everything I've been missing." Jasmine took a sip of her fruity umbrella drink. Smiling from ear to ear.

"Can anybody join this party?" Sadie asked as she approached Madison and Jasmine.

"Sure pull up a lounge chair," Madison invited. "I don't know if you've met Jasmine. She's Xavier's assistant."

"Yes, we've already had the pleasure. I'm glad Xavier allowed you the time. I'm surprised he's not making you work on your vacation," Sadie joked with Jasmine. When Jasmine didn't laugh Sadie's mouth dropped open.

"You've got to be kidding me. I told him no working on my honeymoon. Wait till I see him!" Sadie huffed as she sat down.

"No worries, Sadie, we've already negotiated the terms of payment," Jasmine said, sipping away on her drink a mischievous smile appearing.

"I knew you were a smart woman," Sadie said as she lounged back in her chair. "If I start to doze, please nudge me awake. I was reminded of the punishment I would receive if I got too much sun. I can handle Cameron's punishments. I just wouldn't want to disappoint him on our honeymoon."

"Smart. And having sunburn on your honeymoon would suck," Jasmine commented.

Sadie turned her attention to Madison. "And, how was your first night? I had no idea until Cameron filled me in last night. You must think I'm the worst friend ever. I know I was wrapped up in the wedding, but you could have talked to me about your relationship." She lifted her sunglasses to glare at Madison.

"There was nothing to talk about. I had no idea what they were planning until last night." Madison paused licking her lips. "I think it was the best night of my life." She sat up swinging her legs to the side of her chair. "I never would have thought with Dimitri being the possessive Master he is, that adding Xavier was even an option. He told me that he and Xavier have been getting to know each other. How he had approached Xavier a few months ago." Realization dawned on Madison's face. "During that whole time Xavier had been trying to get me to go out with him. But I refused every time thinking that's what I was supposed to do. I was starting to doubt my relationship with Dimitri because I knew my feelings for Xavier had never gone away. After last night I now know that I don't have to make any decisions. They did it for me."

Madison hesitated sipping her drink, looking at Sadie. "Do you know anything about the room we are staying in? The Midnight Suite?" When Sadie shook her head no, Madison described the room to them. "It's the perfect room. It has everything. And the view, oh my God. I've never seen anything like it. Dimitri told me he designed it with me in mind."

Jasmine chimed in at this point. "So, now what happens? You have to forgive me but, as Xavier's assistant, I typed up the contract." She shrugged her shoulders then continued. "Will you be able to sign the contract?" She didn't want to say anything out loud that Madison might not want Sadie to know about. So she generalized the question. What she really wanted to know was if Madison was going to be able to tell them everything they wanted to know about her.

"We're working on it." Madison smiled as she lounged back in her chair. A comfortable silence fell over them, each of them enjoying the quiet relaxation. Madison rested her head on the headrest and closed her eyes. Thinking about what she had told Dimitri and Xavier last night.

She hadn't thought about Lucy in a while. They had tried to stay in touch, but after faking her death she couldn't stay in touch with anyone from that part of her life. Madison's thoughts started to drift. As her memory pulled Lucy to the front of her brain, she remembered the first time they had meet at the bus terminal in L.A.

"I can't believe you came." Lucy hugged her tight, not wanting to let her go. "For the past four years I've come here and waited for you to show. This was going to be the last year I came. I'm so glad you showed up." Pulling away, she looked at Amber.

"I tried each year, but Madam Mia would always tell me I couldn't. Not till I finished my training and knew my place. She really didn't trust that I would come back. This year I made sure there was no doubt. I told her I would take anyone she wanted to send with me as long as I could go. She looked at me as calm as could be and said, 'Go ahead, you have seventy-two hours. That should give you enough time to fly there, see your little friend, and get back to New York. My plane will fly you and wait at the airport. You will pay me back for the time and the plane. If for some strange reason you are not back when the plane is scheduled to take off, make sure you're dead because when I find you, you will wish you were.' I didn't care what I had to promise her. I just knew I had to come." Amber looked at Lucy.

"I'm just glad you didn't forget. Let's go find a place to eat. Close to the airport. It sounds like Mistress Mia has you on a short rope. I wouldn't want to be the cause of more trouble in your life."

"That sounds great, you can tell me what happened to you after that night. We can catch a cab at the terminal."

"No need," Lucy said smiling. "My driver will take us anywhere I want to go." Lucy pointed to the tinted windowed black limousine. As they approached the vehicle the driver got out to open the door.

"Jerry, can you find a place for us to eat by the airport? Amber has a flight to catch and I don't want her to miss it."

"Yes, Miss Lucy. I know a fine restaurant, it's quiet and has good Italian."

"Okay with you?" Lucy asked Amber.

"Absolutely, I like good Italian. I'm just really glad to see you."

Lucy put her index finger over her lips before she told Jerry, "Thank you, that will be fine." Then she sat back in the seat. She turned her head to look at Amber and whispered, "I will explain."

The ride seemed pretty short even though the I-110 was backed up. When they arrived at the hostess desk, Amber found out that Jerry had called ahead and made a reservation. The hostess took them to a private table away from the other guests. "We are so happy you can join us today, Ms. Jordan. It's always a pleasure. I will send your waiter over right away."

As soon as the hostess left, Lucy held her finger up again. No sooner did her hand hit the folded napkin in front of her, the waiter was at their table. Lucy ordered a bottle of wine and he told them the specials. After he was done, she told him she would wave him over when they were ready to order.

"What the hell is going on?" Amber leaned forward asking in a whisper, placing her napkin in her lap.

"I'll explain everything as soon as I can, but for now please keep the conversation light."

The pleading look in Lucy's eyes told Amber that Lucy was watched more than she was. Amber gave a nod of her head and asked, "I hear the weather has been out of control here lately. How do you deal with it?" She picked up the menu.

"I try not to go out," Lucy said, laughing. She had an infectious laugh and once she got going you couldn't help but laugh with her. "But when I have to, Jerry keeps the car at a comfortable temperature for me."

After the waiter poured their wine, they placed their

order. Finally, alone Lucy started to explain. "You remember the night we were auctioned off?"

"As if I could forget. Everything changed for us that night."

"Well, the stuffy looking lawyer, was just that. A lawyer. He put me in the backseat of a car, took me to the airport and there I met the man who really bought me."

Their food arrived, and Lucy paused her story. "Can I get you anything else?" They both said no and the waiter left them to their meal.

"Okay, so what was he like? Things don't seem that bad for you," Amber questioned.

"No, they really aren't. Except that I can't go anywhere alone." Amber scrunched her forehead. "The man who bought me is a billionaire who lost his only granddaughter. She ran away from home at twenty-one; a few months later they found her body. He wouldn't believe that she was really dead so he continued to search. He was told about the auctions and started searching for any girls who looked like her. He would send his lawyer with a picture and if the lawyer thought the girl was a good match he would buy her. That's how I ended up where I am. In fact, I look so much like his granddaughter he stopped looking for her. He set all the girls he had collected with trust funds and sent them away. He went so far as to adopt me. The only problem is he thinks he's going to lose me. Amber, I've never been happier. I never knew my own grandfather, however, I know with a certainty this man treats me better than my own grandfather would have."

Lucy paused taking a sip of her wine. "I've come to love him. He is the only person, besides you who has ever given a shit about me. He treats me like a princess. Who would have ever thought my life could turn around? I really thought that night I was going to kill myself. If anyone had forced themselves on me I would have. But instead I started a new life. He said he wanted to make sure I never ran away again. So he put me into his will. As long as I stay till he dies, I get the money no questions. His lawyer drew the papers up in front of me and I watched him sign them and his lawyer witnessed it. I don't want for anything. I spend time helping him eat. I read to him and he taught me how to play chess. He brought tutors in to teach me and I got pretty good grades too. I am working on my degree in business. He suggested that as my major. He wanted to make sure I knew how to take care of myself financially after he was gone. The only thing is, I'm not allowed to talk about it. When I told him about our arrangement to meet, I asked if I could tell you. I told him that you were my only friend, and that you wouldn't tell anyone. He agreed, and each year that you didn't show it became easier to ask. I guess he thought you would never show. I promised him that if I did tell you, no one would be able to overhear. So that was what all the secretiveness was."

Amber had finished eating. She sat back sipping her wine mulling over what Lucy had just told her. "So if I had been shorter, with less curves, the lawyer could have bought me too?"

"Probably?"

"Shit. Well, if one of us had to make it I'm glad it was you. After everything you've been through, you deserve this." She raised her glass. "To Lucy, may your grandfather live a long happy life."

They touched glasses. "I hope so too." Lucy added. "So, now what's your story. What have you been doing that you've been kept on such a short leash?"

"I've kind of been doing what you have. I've been going to school. Only I've learned things that will please a man. Be it sports, finance, food, or sex. I know about them all. I speak four languages, I dance, know karate. I can even fly a helicopter, and put a gun back together. I know about art, and literature. Music and the stock market. Anything that a man might bring up in conversation I have some knowledge of it. As far as the sex part, Mistress Mia has only allowed me to go on sex free dates so far. She needed to see how I would handle myself. I have to say so far it's working out." Amber paused as the waiter cleared the table and brought coffee and dessert.

"So you're an escort? Someone to look good on some guy's arm?" Lucy asked.

"I guess you could say that. I still consider myself a prostitute. She gets paid no matter what I have to do. I can also say my wardrobe has expanded. From gowns to school girl clothes. I have to dress the part." Amber started to laugh.

"What's so funny?" Lucy questioned.

"There is a light at the end of my tunnel. I'll be free five years from now." Amber wiped a tear from her eye. She wasn't even sure if it was because of laughing, or if she was leaking tears. "Then again, if I can make two point five million someday, I can buy my freedom. I just don't think that's ever going to happen, but I can still laugh about it. Otherwise I'd cry." Amber drained the rest of her wine. "Lucy, this has been fun, but I really have to get going. I will try again next year. I'm so glad that your life has changed for the better. You deserve it. Do you still want to try again next year?" Amber asked rising from the table.

"Yes, of course I do." Reaching out she tugged Amber into a tight hug. "I just had a thought." Lucy pulled back grinning at Amber. "What if I bought your contract? One day I'm going to have billions. Write down everything about Mistress Mia." Lucy dug in her bag for a pen and paper. "I'll have my lawyer research the information. Amber, if I can do it I will."

"Thank you, Lucy. But in order for that to happen your

new grandfather would have to die. I'm doing all right. Enjoy whatever time you have left with him. Don't wish death on him for me."

Lucy still held the pen and paper out to her. "That's not what I'm doing. I'm just being prepared. Write."

Amber took the paper and pen, writing down what she knew. "Lucy, be careful when you start searching for a man. You know what kind of slimes in fancy clothing there are out there. Don't be fooled, make sure you really know the guy before you fall head over heels. You're my only friend and I care about you."

"I get it. Don't worry about me. I already have a list of qualifications from Grandfather." Lucy started to laugh, and Amber couldn't help but laugh with her.

Madison opened her eyes, her smile still in place from the memory of Lucy's laugh, it had been so real. She turned to see that Sadie had already left, and Jasmine had turned over at some point and was fast asleep. She sat up in her chair, then stood moving to the railing. As her gaze scanned the quests, Madison kept hearing Lucy's laugh. She narrowed her search to a group of subs standing by the Spa and Salon, she just couldn't make out their features. There were four of them, all different heights and hair color. What would be the odds of Lucy being on this ship? Madison thought. Turning from the rail, she shook Jasmine on the shoulder then gathered her things. "Hey, I just wanted to let you know that I'm leaving. I have lunch plans with my Masters, and I want to get cleaned up before I meet them."

"Thanks for waking me. I think I'll do the same. Get cleaned up, I mean. Then it's off to the spa for me. I'll see you at dinner?"

"I'm not sure what the plans are, but we do have to eat. Plus, I'm sure Dimitri has to attend since Cameron and Sadie are now officially on their honeymoon. So yeah, probably."

"Enjoy your lunch."

"I think I will," Madison said, a smile in place as she left. When she got to the area she thought the laugh had been coming from, no one was there. She stood and turned in a circle looking and listening, but she found nothing. She thought to herself it sounded so real. She had missed Lucy. They had met only one more year before Amber faked her death. Lucy still didn't know she was alive. And Madison planned on keeping it that way.

Chapter 11

Madison walked into the Master's Lounge. Standing in the doorway she surveyed the room looking for her Masters. She wore a fern green and pink floral sundress. The built in bra helped hold her chest in place along with the thin straps on her shoulders. A green satin thong was tied on her hips. The floral changed her eye color to a lighter green. Her brunette hair hung down, curling on the ends by her breasts. Mascara and lip gloss were her only makeup. A four-inch pair of wedge sandals wrapped up her calf finished her outfit. She felt like Doris Day without the pig tails. But that had been what was laid out on the bed, so here she was wearing it. Looking at the attire of the other guests in the lounge. She felt over-dressed.

The lay out was similar to the *Onyx* with few differences. The piano and the kitchen doors were on the opposite sides of the bar and the colors were different. The sapphire blue and burgundy walls and accents gave the room a majestic look. The tablecloths were burgundy while the napkins were sapphire. Floral arrangements graced some tables. Others arrangements flicked with light from candles. You could feel the seductive pull of the room as soon as you walked in.

Madison found her Masters at a table close to the piano. Dimitri's sandy blonde hair had grown reaching his ears emphasizing his strong jaw line. His hazel eyes sparkling with the lighting of the room. He wore a black t-shirt with the Midnight Oasis logo on his shoulder. When he rose she saw he was wearing jeans, and not his usual pair of slacks.

She turned her attention to Xavier. He was dressed similar to Dimitri. His chest stretching the material of his V-neck Armani shirt. His light chest hairs peeking out through the opening. He had kept his hair buzzed on the sides, but had let the top grow out. His crystal blue eyes blazed brightly as Madison moved towards them. Approaching Dimitri, she wondered if she should find out if Lucy was on the cruise. But then she thought about the privacy agreement everyone was required to sign. Would he be able to tell her?

They both rose from their chairs as she walked up to the table. "Why are your cheeks red? Didn't you put sunscreen on?" Dimitri questioned as he brushed his lips on each cheek.

She turned towards Xavier to greet him, but he cut her off with a low growl. "If your cheeks are this red what else is red?" He moved the straps slowly across her shoulder, checking her shoulder for more sunburn.

"I'm sorry." Looking back and forth between them. "I did put sunscreen on. I must have been distracted talking with the girls and forgot to do my cheeks. Then I feel asleep on top of that, but it's only my cheeks." She bowed her head waiting for them to display their displeasure. When nothing was said after a few seconds. Madison raised her eyes looking between them, only to see they were waiting for her to look at them.

"Although we are not pleased that you did not take better

care of yourself, you were not given any direct commands while you were away from us to warrant any punishment. However, after seeing your red cheeks, we may have to reconsider that." His beautiful smile made her heart beat faster. "Would you like to sit now?" He held the chair between them.

Madison's smile was hesitant as she sat, knowing she had just dodged a bullet. She knew they would say something about the sunburn. She thought they would at least say hello first. She would make sure to put sunscreen on her cheeks first next time. 'Good afternoon, Madison, we're so glad you could join us.' She mumbled sarcastically under her breath.

"Good afternoon, Madison, we're so glad you could join us," Xavier mimicked her words. Madison froze putting her napkin in her lap. "Your care comes before manners. Always remember that. Now, what should we have? I'm in the mood for a big fat juicy cheeseburger."

The conversation slowed each deciding what they would be eating. They placed their order and the waiter left to get their drink order. Dimitri and Xavier began to make plans for the evening, but Madison's brain couldn't shake the thought that Lucy was on the ship. When the men realized she wasn't paying attention, with a nod of Dimitri's head, each one began running their hands up Madison's leg. Startling her out of her thoughts she almost fell off the chair. Catching her before she hit the floor, Dimitri asked her. "Where were you just now, beautiful?" Concern showed on Dimitri's handsome face as he pushed her gently back onto the seat.

Madison looked between her two Masters. "If I tell you something about my past outside of the Midnight Suite, do the same rules apply?"

Xavier waited for Dimitri to confirm with a head nod before he spoke up. Cupping Madison's hand in his, getting her attention. "If you want to tell us something then yes, Madison, the same rules apply."

"We want you to tell us and free yourself of the burden, but it all has to be in your own time. Where you tell us has no bearing. Madison, we both have things in our pasts we're not proud of. We have just reconciled them and now they stay in the past. That's what we are trying to do for you. Free your mind of the past, so you can focus your thoughts on the present and our future," Dimitri finished.

Madison reached for her water glass. Glancing around her as she drank the ice cooled water. Her attention turned to Dimitri. "Could you tell me if a specific passenger is on board?"

"Is this person a part of your past, and why you were miles away?" He waited for her confirmation before he continued. "I'm not supposed to, but if it's important to you I will."

"What's this all about Madison?" Xavier spoke up.

Madison glanced away, butterflies fluttering in her belly. Not sure if they would think she was crazy. Just because of a dream. She shook her head, putting a genuine smile on her face. "It was just…" she paused. "A thought. I don't want you to break any rules."

"I'm sure if you have a good enough reason Dimitri could ask Alejandro to check the manifest."

The waiter chose that moment to arrive with lunch. "This looks delicious." When they were alone again she looked at Dimitri. "You really don't have to." When both men glared at her, she knew she needed to explain. "I had a dream about an old friend. She had a very distinctive laugh and when I woke earlier…" She laughed with the thought, looking at Dimitri. "Well, anyway, I thought I heard it. When I went to see where it was coming from, there were too many people. I was just curious if you could see if it was her."

"We made some modifications on the ship's computers. Now you can only see someone's bio if they swipe their card and then scan their hand print. After what happened on the *Onyx* we needed to improve on security. As well as a million-dollar privacy disclosure clause being added."

"It's all good. Like I said it was just a dream." She began eating her lunch again. "So, what are the plans for tonight? I told Jasmine I'd see her at dinner."

"That's what we were planning when you faded away," Xavier teased her. "Is there anything special you would like to do?" Madison acknowledged his question with a shake of her head. "Since Dimitri needs to be in attendance tonight, the evening will go as follows. Dinner, show, after party, and then story time. I suggest after lunch you get some rest."

Madison tilted her head to the side mulling over what Xavier had told her. "That might be a good idea. Will I have company?" Hitching her eyebrows up and down. Her expression took a sudden turn.

"What's the matter?" Concern in Dimitri's voice, he reached for Madison's hand.

Xavier watched the encounter at the table. Then his attention was drawn away as his brother and new wife entered the lounge. Concern on their face. "Did Chester come in here?" Cameron asked.

"Chester, who's Chester?" Xavier's voice rising as he felt something brush his leg. Raising the tablecloth, he exposed a black masked apricot colored bull mastiff. Madison's napkin hanging from his mouth.

"That's Chester. Come here, boy." Cameron called him. Tripping over the napkin hanging from his mouth, Chester rolled out from under the table. Gaining his footing on his giant paws, he pranced over to Cameron. He picked up the roly-poly wiggly puppy. "My wedding gift to Sadie was the rights to Todd Phillips new smash hit, *Heroin: Life without*

Needles. Starring Broadway's newest star my wife, Sadie Alexander." Cameron paused for the applause Sadie received. "She gave me Chester. Did you all know about this?"

"Well, I did. She needed to know if he could come on the ship." Dimitri teased the pup with his napkin, making him squirm more in Cameron's arms. "Were you surprised?"

"Extremely!"

"You should have seen how excited she was with the idea. He's cool looking. Just keep him in his appointed areas and we shouldn't have any problems. That means, get him out of here." Dimitri grabbed Chester's jowls, stretching them out, then reaching for his paws. "He's going to be huge."

"I know. It's been awhile since I've had a dog. It was the last thing I would have guessed Sadie would give me."

"Well, you have everything else. You didn't have one of these." She mushed her face to Chester's nose, changing her voice playfully. "And just look at this face." As Chester licked her face.

"I've never owned a pet." Madison's quiet voice came from the table.

"Never?" Sadie questioned looking around the pup at her. "Not even a gold fish?"

"Nope. I had enough to worry about with just myself. Adding another living thing to the equation wasn't an option."

"That sucks!" Sadie exclaimed.

"We better get Chester out of here. See you guys at dinner?" Cameron cut in, as they made their way to the door.

"We'll be there," Xavier answered.

Dimitri and Xavier helped Madison from her chair. "Let's get our girl back to the room. I think a soak in that

139

extra-large tub is just what we need," Xavier said, rolling his shoulders as they exited the lounge.

"Work out with Harley?" Dimitri asked, a knowing grimace on his face.

"Yeah. Don't let his age fool you. I just went over to say hello. The next thing I know I'm in some kind of weight to rep competition. That man kicked my ass."

Dimitri and Madison were laughing by the time he finished. "He's really good at what he does though," Dimitri commented.

"He helped Sadie stay on track. It really helped while she was working and planning the wedding. I'm thinking about hiring him for a month or two."

Dimitri stopped her from walking turning her to face him. "Why would you need to hire him? You're perfect the way you are."

Madison reached up placing her palm on his cheek, she kissed him gently. "You are so cute, thank you for that compliment. But if I'm going to please two Masters now..." She paused, an impish look on her face. "I'm going to need a lot more stamina. I thought working out with Harley would help. Once I had a routine I would be able to continue on my own."

Dimitri looked deep into those moss green eyes. "Another thing to add to our contract. I'm proud of you for taking care of yourself for us." Leaning down he took her lips in a searing kiss.

He released her and Madison's mind was no longer thinking of rest. She gave him a satisfied look. Knowing what she had said made him happy.

They each took a hand and continued on to the suite.

Opening the door to the suite Madison smelled the ocean air. When she walked in, she saw openings in the wall of windows letting in the fresh air. Dropping her things on the couch she continued over to the opening and stood. Dimitri came up behind her. "Come, lets enjoy the view while Xavier gets our bath ready." He walked in front of her taking both hands gently pulling her out onto the clear balcony.

"It's a little weird. I feel like I'm walking on water," Madison said as she hesitantly stepped out of the room on the clear platform.

Dimitri guided her to the railing. Placing her hands on the railing, he moved to gather her to his body from behind, resting his chin on her shoulder. "If finding Lucy is important to you. I can hire someone to search for her." He felt Madison tense up. "Is she someone good or bad from your past? I want the truth, because I will not bring someone who caused you pain back into our lives."

Madison turned in his arms wrapping hers around his neck. "Yes, Master, she is one of the good ones."

Xavier came out the door at that moment. "Everything okay?" he asked, looking at Dimitri's concerned face.

"Yes, everything is fine. Is the bath ready? I'll tell you both about Lucy later. Right now I'd like to enjoy that huge tub with my two Masters." She began removing her clothes as she walked past them back inside. When she arrived at the tub, she was totally naked. Grabbing a hair clip from the assortment by the side of the tub. Madison piled her hair up on top of her head. Then lowered herself into the bubbling hot water. The silky feel of the water told her Xavier had put a scented bath oil in. The calming scent of lavender floated to her nose, combined with a manly cedar scent. She sat and rested her head back on the cushion allowing the hot water to do its job.

She picked her head up as her Masters joined her. Each moving to their own seats in the tub. She sat up straighter looking between them. "Why are you sitting so far away? Is this my punishment for the sunburn on my cheeks?" She bowed her head.

Xavier moved so he could lift her face to his. "This is not a punishment. There will be no punishment." Gathering her onto his lap, he relaxed back into his seat. "Maddie, we know this can't be easy for you. We don't want to overwhelm you. It's new to us as well. I'm still getting used to the fact you're in my arms." She snuggled her head on his shoulder. He ran his hand up her thigh to her hip, pulling her as close as he could get her.

"Being in your arms brings back some really good memories, but…" Twisting to sit on Xavier's lap. She wrapped her legs around one of Dimitri's knees. "I'd like to make some new memories. If that is all right with my Masters?"

Dimitri slid from his seat across the tub. "I've always been one to live in the moment." Dimitri rubbed his rock hard chest up Madison's body. His hands guided her arms up and around the back of Xavier's neck. Taking her hands, he put them on the opposite elbows. Locking her arms in place pushed her breasts up. "Keep your hands locked." He kissed her forehead, then he nipped her nose. When he got to her mouth he whispered against her lips, "Another thing we need to add to our contract. What is your safe word?"

"Patches," Madison replied and pushed her chest forward searching for his kiss. He moved down her body taking first one rose colored nipple then the other in his mouth. Her moan filled the quiet room. When he bit down, the sensation went straight through her stomach to her core, making her push her hips forward, rubbing her center along his hard twitching erection.

Xavier glided his hands to her hips holding her in place. Dimitri began working his way down Madison's body. Her head resting on Xavier's shoulder as she floated on the water.

Taking her knees, he placed them over his shoulders. Dimitri kneeled on the tub floor in front of her waiting body. "You are so beautiful." He ran his fingers along her inner thighs to her weeping apex. He moved her lips back with his index fingers fully exposing her. Rubbing his thumbs up squeezing her clit together. He removed one thumb and brought it to his mouth sucking her juices off. "Your body responds to us as if it knows we own it." He moved forward replacing his fingers with his tongue. Lashing her clit, he slid two of his fingers twisting into her entrance. Pushing in and out preparing her body. He then added another finger hitting her g-spot making her body tense. "Do not come until given permission, Madison." She mumbled her response lost in the moment. Dimitri stopped everything bringing her back to reality. "Was that an answer?"

"I'm sorry, Master. I am not to come without permission," she said clearly if not a little sluggishly.

"That's our girl." Moving back into position, he played with her body as if it were his own special instrument. Xavier closed his knees to help hold the lower half of Madison's body above the water. He used his hands to mold her breasts, working her rosy nipples to erect nubs. Shifting her body up further on his shoulder, he could now dip his head and take her nipple in his mouth. Sucking it, he then began applying pressure. With the sensation Xavier was giving her, and Dimitri working his magical tongue in sync with his fingers, Madison's body was building quickly towards her release. She was hoping she could prolong this feeling, yet she knew that wasn't going to happen. "Masters, may I come? Please?" Madison whimpered deep in her throat, praying her Masters would allow her body to sing with the pleasure they were creating.

"She does beg very sweetly." Xavier's breath a whisper on her body. "And once we get this one out of the way, she'll hold out longer on her next one." Dimitri's skillful tongue was lashing her clit as he gave a head nod. Xavier whispered in her ear, "Yes, Madison come all over Master Dimitri's tongue. Let him lick every last drop of your exquisite tasting cum. Your next one will be at our discretion. No begging. Agreed?" Madison nodded her head vigorously. "No Madison, we need to hear it."

"Yes, Masters," Madison sang out as she exploded with her orgasm. Pressing back against Xavier's shoulder offering herself to Dimitri as he drew it out.

When Dimitri growled, she felt it run through her. Devouring, then slowing down to barely touching her with his tongue. His fingers entering then curving up rubbing her contracting walls drawing her pleasure out, feasting from her, pushing her further. Madison tried to thrust her hips upward. Trying to control where Dimitri touched her, but Xavier held her hips in place. "Remember, Madison, we are in control of your body. We are the ones who will stroke you, pleasure you, punish you and take care of you." Xavier feathered kisses around her ear, down her neck, then back up to her ear. "Come now, my lovely."

As the words left his mouth, Madison convulsed again around Dimitri's fingers. Her clit pulsing on his tongue. She released the breath she had been holding as the scream ripped from her lips. Dimitri started stroking her body down. Little tremors stimulated Madison as her body cooled down. She floated through the water. Xavier moving his knees apart as she landed on his lap, her back resting on his chest. She slit her sensual cat like green colored eyes, a matching smile on her lips. "I thought this was rest time? I think I burned more calories just now, then I have all day." Her eyes playfully looked between her two sublimed Masters.

Smiling back at her as Dimitri joined them on the same side of the tub, Xavier positioned her between them. Her back rested on a set of jets. Closing her eyes again, a look of pure joy on her face. "Can this day get any better?" Madison sighed, her body sinking into the seat.

Xavier smiled, a look of pride in his eyes. Dimitri's look mirrored Xavier's. "Madison, we have all night. Anything can happen."

Madison opened her eyes. Holding her pruned fingers up she exclaimed. "Masters, may we get out now? I don't want this happening to the rest of me." She hoped the excuse sounded plausible. The last thing she wanted to do was get her hopes up. Her whole life had been a series of ups and downs. More downs than ups. She just wanted what was here right now in front of her.

The men exchanged confused looks. They knew they had to tread lightly with her. She was like a wounded animal in the woods. Her trust would not come easy. "Yes, Madison," Xavier said getting out. He wrapped a towel around his waist, then held one out for her.

Dimitri joined them with another towel to help. "We would like it if you would lay down and get some rest. It's not a command; it's a request. We have a busy night ahead of us. You will also need two dresses for tonight." Madison gave him a questioning look. "Dinner and the New Orleans Mardi Gras after party. We have an exquisite mask that will make your eyes sparkle. We are looking forward to putting it on you. But for now, just rest." They escorted her to the bed, sliding a lavender colored negligee over her head then holding the blankets for her to climb in. "We will be here, but if we lay with you…" Dimitri left the sentence hanging as he brushed his lips on her forehead.

Everyone in the room knew what would happen if they joined her. Xavier took the blankets from Dimitri, tucking her in. "Sweet dreams, my lovely." He kissed her as well.

Leaving Madison to rest, Dimitri followed Xavier out onto the balcony. Leaning on the railing, arms folded across his chest watching Madison, Dimitri asked, "What's up?"

Xavier followed suit joining Dimitri on the railing. "This morning at the gym I ran into Caleb. I asked him if he would do an intense search for any information on an Amber Sinclair in the state of Florida." He paused to gauge Dimitri's reaction.

"And?" Dimitri had thought about searching the name himself all morning. The few things Madison had told him about herself only made him want to search the web. He wanted to see for himself what a child selling parent really looked like.

"I'm still waiting to hear from him. I didn't make a big deal about it. I did, however, tell him that it was to be done in the strictest of confidence."

"What kind of a parent sells their child to move in the same circles with the motherfuckers who bought her?" Dimitri growled. "When you searched for her, you didn't read about any of this?"

"Do you know how many Amber Sinclair's there are in the world. Plus, she didn't give me much to go on. I never knew she was from Florida originally. She told me she was from L.A." Xavier ran his hands up and down his face, trying to wipe away the frustration before settling his hands on the railing behind him. "After Marco told me she was dead I stopped looking." He looked Dimitri in the eyes. "I had no more reason to look. She was gone." He dropped his gaze to his feet. "Anything the private investigators had found I burned. I tried to wipe her from my life." Pushing off the railing, he began to pace. "I've also got him looking for that dick Boxwood. I know I've heard the name before. I'm just not placing the face. Probably because he's a waste of life."

"I know exactly who he is, if it's the same one I'm thinking of. Boxwood Pharmaceuticals ring a bell? The location is right; the damn CEO is the right age. If they are one and the same, he's a dead man."

Xavier stopped pacing. "You can't kill the man, but you can make him wish he were dead." He began pacing, then stopped again. "What about Madison? If we do this, that will bring him back into her life. A past life she never wanted anyone to know about."

"How do you make a man wish he were dead?"

"You take everything he owns from him." Xavier looked at Madison sleeping on the bed. "Ever thought of going into the pharmaceutical business? Between us I'm sure we have the capital to buy into the company."

Dimitri caught onto where Xavier was going with his thinking. "I want confirmation before we do anything. Make sure he's the same prick who hurt her. I'll have Alejandro look into the company. See if it's gone public yet. As for Madison..." He stopped Xavier from pacing, grabbing his arm. Xavier focused on Dimitri. "She has to know what we are planning. There is no trust if we don't tell her. Then it's her call if we go after that scum bag. This is her past, Xavier. We have to respect it."

When Dimitri looked at Xavier's confused face, he continued, "She has worked so hard to put her past behind her. If you could have seen her the night of the auction on the *Onyx*, you'd understand. She was terrified. Had I known she had already really been sold twice, and not for her own pleasure, I would never have encouraged her to be a part of it. Even then, she said nothing to me. Her trust is fragile and I don't want to do anything to lose what we have already gained by going behind her back. Any information we gather is not looked at till we have her okay. Understood?"

"Understood, I want what's best for her too. I just…" Xavier wanted to hit something. "I want to hurt him as bad as he hurt her. More than he hurt her. You know what I mean?" The sympathy for what Madison had gone through showed in Xavier's eyes.

"I feel your pain. One way or another he'll get what's coming to him. I also want to look into what her mother has been up to these past years. See how the society she bought her way into is treating her. Make sure Caleb looks for any siblings. I could have sworn Madison mentioned she had a sister. There was a message that said something about her dad being in town. Madison had just deleted it."

"Plus she mentioned her brother Matthew had busted Boxwood's nose the night of that dance. I don't remember her mentioning any other sibling." Xavier was now back resting against the railing.

"Now Lucy." Dimitri started towards the door. "I want her to enjoy herself tonight. I have a feeling we will see two very different Madisons tonight."

"What do you mean?"

"Watch her; during dinner she will be reserved, polite, well-mannered, if you please. When we get to the masked after party, she will be relaxed, open, and able to converse with anyone. The mask gives her the ability to be herself." Bowing his head, he said, "I should have seen the signs. She was like that on the *Onyx*. I wanted her so badly, I didn't see it."

"You see it now; that's what matters. I think she's starting to stir. Let's go seduce her into waking up."

As they began to climb up the bed on either side of her, she sat straight up screaming. "Maddie, wake-up. We're right here for you." Xavier gave a slight shake to her shoulder.

She pulled back as if she had been burned. "I don't want to die. You can't make me do it." She started to struggle out of Xavier's grasp. "I can't breathe." She started gasping for air.

"Madison." Dimitri's commanding voice got her attention. "You are having a dream. No one here will hurt you. You are not going to die. Now wake up." With the command, he snapped his fingers. Madison stopped struggling and opened her eyes. Looking at the concerned faces of her Masters had her shrinking under the covers.

"You were having a bad dream. We were just coming to wake you, when you sat straight up screaming. Do you remember what the dream was about?" Xavier asked.

Madison remembered, she just didn't want to talk about it. So she shook her head no. "I'm sorry if I interrupted what you were doing." She started to climb off the bed around them, but Dimitri grabbed her foot. "I'm just going to the bathroom. I'll be right back." She scrambled off the bed when he let go of her foot.

"What do you make of that?" Xavier asked Dimitri.

"I don't believe her. I think she remembers, she's just not ready to tell us. Let it go for now. We'll wait till later to ask her." He looked towards the bathroom area when he heard the sink water running. "We'll tell her then what we are planning. Right now, I think our beautiful sub needs to please her Masters."

Madison had splashed some water on her face trying to cool her body down from her dream. She looked at her appearance in the mirror; she was pale as a ghost. The memory burned into her brain. She pinched her cheeks bringing a rosy color back to them. She brushed her teeth and hair, then looked again. Feeling more confident, she put a smile on her face and walked back to the bed. She stood at the end waiting for her Masters' command.

They were both laying on the bed, heads resting in the cradle of their hands. Their bodies facing each other, both of them watching Madison. "Take off your night gown," Dimitri commanded.

Madison reached up, sliding her fingers under one strap, then the other, letting the gown slid down her perfect body to pool at her feet. "Have you ever seen anything more beautiful?" Xavier asked, getting to his feet. He walked to the end of the bed. "Undress me," he commanded, standing in front of her.

Dimitri stayed on the bed watching as Madison began. Sliding her hands down Xavier chest, she spread her fingers wide trying to touch as much of his chest as she went. When she got to the waist of his pants, she tugged his tucked in shirt out. Now she slid her hands back up his chest in the same manner, taking his shirt with her. When he stood with his arms over his head, she climbed on the bed to continue with its removal. Her chest the perfect height for his mouth. She then leaned over kissing him sweetly. Tracing his lips with her tongue, teasing him. She started making her way back down off the bed, kissing parts of his body as she went. Planting a kiss on his navel, she knelt in front of him. Releasing his belt, she then pulled it through the loops. She tossed the belt on the bed at Dimitri's feet.

She popped the button on his jeans, then slowly lowered his zipper. Careful not to get anything caught in it, knowing that Xavier went commando most of the time. Once she reached the bottom, she could see his erection waiting to be sprung free. Xavier stopped her from going any further.

Dimitri rolled his body around on the bed. His chin now resting on his folded hands, eye level with Madison's profile. "Before you take Master Xavier's cock into that exquisitely talented mouth, you need to tell us what happened to you that put floggers and canes on your hard limit list."

The smile left Madison's face replaced by a look of fear. Xavier reached down and lifted her face. "We can wait if it's too much."

Knowing she would eventually have to tell them, she said, "It's all right. I knew this topic would need to be addressed sooner or later. I just thought it would be later." Now she was looking at Xavier's semi hard cock with longing.

Taking her hands and pulling her to her feet, Xavier guided her to sit at the end of the bed. "Remember, your trust is invaluable, your safety is also a priority. We will always keep you safe." He sat down next to her, adjusting his cock. This will be hell, Xavier thought. But when we know how to command her body... he paused going to the scene he visualized. His cock jumped, pulling him from his thoughts.

Dimitri rolled on his side, resting his head on his hand while the other reached out to stroke Madison's body. He hated asking her to relive her fears. He wanted her to know they were there for her. But as he stroked her velvety soft tanned skin, he couldn't help thinking if he could flog her how her body would glow. He had to adjust himself. Just the thought was making him semi-hard.

Madison picked up her head holding it high. She inhaled deeply, and released it slowly. She began to paint a picture that her Masters would understand. "I told you Madam Mia wanted me to be well educated right?" They both said yes. "Well, I had searched the web, read books, I even watched BDSM movies. However, nothing compared to going to the dungeon she took me to. To see a scene right in front of me. I could feel everything the sub was experiencing. The Dom was using a bull whip. After the fifth stroke I could see the red rising welts the whip left. They looked painful. But then he moved behind her rubbing something in his hands. He began to massage her ass. Then ever so gently he rubbed the marks he had left." She turned to look at Dimitri her eyes dilated with the picture she was describing. "The spreader she wore on her ankles allowed the audience to see how excited she was as her essence leaked down her legs. Madam Mia knew from my soaking wet panties that I would be a good sub. So, when I turned twenty-one, and she added the option of sex to my dating list. BDSM experience was also added."

She looked towards Xavier his cock still standing proud. Her story described similar scenes he had viewed. Madison's voice brought his attention back. "There was one client who always demanded girls with BDSM experience. So naturally when I was available, he arranged a date. Madam Mia was hesitant the man's reputation was shady, but the amount of money he was willing to pay outweighed his reputation. He was an older man. His wife had died and he was happy being single. He didn't want the complications of a girl-friend." Madison did air quotes when she said girlfriend. "Plus with how much money he had, he didn't trust easy. We went out a few times so I could get to know him. He presented himself as a novice, beginning with things like spankings and anal plugs. I thought he was building up to going to a dungeon. He sent a car for me and it brought me back to his house. A large mansion on a lake. When I arrived, I was escorted to a room and told to 'take my submissive position.' So I did. It was a complete dungeon. I knew then that he was more involved than he pretended. I wasn't sure if that was a good thing or a bad thing. Then I thought if I was at a real dungeon, I would have to trust the Dominant there. Plus, as Madam Mia said, 'he has paid a lot of money for this'."

Madison got off the bed and walked over towards the couch. She turned back leaning on the couch. "He put a blindfold on me, then guided me to bondage bed. He had me lay on my back, as he strapped me to the bed."

Dimitri had gotten off the bed, and was now handing her a glass of water. "Thank you." She looked at him. Taking a sip, she handed it back. "I felt a pinch in my arm." Madison continued. "My head began to swim I could feel things but I couldn't. It felt like my whole body was on Novocain. Putting a ball gag in my mouth he took the blindfold off. He wanted me to watch him. He told me I reminded him of his dead wife and he wanted to punish her for leaving him. When he was finished I was full of red welts. He broke the skin on a few of them when he used the cane. He clamped my nipples so tightly, I couldn't wear a shirt for a week. Not that I wanted to as everything rubbed against the welts. He said if I told Madam Mia, he would deny it and say that I had begged him to hit me harder." The tears streamed down her face.

Dimitri gathered her in his arms. "When and if you're ever ready, I would like to try again. What he did to you was not for your pleasure, it was for his sick obsessive mind. You would be the center of my attention. We would start slowly, with you in total control. No bindings, no ball gag, Master Xavier would be here to guarantee you would be safe." He gathered her face in his hands. "When you're ready." He took her lips in a kiss that promised everything he had just said.

Madison marveled at the way Dimitri had taken what had happened to her. He didn't disregard it. He accepted it. He didn't judge her for a past she couldn't change. He was telling her of a future she could have. She wrapped her arms around his neck deepening the kiss. Needing to feel all of him, she reached down grabbing his shirt. Pushing it up his body, feeling his tight abs constrict as her palms passed over them, breaking away from their kiss to remove his shirt.

Madison reached for his jeans, popping the button and unzipping them. She slid her hands around his hips. Reaching in to grab his ass cheeks in both hands. She pushed his jeans down his legs, out of the way with her forearms.

Xavier came up behind her. "Remember, my lovely, you are in control."

She turned to him saying, "Now, where was I?" She put her finger to her lips. Her expression changed to one of thinking, quickly changing to one of recognition. "Oh, that's right. I was about to suck your cock till you came in my mouth." She licked her lips to emphasize her statement.

"What a good memory our girl has," Xavier stated as Madison moved to her knees in front of him. Sliding his jeans down. Taking his already thick hard cock in her hands. Twisting her hands as she worked them up and down. Creating the pre-cum to leak from his slit. Madison stuck her tongue out, reaching to lick it off him. Continuing her hand movements, ramping him up.

Dimitri came up behind Madison. Never losing eye contact with Xavier, he slid two cushions under her knees. Raising her up. He joined her on her knees. As Madison continued her assault on Xavier taking him deeper into her mouth and sucking him while pumping his shaft which created a flow of fluid between her legs, Dimitri took his thick long dick, rubbing it along the seam of her ass. He moved his cock down to her entrance which was saturated by her excitement, knowing that she was the cause of Xavier's pleasure.

Dimitri slid his body down her back. Pushing her hips up, he laid his head on the pillow between her legs. He inserted his tongue in her entrance, mimicking her movements. The deeper she took Xavier, the deeper Dimitri pushed. Dimitri brought one hand up capturing her extended nipple between his fingers. Squeezing it. He sent a jolt straight to her clit.

Switching his tongue to her clit, he used his other hand to replace the actions of his tongue. Inserting two fingers, Dimitri began his assault.

"You look so perfect in this position. Beautiful. So willing to please your Masters." Dimitri's breath brushed against her body.

Madison loved when Dimitri talked to her. Telling her what he wanted. She didn't want to come before Xavier, but the more Dimitri touched her, the harder it became. She moved her one hand down to Xavier's sac massaging his balls with the same rhythm she had set with her mouth.

"I'm going to come, Madison, and you're going to swallow every drop. Then Master Dimitri is going fuck you till you come all over his throbbing cock."

Xavier reached down wrapping clumps of Madison's hair in his hands, controlling her head, keeping her mouth wrapped around his pulsing cock. Ramping up the speed, he took control. With every draw of her mouth, she took a little more control back. Madison put both hands around him, jerking him off as he came. Madison relaxed her throat to take him deeper. Her throat working to swallow his load, helped prolong his orgasm. Xavier grunted with his release.

When Madison had licked Xavier clean. Dimitri entered her from behind. She was soaking wet from sucking on Xavier's cock so Dimitri needed no extra lube. His slid into her wet tight channel. A satisfied moan escaped his throat. This was where he belonged. Madison's beautiful body posed to submit to his control, to take all he had to give. Between her build up by Xavier and his added stimulation, he knew it wouldn't take long for her to come. "Beautiful, you have been a very good girl. Waiting for your Master to come before you did. That was very unselfish of you. You are so wet I know you must be struggling to not come. I will not make you wait. I want you to come all over my hard wet dick."

Madison tried to hold out for Dimitri, but she was so close she couldn't hold back anymore. Dimitri started pounding into her and that pushed her over. She came with a scream, her walls clamping down on Dimitri's cock, milking it with each spasm. Dimitri moved his hands up her chest. Shifting her body so that she was sitting on his thighs pushed him deeper into her, his cock brushing her cervix. Dimitri wanted her to come again before they were finished.

In this position Xavier could kneel in front of her. Taking her nipple in his mouth he sucked on it as she had sucked on his cock. Nibbling and lashing his tongue around it, he then bit down with enough pressure to entice her, not hurt her. When Dimitri started sliding in and out of her with a slow grinding motion, she thought she had died and gone to heaven. Her Masters were there for her. She knew in this moment they would always take care of her. The feelings that ran through her were so pure and real. Dimitri started moving fast. She could feel his dick swelling in her, getting ready to come. "Madison, Master Xavier is going to tap your clit, and you are going to come at the same time as me. I want to feel those tight walls of yours milk me dry." Dimitri pumped four more times and on the fifth Xavier flicked her clit. She clamped down on Dimitri's cock as she exploded. Xavier coaxed her orgasm with his fingers on her clit. At the same time Dimitri roared with his orgasm. Pumping into Madison, he emptied his load into her.

Madison rested her exhausted sweaty head on Dimitri's shoulder as Xavier took her mouth in a gentle kiss. "That was exquisite. A perfect way to start our night. Thank you, my lovely. First for the best blow job I've had in years, second, for telling us what happened. I would love to be able to tell you with us it will be different, but that's something we know you will need time with." He brushed his knuckles down the side of her face.

"I agree with Master Xavier. Only you will know when or even if you will want to try the flogger or cane with us. We are patient men and we have time. No rush, beautiful." He changed the subject after looking at the time. "Now, let's go get cleaned up. We can't be late for dinner tonight." Pulling out of Madison, Dimitri turned her in his arms. "I'm looking forward to tonight. We will get to show you off as ours. I've waited a long time for this moment. Madison, we will be so proud to have you on our arms. Now, go get into the shower." With that, he kissed her on the nose and smacked her ass as she moved away. Madison bit her lip. A smile planted on her face, she sashayed her way to the bathroom.

Both men collapsed on the floor. Both of them breathing heavy. "I think we may need some extra time with Harley if we're going to keep up with her!" Xavier said with a smile.

"You might be right about that. What do you make of what Madison was saying in her dream? 'You can't make me' and 'I can't breathe.' She didn't say anything like that in her story."

"Maybe she will. I think the more she tells us the worse her dreams might get. Hopefully after she's tells us everything, she'll finally be able to sleep peacefully."

Dimitri pushed himself up off the floor, holding a hand down to Xavier. "At least there are two of us. We'll be there to catch her. Now, let's go make our girl all pretty. It's special night for all of us." He patted Xavier on the shoulder as they followed Madison into the bathroom.

Chapter 12

Their girl looked beautiful on their arms. The black Dior dress hugged Madison's curves as if it had been designed for her. The top black strapless corset was lined with beads and crystals. Stopping above her ass in the back, the front came to a point at the apex of her thighs. The bottom half was a court train design. The dress came to her mid-thigh in the front, then wrapped around the back to the floor. Ruffles of organza created the wavy bottom. Madison had worn her hair swept up off her neck. Black sapphire stones dangled from her ears. Nothing adorned her neck, however, now on her wrists she wore cuffs. Dimitri and Xavier wanted to make sure from now on that everyone knew she belonged to them. The delicate looking pieces were about two inches wide. One in yellow gold, one in white. Both had animal symbols on them.

Dimitri explained how he had them made after Xavier returned his signed contract. Each had their own brand. Making it easy for club members to recognize she was theirs. Dimitri's cuff was made of the white gold. A Siberian white tiger was worked into the cuff. A tiger for valor and fierceness. The black represented grief and constancy. The white, peace and sincerity. Throughout the design the jeweler had placed gem stones. Black diamonds for eyes, with Mother of pearl and black onyx creating the tiger.

Engraved into the gold was a lion with a full mane of hair. This was Xavier's crest. Emerald green diamond eyes glowed when the light hit them. The face and mane of the lion were made with yellow and black diamonds. Each of the gems was placed with precision to create the regal animal.

Dimitri had sat at the end of the Captain's table. Madison to his right, with Xavier next to her. Xavier had watched Madison throughout dinner. Her beauty was flawless her smile contagious. But Dimitri had been right. Although she laughed, and interacted with the other guests and crew at the table, she held a part of herself in reserve. She made sure everything she did was perfect, her table manners and knowing what fork and glass to use for each course. She was knowledgeable no matter what the topic.

Yet, when she didn't think anyone was looking she would revert back into herself. Just sitting at the table sipping her water. She resembled the woman she described last night, a sponge. Sucking up everything that was being said around her, trying to be invisible.

Xavier had watched her all through dinner. During the show, her attention was directed at the stage. However, with Dimitri on one side and Xavier on the other, she would make sure to smile back and forth between them. She seemed to be checking on them. Making sure if she was laughing, they were too.

Xavier was still waiting to hear from Caleb, but they were pretty sure what they were going to find. Pleasing others before herself had been bred into her. Following directions, another. They had one more appearance to make tonight. Besides Sadie and Cameron's Halloween reception party at the end of the cruise, the Mardi Gras after party was the party everyone would be at. Xavier glided his hand in his pocket. A secret smile played on his lips.

Madison sat between her Masters. The show was coming to an end and then it would be time to get changed. She started to map out how she would go about making the switch. When all of a sudden, her panties began to vibrate on her clit. Madison sat straighter in the chair, trying not to look too obvious, and then it stopped. Easing herself back in the chair, she tried to figure out which one of them had the control. A dazzling smile was on her face.

Dimitri knew exactly what had happened to Madison. He played with the control in his pocket setting it to the slowest setting. Madison's groan coincided with the groan coming from the actress on the stage. Then he shut it off. The tension in Madison's face eased. Her back rested on her chair, another smile on her face.

Xavier glanced over at her and whispered in her ear. "If you can guess which one of us has the control, we will let you come by the end of the show. If you can't guess, we will tell you. Although you will have to wear them till the end of the after party."

Madison's first thought was that she'd be coming throughout the party. Not a bad thought, but very distracting while trying to pay attention to someone. Then she thought, they weren't going to let her come. They were going to torture her till the end. The men watched with fascination as Madison's thought process played out across her features.

When they both hit different buttons on their controls, Madison's body sat straighter in the chair. A sneaky smile spread across her face. "You both have one."

You could see the shocked face of Xavier, while Dimitri had a satisfied smile on his face. "I told you she would guess."

Xavier asked her quietly, "How did you know?"

"You each chose a different speed." She grinned.

Xavier looked around behind her at Dimitri. Dimitri tipped his head. "I love watching our girl come. Plus, I want that pink pussy hungry for my cock later. Not so abused she walks bow legged."

"Okay, I see your point." With another head nod to Dimitri, the bullet started to pulse. Then it began to go faster. The show began doing its final scene. Madison shifted in her seat, setting the bullet exactly where she wanted it. Xavier couldn't take watching her anymore. He needed to touch her. Reaching over to her, he guided her head towards his. Taking her lips in a possessive kiss, he captured her scream in his mouth. The vibrator began its descent, milking Madison's orgasm. She sat in the chair drawing ragged breaths.

The applause started for the actors on the stage as the show had just finished. Her strength renewed, Madison sat straighter in her chair applauding. She was, however, applauding her Masters. But the show had been a close second.

Standing in her cabin before the full length mirror, Madison gazed at her reflection. All her life she had been told she was sexy and exotic, but right now she truly felt it. She knew Xavier and Dimitri would recognize her when they saw her, yet she still wanted to add an element of surprise when they did.

She had kept what she was wearing hidden in her reserved cabin. Alice and Lexi from the spa and salon met her there for her makeup and hair. The men had given their approval for her to get ready in her cabin, and to meet them at the Mardi Gras party. They didn't like it apparently and put a stipulation on it. If she was not walking thru the door at the appointed time, there would be a punishment for her when they got back to their suite. Madison had agreed. Excited to be on her way, she had kissed them both. The promise behind each kiss left them both stunned.

Now, as she stood looking, she couldn't thank the girls enough for the perfect job they had done. She had explained what she had wanted and they had accomplished exactly what she had described. Neither was attending the party tonight, both had long work schedules tomorrow.

Her hair was piled on her head, curls falling haphazardly. The smoky green eye shadow made her eyes glow pine green. The black corset with shamrock green satin stripes hugged her center while the black lace and green satin rippled along the edge of her pushed up cleavage. A shamrock colored satin rose rested in the center. Two pieces of the green satin crisscrossed across her chest, tying at her neck. They weren't necessary, but they looked good. Feathers in black, green, and gold created the bottom section of her outfit. They ran across the front just covering her muff and ran over her hips around to the back falling into a vee to land just behind her knees. She wore a black thong with a garter belt holding her stockings in place. On her feet she wore a pair of Guiseppe Zanotti sandals.

The final touch was in the box on the bed. Dimitri had it delivered while she was dressing. Madison opened to find a gold half face mask. Split by the nose, a butterfly covered the left eye. Its wings spread from her forehead down to her chin. Emeralds and black diamonds colored the butterfly wings. The other half of the mask was filled with gold filigree and a black swirled design. Madison lifted it from the box and walked to the mirror. Tying it behind her head, she looked in the mirror. The mask was perfect. She was ready to go. Looking at the clock in the room she couldn't believe she was on time. Smiling with the thought she could always be late on purpose. Shaking her tail of feathers, the thought of what her punishment would be got her panties wet. Before her thoughts got her into trouble, she grabbed her bag and cabin key. Touching up her lipstick once more before she left, she took in a big gulp of air and let it out slowly. She could do this. With that thought she headed for the party.

All the after parties on the *Sapphire* took place around the dungeon arena. Madison was thankful her cabin was on the same deck. It made it easy for her to slip into the party. She knew once Dimitri and Xavier found her everyone would know who she was. For a few minutes she wanted to be unknown. She stood off to the side and observed the area. A demonstration with a flogger was the center of attention in the arena.

At first Madison froze in her steps. She knew the sound of the flogger. She looked towards where she had heard the sound. She recognized Raven as the sub on the table. As she gazed at Raven's face she saw no fear or pain. All she saw was pure pleasure. With fascination Madison watched Raven's face. When the flogger hit she would bite her lip. Then her tongue would sneak out and slide seductively across her lips. Like she was hiding a secret.

Madison started making her way around the outside of the arena. Her concentration centered on what she was watching. The flogger had gold tipped ends, and sparkled when they hit the light. She knew they had to bite into the Raven's skin, but the look Madison saw on her face was not one of pain. Her back was shaded pink with redder spots where the tips bit in. Master Greyson tossed the flogger on the floor, then moved behind Raven. Removing his leather pants, he rolled the condom down his stiff dick and entered her with one push. Holding himself still, he let her adjust to him. Then he began to pump into her still withholding her orgasm. The sweat dripped from both of them their bodies moving as one. The quiet was broken when he said to her, "Fly with me, Raven." As soon as the words left his mouth they both yelled their release.

He pulled out of her, removing the condom and placing it into a waiting garbage can. Getting dressed, he reached over grabbing a warmed blanket, he placed it over her as he removed the bindings holding her on the table. He rubbed her limbs, getting the circulation to flow freely again. He whispered in her ear. Then with a head nod, he picked her up, wrapped in the blanket and they began leaving the arena to the sound of applause.

Madison was pulled from the scene by a hand on her arm. "Are you okay?"

Startled she pulled her arm back. "Yes, I'm fine." She realized it was Jasmine dressed in a blue corset that laced up the side. Blue and peach beading draped along the top and bottom of it and was coupled with peach ruffled panties. She wore a pair of wedged sandals on her feet. "I never realized how fierce a flogging scene could be. I've never watched one before."

"I think your Masters will be happy to hear that," Jasmine said.

"How did you know?"

"The cuffs of course. Without those I would have never recognized you." Jasmine gave a little laugh.

"Do they know I'm here as well?"

"No, they've been talking shop with the menfolk," Jasmine teased. "I think you have maybe... ten minutes before that changes. And if you want to really hide who you are, clasp your hands behind your back. The cuffs are a dead giveaway."

"Thank you, if you run into them let them know you've seen me please. Otherwise, they have promised a punishment for tardiness."

Jasmine laughed again. "Just let them try. I know exactly when you got here. There should have been a counter bet." Madison looked blankly at her. "If they didn't find you as soon as you walked in, you get to choose how many orgasms they have to give you. Or something like that!"

"You really have a devious mind don't you?" Madison smiled big. "Okay, I'm off for a few more moments. Thank you, Jasmine."

"No problem, I'll see you around."

Madison started wandering around the party. She headed to the bar for a glass of wine. Then she knew it was time to find her Masters. Another scene was being demonstrated on the St. Andrew's cross. As Madison came around the far side of the arena, she spotted them. Both wore plain Domino masks, but their clothing differed. Dimitri wore a black button down shirt with his leather pants. Xavier wore a double breasted velvet vest with a black satin lining. Five buttons ran up and down on either side with a stand up collar and sweeping lapels. His washed out blue jeans hugged low on his hips. She stood for a moment just looking at them. She watched more than one woman glance their way. As she came into their view, it was like time stood still. She stood where she was as they stalked her. Nothing and no one was stopping them from getting to their girl.

They approached her stopping on either side of her. "You look stunning tonight. Even with the mask I would know who you were, beautiful." Dimitri kissed her cheek.

"I couldn't agree more. Every Dom and Master watched as you moved past them wishing you were theirs. Till they saw our cuffs," Xavier said, giving her a kiss. "Again you escaped another punishment."

Madison smiled. "You knew I was here?"

"The minute you stepped onto the floor." Leaning closer to her ear, Xavier asked, "How did you like the scene? We wanted you to see how a sub should feel during and after being flogged. For you to see how incredible with the right person it can be. The look of pure amazement showed in your body language. We were pleased to see your reaction." He reached between her legs, swiping his finger along her panties. "Just as we suspected."

They had asked Master Greyson to position Raven so she would face the entrance Madison would walk through. Then they put themselves into position so they would see her immediately when she arrived. Dimitri had started to go to her when her face had first showed her fear. Xavier had held him back and he was glad he had. Allowing Madison to see her friend on the receiving end of the flogger let her know it could be safe. Once she had overcome her fear, she allowed the excitement of what she was seeing sink in which allowed her body to show them what she couldn't say. She had enjoyed watching the scene.

"It is still up to you, Madison. For now, let's enjoy ourselves. I need to meet some possible new investors for the international line. I would like the two of you to meet them as well. If I can locate them... there they are at the table by the bar." Dimitri lead the way to the table.

When they arrived, Dimitri did the introductions. "Good evening, Sheikh Ahmed. We're so glad you could join us on this maiden voyage of the *Sapphire*. Seeing firsthand what the Midnight Oasis Cruise Line can bring to an international cruise ship. Being from Dubai, we are hoping you could tell us how to get our cruise line in there. But enough business talk for now. I would like to introduce you to Xavier Legend and Madison MacIntyre."

"A pleasure. Please call me Colin, that is what my wife has called me since we met. May I present my beautiful wife Lucy." He paused as hands were shook around the table. "She couldn't pronounce my given name, so Colin is what she chose. I had it legally changed before we married." Looking in Lucy's eyes, he ran his hand along her chin, a look of pure desire showing. "She did learn to say it, but she only uses it in our bedroom. Isn't that right, little dove?" He pulled her in for a gentle kiss. Turning back to his guests, he continued, "Legend? Any relations to Legend Vine?" The sheikh asked Xavier.

"Yes, that would be my family," Xavier answered.

Madison started seeing little black dots in front of her eyes. The room began to spin as she grabbed onto the back of the chair. This stunning man that looked like he just stepped off the front of a GQ Magazine had just said Lucy was his wife. Madison had been right. She had heard Lucy's laugh.

Xavier steadied her asking. "Are you all right?"

"Yes, I've never met a real sheikh." Looking at him. "Plus you don't really look like one." She smiled as she said it. "It's a pleasure to meet you both. How long have you been married?" Trying to stay calm.

"We've been married for about ten wonderful years now," Lucy said, nuzzling closer to him.

"I see both of these men have already placed their claim on you by your cuffs. What a shame, I have a brother looking for a woman. You would have been perfect. Such long slender legs."

"Thank you for the compliment," Dimitri cut in. "Tomorrow if you have some time, maybe we could sit and talk some business?"

"That would be perfect." Lucy jumped excitedly in her chair. "Madison and I can get to know each other better. We could have lunch while they talk. If you're free?" Making a pouty face.

Madison didn't know what to say. She had hoped tonight was going to be a break through night for her. And it would have been if this complication had not just been introduced to her. "I have no plans," Her voice squeaked out.

"Fabulous, I'll meet you at the Masters Lounge say around twelve-thirty?"

"That will be great." Madison didn't recognize her own voice.

"It's a date." Lucy clapped her hands.

"Your office, twelve-thirty. Apparently I'll be free at that time." He butted his head lightly with Lucy.

"We'll be there. Thank you, enjoy the rest of your evening." Dimitri shook hands with the sheikh.

Xavier gently clasped Madison's elbow saying their good-byes. He led them out to the railing. "You were fine up until you met the sheikh's wife. Is she the Lucy you were talking about earlier?" Madison nodded her approval. Xavier let out a breath, running his hands through his hair. "Okay, you said she was a good part of your past. You will need to tell us about her tonight. Are you all right to stay, or would you like to go back to the suite?"

"I was enjoying myself. I enjoyed watching Master Greyson and Raven." She looked between them continuing. "Would it be all right if we went back to the suite? I know neither one of you is going to relax until I tell you about Lucy. Plus, I need to pick out my outfit for lunch tomorrow," she teased as she wrapped her arms through theirs.

"She makes a valid point. I know I would like to hear about the mysterious Lucy." Dimitri ran his hand over hers. "Are you sure you're all right?"

"Yes. You will understand when I tell you about her."

Chapter 13

Back in their suite, Madison had changed into a short robe and took off her makeup, leaving her cuffs in place. She placed the butterfly mask on the table near the door next to a yellow sealed envelope. She now sat in front of Xavier and Dimitri on the floor. Pins from her up do being tossed on the table from both sides. "Thank you for the beautiful mask. I left it by the door."

"Beautiful, that is for you. Put it wherever you want it," Dimitri said over her shoulder.

"Madison, we want you to know what we did before you begin telling us about Lucy."

She looked at both their solemn faces. "There is nothing you could do that would change how I feel about either of you. You, however, might change how you feel about me after I tell you what I did." She turned and sat forward again.

Once the pins were removed from her hair, they both ran their fingers through it massaging her scalp. Madison moaned with satisfaction. Xavier got off the couch and got the envelope. Madison in the meantime climbed up on the

169

couch between them. Xavier sat in his jeans. Dimitri in lounge pants.

"In this envelope is whatever history Caleb could find on an Amber Sinclair." He watched Madison's face turn white. "Before you lose it on us, we have not opened it. After what you told us last night we both wanted to know. We don't have to open it now. We don't have to open it ever. But it could help us to fill in some blanks and for you to see what has happened to your brother and sister."

"How do you know about them? I thought you said you didn't look?"

Dimitri spoke up making Madison whip her head around to him. "We didn't. You received a message from your sister at the apartment. Remember? About your dad being in town."

"That wasn't my real sister. It was Marco. He likes to call and leave weird messages all the time." Madison looked at Dimitri. "I just happen to have a sister though."

"Then, last night you mentioned your brother Matthew. He broke Boxwood's nose. We thought you would want to know. When was the last time you saw them?"

Madison spoke in a small voice. "The night of the ball. You'll understand why I know nothing about them after I tell you about Lucy." She paused getting comfortable on the couch. Taking a sip of water, she began to tell them about the night she became Madison MacIntyre.

"Marco and I had been friends back in Florida. We had gone to the same school, but we didn't run with the same crowds. No one in school knew we were friends. My parents would have never let a 'queer' into our house. When I came to L.A. we happened to be in the same coffee shop. We reconnected, exchanged numbers and said goodbye. I never thought he would call, but he did. Almost weekly. It was nice to have a friend."

"And Lucy?" Xavier asked.

"I'll get to her," she acknowledged. "I had a date at Marco's BDSM club. I told him to meet me there and afterwards we could have a couple drinks. When I got to the club, he was at the bar. My date hadn't arrived so we had a drink. When my date arrived, I couldn't believe it was Ryan." They both gave her confused looks. "Ryan, picked me up at the bus station Ryan. Uncle sold me to the highest bidder." When their faces showed the recognition, she continued. "He had used the name Ryan Smith so I had no idea till then. Most guys never gave their real name."

"At first I was excited to see him. He had never done anything really bad to me. When he told me he had always wanted me, I began to get creeped out. But a job is a job. So, I told Marco to give me exactly one hour and I'd be back. Then I followed Ryan to the room. When we got there, I followed him in and he locked the door behind us. The room he had chosen was dressed as an eighteenth century real dungeon. It had the chains on the walls next to lit torches. There was what looked like a rack in the middle of the room, and a whipping post on the other side." Madison stopped talking, just staring blankly into space.

"We're right here, baby. Keep going." Dimitri rubbed her arm bringing her attention back.

"He told me to strip and get on the table. After I was bound, he put a blindfold on me. With my hearing heightened I heard someone trying to get in the room. The next thing I heard were voices getting louder as they entered the room. I couldn't believe he would let someone else in. So, I started to tell him that. 'This wasn't an appointment for more than one. Madam Mia will want her cut.' The voice that whispered in my ear was a woman's and it had sounded so familiar, but I couldn't place it. 'Don't worry, honey, she already got her cut.' Then there was yelling, another man and Ryan. I heard what sounded like skin hitting skin, and something heavy hit the floor.

"I felt a pinch in my arm, and things started getting fuzzy. I tried to fight when they unbound me and turned me over, but I couldn't make my limbs move. A bag was placed over my head and I couldn't breathe. I started gasping for air, and that's when he said to me, 'I always wanted this ass, but my nephew watched you like a hawk. Now, I get to fuck you the way I want and he can't do a thing to stop me. Look how the bag moves as she tries to get air. Release the bag.'

"Madison we get the picture. I can feel you trembling." Xavier couldn't bear to hear what his sick ass father had done to her. He thanked God his father was already in jail. Because if he wasn't, Xavier would probably kill him. "Skip to what happened after. How did you survive?"

"Marco."

"Marco?" Xavier asked. "I talked to him. Why didn't he tell me?"

"We both swore to take it to the grave. Now you understand why this part of our contract was so hard. He has never told a soul. I feel like I'm betraying him." Madison paused, looking at Xavier. "I'm sorry I hurt you. You were a part of my good days. I wanted to call you, but I knew I couldn't. It would have just made it harder to stay away."

"You're here now and that's all that matters." He rubbed his knuckles down her cheek.

"Marco will understand. It's your story to tell," Dimitri commented.

"But he did things that could put him away for a long time. He faked my death." Madison's voice started to raise defending her friend. "He put his life on the line for me. I knew I could never repay him. So keeping this secret was important."

"He'll understand, Madison. He loves you. He'll want you to be happy. We will invite him to dinner and let him know. The same rules apply for Marco as well. Nothing will leave this room." Dimitri pulled her into his lap. Xavier moving closer. "Now, please tell us how Marco pulled that off?"

"He had a few favors he called in. The medical examiner declared the body dead, the forensic evidence somehow became contaminated, and the funeral director produced a casket. When people are paid enough, they'll do anything. He had a full funeral. Including the burial of an empty casket. A few months later a head stone buried Amber Sinclair."

Madison stretched for her glass of water on the table. Xavier handed it to her. "He then had an entire identity created for me. Got me a condo, car, money in the bank, and a resume that lead me to the *Onyx*." She tilted her head at Dimitri. "Most of what's on it is real. Just the degrees aren't."

He kissed her on the forehead. "Pretty good credentials. Caleb never picked up on it. Marco must be a magician."

"Marco doesn't come off as having that kind of funds. What did you need to do to repay him?" Xavier grunted out.

Madison put a calming hand on Xavier's arm. "It's not like that. Marco is loaded. When his family found out he was gay, they disowned him. He threatened to come out on national television if they cut him off. So needless to say, they set up an account. He's never had to work a day in his life and I think he's had more jobs than me. When I needed it, he gave it. No questions. No conditions. He really is my best friend." A tear escaped the corner of her eye.

Xavier kissed the tear away. "I'm thinking Lucy found out the same way I did? You said you gave her Madam Mia's information. She must have been sad to hear of your passing?"

"I don't know. I haven't seen her since we met in L.A. I couldn't risk her recognizing me. Technically, I never finished my contract with Madam Mia. Tonight with the mask on she couldn't really see my face. What do I do tomorrow during lunch? I can't very well wear the mask!"

"It's up to you what you tell her. We are both considering getting into business with her husband. If that helps any," Dimitri told her.

"If she says you look like Amber, say people always think you look like someone they know." Xavier smiled.

"I'm kind of excited to talk to her tomorrow. I have missed her. She has changed so much. She's married to a sheik. I can't wait to hear how that happened."

"I think you will find all that out tomorrow. Right now I think it's time we get our girl to bed," Dimitri suggested, standing up with Madison in his arms.

"I think you may be right. I see a very erect nipple poking through the opening of the flimsy piece of cloth." Xavier leaned down taking her nipple in his mouth. "Finally the dessert I've wanted all night."

They moved towards the bed when Madison spoke up, "Masters if you have a rabbit fur flogger. I would like to try."

Both men stopped walking and looked at her. "After the stories you have told us are you really sure?" Dimitri was surprised by her request.

"I have never felt safer than when I'm with the two of you. You have let it be known that this is something you enjoy. Plus, after seeing Raven tonight, if that is how you can make me feel, then I would really like to try."

Dimitri changed directions and walked behind the clear brick wall into the dungeon area. "You choose."

"The whipping bench?" Head tilted in a question.

"Beautiful, we have a scene for every piece of equipment. Designed just for you," Dimitri said. Standing her on her feet.

Xavier removed her robe minus the cuffs. He leaned down kissing each one. "Seeing you wear our cuffs tonight and everyone knowing you were ours, made this night perfect, now this. You are exquisite."

Dimitri moved over and pulled a flogger from the rack. "Madison feel the flogger with your hands." She felt the soft fur running around on the eight straps with another three leather ones. The way her hand floated over the fur, caressing it, made Dimitri's semi erect hard-on grow to a full fledge erection. "Oh, baby, you're killing me." Grabbing her by her neck, he kissed her, their tongues dueling.

Xavier came up behind them, his jeans gone, his cock wedged against her ass. "Let's get our girl in position. I don't know how much longer I can hold out." He had been a Master for many years, and this woman made him feel like a teenage boy.

They guided her to the whipping bench and positioned her. Xavier put straps in Madison's hands. "Maddie, we are not going to bind you. You are to hold these straps. If for any reason you want to stop, drop the straps. I will let Dimitri know immediately." He moved her hair back from her face. "I want you to know how proud we are of you. They say men are stronger physically, but you bring me to my knees." He leaned over ravishing her mouth. When he pulled back, her red lips were puffy. Her cheeks flushed with color and her eyes glazed with desire.

Dimitri came up, the flogger in his hand, his erection in line with her mouth. He kneeled down. "Beautiful, I'm going to tie your ankles, I need to keep you steady." He waited for her confirmation.

"Yes, Master."

"Then, I'm going to use this all over your body. From your shoulders to your toes. And you are going to love every moment. The softness of the rabbit combined with the leather. The pleasure with the pain. Your juices will be dripping down your leg. You will beg me to fuck you because your pussy will be throbbing for release. But you will not come till you are given permission. Now, what is your safe word?"

"Patches."

"Thank you, beautiful. I promise to catch you." Dimitri kissed her. Then he moved to where her legs were spread, her feet resting on the pads. He leaned down, wrapping the straps around her ankles, making sure they weren't too tight. As he rose to a standing position, he tickled the flogger up the inseam of her leg slowly. When he reached her apex, he let the flogger drift over her weeping pussy. Sweeping them up, he brought the flogger down on her ass cheeks.

Madison jumped with surprise, but held firm to the straps. A hiss escaping from the sensation. The flogger hit along her lower back. Being prepared, she didn't jump but let the pleasure sink in. The next hit in the middle of her back. The next near her shoulders. With each strike, her fear dissipated and her arousal began to build. The moans now coming from Madison encouraged Dimitri to continue.

While Dimitri was flogging Madison, Xavier stood to the side. Watching Madison's face change with each strike of the flogger. He saw the fear replaced with ecstasy. He wanted her warm inviting mouth wrapped around his throbbing dick. He began jerking his cock each time the flogger hit. Finally, Dimitri moved back to where he had started. He took his tongue, licking the juices dripping down her leg, running his tongue all the way up through her sopping wet pussy. "Are you ready to come like you've never come before, beautiful?"

"Yes, Master. Please I'm begging you. Make me come."

Dimitri smacked the flogger down on her labia three more times. Then he was behind her grabbing handfuls of her ass. Spreading her open he pushed clear to her womb, holding himself still. Madison tried to move, but he smacked her ass. "Beautiful, stay still. I've waited for this moment since I met you and I want to savor every moment of it. I want to feel your walls tighten as I push in and release as I pull out. I want you to milk me dry. I want you to make me come so hard, the whole ship hears my release," Dimitri said thru gritted teeth.

As soon as Dimitri moved behind Madison, Xavier moved forward. He slipped his cock along Madison's lips. She opened her mouth and Xavier grabbed a hand full of her hair. Pushing his cock to the back of her mouth. Madison relaxing her throat to take as much of him as she could. Xavier began fucking her mouth. He set the same pace as Dimitri, the pressure building for all three of them.

Madison dropped the strap. Removing Xavier's cock, she said, "Masters please I'm begging you. Can I come?"

"Yes, Madison. You have been a perfect sub tonight."

Madison tugged Xavier's cock back into her mouth, sucking while massaging his balls with her hand. Knowing how close he was to coming, she sucked him deeper down her throat. Her groan pushed Xavier over, his salty cum spurting down her throat. Xavier yelled as he erupted. He stroked Madison's hair as she lapped up every drop, loving the feel of his cock in her mouth.

Xavier's release, had Madison screaming her own. Never in her life had she so freely given herself. However, if this intoxicating feeling was the reward, she was all for it. Madison almost purred.

Dimitri savored the staggering feeling of her contracting muscles. He loved the sight before him. Madison spread across the table. Her hair a tangled mess. Xavier's cock being licked and worshipped by her mouth. But what put Dimitri over the edge were the marks she so trustingly allowed him to put there. Dimitri couldn't hold back any longer. He pushed one last time into Madison, letting her muscles pulse around him, blinding him with the love he felt. He was sure the entire ship had heard them.

Leaning over her trying to catch his breath, Dimitri kissed every small red mark on her back. Xavier had gone and gotten cream to rub on. Helping her up, Dimitri released her ankles. She sat on the end of the table and Xavier placed a warmed blanket around her. Dimitri carried her into the bedroom, setting her in the middle of the bed, propping her up on the pillow. He climbed in next to her, needing to make sure she felt safe, and protected.

Handing her a glass of orange juice and then climbing in on the other side of the bed. Xavier asked, "How are you feeling?"

"I don't think I've ever felt this good." She looked between them. "I'm not kidding. That was amazing. I'm glad you pushed my limits to try. I don't know when I'll be ready for the gold tipped one Master Greyson used, but I'll try, as long as it's with the two of you." She kissed each one with the love that flowed thru her for them. Tonight confirmed it for her. She was truly and deeply in love with her Masters. She still needed to keep that from them though. She had been hit by too many blind sides in her lifetime, to let them know yet. It was still too early. Besides whatever was in that envelope could very easily ruin everything for her. Why did they have to look?

"What's that face for? You look like you might be sick. Are you okay?" Dimitri asked.

She shook the thought away. "No, I'm just fine. So fine, that this blanket is way too heavy for me." She began sliding it slowly down her body, exposing one hard nipple, then the other.

The men left Madison sleeping, while they had their coffee. "Do you think she'll want to open the envelope?" Xavier eyed it sitting on the coffee table.

"I think if I was her, I wouldn't. She has a new life, friends, a job if she wants to keep working. But most of all, she has us. What if something in that envelope spooks her out of our lives? I'm not so sure now why we did this. We want her to trust us, feel safe with us." He picked up the envelope waving it. "This doesn't say trust." He tossed it back on the table.

"What do you think she'll do with Lucy? Do you think she'll tell her?"

"If Lucy doesn't realize it's her, no, I don't think she will. Then there is the chance that Lucy could recognize her. I think Madison would like to have her friend back in her life. They shared an experience no one else could ever under- stand. Then there's the fact that we could be doing business with Lucy's husband. Putting her in close proximity with Lucy on a regular basis when we go to Dubai."

"Well, whatever she chooses, we will be there for her," Xavier said, watching Madison stretch in bed. "God, she's beautiful."

That had Dimitri up on his feet, walking to the bed. Leaning down and kissing her forehead, asking, "Tea, coffee, hot chocolate, or orange juice?"

Madison turned her head opening her bright green eyes. She reached up pulling him down for a proper good morning kiss. Then she said, "Tea please. Thank you, Master." She felt Xavier climb on the bed behind her. Rolling over, she also kissed him good morning.

Dimitri returned with her tea. "We've docked in Cabo San Lucas. Besides lunch with Lucy at twelve-thirty, did you want to go into town? There is this quiet place called Capo San Giovanni. They serve a specialty there that oh… it makes my mouth water. We could have dinner there?"

"Or!" Xavier chimed in. "We could go to Pocho's Seafood. They have tableside cooking and the flambé takes center stage. The crowd is less snotty and a lot more fun." Xavier had a devilish smile. "We could extend the invite to Lucy and Colin? Totally up to you."

"Let's see how lunch goes first. If it's all right with you two, I want to have Marco come to the room. I'd like to talk to him before I talk with Lucy."

"Beautiful, if talking to Marco is going to ease your mind, then yes, have him come here. If you want us here when you tell him, we'll stay as well. If not, let him know we will never speak of it after this cruise. Tell him that we are very grateful that he was there to help when we were not," Dimitri said as he sat next to her on the bed.

Madison had propped herself up and was sipping her tea. "I'm sure you both have things to do this morning. I can see if Marco can come and talk, meet Lucy for lunch, then dinner. Sounds like a wonderful day. In between…"

Madison paused as Xavier swooped down taking her nipple in his mouth. Causing her to jump and spill some of her tea on him. "Ouch, I didn't think your tea was so hot." He smiled rubbing his shoulder where the tea landed. "It was worth it though to watch your rosy red nipple harden for me."

Madison swatted his arm. "Can you be serious for a moment?" Smiling at him she set her tea down on the nightstand. She loved the way her body reacted to her Masters.

She was already wet, but she needed to ask her question before she lost her nerve. "As I was saying, Dimitri, Xavier?" This got both of their attention. "Can I open the envelope alone? I promise I won't destroy anything. I would just like to be by myself and process what's in there. So then I may be able to explain it to you both. The only thing that was typical about my family was the number. Two parents, three kids. Besides that, nothing was normal."

"If that is what you wish. I would prefer to stay but we will abide by your wishes. However, the minute we get back in this room tonight we all find out what is in that envelope." Dimitri ran his fingers down her face. "You are the most important person to us. Nothing in that envelope will change how I or Xavier feel about you."

"I agree with Dimitri. I'm not losing you again. Do you hear me?" She nodded her head, feeling their emotions. "Madison there is also other information in the envelope. I don't want you to be alarmed when you see it."

"You already looked at the information?" She demanded.

"No, beautiful, we told you we would wait for you. I just want you to know besides your family, we had a search done on that prick Brian Boxwood." Dimitri waited for that to sink in. "The best way to ruin a man is to know everything about him. That's what we plan to do."

Madison didn't know what to do with that information. What had happened to her at the hands of Brian happened so long ago. She didn't want to bring that to the forefront of her life. But then, on the other hand, if it wasn't for that bastard maybe the horrible domino effect that happened to her after he raped and beat her might not have happened. He deserved to be in jail, but that was never going to happen. "Can we talk about this after I see what's in the envelope?" She gazed at Dimitri. "Thanks for the heads up."

"Madison know this. If there is a way, we can make that

motherfucker pay for what he did to you, I'm sorry but we're doing it. That man is going to wish he never crossed paths with you."

"I feel like that's just ripping the band aid off. His family was and probably still is very well connected. I don't want anything to happen to either one of you."

Knowing he had said his peace about it, Xavier said, "Well, I'm off to the gym. You take all the time you need with this. If you need me, you know where I'll be." Xavier rolled over Madison, pinning her to the bed. "Baby, Dimitri and I have our own connections. Add Marco's and that bastard won't know what the fuck hit him." He slowly lowered his lips to hers and said, "You no longer have to fight by yourself, baby. We won't tolerate anyone hurting you." Then he sealed those words with a searing kiss. Releasing her, he kissed her on the nose. "I'll see you later, my lovely. Dimitri." Xavier got off the bed and headed to the gym.

While Xavier had been saying goodbye, Dimitri had called Cameron. He wanted him present when he met with Colin. He also suggested that Sadie join the women for lunch. He came to the bed and sat alongside Madison. "Sadie is going to pop up during your lunch. I thought that could take some pressure off of you. As well as Lucy getting to know her. If we go into business with the sheikh I'm sure we'll be spending more time with them socially. It would help if all the women got along."

"We will all get along fine. Lucy is great. What are your plans for today?"

"Well, after I make love to you. I have some work to do before the meeting. Now, spread those legs. I need my breakfast, honey."

Madison laid back on the bed legs spread wide. Dimitri moved between them his shoulder pushing them wider. "Look how wet you are just waiting for my tongue to do this." Dimitri took his tongue and flicked it across her clit. Back and forth, up and down. "You were so gorgeous last night." His breath was blowing across her. "Your trust in me meant the world."

He began prodding her opening. "Tonight, beautiful, I will have this ass. For now, I just want to feel you come all over my fingers. Then you're going to come all over my cock." Dimitri pushed two fingers in her as he continued his assault on her clit.

The sensations combined was driving Madison crazy. His tongue flicked her clit. Her breathing came in short gasps. "Holy crap, Dimitri, I'm going to come."

Dimitri added a third finger and Madison stiffened as the orgasm ripped through her body. He kept the pressure on her clit sustaining the ripples flexing her muscles. With one last lick of his tongue, he crawled up her body. His dick slid easily into her wet channel. He began with a slow pace. His hands held him above her as he watched her. Her nails dug into his rock hard ass, as she spread her legs wider.

He started picking up the pace. He loved when her nails scored his ass. It told him exactly what she wanted. They were no longer making-love. She wanted it hard and fast. Exactly what he wanted and that's what he gave her.

Madison's head whipped on the pillow as Dimitri began surging into her tight warmth. He knew exactly what she needed and he held nothing back.

"Open those stunning eyes. I want you to see how beautiful you are when you come." Dimitri pushed Madison over the edge. Her muscles contracting around him had Dimitri erupting with her. Her eyes glazed with desire.

Madison focused on what she was seeing. Above the bed was a mirror, but not your typical mirror. This one appeared to be directly above them, not twelve feet above. A gasp escaped from her mouth. She looked at her face. A face she had seen many times, but had never seen it look like this. A look of pure elation. Total abandonment. Her lips were swollen from his kisses, and her cheeks were flushed as if she had run a mile. Her hair would need the most care. It was a tangled snarled up mess. But she smiled as Dimitri nuzzled her neck. "Now you see what we see."

She reached her arm up, but felt only air. "How is it doing that? I feel like it's right above me."

Dimitri flopped down next to her looking at her profile. "We had it specially made. Having a mirror above the bed is nice, but you miss a lot because of the distance. We didn't want to miss a thing. You'll see what I mean tonight." He kissed her on the nose then got out of bed.

"Hey, you can't just say something like that then not tell me," she whined, throwing a pillow at his incredible body.

Catching it easily, he said, "Yes I can and I just did. I'm getting in the shower. Care to join me?" He tossed the pillow back at her.

She smiled, tucking the pillow behind her head as she reclined back stretching as she did. Teasing him with her hard tight nipples and wide spread legs. "No, I think I'm going to just lounge around for now." She spread her arms wide as well.

"Shit, you make it hard for a man to go to work. Next cruise I'm taking a vacation," he mumbled under his breath as he headed for the shower, leaving a giggling Madison in bed. "I hear you and you will pay for your teasing tonight," Dimitri shouted as the cold water hit him.

That only made her laugh more. She got out of bed. Picking up the envelope on the table as if testing the weight. It felt light, but she knew a ton of bricks were waiting to fall when she opened it. Tossing it back on the table, she called Marco's cabin hoping he was still there. "Hey, could you come to the Midnight Suite? I really need to talk to you."

"Be there in thirty. That good?"

"Perfect see you then."

Dimitri was drying himself as he walked towards her. "On his way?"

"Yeah, in thirty. Just enough time to jump in and out of the shower. And for you to be on your way." She yanked his towel from his body, as she sprinted to the bathroom.

"You are just itching for a punishment aren't you?" A smile was plastered on his face as he walked into the closet to get dressed.

He was waiting for her when she came from the bathroom. He was so handsome, even casually dressed. He wore a golf shirt with the Midnight Oasis logo on the pocket. His black slacks were tailored perfectly to him. "Whatever you decide, we are here for you. Now, I have to check in with Captain Russell then Wyatt and Cooper. If you need me call the security desk and they'll find me for you." He leaned down kissing her. "Everything will be all right. I promise." Then he headed for the door yanking her towel as he went. "All's fair." He laughed as he opened the door to see Marco standing in the knocking position.

"Well, good morning, sunshine. I see someone has started their day very clean," Marco teased as Dimitri tossed the towel back at Madison.

"Put that back on. I had no idea he was there." Dimitri sounded all indignant.

"Oh, honey, it's not like I haven't seen every inch of all her glory." Marco sashayed past Dimitri.

"Yes, but that was before she had two very protective Masters. I don't care where your preferences lay, you still have a dick swinging between your legs. You'll respect our woman."

"Oh, Maddie, I had no idea he was so possessive." Marco turned to Dimitri standing by the now closed door. "Just remember, she was mine first. Like the song says 'Always and Forever.' That's us. Get used to it." He walked further into the room. "Holy shit, I had no idea what this room looked like. Wow, what a view. Good job, boss."

Dimitri just shook his head. He knew Marco was right. Madison walked around the wall wearing her yoga pants and a sports bra. Her hair was wrapped turban style on her head. "Like that's any better." He picked up the paperwork he needed, then walked to Madison. Wrapping his free arm around her waist, he pulled her close. "I'll see you after lunch. When you are done, come to my office. Bring Lucy and Sadie. You never know we could be starting a whole new kind of partnership today." He kissed her goodbye. Then to Marco, he said, "Yes, they did a fabulous job on the room." Releasing Madison, he waved his arm. "Exactly how I envisioned it. Oh, and Marco?" When he had his full attention, he continued, "You may have been her first, Xavier and I will be her only. Take care of our girl." He gave Marco a head nod.

"You got it, boss. Anything for our girl." He started walking towards the window wall. "I have to walk out there."

"He's like a giant child some days." Madison laughed. "But he'll always be there for me." She hugged Dimitri. "Go you have things to do, and I have to talk to him. I'll see you after lunch." Then she opened the door for him.

"Don't let him fall off." He cupped her cheek in his hand. "Beautiful, I understand you feel better opening the envelope with Marco. He's always been safe to you. But I look forward to the day when you have that kind of trust with Xavier and me." He kissed her cheek and then he was gone.

Chapter 14

Madison watched Marco come back in the room as soon as he heard the door close. She met him at the couch and they both plopped down.

"So, why am I here? You have two adorningly handsome Masters who seem to really care for you." She went to say something, but he put up his hand stopping her. "Don't tell me what my eyes have seen. You know it as well don't you?" He gave a tilted head nod. "Uh huh, I knew it. You fell in love didn't you?"

"That's not why you're here though."

"Oh, baby doll. I'm so happy for you." He reached across and grabbed both her hands, pulling her into a hug. "If there is anyone in this world who deserves love. It's you. So, spill what's your dilemma?" He sat back on the couch.

Madison handed him her contract with Dimitri and Xavier. "This is why you're here."

Marco looked at the folded papers in his hand. "Why would you show me this. Better yet, why are your Masters allowing you to show me your contract?"

"Because of the first paragraph."

Marco flipped the cover page, reading the paragraph. "You have got to be shitting me?"

"It's the only paragraph in the contract they will not budge on. Now, do you understand why you're here?"

"What have you told them so far?" Marco inquired.

"I told them almost everything. I left out a few details. Like how you found me right after I had passed out from lack of oxygen. That if you hadn't found me when you did, I would have really been dead. I still need to tell them about Madison's life till now. Thank God, those years are not so eventful. That's not my only problem though." She tossed him the yellow envelope.

"What do we have here?" A blank look on his face.

"They had Caleb and Alejandro do complete searches. One for Amber Sinclair, the other Brian Boxwood. They haven't looked at the information and I promised I wouldn't destroy anything."

"You promised, I didn't."

"No, I promised. That's the one that counts. Trust works both ways you know?"

"Yes, baby doll. I know. So wait right here for one minute." Marco got up and went to the bar. Taking a bottle of wine and two glasses, he headed back to her."

"Oh, you're funny! It's ten o'clock in the morning. Oh, and did I tell you I'm having lunch with Sheikh Colin Ahmed's wife at twelve-thirty?"

"Another reason to have a drink. You open the envelope I'll brush out your hair. You want me to see something, show me. If not, put it away. I'm just here if you need me."

"No, you don't understand! The sheikh's wife is none other than Lucy Jordan. Do you believe that? We met last night."

"Your Lucy Jordan? Get the hell out of here. Apparently she didn't recognize you?"

"No. I was wearing that remarkable mask. Isn't it gorgeous?" Madison pointed at the table that held the mask.

"Exquisite. They have superb taste." Picking the brush up from the table, he continued. "They picked you didn't they? Now turn around. Scoot back and just know nothing in that envelope is going to change how they feel about you." He brought his hands up to remove the towel, massaging her scalp as he did.

"You say that as if it's so easy. I can only imagine what my mother the bitch has been up to." Madison had never kept up on her family. As far as she was concerned they died the same day she did.

"You won't know until you open it." He began working the knots out of her hair. "What are you wearing to lunch?"

"Really?" Madison turned her head to look at him, a dumbfounded look on her face. "Really, that's what I'm supposed to be worried about?"

"I just wasn't sure what a dead person wears to come back to the land of the living."

She smacked his arm. "You're an ass. I'm not telling her who I am. Better to leave things as they are. I'm not taking it totally off the table. Dimitri and Xavier are considering going into business with the sheikh."

"The international line?"

"Yeah." Madison unsealed the envelope. She removed the two manila folders. She opened the one titled family. A photo of her at the age of seventeen was the first thing she saw. It was attached to a missing person's report. "I mean I know to my mom I was nothing but a piece of meat to be purchased by society. But this really proves it. My brother filed the report ten days after I didn't come home. I guess if I wasn't there I didn't exist."

Marco didn't say anything. He just let Madison rave about the file. Some good, most bad. The upside to it all was her mother was right where she belonged. Someone had finally gotten smart to her skimming from every charity and started investigating her. The feds had finally gotten her on embezzlement charges. Right before her trial was to begin for that, they found out about her involvement with a Ponzi scheme. Her mother would hopefully never see the outside of a prison for years. If not for life. Sad, Madison thought. She was truly happy her mom was in jail. She'd have to talk to her therapist about these feelings next time they met.

Her dad had divorced her mother and married some hot twenty-year old with a trust fund. He was living in California. Her brother finished college and moved to Denver. An injury ended his baseball career, so he opened a medical/social marijuana store. According to the file, he was one of the first and he had tripled his investment so far. Making him one of the richest men in Colorado. It showed he owned a ranch in Aurora with his wife, son and daughter. It also showed that until the police produced the file showing she was dead. Matthew had called them weekly to make sure she was never forgotten. Marco handed her a tissue.

"He was your protector. He felt like he failed you because he wasn't there to help you. Does it show his medical history? Not to make you feel bad, but I think he had a break down when he heard you were dead." Marco started French braiding her hair.

The last thing in the file was about her sister Sarah. It said she had recently been hospitalized for a heroin overdose. She had been released and her brother had moved her to a rehab center closer to him. "Seems ironic my brother sells pot for a living, and he's helping my heroin addicted sister. What's wrong with that picture?" She tossed the file on the table.

Opening up the Boxwood file she almost threw up when she saw his picture. He looked similar to how he looked in school only thinner. Once Madison had met the real Brian Boxwood, she had begun to see what he was really like. Unlike the other girls in school who still drooled over the quarterback, Madison knew the truth.

Looking at that picture she saw the same beady evil eyes staring blankly back at her. The fake smile looked impatient. The write up on him showed he and his mother were key witnesses at her mother's trial. They had the proof that her mother had been skimming from the charity Pamela appointed her too. That just made it easier for the jury to believe she was the ring leader of the Ponzi scheme.

Right after her mother's three-year trial finished, the Boxwoods bought a failing pharmaceutical company. Last year its worth was estimated at over fifty-four billion dollars. His mother was still running things with Brian second in command. He had a knack for finding companies that were in financial trouble. He would wait them out until they were desperate then swoop in and buy the company for rock bottom prices.

"Hey, Marco, get this. It says this piece of shit is looking to acquire another pharmaceutical company here in Mexico. Some place in Puerto Vallarta, that's our last stop. Right?" A sick feeling sank into Madison's stomach. Then she thought of her men. She wondered if the information she was holding could help them with whatever plan they had for Boxwood.

"Yeah, I think you're correct. Why what's up? You've been seriously quiet?" Marco rubbed her back as he sat next to her on the couch.

"This is the motherfucker who used me like a punching blow-up doll. I don't think my church going grandmother would get mad at me for wishing the worst kind of pain on him and his fucking family. Do you?"

She handed him the picture. "I've seen this guy before. I can't place where right now, but I know I've seen him," Marco said looking closely at the picture.

"Well, for a while apparently he was the poster child for the company. Look here's a picture of it. You could have seen the ad. It says he had some kind of weird infection. The research and testing of a new antibiotic the company was working on saved his life."

Marco took the file from her and tossed it to the table like she did the other one. "Enough about this asshole. Let's go make you beautiful." He pulled her to her feet after he stood. "Save this one for later with Xavier and Dimitri. I think they would be very appreciative."

"Maybe you're right. I don't want to be later for my lunch. Marco what should I do if Lucy recognizes me? I told them earlier I wasn't going to tell her it was me. Now I'm not so sure. I miss my friend, but if it gets out I'm alive Madam Mia will come looking for me again. I can't go back to that."

"Baby doll, first off if you want your friend back then tell her. If you don't, well then you don't. But as far as Madam Mia looking for you that will not happen."

"But it could, she could say I owe her the years I wasn't there," she interrupted him. Madison was mumbling under her breath.

"Sweetie," he grabbed both her upper arms to get her focus on him. "I paid her what was left of your contract."

"You what?"

"I paid the rest of your contract off."

"Why would you do that? I was already declared dead."

"Because I knew you weren't, and no one was taking you from me again."

"What did you tell her when you did it? Why didn't you ever tell me? How much do I owe you?"

"I told her I was your brother and that I wanted you to leave this world owing no one your life. Second, I saw no reason. I knew you wouldn't run into the woman. You were doing so good. You were building a new life for yourself. Finally, if I had told you, you would have been building a life to pay me back. Which isn't an option. Now do you understand why I didn't tell you?"

Madison wrapped her arms around Marco giving him a hug saying, "I love you too. Thank you." Tears choked her as she spoke.

"You have always been there for me. Except when you disappeared after that fucking ball. You are never to leave me like you did then. When I helped you that night in the dungeon, I was so scared." Marco hugged her tighter. "We had just reconnected, it was like a light reignited inside me. Finding you in that room barely alive, for just a moment I became very selfish. I was mad at you for coming back into my life. Only to leave again. I wasn't letting you go. That's how much you mean to me, baby doll." Marco was wiping the tears running down his face as they separated. "I really do love you. Don't ever leave without saying goodbye. I couldn't take it again."

"I promise I won't." She wiped at her tears. "Now, look what you did. I'm going to have runny eyes, and a red nose for lunch." She went to the mirror. "Maybe she'll think I'm sick?" Madison laughed.

"You'll be your beautiful self in a few minutes. Now, I'm going into this amazing closet and picking out your clothes." Marco picked out an army green cross fold bondage mini skirt. It would hug her curved ass, landing mid-thigh. Her black bustier crop top had a zipper in the middle with rhinestones across the front of it. Finishing the outfit were a pair of open toed wedged sandals which buckled around her ankle.

Then he sat her at the vanity and did her makeup. A dark green eye shadow rimmed her eyes. Black mascara and eyeliner accented her lashes. Loop earrings hung from her ears. A chain with a green colored stone weighing it down hung to her cleavage. Her cuffs remained firmly in place. All she needed was her lipstick. Marco walked her to the full length mirror. "See. Beautiful. No one would ever know you had water leaking from your eyes."

Madison looked at herself in the mirror. Marco had transformed her into someone else. The makeup made the dark flecks of green in her eyes dominate her pupils. The soft French braid hung down her back. Wisps of hair escaping it framed her face, giving her a gentle look. "Wow, where did you learn to do makeup like this?"

"I was a showgirl in Vegas for a season, till the manager learned I was a man. It was a really good gig. Learned a whole lot about makeup and hair. I'll tell you someday. Now, get your bag and key. I'll walk with you to the lounge, after that you're on your own."

She stopped him before he opened the door. "Marco, you're really not mad at me for telling them?"

"Baby doll. I checked out the rest of that contract while you were traveling down memory lane. They aren't looking for a contract for few months. They are looking for a lifetime contract. You can tell them anything, sweetheart."

"How do you know that?"

"Baby, they could have looked at your hard and soft limits and said 'okay this is what we are working with', but they didn't. They took a blank piece of paper and put it where your limits should be. I only see ball gag as your hard limit. What happened to all the rest?"

"Dimitri said we are rewriting my limits list to suit us not past history. So we are trying things slowly." She looked at Marco. "And I think it's working. Last night Dimitri used a rabbit fur flogger on me. I couldn't believe I didn't hyperventilate or have a panic attack. They tied my ankles, but they had me hold the front straps. Xavier stood to the side watching. Marco, I never felt safer. It made it so I could relax and really feel what was happening to my body. And let me tell you it was amazing."

"I'm sure it was. Dimitri is one of the best at handling the flogger. When you move up to caning, you have another expert. I think once the three of you settle into a routine, things will get easier. You'll see." He opened the door. "Today at lunch, feel your friend out. If you feel she is trustworthy, do what you have to. I trust you, Madison. I always have I always will." He took her hand, kissed the back of it then twirled her out the door. "Damn you look hot if I do say so myself."

Then she lightly smacked his shoulder. "Don't let Dimitri hear you say that. You know how he can be."

"Oh yes I do and I couldn't be happier. He and Xavier are going to take very good care of you. And it's about damn time." They arrived at the lounge. "I love you, sweetie. I'll talk with you later."

Madison kissed him on the cheek as she walked thru the open door. "What would I do without you?"

Madison heard Marco say as the door closed. "Let's not find out okay?"

With a smile on her face she waited for her eyes to adjust to the darker room. Gaining her sight, she looked around the room for Lucy. Seeing she hadn't arrived yet, Madison took a table opposite the piano. When she looked towards the door the next time, she saw Colin kissing Lucy goodbye. They spoke quietly, Lucy nodding her head. Colin pointed to the extremely large man behind him. Again Lucy nodded. Then stood for a minute looking at her. Madison could feel his love for Lucy. He gazed into her eyes, lowering his head, he gently kissed her cheek. He murmured something that Madison assumed was very naughty by the way Lucy melted into his arms. He set her away, kissed her cheek, and then he left.

Madison stood up when Lucy walked up to the table. The smile left her face as she whispered. "Amber?"

"Excuse me? Are you okay? Do you need some water?" Madison was glad for the lighting in the lounge. Lucy couldn't see how pale she had turned.

"No, no I'm all right. It's just that for a minute you reminded me of a friend I lost. It's uncanny how much you look like her. Here look." Lucy dug into her bag. Pulling out her wallet Lucy opened it to a photo of (Amber) her. It was a wallet size of Amber posing in a black and white striped pants suit. "See what I mean."

Madison looked at the picture. She remembered that day. The girls at the house had called it 'animal print day.' Each girl had picked their print. Lucy had chosen the cheetah, Amber the zebra. "What happened to her?"

"She died way before her time."

"I'm very sorry to hear that. She must have been very special friend. You're still carrying her picture."

"She was. She was really my only friend. She came into my life at a very bad time, but somehow she made it better." Lucy put the picture away and sat down.

"So," Lucy said, a smile returning to her face as she smacked her hands on the table, "our men are thinking about going into business together. What do you think of that?"

Wanting to change the subject to anything other than

'Amber' Madison smiled. Knowing Lucy wanted the subject change as well. "Can I answer that question at the end of our lunch?" Madison asked, placing her napkin in her lap.

"My first reaction was to ask you why? But I think I understand." Lucy placed her napkin as well. "What do you like to do? Besides the obvious." Lucy laughed.

Madison picked up on her meaning laughing as well. "I enjoy dancing. In fact, that's how I met Dimitri. He is my boss? Was my boss? I'm not really sure anymore." Lucy had a confused look on her face. "Oh, sorry I was thinking out loud. You see I worked for him on the *Onyx*, their first cruise ship. At the crewmember auction Dimitri bought me, and we've been together since." Madison watched Lucy pale at the mention of the auction. She continued on. "This cruise I'm on vacation. Our friends Sadie and Cameron got married right before we left port. So Cameron and Dimitri put the *Onyx* in for any repairs or improvements this week. I know they are updating the computer system to the same one as we have on the *Sapphire*. This allowed crewmembers who knew the Alexanders the chance to come to the wedding. How did you meet the sheikh?"

"After my friend died I was very depressed. My grandfather decided to cheer me up and took me on a trip around the world. We were on our second stop in Dubai. Which by the way is very beautiful! He had made reservations at this upscale restaurant. While we were waiting for our table, a group of men came in. They pushed their way thru the waiting line at the reservation desk. While pushing their way thru, they almost knocked over my grandfather. So being the outspoken spoiled American I am, I spoke up. I told them, 'Hey if you haven't noticed there is a line, and it starts back there.' But as I turned to point to the end of the line, Colin appeared."

A dreamy look flashed across her face. "He looked at me

and politely said in an arrogant tone. 'I wait for no one.' To which I replied. 'Well, you should learn.' Before I knew what was happening he was stopping his guard from striking me. I stood and watched as he calmly berated his guard. Then Malik came over and apologized for almost striking me. I accepted his apology and I thought that was the end of it. Their table was ready and the hostess was waiting to escort them. The guards started moving forward, but Colin stood still watching me. Then he asked. 'Would you please accept my apologies for Malik and join me for dinner?' I looked at my grandfather and he gave me the head nod so I accepted."

Lucy paused her story as the waiter took their order. Then she continued. "My grandfather was thrilled to be sitting at the same table with a real live sheikh. Neither one of us could pronounce his name so I just called him Colin. Grandfather and Colin hit it off from the beginning. I was still hesitant. He made my stomach flutter as if a hundred butterflies had been let loose in it. I however, kept my guard up. My grandfather had a lot of money, and I wasn't going to have him involved with any shady dealings."

Their lunch arrived and Lucy continued. "By the end of dinner we were going to be staying at his palace so he and grandfather could do business. When we were walking out of the restaurant, Colin came up behind me as whispered in my ear. 'Little dove, do not fight your desires. I already have your grandfather in the palm of my hand. Now, I intend to have my palm on your ass. That sweet little mouth has earned you a good spanking.' I looked at him like he was crazy and told him to kiss my ass. My grandfather would never allow that." Lucy had changed her voice to sound like her grandfather. "What I didn't know was Colin had already told my grandfather he was going to marry me, and my grandfather had given his blessing. Providing he had no other wives then or in the future, and

Colin had agreed. Over dinner could you believe that. I couldn't."

Lucy downed half of her wine then continued. "We arrived at his palace and I couldn't believe what I was looking at. It was bigger than some hotels we had stayed at. We were given our own wing, and we settled in. That's when grandfather told me what he had done. 'Why would you do that? You told me you wanted me to marry for love. How can I do that? You already told him I would marry him. I have no idea who he is, what he does. Shit, Grandfather I can't even pronounce his name. What were you thinking?' I had railed at him, and he just sat there letting me. When I was finished, he very calmly said. 'I know he is the man for you. You may not know him, but I do. What do you think I do all day, Lucy?' He had asked and I had just shrugged my shoulders. 'I sit on the computer mostly doing business, but the rest of the time I'm searching for possible husbands for you. I'm not going to be here much longer and I need to know you will be taken care of. I'm very sorry your friend died. But this trip gave me the excuse to get you out of the mansion. I knew if you thought it would please me you would do it.'

"The sly old fox had played me like a fiddle. He just didn't realize that after Colin and I met his search would stop there. We spent the rest of our vacation there. Colin asked me to marry him, I accepted, and we had the wedding. My grandfather was there to walk me down the aisle. About a month after the wedding he died. Colin made all the arrangements to have him shipped back to the states. While we were settling his estate, Colin applied for dual citizenship and was accepted. It had taken four months, but he wanted to do it for me. This allows us to travel back and forth easier."

The waiter came asking about desert. Lucy ordered the

cheesecake. Madison got the fudge brownie with ice cream. "So if your friend hadn't died, you wouldn't have gone on the trip. You might not have met Colin?" Madison asked.

"Oh no, he was high on my grandfather's list of…"

"Qualifications?" Madison filled in for Lucy. Smiling, as she put a scoop of brownie in her mouth. Stopping with that one word, she looked at Lucy's stunned face.

"Yes! How did you know that?"

Madison realized her mistake. Covering quickly, she shoved another mouthful in and shrugged her shoulders. Talking with a full mouth she said. "Good guess?"

Lucy wasn't convinced, but she let it go. "Yes, qualifications. If we had not taken the trip grandfather would have brought them to the United States to meet me. So, although I'm sad she passed, I was happy that I found my husband on our trip. It was the last one for grandfather. I knew he wanted to travel, but he wouldn't leave me."

"What do you mean, 'he wouldn't leave you?'"

"I had hired a security team to follow my friend in the picture." Madison's face went white. Grabbing her water glass, she took a long drink. "Are you okay?"

"Yes. Please continue," Madison choked out.

"Well, when they told me that she had died after a date she had been on, there was nothing more I could do." Under her breath she whispered. I had been so close. To Madison she said. "She needed some financial help, but I was too late to give it to her. How did we get back to her?" Lucy shook out her hands. Waving away the bad vibes.

"My turn!" Lucy said excitedly clapping her hands. "How did you meet your two unbelievably handsome Masters?"

"Well, as I said earlier Dimitri was my boss on the *Onyx*. Xavier I had met years before. We reconnected the first night of the cruise with the help of Dimitri."

"Oh, they are special aren't they?"

By now Madison had had two glasses of wine, and was feeling the effects. "Yes, they are very special. How long have you been involved with the BDSM lifestyle?" She asked. Then giggled. "I'm so sorry. That was so inappropriate."

"Really! Look where we are." She lifted her arms waving them around the room.

"You make a good point." She giggled again.

"Colin and I have always been involved. He introduced me to it, and I can truly say it keeps a marriage interesting." Lucy grinned, fingering her diamond collar.

Madison looked at it with envy. Not for the jewels, but for the meaning. "Are you ready to get going? Dimitri wanted me to bring you to his office when we were finished." She looked around the room, just realizing Sadie had never showed up when she burst through the door.

"I'm so sorry. Cameron left me with Chester, and I lost track of time."

Lucy looked at Madison as to say who is this? "Lucy I'd like to introduce you to Sadie Alexander." They shook hands. "She married Dimitri's business partner, and Xavier's half-brother."

Sadie looked at Madison with wide eyes. No one was supposed to know that information. Because of who Xavier's biological father was. Realizing her error Madison thought to correct it but changed her mind. "Sadie, I'd like you to meet Lucy. She is Sheikh Colin Ahmed's wife."

Shaking her hand. "Colin Ahmed, the same one our men are meeting with?" Sadie asked understanding what Madison meant. "It's a pleasure to meet you. Trust is a big part of our lifestyle. I'm hoping you feel the same way?" Lucy nodded in agreement. Sadie continued quietly. "Xavier's real father is a walking nightmare. We can only hope he rots and dies in prison. I know that sounds harsh, but you wanted the truth."

"Thank you for trusting me. We were just leaving to meet the men, but if you're hungry?"

"No, no I'm good. Let's go get some air on our walk. If that's okay. I feel like I haven't seen the sun in days," Sadie commented as they left the lounge and headed outside towards the railing. "It's beautiful here." Looking over the rail at the port.

Madison asked Lucy. "How do you feel about our men in business together?"

"I think it's a fabulous idea. You'll love Dubai. Have you ever been?"

"No, can't say I have." Lucy didn't realize Madison's undertone.

"You must do a lot of traveling for business Lucy, do you and the sheikh own your own private plane? Cameron and I are thinking about getting one."

"Yes, we do travel be it for business or pleasure. It just so happens besides this business meeting Colin also has one in Puerto Vallarta on Thursday. So we got to combine business with pleasure."

Madison's hearing picked up when she heard where the meeting was supposed to take place. "I'm sorry," she interrupted. "Who is Colin meeting with in Puerto Vallarta?" Madison started to have a panic attack. As a sick feeling hit her. Sadie and Lucy rushed to her side.

"Are you okay?" Lucy asked with concern.

"She's having a panic attack," Sadie said to Lucy. To Madison she said, "Maddie, slow down. Breathe, in… out…" Sadie started breathing with her.

"What's the name?" Madison asked through breaths.

"I don't know. Madison, are you sure you're all right?" Lucy asked with concern. "I'll ask him as soon as we get to Dimitri's office. Come let's go."

Madison was breathing normally again. "Yes, I think that

would be a good idea. Because if it's who I think it is," Madison said, looking straight at Lucy, "you don't want anything to do with this guy." Then she headed to the stairs to get to the bridge and Dimitri's office next to it.

Madison thought as they got closer to the office. What if they are supposed to meet with Boxwood? What if Colin is going to invest with that pig as well as Dimitri, Xavier, and Cameron? This can't be happening Madison thought just as they got to the office.

Chapter 15

She knocked lightly on the door before sticking her head in. "Are we interrupting?" she asked as the three of them walked into the office.

Dimitri stood up from behind his desk and walked over to Madison. Taking her hand and kissing her palm, he escorted her to his chair sitting down with her in his lap.

Xavier came over and kissed her as well. "We have just finished up. Say hello to our new partner for our international line." He nodded his head toward Colin smiling.

"Congratulations. I'm very happy for you." Gathering her courage, she asked Colin. "Could I ask you a question, Colin?"

"Of course."

"Who are you meeting with in Puerto Vallarta?"

Colin looked at Lucy as she said. "I told her we were mixing pleasure with business. I couldn't remember the company name otherwise I would have told her. She started having a panic attack as soon as I mentioned the meeting in Puerto Vallarta."

"Are you okay, Madison?" Xavier asked with concern, touching her shoulder.

"I need to hear the name and when I do. Then you'll understand." Looking at Xavier.

Everyone's vision turned to Colin and Lucy. "His name is Boxwood. Brian I think. We have spoken over the phone. He's looking for a partner in a new pharmaceutical company in Mexico. I thought it would be a good investment. It will not interfere with our arrangement."

"It might," Dimitri said. "How set are you on doing business with him?"

"I've looked into the profit margin. The numbers look good. You would have to give me a really good reason to change my mind," Colin responded.

Dimitri turned Madison so she was looking at him. "How did you know the meeting was with Boxwood?"

"The file you gave me this morning said it. It was the only thing in the file I saw before Marco ripped it out of my hand. He told me I should look at that one with the two of you."

"I think you have to give Marco a raise," Xavier said to Dimitri.

"Madison this is your call." Her big green eyes looked at Dimitri and Xavier and gave a head nod. "Before we do this I'd like to see what's in that file in our suite. Colin would you indulge us and come to our suite in thirty minutes?"

"I think that's a good plan." Colin paused before continuing, "The information that you will be sharing with me..." Colin stressed his words. Then waited for them to sink in. "How reliable is your source?"

"Very. Why?"

"Because I think I'm going to be looking for a new hacker. I had a thorough investigation done on this Boxwood. If one piece of information is different he's fired.

Then I'm going to give him to Lucy's body guard Malik to find out why."

They all rose from their chairs. "Thirty minutes, Midnight Suite. I'm confident that once you hear what we have to say, you will be changing your mind. See you there," Dimitri commented.

Entering the suite, Dimitri and Xavier headed for the couch area where the folder sat on the table. Madison lagged behind. "Beautiful, do you want to look with us?" Dimitri questioned.

"No, I think I'm going to get a glass of wine and go out on the balcony. You can send the women out when they get here." She turned from the bar with a bottle of wine and three glasses. "I'm going to tell Lucy and Sadie who I really am. They need to know. I want them to know. I trust them to keep it to themselves."

"It sounds like you're trying to convince yourself not us," Dimitri said.

"Maybe I am." She bit her lip. "Xavier, it slipped out to Lucy that you're Cameron's half-brother. I didn't mean to tell her. It just came out."

Xavier placed his hands on her hips stopping her. "I've been waiting to tell you this since you walked into Dimitri's office. Damn woman you are sexy as hell!" He then kissed her deeply. "You taste even better." The bondage mini skirt hugged her ass. The black halter bustier pushed her breasts up as an offering. Her green four-inch wedge sandals, put her at an ideal height for both her Masters.

Dimitri came up behind her grabbing both her ass cheeks. "Marco dressed you today didn't he?" he said in her ear, as he leaned his chin on her shoulder. "Xavier is right though. You are sexy as hell. I'm going to talk to Marco. We may have to hire him as your personal shopper." He slipped his hands down her thighs as he stepped up behind her pushing his erection against her ass. "I've been like this since you walked into my office. Xavier, what do you think? Our girl got out of another punishment with this outfit?" He kissed her cheek. "This will have to wait till everyone leaves." He pushed his hips forward. "I know I won't be able to wait till after dinner though."

"I agree with Master Dimitri. There will be no punishment for your little slip. Just keep in mind, if it happens again I make no promises. Now, take your glasses and wine. We will send the girls out. Relax, my lovely, we will make this as right as we can." He kissed her forehead, and sent her on her way.

"Dimitri?" Gaining his attention, Xavier asked after Madison was out on the balcony, "This can't be that easy?" Making his way back to the couch where Dimitri was flipping through the file, Xavier picked up her family folder.

They sat scanning the pages. Both engrossed in what they were looking at, when the knock arrived on the door. "Pull the information on Madison's sister out, and put the rest of the file in the safe." Holding the papers in his hand, he added, "I don't know why, but I have a feeling her addiction is related to him somehow."

Dimitri answered the door. The ladies walked in before Colin and Cameron. "Ladies, if your Masters will allow it, Madison is on the balcony with a bottle of wine, and glasses." Both women looked to their men for approval.

Cameron grabbed Sadie's chin. "We are still on our honeymoon, and you're a light weight with alcohol. A half glass for you." She made a face at him. "Did you eat lunch?" When she kept her head down. "You're lucky you're even getting that. I should have you drink water." She made a sad face and looked at him. "Go, before I change my mind." She smiled big, giving him a quick peck on the cheek.

"Lucy, we have dinner plans with Dimitri, Xavier, and Madison in town tonight. Keep that in mind."

She kissed him putting all her love behind the kiss. "I look forward to it. Enjoy your meeting." She grabbed Sadie's hand and they went out the balcony door.

They could hear the women praising the balcony. Colin sat in one chair looking around the suite. "Very impressive. We will need three of these suites for the international ship. Lucy has never requested one of the luxuries I have given to her. However, I still like to give them to her. Will that be a problem?" Dimitri shook his head to let Colin know it could be done. While Cameron took the other seat, Colin asked. "So how bad is it, Dimitri?"

"It's bad. Before we deal with Boxwood…" Dimitri looked at the men sitting with him then said, "Nothing leaves this room. We promised Madison and we intend to keep that promise. Do we understand each other."

Both men gave their word. Then they sat back as Dimitri and Xavier began to tell them what they knew about Boxwood. They only told them what they needed to know. "Now, as far as that motherfucker goes, the planning begins right now. Between the four of us we are going to come up with a plan. We have two options. Option one, we ruin him financially. Option two, we ruin his family life," Xavier commented.

"I'd like to go with option three. Ruin his family and take his company," Colin chimed in. "I had no idea what a slimy bastard he was. None of this information was available to me. I can see your brain is working, Dimitri. What do you have in mind?"

"Oh, yeah my mind is working. I'm thinking he should get strapped to a St. Andrew's cross. A testicular cuff locked tight on his balls, a ball gag shoved in his mouth, and a bull whip used to flay the skin from his body. Then after about a week of torturing him, we drop a dozen hungry rats over his head and let them finish him off." Dimitri was seething by the time he was finished.

Xavier gave a little chuckle. "Man your Russian is really coming out now isn't it?"

"You have no idea of the things I've seen. What I described was a walk in the park. I watched a man have every finger nail ripped from his nail beds, feet included. And that was just the start of what they did to him."

"In my country we find messing with the mind very effective and permanent," Colin said with an evil grin on his face.

"There is something else we need to tell you about Madison. I think right about now she's telling your wives." Dimitri had their attention.

Colin stood up hearing Lucy shouting. He started heading towards the balcony doors. Dimitri put a hand on his arm stopping him. "Your wife is fine. She's just angry, probably excited, and stunned."

Colin looked out the window and saw that Dimitri was right. Lucy was now hugging Madison. "What just happened?"

"That's what I was trying to tell you. Madison is not really Madison. Her real name is Amber Sinclair, and technically she's dead." Dimitri had their attention.

Madison poured wine for Sadie and Lucy. "Half a glass for me. Cameron has already warned me." Sadie looked at Madison as she sat back down on the lounge chair. "Maddie, you look like you lost your best friend. Whatever it is we'll help you."

"There's a chance I might. I have to tell you both something. All I ask is that you listen to my whole story before you pass judgment. Just know I did what I thought I had to do." Madison took a gulp of wine. "Here goes. Lucy, you were right earlier. I am Amber. I'm the girl in that picture. Sadie, give me a minute and I'll catch you up." Sadie gave an understanding nod.

Lucy stood up from her chair and walked over to Madison. She touched her face like it was a fragile piece of art. "I knew it was you. I wanted it to be you so badly. I've missed you so much. I never forgot you." The tears started trailing down her cheeks. "You could have told me; I would have protected you. Why didn't you come to me?" Lucy started shouting at Madison.

"Do you remember at lunch when you told me about the security following me… Amber?"

"Yes. It was only a couple of hours ago," Lucy snapped back. "That was the night they told me you were dead."

"Well, technically I was." Lucy sipped her wine. "I had a date that night that turned into a mess. If Marco hadn't been there I would have been dead." Madison explained what had happened. She told Sadie how she knew Ryan Arcola aka Smith, aka Romano and his uncle, the piece of shit. She told them of the shape she had been in when Marco had found her.

Finally, she told them of the plan that Marco had come up with. That she had to make that split decision right at that moment. "Once I made the decision, there was no going back. I had to forget about everyone I ever knew as Amber Sinclair. I couldn't tell anyone."

Madison stood up and took Lucy's hands in her hands. "You and…" Madison looked over Lucy's shoulder at Xavier. The expression on her face softened. She had hurt him as well. Looking back at Lucy, Madison stood a little taller.

"Xavier, were the only ones I was worried about hurting. You had always been nice to me. You were my only friend. Then, Marco told me that I had to make that life changing decision right then. I never meant to hurt you, and I'm so sorry. If you never want to see me again I would understand. But please don't let what I did effect Dimitri's business dealings with Colin."

"Do you think me so shallow that I would allow my personal life to affect my husband's business dealing?" Lucy asked, still holding Madison's hands.

"Absolutely not. I know what kind of a woman you are. But people can change, and the love of a man can also influence a woman's decision. I also know how much a man relies on his woman's opinion. I'm sure when Colin asks you he's looking for your input. That's all I'm saying."

Lucy pulled Madison into her arms hugging her. "Don't think because I'm hugging you it means I'm still not mad at you. I know Colin heard me yelling. I just wanted to let him know everything was all right." Lucy held Madison at arm's length then sat in her chair. "Why are you telling me this now? You could have told me at lunch. What happened?"

"Brian Boxwood." Was all Madison replied.

"What does 'Brian Boxwood' mean?"

"He is the reason I ended up with the Arcolas to begin with." Madison continued on telling them what had happened between her and Brian. From the very beginning. "So, now you know everything. Dimitri and Xavier dug up information on him. I was starting to look at it this morning. That's how I knew about your husband's meeting with him. Lucy believe me when I say he was bad news, and he probably still is."

"Amber... Madison, what do I call you?" Lucy asked frustrated.

"Madison. Please."

Lucy took a deep breath in and let it out slowly. "Okay. So let me see if I have this straight. Boxwood chased you like a dog. When he couldn't get you the normal way, he had his mommy basically buy you for him. He used you, beat you, and then threw you away. Pretty close?" When Madison nodded in agreement. Lucy stood up from her chair and walked to the balcony doors. "Colin?" Getting his full attention, she then continued. "Don't even think about doing business with that Boxwood piece of crap. In fact, I want you to sit with these gentlemen until you have a solid plan for taking everything that dick has. He hurt my friend, and now I want him hurt. You'll do that for me right, sweetheart?"

Madison couldn't hear Colin's response. She didn't need to. When Lucy came back to the sitting area she had a huge smile on her face. Grabbing the wine bottle, she poured more into her and Madison's glass. Looking at Sadie who shook her head no, Lucy put the bottle down. "Now that all that bullshit is out of the way let's have some fun. I still can't believe you're here."

Madison and Sadie looked at each other. "What just happened?" Madison asked.

"Colin hates when I'm unhappy. I have no worries that this Boxwood character will be taking care of. The proper way. So, now we can focus on other things, like having fun. As far as what Madison just told us about her experiences. God, I wish there was a way I could make them all go away. But I can't. What I can do is thank God because she's sitting in that chair in front of me. I can make sure the person who caused her pain, gets punished. Until that can be accomplished, I plan on enjoying the fact I have my friend back. I'm not going to lose her again. So, the only way to do that is to move on. Now, let's get reacquainted." Lucy looked at Sadie. "What do you do, Sadie?"

"I star in a Broadway play." Sadie answered hesitantly.

Not sure if Lucy could be bi-polar? She had never seen someone go from anger to easy going so fast.

"Which one? Colin and I saw a bunch when we stopped in New York."

"*Heroin-Life Without Needles*."

"You're kidding me? We saw that one. You were amazing in that play. It was the only one Colin didn't fall asleep at. In Dubai, we have very strict laws for opiates. Minimum of four years just for carrying a prescription not registered with the Ministry of Health. What Todd Phillips is doing by getting the word out is admirable. I know that mental health in this country is not taken as seriously as in other countries. We are in the process of building a four hundred ninety-five-million-dollar facility, to house two hundred seventy-seven beds. Although, the law is in place we still have trouble with illegal drugs on the streets. The ones looking for help need a place they can go to get it. We're trying to give it to them. Anyway, getting back to the play. I loved the last song you sang in the finale. What was the name of it? Something about family?"

"The name of the song is *Stronger with My Family*. One of Todd's nieces overdosed on heroin. He thought he could get the word out in another way. There's an epidemic going on in this country. Heroin is everywhere in every town, it doesn't discriminate age, race or status. You see news stories about it on every channel. But no one can seem to stop it from getting out on the streets. Anyway, we are trying to get the word out there. Hoping one day someone will have the balls to stop it. I'm glad I'm a part of the solution."

"I've heard talk of a Tony for you for your part." Lucy raised her glass to Sadie. "If I could vote for you I would."

"I think it's a little early to be talking Tony award, but thank you."

"When you come to Dubai maybe we can talk your producer into bringing the play as well. The DUCTAC-

Dubai Theatre seats five hundred plus. I think this play should be shared. Then there's the fact that Colin stayed awake. That says a lot." They all started laughing. "Okay, ladies. Let's go find out what diabolical plans our men have cooked up." Lucy rose from her chair, and was the first to walk in from the balcony."

"Madison, I'm sorry those things happened to you. I wish there was something I could say to make everything go away. But I know I can't do that. I can only be your friend. I hope you know how much you mean to Cameron and me," Sadie said to Madison before they walked in. "I agree with Lucy though, let's twist this guy's nuts in knots. Then cut them off."

Madison hugged Sadie. "I don't know if they can do that, but I'll ask," she teased Sadie as they walked through the balcony entry.

"All right gentlemen, calm down. We only have a day and a half to figure this shit out. So, let's stop fucking around and get down to some serious planning," Dimitri announced.

"What have you come up so far?" Madison asked as the women approached.

Dimitri and Xavier moved apart, making room for Madison on the couch. Lucy walked over and sat on Colin's lap. Sadie stood behind Cameron swaddling his neck with her arms, leaning on his back.

"Ladies, why don't you go down to the spa. Massages on me," Colin spoke up.

Madison and Sadie looked at their men. "You do remember what happened the last time plans were made without our knowledge?" Sadie stood up speaking out, resting her hands on Cameron's shoulders.

He reached up taking her hand, he pulled her into his lap. Nuzzling her neck. "Yes, we remember." Pulling his head away from her neck, he said, "We are not sending the women out, Colin. They need to hear what's going to happen. We kept vital information from them once before, and it did not work in our favor. That's a story for another day." He took Sadie's face in his hands, looking deeply in her eyes. "I'm very lucky to have this woman on my lap. She was almost lost to me, and I'm not risking that again." Cameron gently kissed Sadie on the forehead.

Dimitri turned to Colin. "I agree with Cameron. If you would prefer to have Lucy uninvolved we understand. Malik can escort her…"

"No fucking way. I'm staying!" Lucy demanded.

"Lucy, your mouth!" The stern sound in his voice told her she was in trouble. "Defiance as well?" He raised his eyebrows. "Oh, you can look forward to a very red ass tonight. And I will enjoy carrying it out."

His erection evident under her ass, she said, "Sorry, Sir. I would very much like to stay and help my friend." She looked at Madison smiling. "Colin meet Amber Sinclair, my friend." She turned back to Colin. "She prefers Madison now."

To Madison he said, "You do look like the girl in the picture." To Lucy, he added, "Dimitri and Xavier have informed us of Amber's demise, and Madison's birth." Seeing the set look on her face he said. "Even if I ask, you're still not going to stay out of it are you?" She shook her head in agreement. "Fine, but you will follow every direction to the letter. Otherwise, I will bind you to our bed and not release you till we are docking." Lucy started kissing him all over his face. "I'm not joking, Lucy. Every direction."

"Yes, Sir, yes, Sir, yes, Sir." Continuing to kiss him, she added, "Every direction, got it. Okay." She finished by taking possession of his mouth. Showing her appreciation with her kiss.

"Colin, we have a crew of very capable ex-military special ops personal. We would be smart to enlist their help with whatever we decide to do. Are you okay with that?"

"That might be advisable. If he's done his homework on me, he'll know my personnel," Colin replied.

"Did Boxwood reach out to you, or vice-versa?" Xavier asked.

"He contacted me. My media staff had put out a notice I would be on this vacation. Two days later, my strategic manager came to me with Boxwood's proposal."

"Did you bring the proposal?" Dimitri asked.

"Of course. It's in my cabin. I'll bring it to dinner."

"Good. That's a start. I'm going to have Caleb dig deeper into this pharmaceutical company. Colin could you tell us the terms of the proposal?"

"He's looking for cash."

Dimitri got off of the couch and started pacing. "I guarantee he's doing something shady. If he needed cash why didn't he just get it from his mommy?"

"It could be something he doesn't want mommy to know about. And if that's the case, it's probably illegal," Xavier interjected.

"We need to know what's going on under the radar at that pharmaceutical company. Cameron, call Greyson to see if has anybody who can do re-con on the ground in Puerto Vallarta. We have to know what we're walking into," Dimitri asked.

Cameron got out of his seat with Sadie in his arms. Placing her on the seat, he fished his phone from his pocket. Walking into the dungeon area, he called Greyson.

Madison sat flipping through the report on Brian Boxwood. She kept going back to the picture. The file had his school records, college, and sporting statistics. His wedding, first divorce, when his grandmother died. All his addresses, phones numbers, and cars registered to him. It showed his net worth, and his present bank balances. Madison sat a little straighter, setting the file flat on her lap. She methodically searched the file. She looked at Xavier and said, "It's not in here." A confused look on his face prompted her to go on. "It's not here," she repeated.

"What's not in there?" Lucy asked.

Madison's eyes seemed to twinkle when she looked at Lucy. "His medical records. I looked thru this entire file. The only thing it mentions is the antibiotic ads he starred in. Marco told me his last year of college his knee got crushed in a football game. It's not in here," she said waving the file. "I was also looking to see how he was health wise after using this miracle antibiotic. Again, it's not in here. Where is the rest of it?" She smacked the file against her hand. Looking at Colin. "Did your research on him show any medical information?"

Colin looked thoughtful. "I believe you're right. I don't recall any medical records. I wouldn't normally look for them though. Why do they matter?"

Madison reached in the file and pulled out Brian's photo. Handing it to Colin she said. "Does this look like a healthy man to you? He's buying a medical company in Mexico! What if he has to have some weird experimental drug and the only place that makes it is this company? You could back out and he wouldn't get the medicine he needs?"

"Beautiful, he'd just find someone else to fund it. If Colin backs out, we lose our edge."

"But, Dimitri, then that puts Colin in close proximity with Boxwood. What if he gets hurt? I couldn't live with that."

"Madison dear, I will have my security with me."

"Us." Lucy corrected. "If I don't go he will wonder where your wife is."

"Greyson knows a team that's available. He needs whatever intel we have on Boxwood, and the location. He'll have them there by tonight. That gives us at least a day's surveillance." Cameron came back into the living area.

"Tell him Alejandro can give him that information. Xavier ask Caleb to dig deeper. I think Madison might be onto something. We need those medical records."

"Sadie," Cameron held his hand out for her. "We need to go get Chester."

Sadie stood up. "But what about the plan?"

"There can be no plan until we have all the intelligence. Let's meet here tomorrow after dinner. That should give the team enough time to get a feel for what's happening at the pharmaceutical company. Until then we are still on our honeymoon."

"Yes we are, aren't we?" Sadie smiled.

"Gentlemen, ladies, if you need us, you know where to find us. Enjoy dinner." Cameron shook the men's hands.

Sadie gave departing kisses to the women. "We dock tomorrow at Mazatlán. Cameron and I going horseback riding. Would you guys like to go tomorrow? The car is picking us up at 10:00 a.m. It might take your mind off all this shit."

"It sounds wonderful to me. I'll need a distraction," Lucy answered.

"I haven't ridden a horse in years. It does sound fun." Madison sounded excited. "But I think I should be here." The excitement left her voice.

"Madison, we all could go if you like? I agree with Lucy horseback riding would be a good distraction. At least a distraction off the ship." Dimitri came up behind Madison sitting on the couch. Rubbing down her arms, he said, "If we stay on the ship I'm sure we could find another way to distract ourselves." He began kissing her from her ear down to her neck.

"I think that's our cue to leave. Dimitri, Cameron, we will talk more tomorrow on our business deal. Xavier, I would also like to talk to you about the wine industry. Sadie, I'm sure we will be seeing more of each other. Madison, I look forward to dinner. I'd like to get to know my wife's best friend. The woman you are today." Colin kissed the back of Madison's hand. "The car will pick us up at the pier around six o'clock." Grabbing Lucy around her waist, he crisscrossed his arms over her abdomen, grinding his dick against her bottom as he pulled her back against him. His knees pushed behind her knees, making her walk forward towards the door. "I have some ideas on how I will be spending my time till then."

Lucy tried to spin out of his arms but he caught her. "Oh, I thought I had a punishment coming?"

"You do. But that's not till after dinner. I want you to enjoy your meal sitting down," Colin commented casually. "I also don't want to rush your spanking. I like to admire my work."

"I look forward to it, Sir." Lucy's voice jumped as Colin swatted her ass out the door.

"See you guys tomorrow. Try not to think too much on this tonight. There really is nothing you can do. Enjoy dinner." Sadie and Cameron followed Lucy and Colin out the door, leaving Madison with her Masters.

"We have three hours to kill before dinner. Any ideas on what we should do?" Xavier sat on the coffee table in front of Madison.

Dimitri still leaning over the back of the couch brought his hand up, unzipping her bustier. Pushing it out of the way Xavier leaned forward taking her nipple in his mouth.

Lashing his tongue around, then biting gently. "I think I have one." Pushing his hands up Madison's thighs, he took her skirt with them. "You may be onto something, Dimitri. Maybe we should hire Marco. He has dressed our girl just the way we like her. Panty free." He moved his hands up and over her thighs. Brushing his thumbs over her wet lips. "I've been waiting for this all day." He kneeled before her, taking Madison's legs and putting them on either side of his head. Moving forward, his tongue followed a path through her wet folds to her entrance. Pulling back, Xavier said, "We need to move this to the bed now. I want to feast in comfort, not kneeling on the floor." He scooped her up and carried her to the bed. He set her on the bed.

Madison picked up her head and looked at her Masters. "I'm sure neither one of you banked on all my problems. I'd understand if you didn't want to have anything more to do with me. But I would like a farewell fuck."

Xavier had her over his lap so fast her head was spinning. "Would you like the first one or should I?" he asked Dimitri.

"I think our little sub has just earned her first punishment. There will be no reprieve from this one, beautiful," Dimitri said as his hand came down with a smack on her ass. Jumping when his hand hit, Madison tried to move, but Xavier held fast. "Why would you think because you have problems we would leave you? You really have no idea how we feel about you do you?" Madison just kept her head bowed down. "I think we are just going to have to show her."

Chapter 16

Dimitri and Xavier combined gave Madison ten smacks, as well as ten rubs. Xavier lifted Madison up to sit on the bed next to him. Looking at her tear stained face pulled at his heart. But he knew if he ran his finger through her lips she would be slick with wetness. "Madison, look at me." Xavier's voice deepened to his Master's voice. She picked up her head. When her eyes locked with Xavier's, he picked up her wrist. "Do you think we gave you these as pieces of jewelry? They might not be a collar, but they still claim you as ours to all who see them."

"We understand we have asked you to relive some of the worst times of your life. We expect you to feel that pain. We do not want you doubting yourself or us. Beautiful, we are here for the long haul," Dimitri gently added, moving her hair off her shoulder.

"I've had some terrible things done to me. I've done some terrible things." She looked at Xavier. "I hope you can forgive me for not trusting you. But if I had, and not listened to Marco," she paused, looking at Dimitri, "I would have never met you." She touched his scruffy cheek, a day's growth bristled under her fingers. "When I think of my life without one of you, my chest hurts."

"Madison, I think it's time for us to show you how much you mean to us." Xavier got off the bed and went into the closet.

Dimitri looked at her sitting on the bed. "Let's get you ready." He finished taking off her bustier and slid the skirt down her legs. He kneeled at her feet unbuckling her shoes, tossing them off to the side. Xavier returned and kneeled next to Dimitri. In his hand he held two ring boxes.

When she realized what they were doing. Her hands flew to her mouth and the tears began to fall from her eyes.

"Once upon a time, I fell in love with a woman, but she left this world too early. Now, I've been given a second chance to have that love again." Xavier reached up and took her hand kissing her palm. Then, gazing into her eyes with such longing, he continued, "I know we all come with baggage. Hell, my father is the Devil himself." His voice raised as he spoke about his father. "I wish I never knew about him."

Xavier's voice softened. "But then I never would have known about Cameron, and through him, I found you. I don't want to lose you again. I want to fall asleep and wake up every day for the rest of my life looking at you. At the amazing woman you've become. If you choose, the mother of our children. We can have that future we talked about all those years ago. With one deviation from that road."

Xavier looked at Dimitri. "When we made those plans, Madison. I never expected you to bring another lover with you when we did finally get back together." Madison laughed wiping her eyes. "But if it had to be anybody, I'm happy it was Dimitri. You've introduced me to a man I can admire. Who thinks like me! Is a lot more presumptuous than me, but we wouldn't be complete without him. I love you both and I would like to spend the rest of my days with the both of you. If you will have me?" Xavier asked.

Dimitri reached up taking Madison's other hand. Like Xavier he kissed her palm. Then drew a circle with his tongue and licked up her wrist. Smiling that beautiful smile at her. "When I first saw you sitting in my office, I thought I had found my new sub. At least for the length of the maiden voyage of the *Onyx*." Dimitri laughed. "Then as I watched you and got to know you, I hated how you withdrew into yourself. I wanted to be the one to protect you. But I didn't know who or what I was fighting." Dimitri looked at Xavier. "The way you looked at Xavier the first time on the *Onyx*, I knew you had a history, but you wouldn't tell me. I followed you the day you met him on the docks." Dimitri's gaze went back to Madison. "After that, you were different. Happier. I knew then that if I wanted you, I needed him."

He smiled at Xavier. "He is a cocky prick, but when we are together… something just clicks. Like pieces to a puzzle, we are complete. You will never be alone again. We want to be your husbands, lovers, and Masters for the rest of our lives. What do you say? Will you marry us?"

Madison watched Xavier hand Dimitri one of the boxes. He lifted the lid of the jewelry box. Sitting on the black velvet cushion was a ring. It kind of looked like a school graduation ring. But when you looked closer you saw a wide band engagement ring. On one side was the face of a Siberian tiger in white and black diamonds. On the other side was the face of a lion in yellow diamonds. Red rubies for his eyes. Centered in the middle was a five carat emerald cut diamond.

"Marry us, Madison?" They asked together.

Looking at Dimitri, she said, "When you said get me ready, this was the last thing I would have ever thought was going to happen."

"Sitting naked on your bed is not the way you probably dreamed of being proposed to. We had planned on doing it right, but you need to know right now. We aren't going anywhere."

"Yes." Was all she said.

"Yes. She said yes?" Xavier asked.

"Yes. She's all ours." They each held the ring in their fingers, and slid it on her finger. Then one after the other, they sealed it to her finger with a kiss.

Madison held her hand up to admire the one of a kind ring. Bringing her hand down, she looked at the second box. "Now, can I see what's in the other ring box? Was that the ring for if I said no?" Madison teased.

"I think our girl is teasing us. Like she would say no to us?" Dimitri teased right back.

"No, Madison. These are our rings!" Xavier lifted the other lid. Inside were two rings. One a tiger, the other a lion. "We had them specially made. Why should only women get to wear the bling!" he added.

Xavier took the gold lion out. Holding it so Madison could hold it with him. Xavier said, sliding the ring on Dimitri, "We give you this ring, as a symbol of our commitment to you. As partners, friends, and lovers. To show everyone that you have been claimed by us."

Dimitri and Madison did the same with the white tiger ring. To Xavier, Dimitri said, "Wear this ring as a symbol of our commitment to you as partners, friends, and lovers. To show everyone that you have been claimed by us."

They stood up bringing Madison with them. "Now, do you see how much you mean to us? We love you, Madison, and we want you with us. Always," Xavier said as he kissed her.

"You belong with us." Then holding her hand with the ring, Dimitri kissed her. "Now, you belong to us. Believe what

Xavier said. We do love you. Now, I think our sub should receive some form of punishment for making us do this before we had the perfect setting. What do you think Master Xavier?"

"For doubting her Masters maybe, but not for such a happy occasion. Do you doubt your Masters anymore?"

"No, Sirs. I feel like… I don't know what I feel. There is so much going on."

"Madison, get up on the bed. Arms and legs spread." When she stood there, Dimitri voice softened. "Beautiful, we are going to leave the bindings loose. Trust us to take care of you." To Xavier, he said, "Go get some lube from the dungeon area."

"With pleasure." Xavier danced off.

"Madison we are going to punish you with pleasure. Then when we think you've had enough, we are going to make you come so hard around my dick. Xavier is going to feel it in your ass."

Madison happily laid on the bed. She wanted to please her Masters for this wonderful gift they had given to her. For a brief second, she had been disappointed that her Masters had not given her a collar. But she had her cuffs, and now this incredibly unique radiant ring. In Madison's mind marriage was forever, and that meant something too.

By the time Xavier came back to the bed, he had shed his clothes. Dimitri as well. They looked at Madison each standing on opposite sides of the bed. She couldn't believe these two incredible men wanted her. Not just as a sub but also as their wife. Even with all the shit she'd been through, they still wanted her.

They laid on the bed next to her. Dimitri framed her face in his hand. "How are you feeling?"

"Overwhelmed! Excited, in awe. A little scared. Overall, happy."

Dimitri leaned down taking her lips in a gently kiss. "Why are you scared, beautiful?"

Dimitri leaned up on his elbow. Head in his palm, he looked down at her. Xavier took the same position on her other side.

Madison didn't want to ruin the mood. She would tell them later why she was really scared. So instead she told them, "I'm scared that this is a dream. That my wistful mind is creating this moment, only to have me wake up in some fucked-up nightmare."

Xavier latched onto the nipple closest to him. Laving it, then biting down.

Pain radiated thru Madison's breast straight to her core. Caught off guard, Madison screamed and yelled at Xavier, "Ouch, what the hell was that for?"

Xavier smiled leaning down to her face as his hand gently massaged the pain from her nipple. "Making sure you knew this was real. Madison, we are going to show you how truly special you are to us." Xavier's kiss was rough and deep. More demanding.

He broke the kiss and Dimitri replaced him, trailing his tongue along her lips. Licking and sucking, Dimitri started a trail down her chin coming to her ear. Circling the rim of her ear, he said, "We are going to love you for the rest of your days. We will fight." His tongue looped in her ear. He could feel the chill run through her. "We will argue." His lips were nipping their way down her neck. "But, we will never bring that to our bed. Never be scared with us. Our beautiful Madison." When Dimitri kissed away her salty tears, he commanded Madison. "Open your eyes." When she complied, he continued. "No punishment will ever be given in anger. This is our oath to you." He sealed his lips over hers. Their tongues advancing then retreating, dancing around aggressively.

Xavier's tattooed biceps flexed holding his body above Madison's as he crept down her body. He kissed a trail from her neck to her collar bone. Reaching her chest, his tongue came out to taste her essence. Her unique scent mixed with her perfume. If he lived to one hundred, he would never get enough of her. He replaced his hand with his mouth. Still holding himself above Madison, he molded both of her breasts in his hands. He held both nipples up. Licking back and forth between them, he lashed his tongue with a rapid movement.

Madison moaned with the sensations they were stirring up in her body. Dimitri distracting her with his talented mouth, Xavier moving further down her body. His tongue swirled around her navel creating butterflies in her flat stomach. He licked and sucked his way down, till he was settled between her legs. Madison could feel his hot breath on her mixing with the wetness that had formed through her folds. His tongue slid through her sex and Madison bucked off the bed with the sensation.

Xavier followed her body up then down never losing contact. When Madison's body landed back on the bed, he positioned his hands on her thighs. He could now control her lower body.

Xavier continued his assault on her. His tongue grinding on her clit. He released one thigh and moved his fingers up through her lips, latching onto her clit. Holding her exposed her little bud out, he gently bit down, then brushed his tongue over, soothing the sting. The mixture of pain and pleasure was driving Madison insane. She knew she couldn't come without permission.

She moaned deep into Dimitri's mouth when Xavier tapped his fingers on her clit. Then he slid two of them into her entrance. Her walls clamping onto Xavier's fingers told him she was close. So he pulled back from all he was doing.

Madison had gone from moaning to whining in a matter of seconds. "Our girl is being so good. But a punishment needs to be followed through on." Xavier took his two fingers and repositioned them at her entrance. "My lovely, do you like when my fingers slide in and out?" Madison just groaned when he pushed inside her. "Is it better when it's just my tongue?" He removed his fingers and replaced them with his tongue. In and out he pushed. "Or is what you really want the combination of the two?" Xavier did as he described. "What if I do this?" Xavier took his other hand, and pulled her labia lips up tight. Exposing her swollen clit. "Will this make our girl come without permission?" He lashed her clit, while pushing another finger into her. Again, just as her walls started to clamp down on his fingers, he stopped.

The time Madison screamed her frustration into Dimitri's mouth. "I think you have punished her enough. Madison release your hold of the straps." When she did, he rubbed the feeling back into her arms.

Xavier climbed up her body. She could taste herself on Xavier's lips as he captured her mouth. "Your Master feels you have been punished enough. I want you to know I enjoyed every minute of your torture. Now, your reward for following our instructions."

Xavier pulled Madison into a sitting position on the bed, as Dimitri stretched out. "Madison, climb onto Master Dimitri."

"With pleasure," Madison responded. Dimitri positioned her above his throbbing shaft. She lowered herself slowly as to savor every moment of the loving. When she was fully seated, she could feel his dick rubbing her cervix. Xavier gently pushed her forward her hands landing on Dimitri's unbelievably hard chest. This position prompted more sounds from Madison.

"Are you looking at this? I don't think I've seen a more

outstanding picture than what I'm looking at right now," Dimitri said looking up at the mirror.

Xavier had retrieved the lube. She felt the cold lube warm as Xavier rubbed it around her puckered entrance. Then his finger entered her. The feeling of Dimitri filling her tightened. Adding another finger, Xavier started to move them in and out preparing her. He added more lube and a third finger. "Are you ready for me, Madison? Because I can't wait any longer. Seeing your Master's dick in you, while I prepare to slide into your tight opening has my cock jumping." With that Xavier removed his fingers and pushed gently into her. "Push back, baby. Open yourself to me."

Madison pushed back as Xavier entered her, seating himself all the way to his balls. Madison felt so full. In all the things she had done as an escort, she had never done this and now she knew why. It was never right. This felt right, better then right. Madison moved her hips forward. Letting them know she needed more.

"Go easy, Madison. We don't want to hurt you," Xavier said, as he slowly withdrew. Then pushed back in. Starting with the pace that they knew would ignite her passion again.

At the same time Dimitri withdrew his hips, almost pulling out of her. He surged his hips up, plunging back into her. Feeling Xavier's cock through her perineal, heightened his desire. Knowing that they were building Madison to a climax that none of them were ever going to forget, drove him, pushed him. He knew she was close. He looked up at her face flushed with color. Her eyes opened looking down at him. What he saw there almost put him over.

He looked past her shoulder at Xavier. His hand was on one of Madison's shoulder, keeping her in place, guiding her. Dimitri could tell from his face that he was holding back, but only by a thread. They were both holding back, waiting for Madison. They needed her to ask.

Madison knew she couldn't take much more. She didn't want to disappoint her Masters. Gasping for her breath, she said, "Masters, you have done something no one else has ever done to me. I can't take anymore. Please Sirs, may I come?"

Something in the sound of Madison's voice told them that this was a good thing. Not knowing what she meant didn't matter right now. "Yes, Madison. Come now. I want to feel your walls milk my cock as Xavier pumps into that tight ass of yours."

Dimitri reached up, and molded his hands over her breasts. He pinched her nipples. Sending Madison over, the scream left her mouth.

Her body tightened with her orgasm. Dimitri reached between them, playing with her clit, prolonging her orgasm, rolling his fingers over and over. Madison felt a different sensation, something she had never felt before. It spiraled around her clit. His fingers continued their assault. With both Dimitri and Xavier still deep within her, her clit started to convulse and Madison felt warm fluid as she squirted. Throwing back her head, Madison screamed with another orgasm.

Dimitri looked at Madison's face. The pure elation. Tears sliding down her cheeks. She was fantastic. He had never been with a woman who squirted. The minute Madison did, he couldn't hold back any longer. With a growl Dimitri came harder than he had ever come in his life. Pushing deeper into her.

Xavier released at the same time as Dimitri, looking at Dimitri's face Madison's head thrown back in pleasure. Feeling her walls convulsing, Xavier couldn't hold back anymore if he wanted to. His roar came with his release.

Madison collapsed on Dimitri, as Xavier pulled out of her to fall on the bed next to them. Their breathing slowing down, almost back to normal, Xavier asked Madison, "What did you mean by 'we did something no else had'?"

Madison leaned her chin on her hands that were resting on Dimitri's chest. Looking first at Dimitri, then Xavier. "I've never been double penetrated. In fact, we've had a lot of first's tonight. I've never squirted before either. That was fucking intense." Her smile spread across her face.

"I have to agree. That was intense," Dimitri added. Pulling out of Madison and putting her between them, he rolled to his side.

"Never? Please tell me you wanted to?" Scared for a minute that they may have violated her somehow, Xavier's face showed his concern.

"Yes, yes I did." She placed a calming hand on his chest. He flopped back on the bed, relieved. "It never felt right. This did."

Dimitri reached into the night stand draw removing the wipes. Pulling some out, he cleaned himself and Madison. Then he threw the container at Xavier. When they were settled back in bed, he said to her, "Thank you for that gift. We would never want you to do something you didn't want to. This was on neither your soft or hard limits."

"Because I've never done it. I knew one day I would want to try it. I was just waiting for the right men to come along."

"Well, your wait is over and trust me, darling, we will be doing that a lot more," Xavier commented. "Dimitri how much time do we have before dinner?"

Dimitri looked at the clock. "Not enough time to do it again. But if Madison would like to close her eyes for a half hour. It would be just fine."

"That sounds heavenly." She stretched her arms up.

"If you keep tempting us with those magnificent tits, you may not get any sleep!" Xavier said as his mouth latched onto her nipple making Madison squirm. Releasing it, he said to her, "Get some rest. We'll wake you in time to be ready." Then he kissed her nose and got out of bed.

Madison turned her head to look at Dimitri. "We won't be far if you need us. Sleep tight, beautiful." He placed a kiss on her forehead. Then they left her to doze.

"Any ideas on what they might find at the pharmaceutical building?" Xavier asked Dimitri. They had each thrown on lounge pants and settled into the chairs facing the bed, drinks in their hands.

"I'm not banking on anything good. You're a business man. How do you know you're getting into a good deal or not?"

"In business, I go with my gut. That's why I asked. You have a sick feeling about this too?"

"I get the feeling what they find there isn't going to be good," Dimitri said, picking up the file on Boxwood and flipping through it. "Nothing in here is good. This piece of shit has bounced through life without a fucking care. What she went through at his hands… I want to kill him!" Dimitri had to get out of the chair. He hated when his hands felt like they were tied. It frustrated the shit out of him.

"Keep your shit together. We don't need her dwelling on this." That got Dimitri's attention. Xavier looked at the paperwork on the table. "You know you're not the only one who wants a piece of that douchebag. I think Cameron had the right idea. Beat the piss out of him in a ring. Then have his ass thrown in jail. We just need to find something on him to make that happen. At least the jail part."

"Why is he doing this deal without his mommy?"

"Good question."

"That has to say something. All his life he's been a

momma's boy. What would make him feel grown up enough to venture into what they already know is a money making business? Without her?" Dimitri's mind was working in overdrive.

Looking at the bed, Xavier's voice carried quietly to Dimitri, "How do we keep her safe? Keep her from being hurt anymore? I want to put her in a protective bubble. Where nothing bad can touch her." Dimitri had stopped pacing and was now looking at Madison stretched out on the bed. "I can't lose her again. It hurt so bad the last time." Xavier finished his drink. "Not going to happen again."

"No. You're right about that. We have friends who will do everything they can to help." Dimitri downed his drink. "When we were on the *Onyx*, you saw firsthand what they can do. They'll do that for us as well. I just hope we find something to put that son of a bitch away for a long time."

"Thank you Dimitri." When Dimitri just looked at him, he continued, "That day in the deli I thought you were going to warn me off. Instead you did the total opposite. You made us a family. I will never forget that."

"She needs both of us. Deep down she's still that little girl. The little girl who dreamed of a wedding to her dream man. Looking for the approval from a mother she was never going to get it from." Dimitri stood behind Xavier putting his hands on his shoulders. "We are going to change all of that. We've already started and we have the rest of our lives to keep showing her."

"I hate to wake her she looks so peaceful." They had moved to the end of the bed.

"If we don't, she won't be ready for dinner. As it is, she only has forty-five minutes now. I'm sure she won't want to be late. You wake her up. I'm going to take a shower." Dimitri smiled at Xavier, as he turned away.

Xavier stood for a moment. Hearing the shower, he

climbed up the bed. Climbing over Madison waking her when he paused over her breasts. Moving the blanket down, he exposed her chest to him, watching her nipples tighten with desire. He looked up into moss green eyes dilated with love. Xavier smiled. "We don't have much time. So, this is going to be fast and hard. Open for me, my lovely."

Madison pushed the blanket down her naked body, as Xavier shed his pants. Taking his hand straight to her core he found her already wet for him. He guided his stiff cock to her entrance. Pushing in, he paused savoring the feeling. Her warm walls gripped him clamping down, not wanting to let go. A feeling of home ran through him. Looking in her eyes, he leaned down. "So tight and wet." He eased his hips back, slowly. "So ready." With that, Xavier began to drive into her. Pumping his hips, he found the spot that would send her over.

"Xavier, may I come?" Madison asked through heaving breaths.

He knew he wasn't going to last. When she used his christen name. It pulled him over. "Yes… Madison!" Xavier gasped. He gyrated his hips, grinding into her until he felt her muscles quivering around his throbbing cock. The pressure building in him released with her scream. Pumping till she milked him dry. He stilled above her. Capturing her lips, he kissed her with all the passion and love he was feeling.

"Now, go get ready. You don't have much time." With a kiss on her nose, he got out of bed, bringing her with him.

"Are you going to join me? It will save water." She kissed his chest as she walked by.

"It might save water, but it won't save time. Go!" Xavier demanded.

Madison danced off happily to the bath area, smiling.

Chapter 17

Dinner had been a time for them all to get to know each other. The women fawned over Madison's engagement ring. The men toasted Dimitri and Xavier, then broke out the cigars. This only added to the fun of horseback riding the next day in Mazatlán. Everyone was a little on edge waiting for word, but not letting it ruin their time. The six-hour tour helped. They laid on the beach, played volleyball, and drank rum punch. Dimitri invited Kristoff to join them. He had second guessed himself when he introduced Kristoff to Colin, and the sheikh had recognized him as Sabastian.

Colin had been a huge contributor to the Emirates Hockey League, the EHL. He knew exactly who he was and had won a lot of money betting on his team. He had also heard through the grapevine he was in some trouble. The apparent hidden identity solidified his suspicion. Colin offered his assistance, if Kristoff would play for the Dubai Mighty Camels. His contract would include a penthouse, living expenses, and a car. However, his salary for the first two seasons would be forfeited for Colin's help. Kristoff had agreed with Dimitri's approval.

Arriving back at the ship everyone separated with the promise to meet after dinner. Kristoff and Jasmine had followed them back to the suite. Jasmine had jumped down Kristoff's throat for not telling her. Jasmine had been ready to walk out, when Xavier spoke up for Kristoff. Something Kristoff didn't know how he would be able to repay. He was not sure if it was love, but Kristoff knew he wanted the chance to find out. In turn, Dimitri brought his brother up to speed on the Boxwood project, inviting him to join them after dinner. Kristoff had hugged Dimitri so hard when they were leaving, he thought for sure he had broken a rib.

Leaving Madison to get some rest. Dimitri went to get updates from the crew, while Xavier went to talk with Cameron. They hadn't spent much time together with Cameron's busy schedule before the wedding.

Madison laid in bed listening as the door closed behind her men. Snuggling down in the soft sheets, she had a smile on her face. She was so happy. Then her smile fell. Normally, when she was this happy something always happened to ruin it. Just like now. She knew something horrible was going to happen and she was going to lose them. She knew that somehow this whole connection between Colin and Boxwood wasn't a coincidence. Fate was going to rip her heart out. Only this time it would be her whole heart as each one of her men held a portion.

Madison shook the bad thoughts from her mind and focused on the present. She had them now, and she wasn't letting go without a fight this time. She was done running. Whatever came their way, together they would be able to work it out. She hoped! The smile back on her face, she dozed off thinking of when she met Xavier.

Madam Mia had booked her with a new client. She had said he would be in town for the night and that he was just looking for company. She was to have a car drop her off at the restaurant. If he enjoyed dinner with her, he would bring her back to the room. If he didn't, the car was to wait to take her home. Madam Mia expressed to her how important it was for her to keep him happy. Because although the client might only be spending dinner with her, he had paid for the night. Without question that was the type of clients Madam Mia loved.

At first Amber had been offended that he might not take her back to the room. But after she thought about it, it made sense. She wouldn't want to spend the night with someone she couldn't talk to either.

She took her time getting ready that night. Made sure every part of her bronze body was waxed and smooth. Her makeup was done in a smoky green, that brought out the moss green flecks in her eyes. Her brunette hair cascaded over her shoulders in big waves. She wore a jade and black cocktail dress. The bustier top in jade hugged and lifted her breasts up for an inviting view. The bottom came to the front of her thighs, but ran to the ground in the back. A black bolero jacket and two inch heels finished her outfit. Amber was taller than most girls she worked with and a lot of her clients. So, she always wore low heels on a first date.

She arrived at the appointed time, going to the bar as directed by the hostess. Amber walked in and stood in the doorway letting her eyes adjust. Scanning the room, she looked for the man Madam Mia had described to her. He stood with his profile to the her. He was spinning his drink on the bar as if he was impatient. She stepped further into the room as he lifted his head. His expression went from solemn to smiling in zero point three seconds, looking more relieved as she got closer. He was handsome beyond anything Amber had imagined, and taller. His blonde hair was cut short on the top and sides. His strong jawline and high cheeks accented his aquiline nose. His black suit was tailored to fit his wide shoulders down to his trim waist. His slacks brushed the tops of his shoes. But what held Amber transfixed were his crystal blue eyes. They seemed to look through her seeing all of her secrets.

"Good evening. I'm Amber. Xavier?"

"Yes. Nice to meet you. Shall we, our table is ready?" he asked. Taking her by the elbow, he led her back to the hostess.

He wasn't rough with her but he was demanding. Moving his hand to the small of her back he guided her. The hostess showed them to their table in a secluded area near the back. He held her chair for her. Then took the opposite seat, moving the center piece out of his line of sight. To the waiter he said, "Cruzan single barrel." Looking at Amber. "For you."

"Cabernet Sauvignon, please."

Xavier remained quiet until the waiter left the table before he said, "You are so beautiful." Gazing at her.

"You sound so surprised. First time?" Amber smiled. She was trying hard to remain professional. However, the butterflies this man was creating in her stomach were making it almost impossible.

"What gave it away?" Xavier sat back in his chair.

"You still have manners," Amber said with all sincerity. "After a while, all the preliminaries stop. The hotels still stay five star though." Amber picked up her menu. Trying to hide how that thought sped up her breathing. "Any recommendations?"

"I've heard the chateaubriand in wine sauce is excellent," Xavier replied, not looking at the menu.

Putting her menu back on the table she agreed, "That sounds good to me."

The waiter had returned with their drinks. Xavier ordered for them and sent the waiter on his way. Amber was sipping her wine when he asked her, "Why do you do this?"

Almost spitting out her wine. Amber grabbed her napkin. "Nothing like being too forward," she stated then added. "It pays the bills. What do you do?"

"My family owns Legend Vineyard. I believe what you're drinking is from one of our vintage stock."

"How could you possibly know that by looking at what I'm drinking?" She held the glass up.

"I had a variety of bottles sent over from our closest location. I wasn't sure what you would like."

"It's very good." Looking at the drink in his hand. "You don't drink wine?"

"After seeing you I needed something much stronger."

Amber had laughed at his comment. The rest of the dinner progressed with them getting to know each other. Something Amber had never really enjoyed with any of her other clients. For some reason, she felt safe with him. Xavier asked a lot of questions. Some she answered. Some she blew off. Others she flat out lied. When dinner was finished, he escorted her to his suite. It was an elegant five bay suite, with panoramic views of the mountains and the ocean. Amber had been to some fancy hotels, but never this fancy.

Amber walked in and before her out the windows was the most astonishing view she had ever seen. The lights of the city twinkled, welcoming the setting sun, drawing her. She walked to the window, caressing her fingers on the glass. She stood and watched it disappear. She felt him the minute he stopped behind her. She looked at his reflection in the glass. "That was breathtaking." Her eyes reflecting to his. He had removed his jacket, and tie, rolled up his sleeves and released the top three buttons on his shirt. Getting comfortable.

"Yes, it is." He handed her a glass of wine. His arm grazed against her breast. "Would you like to sit?"

This brought Amber back to the room which she had totally ignored on her walk to the view. Turning she looked at the opulence of the room. Her back was turned to Xavier. She mouthed WOW! To Xavier she laughed. "Where? There are so many places to sit?" Looking over her shoulder she asked. "How many people sleep here?" She started wandering around the living area. She followed it down a short hallway finding the enormous bathroom to her right, and the bedroom at the end. Stopping at the entrance, she saw the one huge bed. "Just you!?"

"Yes, just me. Not that it's any of your business, but I use the entire space for work."

"I didn't mean to insult you," Amber quickly said. "I'm just surprised at how much space there is. This is not the hotel room of a man here for just one night. It feels more like a penthouse than a hotel. That's all I was trying to say."

Xavier guided her further into the bedroom. Sitting down on the bed she looked at Xavier. "My feet are killing me. Do you mind if I take them off?" Other clients liked her to leave them on.

In answer to her question, he got down on his knees before her. Gently taking her foot in his hands he unbuckled her left shoe. Throwing it off to the side, he massaged her foot eliciting a groan from Amber. Smiling he picked up the other foot duplicating his action with the first. Only with this foot he continued a slow massaging up her calf. His hands working their magic.

Amber felt his hands climbing her leg. She had done this

many times before. But somehow this time it was so different. Then it hit her. She wasn't the advancer. She had always been the one to initiate what happened on her dates. Not with Xavier. His lips began to follow his hands up her leg. His hands advanced up to her thigh, brushing against her apex as they reached the top. Amber leaned back on her elbows watching him. He looked right in her green eyes, as his tongue swiped across the thin soaking wet piece of material. Amber's head fell back with the jolt of pleasure that ran through her body. "No." Xavier demanded, "Look at me."

Her head whipped up. "Yes, Sir!" Her breath hitched as he pushed his tongue against her clit hard.

When she had called him Sir, something had snapped inside Xavier. "You have no idea what you are doing to me do you?" He moved so fast Amber had no time to register what was happening. He lunged up over her. Pressing her into the bed with his body, covering her mouth in a demanding kiss. He reached for her one hand, interlocking her fingers with his. He brought it up above her head. "Don't move it. Understand?"

"Yes, Sir," she purred out. Overwhelmed by the way her body was reacting to his demands, her eyes locked onto his.

Xavier groaned with her response. Bringing her other hand up to join the other. "Lock them together, and keep them there." He then stood at the end of the bed looking at Amber. Never moving his eyes from hers, he shed his shirt. Pulling a condom from his pocket, he removed his belt dropping it on the floor. Unbuttoning his pants, he pulled the zipper down. His rock hard erection freeing as they fell to the floor. Amber watched as he rolled the condom on. "I hope you are not too fond of these," he said as he ripped her thong from her body. Tossing it away, he lowered himself over her, pressing her body into the soft cushion of the bed. His hard cock glided along her folds leading to her entrance.

"This one is for me. You are not to come or there will be a punishment to pay." The words were empathized as he slid home, fast and hard. He held himself still as her body adjusted to the size of him. Pulling back slowly, he hissed out, "This is for making me lose control." He grunted as his pushed back in, reaching up to grab her breast though her bustier. She had enticed him all evening. Her submission coming so easily she didn't even know she was doing it. Amber shifted her hips trying to get Xavier to move. "Is this what you want?" He pulled back out, but this time when his hips drove back into her, he continued pounding into her. He could feel her muscles begin to tighten. "Do not come, my lovely, you won't like my punishment."

Amber didn't know how he expected her not to have an orgasm. The only time Amber ever had an orgasm was when she did it herself. Now for the first time in her life, a man was getting her so turned on she was going to come, and he was telling her not to. Who does that she thought? Plus, what the fuck was a punishment. She had read the BDSM books but up until now it had been just vanilla sex. That thought almost put her over. She knew he was close so she took a chance. "Can I come after you? Please, Sir." The answer of yes was ripped from his mouth as he erupted like an untried boy. He continued thrusting his hips, grinding into her.

Xavier couldn't believe what she had done. Her begging had pushed him over. He couldn't stop himself from coming. Feeling her walls clamping down on him. Her satin sheath surrounded his cock milking him dry. Yet, he was still semi-hard. There was no way he could give her up. The smile that met his eyes confirmed what he was feeling. "I'm here for three days. Stay with me." The words were out before he could stop them. Looking at Amber's face, he knew it was the wrong thing to say.

Pulling her arms down, she started pulling away from

him, looking anywhere but at him. "You would have to arrange it with Madam Mia. I need to get going." She shifted up ejecting him from her body.

Stopping her with his body and taking her face in his hands, he forced her to look at him. "What just happened? You're pissed because I asked you to stay? I want to get to know you."

Looking into those amazing eyes, how she wished that could be possible. But her dreams never came true. With the anger she felt at her situation, she told him, "No, you don't. And I don't have the time or the money to be your play thing for a few days. I have to work in order to get paid. I don't own my own business." Amber calmed down. It wasn't his fault. "I'm sorry. I would like nothing more than to spend the time with you. I just don't know if Madam Mia has me booked elsewhere." Plastering a forced smile on her face, she thought to herself, if I spend any more time with him I'm never going to want to let him go. Then eventually, he'll want to know about me, and that's something that wasn't going to happen. He shifted as she pushed her way off the bed.

He laid on the bed watching her walk to the bathroom. The Dom in Xavier wanted this girl. He wanted to master her body and care for her. The man in him wanted to protect her. If she was like the rest of the escorts, she probably didn't have a great upbringing. He knew she doubted what he was saying. Trust was something she would never expect from a client. He needed to become more than a client. If she would let him. "Amber, I've already arranged it."

This stopped her in her tracks. "What do you mean?" Looking back at him.

"I explained what I wanted to Mia and she sent you. So, I have you all to myself for the next few days. It's all arranged." He smiled as if that made it all better.

"I don't have any other clothes with me. She would have

told me to pack a bag." Amber thought to herself, if only she could stay she wouldn't need any clothes, because they would never leave the bed.

"It was a last minute decision." Rising from the bed, he zipped his pants back up.

Meaning to Amber, once he was sure he wanted her to stay then he'd let Mia know. "I'm sure it was. Regardless, I need to confirm that with her. I'll then need to pack a bag." She looked at her cell phone for the time. It was after midnight. "I'm going to leave. I'll pack a bag and be back tomorrow after dinner. How does that sound?"

"No. Whatever you need this hotel can provide." He opened the closet and pulled out a box. "As you will see." He handed it to her then guided her back to the bed. "The choice is yours, Amber. I would very much like you to stay."

She opened the box, pushed away the tissue paper, and pulled out a soft pink floor length negligee. "As much as I would like you to sleep naked with me. I wanted to be prepared if it was something you didn't do? Will you please stay?"

Amber had never stayed the night with a client. So she wouldn't know if she liked sleeping naked. She defiantly wouldn't mind sleeping next to Xavier. She knew it was going to kill her when he left. But she'd be a fool not to enjoy what time they did have.

Xavier could see on her face when her decision was made. "You won't regret staying I promise."

What started as three days, turned into just short of two weeks when Xavier told her he needed to go back home. He had some business he needed to take care of. He told her to stay in the room as it was paid till the end of the month. He also said that when he did come back, he would buy her contract and give it to her.

She had been so excited. Here was this gorgeous man

and he was going to free her. No one had ever done anything this amazing for her. She would be free. Or was he going to use it to control her too?

Madison started tossing and turning on the bed. She had never gotten her chance with Xavier. A few nights after he left, she had gone on the date that had changed her hard limit list. After that had happened she broke all contact with Xavier. He continued trying to see her, but she knew he would never look at her the same. When she had healed. Madam Mia had booked her with Ryan Smith. The night at the BDSM dungeon with Marco. The night Amber Sinclair died.

Xavier was running by the time he got the door open. He had heard Madison's shouts for 'help' and 'no' from outside the door. He rushed to the side of the bed and gently stroked her face calling her name.

When her eyes fluttered open, they were wet with her tears. Realizing Xavier was holding her, she told him, "I was dreaming of when we met and how happy we had been. Then fate stepped in and shit all over it. I can only pray she's done fucking with me." Xavier heard the anger behind her words.

"Watch that mouth, my lovely, or it might get you that punishment we keep promising." He leaned down kissing the tears from her cheeks. "Do you want to talk about your dream?"

"Not now, I need to get ready for dinner. I'd rather wait till we are with Dimitri tonight. Is that okay?" she asked the anger leaving her tone.

As Xavier was answering her, Dimitri walked into the suite. He looked at her with concern. Seeing her tear stained cheeks. "Go take your shower. I will explain it to Dimitri." She forced a smile as she moved to the bathroom area.

When she was out of ear shot, Dimitri looked questioningly at Xavier. "When I came in, she was thrashing around the bed, grabbing at her throat. She said she was dreaming of when we met, but then the dreamed changed. Because she said that's when fate shit all over her life. She's praying it doesn't happen again."

"She still thinks we're going to leave her?"

"No. She's thinking she doesn't deserve us. So in turn, fate will step in and screw it up for her."

"That's ridiculous. We are just going to have to work harder to prove that to her. Until she believes us, nothing will change. She's starting to trust us, in bed at least. We'll continue with the plan we started with. Little by little we will chip away at her defenses and when we're done, she will never question us again," Dimitri stated. "Let's get ready. I get the feeling we aren't going to like what we find out about this facility."

"I think you're right, but let's not jump to any conclusions. We'll know in a couple of hours."

"Let's pick something special out to wear for our sub. I get the feeling she needs some extra loving tonight," Xavier commented moving towards the closet. "Something that shows off that lovely neck of hers. What do you think?"

Dimitri stepped up next to Xavier standing in front of an array of clothing for Madison. "I'll take care of this. I think I know exactly what you're looking for."

Madison tried to pass Xavier on his way to the shower. Snatching her up in his arms and swinging her around, he asked, "Where do you think you are going?"

"I need to get ready."

"You were going to walk right past your Master without giving him a kiss. I now have a reason to punish you."

Bringing her head up, he leaned down gently pressing his lips to hers.

Madison brought her arms up latching them behind his neck melting into his kiss. She opened her mouth, slipping her tongue out and caressed his lips. Sucking his bottom lip in, she bit down gently on it. She let go and told him. "If that's what my Master wants."

The seductive smile she gave him had his semi-hard shaft throbbing with need. "You now we need to get ready for dinner, and yet you play with fire. I think I should carry you right back in the shower to cool you off." He turned heading towards the shower.

Madison started to squirm and twist trying to get out of his arms. "No, please I'm sorry I was trying to be seductive. I guess it back fired. I can't get wet again, I'll never be ready. PLEASE!" When she realized he wasn't going to stop, she went lax in his arms, resolved to fact she was going to take another shower.

He got right to the door of the shower. Placing her feet on the floor he looked at her stunned face. "Baby, you don't have to try to be seductive. Everything about you is erotic. I wasn't going to put you in. I was giving Dimitri time to pick out your clothes." He kissed her then swatted her on her butt. "Go he should be ready."

Dimitri had picked out a backless, scoop neck, court train chiffon evening gown. Their cuffs hugged the regency purple long sleeves to her wrist. She had wrapped her hair in a twist and applied only eyeliner and mascara. The four-inch spike heels she slipped on still only brought her to each of their chins.

She was sitting in one of the chairs watching them run

around getting ready. For once it was nice not to be rushed. Each man wore his own style of suit. Dimitri the double breasted, Xavier a three piece. Both shirts were a shade of purple, as well as their ties.

Dinner for the most part was uneventful. However, when it came to announcing the fantasy winner that night, everyone was excited to hear that it was Kristoff's. Especially Kristoff. When in sunk in he was going to experience something he had dreamt of all his life, his dick got ram rod stiff. He turned to Jasmine and asked her if she would participate instead of Rachel (the shows fantasy coordinator). Not knowing what the fantasy was she agreed immediately.

Dinner ended and Madison, Dimitri, and Xavier headed to the Sapphire Theater wanting good seats. Cameron and Sadie joined them.

Kristoff and Jasmine were back stage getting prepped on the scene. When the fantasy scene was announced, the theater got suddenly still.

The MC announced. "Welcome to tonight's Sapphire Theater fantasy finale. Tonight the creator and one of the stars of this show Kristoff..." He paused for the applause. "Will live out his special fantasy. We have named Kristoff's *Pussy Ice Hockey*." As his words announced the title, the curtain opened. On the stage before them was a simulated ice hockey rink. A section of it was made of actual ice. The rest an inflatable silver air bed was designed as the rest of the ice.

Kristoff stood at the beginning of the real ice. A hockey-stick in his hands. In front of him were specially prepared hockey pucks. At the other end was Jasmine. Her body positioned so that her butt rested on the air mattress, but her wide spread legs hung on the ice. At her entrance a vibrating dildo was poised. As Kristoff shot the fur trimmed pucks across the ice, they pushed the dildo further in. Driving her insane with pleasure. On top of that, each time the puck hit it just right, it changed speeds. And Kristoff was a very good hockey player. With the strict rule that Jasmine was not to come till he sank into her, she was practically screaming by the time Kristoff slid across the ice joining with her.

This had been his true fantasy. To screw someone on the ice of any hockey arena. This wasn't exactly the same thing, but it was a damn good second place. His body was on the ice, yet he was rock hard, and on fire. Jasmine had a lot to do with that. Kristoff didn't think he could be any happier. He had given her permission to come, and the two of them together screamed their release.

The applause that greeted them after the scene had finished was deafening. Many of the men remained in their seats clapping, while the women in the audience stood. Madison heard one woman say, "if only real ice hockey was that exciting. I'd watch it more."

Madison, Xavier, and Dimitri said their farewells and headed to the suite to wait for news from the team checking the pharmaceutical facility. A few minutes after their arrival they were joined by the others. Drinks were handed out and the conversation revolved around Kristoff and Jasmine's scene until the knock came signaling the information they were waiting for had finally arrived.

Dimitri opened the door for them. Greyson, carrying a file in his hand, headed straight to the coffee table. He laid out the plans of the facility for all to look at as he explained what they had found out.

"It's a twenty-four-hour facility. The only problem is the Mexican government doesn't know about the night time operation. From what they could gather, during the day there's a full crew. Office personal, as well as factory workers. Boxes packed with orders wait on the docks for delivery." Greyson paused flipping to a different picture in the file. He pulled the portrait of an evil looking pock marked man to the top of the pile. "We believe at night this man takes over for the day security guard. He's Juan Torres part of the Cartel Pacifico Sur."

Nick took over talking. "When he punches in, he opens the bay doors for a truck to pull in. They unload pounds of heroin. Juan and his crew open the boxes for distribution and repackage them. Sending the heroin into the United States with the pharmaceutical supplies."

"Do you know where they are sending them?" Xavier asked.

"Several locations, from California to New Hampshire. But the bulk of it is being sent to Boxwood Pharmaceutical in Florida." Replied Greyson.

"So, that's why he wants to buy the company. It's a win-win for him. He could become one of the biggest heroin distributers in the United States," Xavier pointed out.

"If this was Russia, the cartels would be hunting Boxwood down. Caleb, anything about his personal life? Wife, kids, animals? These are all very good bargaining chips."

Caleb pulled up the information on his tablet and handed it to Dimitri. He browsed the information for a minute, then sat forward on the couch. "Holy shit," was all he said placing the tablet down. He started rummaging through the papers spread on the table. When he found the one he was looking for, the breath left his lungs. Before he could say anything Colin cut him off.

"Gentleman, if I may," Colin cut in. "I had my lawyers inquire further into the ownership of this pharmaceutical company." He walked forward handing Dimitri a file, putting what he had found to the side. "The owner, a sweet little old man was looking to get out. He heard a rumor that the Cartel Pacifico Sur was looking for a new location. Their new leader is trying to make his mark. Apparently, the owner didn't know they had infiltrated the company already." Colin held his drink in the air. "So as of 3:00 pm this afternoon, I became the new owner of a pharmaceutical company."

The entire room turned to look at Colin with astonished faces. "What?" he asked innocently. "If we own it he can't. I thought that's what you wanted?" Colin asked with all sincerity.

"No. This is good," Greyson injected. He picked through the papers on the table till he found the blueprints for the inside and out. After an intense appraisal of the blueprints a smile formed on his lips. "I've got it. A plan to get rid of the Cartel and put Boxwood in a Mexican jail for the rest of his life. Colin you have a meeting planned for you and Lucy tomorrow correct?" He confirmed that statement. "Good, that will work perfect into my plan." Looking at Colin, he said, "You won't have to worry about Lucy. We will have eyes on the two of you at all times."

Colin smiled at Greyson. "I never worry about Lucy. Malik would die before any harm came to her." His head nodded to the monster of a man off to the side.

The rest of the night the men sketched out a strategy. If a weakness was found, they found a resolution. Each person had a part to play. With Colin having a huge entourage, it made it possible to replace several of Colin's men with Greyson's team.

The women had sat outside listening through the open windows. Chatter was going on all around Madison, but she had tuned it all out. All she could think about was how her life had come to this point. From the scared girl who got off a bus, to a well-educated escort, and now a submissive to the only men she would ever love. This man they were going after was because of her. Because of how he hurt her. These two special men were doing everything they could do to help her get her revenge. Most men would say that it would be better to just forget about it and move on. Not her men. They both came from families that took their responsibilities very seriously. The retribution they were planning would make Brian Boxwood very sorry he had ever met her.

Then the sound from inside went quiet. They were talking, but making sure the women did not hear. Madison wondered why? She shook off the bad feeling and began paying attention to the woman. Caleb had brought Isabella. Greyson had brought Raven. Nicolas had left Payton tucked in bed. When Raven realized Madison was staring at her, she asked if something was wrong.

"No. I'm sorry if I made you feel uncomfortable. I really wanted to say thank you." Raven's face was a blank slate. Not knowing what she was talking about. "The other night. I watched your scene with Master Greyson. It has been a very long time since I could handle a flogging. But after watching you, seeing the euphoria all over your face." Madison had that satisfied look on her face.

"I put my trust in my Masters that night. Let me just tell you, I felt everything your face showed. It was so loving. The strokes were enough to sting, but by the time he was finished…" She looked around to see she had the attention of all the women on the balcony. "I was soaking wet." He cheeks glowed a bright pink. "We are starting with baby steps, but I think in time I will be the sub they need."

"I'm so happy to hear that. When I do a scene, I never know if anybody else gets it. Or if it's just all about the sex. You just confirmed to me it's more than just the sex. Thank you." She gave Madison a quick hug.

Madison looked up as Greyson came out the door looking for Raven. "Are you ready? All this planning has brought back some of the feelings I had every time we went out on a mission. It gets the adrenalin going." He hugged Raven to his chest.

"And other things too? Huh..." She reached down rubbing her hand on his hard shaft. Remembering they weren't alone, Raven pulled back from him smiling. "I'm glad everything worked out, Madison. Once this is over you can concentrate on the wedding. I know everything will be all right. See you tomorrow." Greyson placed his hand on the small of her back leading her out the door. Madison heard her giggle as her lower body jumped through the opening. She smiled watching Raven squirm around so Greyson couldn't get to her ass.

"Well, ladies, I think it's time to say good night." Madison rose as she said this. "I'm sure we will all find out our roles in tomorrow's performance." Walking towards the opening, she added, "Sadie, Isabella, I'm sure your roles will not be too involved." She stopped walking and looked at them. "I think the two of you have been on enough adventures with the last cruise. You two should sit this one out." She grinned at them.

"Don't you think for one minute that I'll be sitting on the sideline," Sadie growled at Madison. "The last time I didn't know what was going on and I almost lost the most important person to me. That is not going to happen again." She looked right at Cameron. "If you're going anywhere near that pharmaceutical company tomorrow, so am I!" Putting her hands on her hips to emphasize her point, she said, "For better or worse, Cameron Alexander." She walked towards him.

When she was close enough, he scooped her up. "I know what I said." Kissing her deeply, she melted into him. "We will discuss it in our cabin. Do you have everything?" he asked, not putting her down.

"Cameron, you can put me down. I'm quite capable of

walking."

"But up here you can't get into any trouble." She smacked his chest.

"Fine," she looked at him. You could feel the love radiating between them. "I have everything I need right here." She wrapped her arms snuggly around his neck, nuzzling her head under his chin.

"Good night all. We will see you all tomorrow. Try and get some rest." He was looking pointedly at Xavier and Dimitri.

As they took their leave, Nicolas, Caleb and Isabella followed them out. Leaving Colin and Lucy. "So, tomorrow I'm going to meet the person who made it possible for me to meet you." Lucy was looking at Madison. "I'm going to hold it together till Colin says. Then I'm going to release the fury I'm feeling inside right now!" Her voice rose.

Colin wrapped his arms around her mid-section, pulling her body back against him. "This emotion is going to make you a wonderful mother." She stiffened in his arms. "Relax, my little dove. I just know everything will be different this time."

Madison's eyes were as big as silver-dollars. "You're pregnant?" The surprise in her voice expressed the feeling in the room.

"Yes," she squealed. "We just found out. I take a test every morning. This way I know if I can drink alcohol that day." She gave an evil look at Colin. "We weren't going to say anything for the first few months." He just grinned at her. "I've already had two miscarriages. I don't want to get my hopes up too high." Her voice had taken on a sad tone.

"We are not losing another child," Colin commanded. "God will not take away another one. You will see."

Madison gathered Lucy in her arms. "I'm so happy for you. We will make sure nothing happens to you or this little one." She put her hand on Lucy's stomach. "Which means…" It was like a light went off in her head. "You can't go to that meeting tomorrow."

"Yes I can. I won't be in any danger. Colin will be with me." The adoring look she gave him, almost had Madison convinced.

"No you can't. You don't know this guy, Lucy. He's fucking nuts."

"But, Madison, he's expecting me and Colin. I have to go."

"Maybe you don't." She looked at Colin. "Public pictures are not to be taking in Dubai without consent. Correct?" He confirmed what she said with a head nod. "That means Brian has no idea what she looks like. So we could replace her with anyone. Shit I could even go." Xavier and Dimitri watched her face and saw when she had come to her decision. "I'll go. I'll pose as Lucy."

"Madison, you can't go." Dimitri stood in front of her, his hands gripping her upper arms. "What if he recognizes you? Lucy proved to you that your looks still resemble Amber Sinclair. Don't you think with how obsessed with you as he was, he won't know it's you?"

Madison looked up into his blue eyes tears glistening in her own. "Lucy can't go. If anything happened to her or the baby. I would feel responsible." She wiped at the tears on her cheeks. "What if Dennis did some light modification? If he can disguise me so you don't know it's me can I do it?" Dennis was the makeup and special effects designer for the ship's show.

"Madison, I don't want you anywhere near this motherfucker. But I have to concede. I don't want to take a chance with Lucy. Maybe we could ask…"

The question was left hanging as Madison spoke up. "No. It has to be me. I can't allow any of our friends to get hurt because of me. I just can't do that. The only reason Colin agreed to this was because he knew how much it meant to Lucy to help me. She knew it was important I get my revenge. Please don't take that away from me," she pleaded.

The room was silent while both men contemplated what was just said. They knew that if they tried to keep Madison out of it she would get into trouble. At least if they agreed, they would have some control over her. Xavier was the first to speak up. "This will be done our way. You will obey every order given to you without question. We will be part of Colin's entourage, so we will always be close." He watched as the grin spread across her face. "I'm serious, Madison. If you get one scratch on that beautiful body, there will be a punishment. Am I making myself clear?"

"Abundantly." She did a little happy dance.

"I don't think you seem to grasp the danger you will be in," Dimitri commented looking at how happy their girl was. "There are going to be Mexican police and cartel involved. They are not the kind of people you dance around happily for." She stopped jumping. "The only reason we are allowing this is because we will be there with you. Otherwise, you wouldn't be doing that little happy dance. Because you would not be going." Empathizing his point, he grabbed her and pulled her into his arms. Glaring into her eyes, he said, "Do you understand now?"

Madison had never seen this side of Dimitri. This was a dangerous man. But she knew in her heart he could never be that way with her. She did, however, understand exactly what he was pointing out to her. Showing not one ounce of fear, she said, "I understand exactly, Master." Gathering him in her arms, her head laid on his chest she could hear how fast his heart was racing. Adrenalin and fear will do that. With her in his arms, he began to relax.

Xavier said to Colin and Lucy, "We will let Greyson know about the change in plans." Madison and Lucy said goodnight and they were gone.

Tomorrow they would be in Puerto Vallarta. Madison would finally get to see the look on that bastard's face as he got arrested. It was a small amount of satisfaction for what she had gone through. But it did give her a great amount of gratification to know he would be spending his time in a Mexican prison. She knew he wouldn't be coddled like they did in the United States.

"Let's get you to bed." Xavier came up behind her as she was standing by the windows. The moon reflecting off the ocean had a calming effect. "We have a busy day ahead of us tomorrow." He unclasped the hold at the back of her dress and it slid slowly down her body. Removing her cuffs allowed the sleeves to fall as well.

Standing in front of them with just her thong, had them both hard in seconds. "You are so incredibly sexy. I could look at you all night," Dimitri said, leading her to the bed.

Removing her thong, she climbed onto the bed where both men joined her. They each made love to her, then tenderly tucked her into bed. Xavier spooning her from behind fast asleep. As she lay draped over Dimitri's exhausted body, Madison laid awake. Her fingers ideally twirled through the light hair on Dimitri's chest, imagining every scenario that could possibly occur tomorrow. Making sure that each one ended with Boxwood getting what he deserved. When she had finally felt she had all her angles covered, she thanked God for the two men laying with her in this bed. Without the two of them none of this would be possible.

She kissed Xavier's hand, then placed a kiss on Dimitri's chest. She snuggled into the warmth of her Masters and fell asleep.

Chapter 18

The next morning Madison woke up later than she had wanted. She took a quick shower, grabbed something to eat and headed down to Dennis. She wanted to give him as much time as he needed to change her into someone else. Xavier and Dimitri had met with Greyson and explained that Madison would be replacing Lucy. The meeting was set for 1:00 pm. This gave the ground team time to get into position. The local cartel and police would be notified but not until they wanted them notified.

They were all to meet at twelve o'clock to finalize plans in Colin and Lucy's suite. Anyone accompanying them would need to be dressed like the sheikh's security team. Dark suits, dark glasses, and ear pieces. Plus, Lucy had sent a dress down to the theater where Madison was getting ready. When the knock came at the door. Lucy opened it, and there stood Madison. The only reason Lucy knew was because of the dress. There was no way Boxwood would ever recognize her.

Dennis had done a wonderful job. The wig she wore was a wheat color blonde. He had put blue contacts in and had used some face putty to change the shape of her nose and chin. The long blue gauze dress just brushed the floor. It gathered at the waist with long sleeves and a high neck. It was embellished with jewels around the neckline waist and cuffs. On her head he had attached a navy blue colored scarf that fell to the middle of her back. She wore a pair of diamond studs in her ears and a gold chain that joined at her cleavage, falling into one piece down to her stomach.

When she walked into the room, everyone seemed to stop talking and just look at her. Xavier broke the silence. "Even blonde hair and blue eyed, I still know who you were." He leaned down talking her lips in a soft kiss. "You do look remarkable though."

Dimitri came up right behind him. "As beautiful as you may look, I'm glad it's just for today. I would miss those exquisite moss green eyes. Those eyes that look almost black when dilated with desire." His kiss was not as gentle as Xavier's. When he released her, he told her, "You will follow every direction given to you. No questions asked. These men know what they are doing. Follow their instructions and no one should get hurt. Once we are in there it will be hard for us to talk to you. Just know that Xavier and I are watching over you." To Colin he said, "She is our everything. Make sure no harm comes to her."

"On my life, Dimitri, Xavier. I will take care of her as if she was my real Lucy." Colin gathered Lucy in his arms. "We will be back. Try not to worry and take care of our little one. I love you, my little dove." He kissed her, then headed out the door. Madison and his entourage following behind him.

They exited the ship onto the pier. Four black Suburbans were waiting for them after they passed through customs. The drive was long. Made only longer by the tension hanging in the air. Madison stared out the window watching the landscape change. From the tourist area, to lush green and colorful grounds, past a rundown area, and finally to the city. From there they followed a curvy dirt road for a couple of miles to end at their destination.

When the door was opened for Madison, she stepped out cautiously, looking around the entire area. There was activity going on everywhere. The building they were standing in front of looked to be a fairly new building. The parking lot was paved and the landscape manicured. Colin came to her side startling her. Catching her hand, he placed it on his forearm. Then whispered to her, "We won't let you fall." To that she smiled brilliantly. Her Masters were with her. She had nothing to fear. Straightening her back, she gathered up all her pent up anger and turned it into a what looked like a "Regal Bitch."

"Are you ready, my dear?" Colin asked her.

Putting a smile on her face, like he was the only man in the world for her, she said, "Let's go see what new toy I have bought this month." Colin smirked at her as he led the group to the front doors.

The inside was similar to the outside. Neat, clean, simple. The reception area was straight ahead, a glass-wall conference room to the right, and offices to the left. Pictures of different work areas were displayed around on the wall. Jafar, Colin's man approached the receptionist giving their names. She in turn replied that Señor Ramirez would be right with them.

Dimitri and Xavier stood on either side of Madison. Their backs were to the doors that opened for Brian Boxwood. "Sheikh Ahmed, welcome to Mexico. I hope this business matter can be handled as quickly as possible so you and your lovely wife can get back to your vacation."

Colin stood with a blank face and looked at Boxwood. Then saying. "And you are?"

"Oh my! Look at me I have forgotten my manners. If my

momma was here she'd box my ears." Extending his hand. "Brian. Brian Boxwood. We've been speaking through emails."

Colin clutched his hand, gripping him harder than he normally would have then released it just as quickly. "Yes, I remember now. Lucy darling, meet Brian. He wants me to invest in this business with him."

Madison's back had been turned to him when he entered. While he had been making a fool of himself in front of Colin she had turned slightly. She needed to see him. Thank God, she had. The shell of a man that stood before her now looked nothing like the high school boy she remembered. As politely as she could, she told him, "You can call me Lucy. Nice to meet you." When he clutched her hand to shake it a frosty chill ran through her. Pulling her hand back as if shocked but Brian didn't release her hand.

"The pleasure is all mine. Lucy what a beautiful name. Does it…" His words were cut off by the knife appearing at his throat.

"Remove your hand from my wife. Dog. You are not worthy of looking at her. Let alone touching her."

Her hand was released immediately. "Do not touch my wife again. I do not like it. Understand?"

Brian hated backing down to anyone, but he needed this money and he needed it bad. He had tapped out every dime he could from his accounts, and he could only take so much from the Boxwood Pharmaceutical account. He would be just fine as soon as this shipment made it to the states. Everything would be put back and no one would be the wiser. A sly smile appeared on his face. Once he was part owner in this business he would be set. His own stash of heroin for his own head. Plus, enough to sell at top dollar on the streets. The best part of this deal was the sheikh would have no idea what was happening. He'd be back in his palace in Dubai, and Brian would be here running things. He couldn't believe his good fortune when the sheikh had responded to his email. Now, if he could get an extra million on top of everything as a signing bonus, all his problems would be solved.

Señor Ramirez appeared at that moment, guiding them into the conference room. The receptionist offered beverages, then left the room. Colin was the first to speak. "Señor Ramirez."

"Tomas, please."

"All right Tomas. Out in the hall are my most trusted men. They will be allowed to walk anywhere they want in this facility. If a door is closed and they want it opened, it will be opened. If a box is closed and they want it opened, it will be opened. If I want to go through your mail, you will allow me. We have all afternoon to inspect this facility. Isn't that right Tomas?"

"We are open until 5:00 pm Señor Colin."

"Sweetheart, I don't know if I want to be here all day. Maybe, the men could do half their inspection today, and the rest tomorrow?" Madison asked sweetly. Knowing full well Brian wanted this deal done today. And they needed to get back to the ship. She glanced over at Brian to see him mopping his brow with a handkerchief. "Does the heat bother you much, Mr. Boxwood. I thought you came from a warm state?"

"No. I just think I ate something that didn't agree with me." Looking at Colin, his grey coloring looked worse with the sweat on his brow. "Do your men really need to inspect every area of this building. I thought we would be signing papers and doing the bank transfer?"

Colin stood, bringing Madison with him. "Yes. Mr. Boxwood. I have never bought into a business I was not intimately involved with." To Madison he said. "Come, my dear, I would very much like to see the floor from the view in

Señor Ramirez's office." Opening the door, he said loud enough for them all to hear. "You two stay with my Lucy." Talking to Xavier and Dimitri. "The rest of you begin your searches. We will be in Señor Ramirez's office if you find anything I need to know about. Señor Ramirez, after you Tomas." When Boxwood didn't move, Colin asked him. "Are you joining us, Mr. Boxwood?" Stressing his name.

Before he could answer Angel the day supervisor rushed up to Ramirez. "Señor Ramirez, we have a problem. We just found three boxes that were supposed to go to Boxwood Pharmaceutical last night. Juan must have misplaced them."

Brian was making his way to the door when Angel announced the error. Señor Ramirez spoke up with authority in his voice. "Angel, make sure those boxes get out, overnight at our expense. This is the last straw with that one. When he comes in tonight, send him immediately to my office. Oh and Angel, on your way back, stop in and have Helena put out the word we are looking for a new night warehouse supervisor. Unless you know someone who you trust that needs a job."

Brian thought he was going to vomit right there. What the fuck was happening? First this stupid inspection. Then, the boxes. Now, the asshole from that cartel was going to be fired. Nothing was going as he planned. Knowing he needed to acknowledge Ramirez, but he also needed to try and save that asshole's job too. "Señor thank you that is appreciated. Sir, I'm sure it was an honest mistake. I would hate to think someone would lose their job over something like this. I would hate to start our new venture with someone who doesn't know the operation."

"You are correct, Sir. As of tomorrow I will no longer be making the decisions. I will leave it in your hands." Señor Ramirez backed away.

"Angel where are these boxes? I would like to see what

my future partner invests in?" Colin spoke up, and with a nod from Ramirez he was off to retrieve them.

Boxwood could only pray the special ones had been shipped already. But the way his day was going it didn't look to promising.

They arrived at the office. The view from the window of the floor showed the packers, as well as the warehouse, and what you couldn't see through the glass cameras on the wall filled in the blanks. There was more security in this building, then most banks had in them.

Throughout this whole time Madison hung to the back with Xavier and Dimitri. She had seen Boxwood's face when Colin had requested the boxes be brought up. He became whiter than he already was. She whispered to Dimitri, "Did you see that? There has to be something in those boxes. What do you think?"

"I think you're right. But it's anyone's guess what this sick bastard might be shipping. I'm sure we'll find out though."

"Dimitri," Colin called out. "Bring the papers that need to be signed. I believe I will be very happy running a pharmaceutical company." Dimitri moved forward opening a folder, and placing it on the desk.

Finally, Boxwood thought. Something was going his way. He moved to the desk. Picking up the pen, he signed all the papers in the appropriate marked spaces. Passing the pen to Colin.

Colin accepted the pen with a satisfied grin, as the door opened for the three boxes to be delivered. Dimitri moved forward closing and taking the file off the desk, making room for the boxes. Colin then stepped forward, producing the knife that had previously been poised at Boxwood's throat. He sliced through the tape sealing the box. Pulling it open they found bottles of antibiotics. The next box had all different kinds of pills. In the third box they found thirty-three pounds of heroin. All eyes turned to Boxwood with questioning looks.

"I have no idea what that is." He tried his best to sound convincing.

"By the looks of it I would say we are looking at about is a street value of eight million dollars' worth of heroin." Señor Tomas spoke up. "These boxes were cleared last night to ship. If they had shipped this heroin would be heading to your company Mr. Boxwood. Can you tell me how this happened?" he demanded.

Again all eyes were on Brian. "This is your facility. Would you like to tell me?" Brian was trying to sound indignant. "If it wasn't for this meeting I wouldn't even be here." With that statement, Brian felt he had explained himself. He Stepped back away from the desk and over to the computer screens. "Is all this security for show? Or can you see what happened last night?" Knowing he was not on any film, he felt confident in this request.

"That is a very good idea, Mr. Boxwood," Colin commented. "Tomas, would you have last night's footage pulled up for us?"

Brian's body seemed to relax. His color was slowly coming back, and with it, his scheming mind. He needed to start weaving a believable tale. If he wanted them to believe it, he needed to make it good. Tomas had sat down at the desk and began typing on his computer. Everyone's eyes went to the screens on the wall. Except for Brian's. With everyone's attention away from him he had eased his way behind Madison. He knew if things didn't go his way, he was going to need a shield. He planned on making the lovely Lucy that shield.

As they watched the footage they came to the part were Juan switched out the supplies in four boxes. Not just one. All of a sudden the sound was turned up and you could hear what Juan was saying. "Julio, come here." When the driver of the truck got there, Juan had already set aside three blocks of the heroin. Handing a sealed box to Julio he said. "Make sure you drop this at the clubhouse. The men know what to do with it."

"Are you sure you want to take three this time? What if Boxwood questions the quantity? He hasn't paid for the full delivery yet. I'm supposed to pick up the rest on delivery. If he realizes it's missing. He won't pay."

"He won't even miss these until it's too late. You'll have already left by the time he opens them. Relax. Just do what I said. This has been a very profitable deal for our cartel. I'm going to put us on the map with it, and this stupid American is going to help me do it."

"I can only pray you're right. I don't even want to think about what could happen." Julio took the box, and stashed it under the front seat.

While Juan finished packing the other boxes. His phone rang. Recognizing the number, he answered it. "Mr. Boxwood, good evening Señor. What can I help you with tonight?" He walked away from the camera so the rest of the conversation was not on the tape. However, while he walked away, they saw why the three boxes missed the truck. Once they had seen and heard proof positive that Boxwood was involved, all eyes in the room turned to him.

Knowing there was no way out for him, he grabbed Madison with his arm, wrapping it around her throat. Putting a gun to her head, he said, "Señor Tomas, I believe we have seen enough. Sheikh Ahmed, I hope you don't mind if I use your wife for a little while. I deserve to get something out of this deal. I'm sure you have another one waiting at home for you."

If Colin looked enraged, it was nothing compared to Xavier and Dimitri. "There is no place for you to go,

Boxwood. My men are crawling all over this facility, and the Mexican police should be pulling up any second. Let Lucy go, and we can talk," Colin pleaded.

"Talk. You want to talk. No. I think right now you want to kill me," Brain taunted. The police were on the way. Colin was right. There was no way out for him, and he didn't want to spend the rest of his life in a Mexican jail. But if he could get away with Lucy as his shield, he just needed to get to the airport. The company jet was waiting. "However, I think you are going to let me walk right out that door. Unless you'd like to see if the inside of Lucy is just as beautiful, as the outside." He moved the barrel of the gun down her face.

Dimitri and Xavier saw the fear on Madison's face. She was starting to shut down. Dimitri had seen her do this before on the *Onyx*. In a few minutes she wouldn't know what was going on around her. She would, as she described it to him "go to her happy place." Dimitri whispered into the ear piece, "Greyson are you hearing all of this?"

"Yes, Dimitri. Let him go. We have put a tracking device on his car, but I'd lay odds he's going straight to the airport. We'll get him before he's off the ground. He won't be leaving Mexico."

"Make sure he doesn't. He has Madison."

"Now if you would be so kind as to put that box onto the dolly. We can get Angel to walk it to my car. Sheikh, I will let your Lucy go as soon as I'm safe. Until then, I suggest you say goodbye." Brian just couldn't stop himself from rubbing it in Colin's nose. "Even with all your security, you couldn't protect the one person you are supposed to love." To Madison he said, "I guess money does buy love because I can't see any reason for a woman to want to suck his dick. Let alone marry him."

"Oh, and speaking about wives," Colin commented to him, the anger and sarcasm in his voice. "Dimitri, the folder please?" Dimitri handed the folder to Colin. "You no longer have one." He flipped through the papers in the file.

"What the fuck are you talking about?" Brian demanded, his grip tightening around Madison's neck.

"I never had any intention of going into business with you. In fact, I bought this business yesterday from Señor Tomas just so you couldn't have it. You hurt a dear friend of my wife's and she requested I didn't do business with you. I did my homework, Mr. Boxwood. She was right."

"What do you mean I no longer have a wife?" Brian enunciated every word.

"Well, I found out in my research that your wife has been begging for a divorce since you put her in the hospital even though the pre-nuptial she signed before the wedding states she gets nothing. However, if you requested the divorce she received half of everything. I wondered why you wouldn't just sign the divorce papers?"

"It's none of your business, Ahmed."

"Then I read the name of your wife. It seems, she is the sister to my wife's friend. You couldn't have Amber, so you settled for her sister. Isn't that right, Boxwood? Well, now you can't have her sister either. The papers you signed were divorce papers. Giving Sarah half of everything you own. Which after the police are finished with you won't be much."

This conversation snapped Madison out of her fear. He had married her sister. Had she heard that right? Not only that, he had put her in the hospital. None of this was in the file she had read. But now she understood how her sister was addicted. This piece of scum, that's how.

Colin, Dimitri, and Xavier knew Madison was hearing everything. They saw her glazed eyes clear, and knew she was back with them again. Colin sat in a chair by the desk making Brian shift his position. He was no longer right by the door. "There is one other thing you should know," Colin continued to egg Brian on. "While you're enjoying the rest and relaxation of the Mexican jail. Your mother will be enjoying a cell of her own. For all we know, she could end up in the same prison as Amber and Sarah's mother. Wouldn't that be fun?"

Brian's face turned white. "What the fuck are you talking about? My mother hasn't done anything. You can't prove she has!" He was spitting his words. If his mother was arrested because of him, he might as well be dead anyway.

"We don't have to prove anything. As soon as those boxes are opened up by the United States DEA they will just take her away. Since of course the boxes were addressed to her directly."

"You're lying. You saw the video. All the boxes were addressed to the company." Boxwood screamed.

"Yes, we did. What you didn't see, was the team of men at the airport who changed them." Colin had a satisfied smile on his face. Especially, because he knew he had flipped the right switch. What he had said enraged Boxwood.

"I will fucking kill you!" he shouted. But before he could point the gun at Colin, Madison elbowed him in his gut.

The gun went off, grazing Madison in the thigh. As she crumped to the floor her weight threw Boxwood's balance off. Before she knew what was happening. Dimitri had gathered her in his arms. Xavier and Colin had Boxwood pinned to the ground while, Greyson and the rest of the team were rushing through the door.

Madison looked up at Dimitri. "You knew he married my sister, and you didn't say anything?" Accusing eyes glared into his until he tightened the belt on her leg, and then her eyes flared with pain.

"I'm sorry, beautiful. I have to try and stop the bleeding before you go into shock." He continued talking to her to keep her focused on him. "I wasn't positive. I had Caleb dig deeper after I saw she was living in a rehab house. I didn't want to be right. I'm so sorry, beautiful." He hugged her to his body as they sat on the floor.

"When I read the report about not signing the divorce papers, it didn't really matter to me who his wife was. We would have helped them just the same, but when I realized it was your sister, we had Max add something like a codicil to the divorce decree. It stated that your sister had no wrong doing in the business. Plus, he signed over the houses and cars. Transferring them into your sister's name as well. This way she would retain the business, since Mother Boxwood, and her son would have to forfeit it. As well as the houses and cars. Now the DEA won't be able to seize them," Dimitri explained. "We only confirmed it was your sister right before we got here. We would have told you if we could have."

She looked up into his worried hazel eyes as Xavier joined them on the floor. "Are you all right?" Another pair of worried eyes looked her over to make sure.

"Yes, I think it just grazed me." She reached up to cup both of their faces in her hands. "Thank you. I'm actually kind of glad you didn't tell me. It's what snapped me out of my panic attack. I had to fight back for her." She moved her hands away, and bowed her head. She quietly added, "And for me."

Dimitri picked her chin up. "We are very proud of you. If you hadn't elbowed him, Colin might be dead right now."

"I agree. You gave us the chance to make a move on him." Looking to where the police were holding a hand-cuffed Boxwood. "He'll be spending a long time in that jail." Xavier smiled. Turning back to Madison. "Now let's get you out of here. Greyson can finish up with Colin."

Dimitri picked Madison up in his arms. "Can you bring me over to him? Please?" she asked as he put her back on the ground. Both Dimitri and Xavier shared confused looks. When she was standing right in front of Boxwood, police on either side holding him in custody, Madison hauled off and punched him in the face. His body boomeranged from the blow. Shaking her hand to relieve the pain, she whispered to him. "That was for a seventeen-year-old girl who you left beaten and broken. I hope you get everything you deserve in that jail." She turned to the policemen holding him and told them, "I hear he's a pedophile as well." The looks they gave Boxwood had the man peeing his pants.

Explaining to Colin they were leaving, and that they would get together later on the ship, Dimitri picked her back up. He carried a smiling Madison from the building to the car. On the ride back, Madison had passed out. She would never see her two Masters shed the tears that had fallen for her. Never see the fear in their eyes just as her head dropped forward, thinking she had gone into shock. But right there and then they pledged that they would keep her safe, happy, and most of all loved.

Once they had her settled with Doc he sent them on their way, explaining she would sleep for a while after the shot he had given her. He would call when she was up.

Both men went back to the suite to clean up. Drinks in hands they sat knowing the wait for word on Madison would be torture. They knew she would be fine, but not having her with them was killing them. Just when they didn't think they could take anymore. Greyson showed up to fill them in on what they had missed.

Chapter 19

Madison woke up lying on a very comfortable mattress. The room was gently lit. When she turned her head to see where she was, her head started swimming. Closing her eyes again, she willed it to stop.

"The spinning will subside, have no fear. Besides that, how are you feeling?"

Madison knew who was talking to her. "My leg feels like it's on fire. Will that go away too, Doc?"

He pulled a chair close to the bed. "Yes, my dear, it will. I heard you had some adventure huh?"

"Nothing I would ever want to do again. Can I go back to my cabin, Doc?"

"If I let you go before those two over grown bullies know, I think I'll be needing that bed next." He laughed. "I see they finally did right by you." Looking at the ring on her finger, he continued, "They are good men, I've known Dimitri a long time and I've never seen him this content. Xavier not so long, but if he's anything like Cameron, you will be very happy."

He stood next to her. "Now, let's try and sit you up. Make

sure you're not unbalanced." He helped her into a sitting position. Jerking her leg, she moaned in pain. "Once the boys tuck you in, I want you to take these pills. One is an antibiotic, the other is something to help you sleep." He handed her the bottles. "Then tomorrow, just continuing taking the antibiotics till you finish them. Understood? You were very lucky the bullet just grazed you. If it had gone in, I don't know if you would have made it. You've been blessed."

"I most certainly have." A totally dreamy look came over Madison's face, as her two Masters walked into the sick bay. They could be frightening to other people with their size, but to her they were perfect. Both big and solidly built. Their dominance came out as they walked towards her. The break in their flawless façade were their eyes. Both were filled with worry.

"She would like to go back to her cabin. She has some medicine to take, and she needs to rest. Am I making myself perfectly clear?" Doc's voice held a stern tone.

"We will take care of our girl, Doc. Don't worry. Thank you for everything." Dimitri walked straight to her, and had basically dismissed Doc. His eyes on Madison, he asked, "How are you?"

"I wish people would stop asking me that. I'm fine," she stressed. Swinging her legs over the bedside a grimace crossed her face with the pain. Thankful there was no dizziness, she tried to stand.

"What do you think you're doing?"

"I was going to walk to my cabin." She stood up and the pain that seared through her caused her to sit right back down. "Okay, so maybe I need a little help?" The coy look on her face didn't fool either of them. She was in pain.

Xavier came to her side. "You can ride in the wheelchair or I can carry you? Your choice."

Why would she ever want to ride in a wheelchair when

she could be carried, held close, cared for? "You of course!" she said as if that was the only answer to give. "Thank you, Doc, for everything."

"You're, welcome, sweetheart. Change the bandage tomorrow. If it looks red, irritated or puffy, bring her right back to me. Here's some cream to put on. It might help with the burning. Take care, my dear." He gave her a fatherly kiss on the forehead. "Sleep well."

"Let's get you to bed," Dimitri said to her, turning to the doctor, he added, "Thank you. Have you reconsidered coming on the international cruise yet?"

"I'll let you know, so far I've been needed in both oceans. But then again you did promise me adventure." He chuckled, and placed a hand on his shoulder. "She's a special one. I'm happy you found her."

Dimitri's head turned, watching Xavier carry Madison to the door. "You don't have to tell me." Turning back to Doc, he said, "By the time this cruise is over, she will be well and truly ours. Have a good night." Then he followed them out the door.

Madison had slept through the night and most of the next day while they were at sea heading home. While she had been awake and eating, Dimitri and Xavier explained what had happened after they had left. Greyson told them that Boxwood had tried to escape and had been shot dead in the process. They all figured he'd rather be dead then in jail. His mother had been arrested in the states, their property seized, and was sitting in jail awaiting her trial. Once she was arrested on heroin distribution charges, all of her friends deserted her. She was lucky she had a lawyer. Plus, the cartel members were rounded up and arrested as well.

They had also explained that because Max had filed the papers for the divorce, her sister would still maintain the business once she was on her feet again. Till then they had sent people from their own businesses to run things till she could. They didn't want Madison worrying about anything for the rest of the cruise. They had something special planned and worrying wasn't part of those plans. Tonight was the Halloween party as well as Cameron and Sadie's reception.

Madison's leg was only mildly annoying by the time she was getting dressed for the party. Her musketeer costume allowed for nothing constricting on her wound. The rich purple velvet tabard fell to just above her wound. Where there should have been a white puff sleeved shirt underneath it, Madison's was shirtless allowing the sides of her naked body to show. Her thigh high, flat black boots hid her bandage. A leather feathered hat covered her braided hair. A belted sword hung at her waist finishing her costume. On a normal tabard there was a white cross in the middle. Madison's had been designed just her. On it were a snow white Siberian tiger and a lion roaring. Each animal climbed over her breasts. Protecting what was theirs.

Dimitri and Xavier both wore worn leather doublets with snippets of a white linen shirts at the collar and cuffs. Their leather pants were tucked into swashbuckler boots. Leather hats with feather plumes on their heads. Belted to their waist on one side they wore swords. On the other a single shot original musket pistol rested. They looked so dashing, more like swashbuckler's then musketeers.

They arrived at the dungeon area that had been totally decorated for the party. Soft music played in the background. Black and orange swag wrapped the railing with purple lights flickering within it. Pumpkins and jock-o-lanterns resting on bales of hay with others scattered about. Eerie trees, spider webs, and tombstones were cleverly placed about. The bars were decorated with spider webs, skulls, ghosts, and gnomes. Other decorations were part of the scenes set up around the area. Dracula in a coffin, a witch stirring her witch's brew in a smoking caldron with green goo bubbling and hissing.

All the servers at the party were dressed as zombies. There was spider-web soup and eye ball deviled eggs. A dessert table overflowed with cupcakes designed with purple and orange frosting swirled on top. Pieces of chocolate made to look like pumpkins, bat wings, and black cats were scattered amongst the desserts.

The silver colored wedding cake however, dominated the table. The five tier cake with black colored shapes was decorated for the occasion. The bottom was designed to resemble a haunted forest. Moving up to the next tier the forest grew into a grave yard. The third tier had spider webs, the second had vine work with tiny orange pumpkins. The final piece had two skulls bumping heads sitting on red raspberry glaze that dripped off the side and down the entire cake. Separating the layers, roses in black and red alternated as they wrapped around the individual tiers.

Guest in costumes were mingling about drinking and conversing waiting for the guests of honor. There were Spartans, kings and queens. Queens that were kings. Cavemen, harem girls, super heroes, ninjas, marvel comic heroes, and even Star-wars characters. The array of costumes astounded Madison. They had found their table joining Greyson and Raven, as well as Marco and Jace. The last two to join them were Caleb and Isabella. The party would progress like a normal reception with the exception of the use of the dungeon arena. After the happy couple arrived, the arena would be opened.

Once everyone was seated the DJ turned down the music and announced the arrival of the bride and groom

Cinderella and Prince Charming. Sadie's gown was a perfect replica of the princess's gown. Although, she had made a few modifications to it. The DJ then played their wedding song to start the party, inviting guests to join them on the floor. Towards the end of the song, Cameron tore the bottom part of her gown off in a spinning motion. Leaving an off the shoulder blue satin corset with a plunging neckline and a sky blue leather mini skirt. The lace overlay that fell to the floor behind her was embroidered with beading and pearls. White thigh highs and five-inch clear peep toed shoes finished the sexy Cinderella costume.

Madison, Xavier and Dimitri joined them on the floor with Madison in between their bodies swaying to the music. "This will be us in a few months, and I for one cannot wait." Xavier exclaimed kissing her ring on her finger. "We have discussed it, and if it's all right with you, Dimitri will be your groom. However, we will add my name. You would then be Madison Zilkin-Legend. Does that sound all right with you?" Before she could answer he finished saying, "This way our children will carry both our names."

Madison looked at both of their faces. For them to have thought this far in advance told Madison she finally had fate on her side. She had a future to look forward too. The way they were staring at her told her this was important to them. "I wish I could legally marry you both, but I'm happy you made the decision for me. I would never have been able to choose between you."

"So does that mean yes?" Dimitri questioned.

She moved back a step so she could wrap her hands around both their necks before she stepped back up to them. "That's a yes." Stretching up, she kissed both of them, rubbing her body up them as she did.

Groaning in unison, they each slid a hand up her thigh,

wrapping around to grope her ass. Her warm soft skin fitting perfectly in their hands.

"Masters if you continue to do that, I don't think we will be here long," she whispered to them, moving out of their reach holding them at arm's length. "But, before we do leave. I need to talk to Colin and Lucy. I want to thank them for everything they did. I thought I saw them while we were dancing." She dropped their hands and turned to where she had seen them.

"We will come with you, Madison. We would like offer our gratitude as well." They each took a hand, as Xavier led the way.

Colin and Lucy had chosen Bonnie and Clyde for their costumes. Right down to the old Browning rifle, and Bonnie's "Whippet" gun. Reaching the table, Colin rose from his chair saying. "Madison, what are you doing? You should be resting." Pushing his way past Xavier he guided her to his chair next to Lucy, kissing her cheeks before she sat. "Sit here with Lucy." To Jafar and Malik standing to the side. "Do not let them leave and let no one near them. Understood!"

"It will be done, your Highness!" they both exclaimed, moving forward.

"You two stay here; we will be back." Kissing Lucy soundly, he added, "Madison, what would you like to drink?" She told him what she wanted and the men were on their way.

Madison leaned over and hugged Lucy. Surprised by the show of affection at first, Lucy then melted into the hug. "I don't know how I will ever be able to repay all you and Colin have done for me." Tears glistened in her eyes. "You could have been a real bitch after what I did. Thank you."

"I was so worried for you when Colin told me you had been shot. Even though he said it just grazed you." She paused, looking down at the hand that clutched Madison's on the table. Giving it a squeeze, she raised watery eyes to Madison, her face stern as if resolved to say something. "I need to thank you for something." Lowering her voice, she said, "Colin is the only person I have ever told this too." She looked at her with pleading eyes.

"Lucy, please don't tell me something I can't tell my Masters. I promised them I would hide nothing from them. I'm sorry," she said, thinking that Lucy would not tell her what she wanted to say.

"I understand, but what I have to say involves you. So, you can tell them if you have to. That's what I love so much about you. Your loyalty. Once it's given, you stay true to it."

The tender look she gave her swelled Madison's heart. Searching for her men, she said, "I would do anything for them."

Lucy pulled her attention back to her. "Do you remember the day you found Tia crying to Mildred?"

Lucy had Madison's attention. "Of course I do. It was the only day I thought that girl had a heart!"

Lucy bowed her head and in a mouse like tone she told Madison. "I know what she was talking about, by being different." She picked her head up to look at Madison's stunned face.

"When I told you what happened in the kitchen, why didn't you say anything?"

"She threatened to cut my face up if I told anyone. Besides, I was too embarrassed." Wiping the tears from her cheeks, seeming to gain her courage. She blurted out. "Tia, was a he/she. There I said it." Madison looked at her, a confused expression on her face. "She has both male, and female parts. The reason I know this is because one day she caught me in the shower alone. I was too shocked to do anything. After it was over, she told me in her crude way that

I would now be worth more, cause my ass was no longer virgin." Taking a sip of water, she continued. "She told me she had done it to all the girls. Everyone but you."

"What do you mean? How did I not know any of this?"

"Arcola, removed her from the house when he found out. I have no idea what happened to her, I was just glad she was gone. I think it was because of you."

Madison now understood what Sadie had meant. Tia had talked about her on the *Onyx*. "Tia had said something about unfinished business pertaining to me to someone I know. I just didn't understand it."

"Arcola, knew what she was planning to do to you, and he had already set up the party for us. With us leaving the house, we were off limits. So, he couldn't have her abusing you. Plus, I think he had a tender place for you that Tia always hated."

Lucy could not have been more off the mark. "Oh, he had a tender place for me. I told you how I ended up dying. She was there that night. It all makes sense now." Madison thought back to the night at the club. She had heard a woman's voice that had sounded familiar. Now she knew it had to have been Tia. "She was there that night. I couldn't place the voice until you just told me all of this."

"You never knew, but you saved me from her so many times. We will never lose each other again. I've made sure of that. Colin has already signed the papers with both your men. Dimitri for the Midnight Oasis Cruise Line to have a home port in Dubai. Xavier, to bring his family's wine business to Dubai as well. You and I will get to see each other all the time. Like it should have been." A huge grin was on her face.

"I would imagine so, since I will need my maid of honor's help planning my wedding."

Tears filled Lucy's eyes again, but the smile on her face

told Madison they were happy tears. "I would be honored to stand with you when you marry…" Lucy left the name hanging.

"Dimitri"

"Yes. When you marry Dimitri. I'm so happy for you." She jumped out her chair bringing Madison with her in a bear hug.

"Why is your wife mauling our woman?" Dimitri kidded with Colin.

"The only time she's like this is if she's really happy," Colin replied as they approached the table.

He discovered why she was happy when he heard her saying, "We have to plan it soon otherwise I will be too fat. We could wait until after the baby too? Whatever you want. I'm just so excited." Almost spilling the drinks Colin carried, she spun towards him. "I'm going to be Madison's maid of honor! Isn't that wonderful?"

Over hearing the news Lucy had just announced Marco was pulled from his own conversation. Walking to Madison, throwing his hip out his hand resting on it. His other hand waving in her face. "Did I just hear her correctly? She!" He stressed the word. "Is going to be your maid of honor?" His eyes flared wide, his lips pursed together.

All Madison could do was smile. "Excuse me, Lucy, I meant to say co-maid of honor."

"Ahem." Was all Marco said. Very pleased with himself.

"I'll explain later, Lucy." Then looking at Marco, she teased, "Did you really think I would get married without you by my side? You, silly little man."

He kissed both her cheeks. "You're not dancing tonight are you?"

"No, and thank you for not asking." He knew she was tired of people asking how she was. This afternoon when he had gone to see her she had explained that to him. In great detail. "Did you bring it?"

Marco was dressed as Cher to Jace's Sonny. Opened his sparkled-shirt a little to show her the papers tucked in his bra. "I kept them in a safe place," he whispered.

"I will need them in a bit. Keep holding them till then," she quickly said so her Masters would not hear. "Lucy, I will talk with you tomorrow. I would imagine breakfast will be served before everyone departs. We will see you then. Enjoy the rest of your night." Madison hugged her again.

Colin engulfed her in a hug, whispering in her ear, "If you ever need anything, we will be there for you. You have put a spark back into my Lucy. I will make sure it doesn't go out."

"Thank you again for everything, Colin, and for taking such good care of Lucy. She's pretty special."

"I'm lucky to have her. Just like they are lucky to have you." He looked at the daggers being directed at him from her Masters.

"Let me go. We will see you at breakfast." She slipped out of his arms and strolled to her Masters.

"Say your goodbyes tonight, Madison. We will not be making breakfast," Dimitri commanded. "Don't worry. You will see Lucy back in New York. We have dinner already planned."

She said her goodbyes to Lucy and Colin. The party continued with the throwing of the flowers which Jasmine caught. Followed by the garter, surprisingly caught by Kristoff. The dungeon arena opened and was in full use. Turning the celebration into a sensual setting.

Madison tried to hide a yawn behind her hand, but Xavier caught a glimpse of her at the right moment. Leaning to Dimitri he said something to him quietly. Dimitri turned his full attention to Madison. "If you are tired we can leave, the only thing left is the cake."

Not wanting to leave, but knowing her Masters would be mad if she pushed herself, she decided to leave. "Could we have some cake sent to the room? I can think of a few ways we could eat it." Understanding her suggestion, both men rose at the same time. "I need to get something from Marco. Can you wait here for me?"

"We will be by Cameron and Sadie."

Madison found Marco and retrieved the papers. She was saying good night when the music stopped, and Dimitri's voice came over the speakers. "Can I have everyone's attention please?" Finding her in the crowd, he said, "Madison join us please." Too stunned to move, Marco escorted her to them, sitting her in the chair Xavier had retrieved.

Speaking to Madison he began, "During this cruise we created a new beginning. Your trust in us to take care of you did not come easy. We will do everything in our power to never lose it." Dimitri began speaking from his heart. "You have changed my life. I never thought I would feel this magnetism towards one person let alone two. I may be your Master, but you have mastered me since the day I met you. I love you, Madison. I always will." He handed the microphone to Xavier.

"When Dimitri approached me with the idea of the three of us, to say I was floored would have been an understatement." Looking at Dimitri, he said, "I would like to think I would have thought of her before myself had our roles been reversed." Kneeling down before Madison, he continued, "I never thought you would be a part of my life. Seeing you on the *Onyx* with someone else, knowing you would never be mine again didn't change how I felt about you. I still couldn't get you out of mind. I wish I could say it will be smooth sailing from here, but no one knows what the future holds.

We only have today, and I for one don't want to let fate 'fuck with us anymore.'" Using her own words. "You have already made us very happy by agreeing to marry us. That is only a legality, what matters to us and everyone here is will you accept us as your only Masters? Will you serve us of your own free will? Trusting us to know what is best for you both in and out of bed?" Xavier stood next to Dimitri, as he opened the box with her collar in it. "Will you submit to us your body to pleasure and punish as we see fit? Will you love us till your dying breath?"

Marco handed her a napkin to wipe the tears rolling down her face. "When the two of you ambushed me with this idea, I was terrified you'd kill each other. Both of you are so dominate and possessive. Then you handed me this." She held the contract in front of her. "Not knowing my limits, my history, if I would even want to be a part of this ménage. You both signed it anyway. It's amazing you are both so successful in your business dealings, if this is how you do business," she teased them. "As you can see, I'm a little handicapped right now. Otherwise, I would be kneeling before you. Trust is mutual, it can't be one sided. It's not easy to hand over something so fragile. I've been waiting my whole life for the two of you." The tears slipped down her face, catching a sob. She sat a little straighter, courage in her voice.

"I vow to submit to both Master Dimitri and Master Xavier of my own free will. I promise I will try to accept my punishments without too much complaining. I will submit my body to my Masters for them to pleasure as they see fit. To love them till my dying breath." She handed Dimitri the signed contract. Opening it he showed it to Xavier with a big grin on his face. Across the area for her hard limits was written "to be determined." "Signing this contract solidifies us. It's more precious to me than a marriage license. I love you both so much, sometimes it hurts my heart."

They removed the collar from the box. Dimitri holding the white gold side, molded into the shape of a tiger. Xavier held the gold side, this one molded in the shape of a lion. Their heads intertwined in the middle of the collar while their bodies hugged her neck. Emerald green eyes, glowed from the tiger. Rubies flared brightly in the eyes of the lion. It was both delicate and commanding. The detail was defined perfectly. They locked the collar on her neck. Handing her the key. In unison they both said, "We give this key to you to protect. It is a symbol of our commitment to you. As our submissive, we will provide for you. We will clothe you, feed you, pleasure you, but most of all we will treasure you. We will guide and care for you. We will love and strive to fulfill your every want and desire, to push you to your sexual limits. Never to abuse, or take for granted the gift you give to us freely."

"I love you, Madison." The spoke individually.

"I accept this key, and with it the two men giving it to me. I promise to submit my body to the fulfillment of our sexual, emotional, and intellectual needs. To rely on them for all my wants, giving them the power to dominate me as they see fit while wearing their collar. To submit to their wants and desires. I will proudly wear their collar to show the world how honored I am to call them mine. To never abuse or take for granted the gift they have given me. I love you both very much."

They helped her stand. She leaned to Dimitri pressing her lips to his. Her tongue running along the seam of his till he gave in. Gathering her in his arms, he pressed her against his rock hard cock and sealed their contract with a searing kiss. Reluctantly, he released her into Xavier's arms.

Xavier held her face in his hands as if he was seeing her for the first time. "You are finally ours." His lips captured hers, trying to be gentle but not succeeding. His hands slid down to her hips, pulling her tight to him. Releasing her from the kiss, he said, "We need to leave. Say your good-byes." He grinned at her.

When he stepped back, Madison wavered. Not because of her legs, but because he had moved out of reach. They steadied her, concern showing on their faces. "I'm fine." Color bloomed in her cheeks. "I just got caught up in the moment. All right?"

Both men looked at each other smiling. "Let's get our girl back to the suite and tucked in. Dimitri swept her up in his arms. "Good night all," and they were gone.

Arriving back at the suite, Madison thought there would be a frenzy of them all getting out of their costumes. But that was not the case. Removing their belts and doublets, they began by placing little kisses and nips along her ears and neck, slowly unwrapping her. The gold belt fell away to the floor, her hat followed, and then they lifted the Tabard over her head. Leaving her collar in place, she stood before them naked and proud. Her nipples were hard little nubs, antici-pating the feel of their hands that hadn't touched her yet. "Sit on the bed," Xavier commanded.

They each approached her kneeling by her side. They slid the zippers down on her boots, spreading her legs open in the process. Dimitri dipped his nose between her legs inhaling. "I can't wait to dive between your legs and devour that little clit until you are screaming. Then when you think you can't take anymore, I'm going bury my cock in your warm tight convulsing channel and make you scream again."

They each began their assault on her body. Sliding her boots off, checking her wound to making sure it was healing, they continued to overwhelm every nerve ending on her body. From her feet up to her head, there was not a spot that they didn't nip suck or touch. Her body was on fire, like she had never felt before. Her breaths were coming in short pants.

Her body was no longer hers, it belonged to her Masters and they were proving that to her right now. She started to lay back on the bed, but they had something different in mind. "Madison," Dimitri paused watching her eyes clear. "Go into the dungeon area. And sit on the spanking table."

They helped her up from the bed and guided her in the room. Setting her on the table, they began to undress. Making her watch, but not touching them was driving her insane. With each piece revealing their perfect bodies, shirts fell to the floor, boots were thrown to the corner. They unzipped their pants, freeing their jutting hard cocks.

Xavier walked to her, a blindfold in his hands. "We are going to put this on. We are the only ones here, and you know you are safe with us, correct?"

"Yes, Master." She picked her head up, a pleased look on her face. Closing her eyes, he slid the blindfold over her eyes. Thrown into the darkness, she now had no idea at first who was kissing or touching her.

Sitting on the table waiting for her Masters heightened Madison's other senses. Anticipating what they would do pulled her nipples taut, and had her juices flowing. Music softly drifted into the room, but Madison was hardly aware of it. Gliding her body down on the table, each of her Masters chose a different part of her body to touch, setting her on fire all over again. She felt everything. Her nipples were sucked, nipped and even bitten. Her breasts molded in her Masters' hands making her wetter then she had ever been. She had never had an orgasm brought on by someone manipulating her breasts, but she was damn close to coming right now.

Knowing she must have been close, Dimitri told her, "Although we are in the dungeon, tonight is about pleasure, and celebrating. No permission is needed, Madison. Doesn't our girl look beautiful in our collar?"

"I've seen nothing that can compare," Xavier whispered in awe.

She silently thanked God for her Masters. A warm mouth latched onto her breast. His tongue lashing around her taut nipple, biting down. Madison came, her head thrown back, pushing her breasts up for more. Reaching out, she grabbed a hand full of hair, her nails scraping along his scalp.

Taking her hands from his head, he pulled them above her head. Moving away from her body, they turned her on her stomach. He handed her two straps. At the same time her knees where pushed to the side, hugging the table. Leaving her spread open at the end of the table, Dimitri's voice sounded right next to her, "If you release them, there will be a spanking punishment. Understood?"

"Yes, Master."

"What is your safe word, Madison?"

"Patches. Master"

From that point on there wasn't much talking as both Dimitri and Xavier continued to torture her. After her first orgasm, they wanted to prolong the next one for as long as they could. She was a human sacrifice, and they were going to take everything she offered. She gave them her trust and love, and it showed in her submission to them. Dimitri was between her legs. Xavier had a suede wide strap flogger in his hand.

The anticipation had her soaking wet and it was all because of them. When his tongue first touched her, she thought she was going to fly off the table. Holding onto the straps she tightened her grip. Circling around her lips, his tongue moved slowly up separating them, climbing higher, latching onto her clit. Lightly, sucking, then nipping down as he eased two fingers in as the first strike of the flogger hit.

Madison felt the difference in the flogger immediately. The lashes were of a wide soft suede, a step up from the rabbit fur. The sensations running through her body was indescribable. The tongue lashing her clit, the fingers thrusting in and out of her, set a rhythm sure to send her into another realm. The lashes from the flogger left her skin a pink rosy color, warming where the precise strikes of the flogger landed.

Dimitri left his fingers in her, backing away for the flogger to land on her clit. When Madison screamed, Xavier asked her, "What color are you?"

Her response was immediate. "Green, Master!" she said, panting her answer.

The grin Dimitri gave Xavier had the lashes hitting her ass. His fingers working with the flogger to bring on the longest orgasm Madison had ever had. As her orgasm hit, Dimitri drove into her. Her tight satin walls pulsed around him. As Xavier continued striking her body with the flogger. Dimitri was on the verge of coming. Pulling almost out of Madison, Xavier brought the flogger down, hitting Dimitri's cock. As it landed on Madison's clit. Dimitri, couldn't hold back any longer, shoving his shaft to Madison's cervix shouting as he did.

Madison felt Dimitri unload his cum into her. Making her come again. She was starting to lose count. Dimitri pulled out of her body from behind. Xavier took the straps from her hands. He placed a blanket on her and removed her blindfold. While Dimitri cleaned himself as well as Madison, Xavier positioned Madison so he could pick her up. Dimitri followed them out onto the balcony.

A few changes had been done on the balcony while they

were out of the room. On the balcony, Dimitri had the crew set up a three-person hammock. Xavier carried her to the hammock, while Dimitri got her something to drink. Climbing into the hammock, Madison snuggled close to Xavier, waiting for Dimitri.

When all three were comfortable looking up at the thousands of stars above them, Madison broke the silence. Fingering her collar, she said, "Thank you both for everything that you did. Knowing that Brian Boxwood won't be able to hurt anyone again means a lot. You've also given me back a friend that I probably don't deserve, but I'm grateful for."

"Of course you deserve her. If fact, she's lucky to have you as a friend. Madison, you are a very special person. Who else could bring together two very dominate jealous Masters?" She shrugged her shoulders. "Not only did you do that, you bonded us as a family. We should thank you," Dimitri explained. Caressing her face, his hand moved down to her collar. "I don't think I've ever seen anything more breathtaking then you in the moonlight wearing nothing but our collar." He turned her face to capture her lips in a tender kiss. "Don't get too comfortable, beautiful. We have more planned for you tonight." He pecked a kiss on her nose.

Reaching over, she began stroking Xavier's long hard thick cock. "I have to agree, Master Dimitri," she said, watching her hand gliding up and down knowing exactly what she was doing to him. "This is one awesome view."

"If you continue to do that, your time in this hammock will be cut extremely short." Xavier groaned out as her hand moved down further, gripping his swollen balls in her hand. "We planned this time out here to give your body a chance to recover. Have no fear, my little sub. You will soon be relieving the ache your hand is creating." She went to pull her hand away, but he caught it. Putting it back on his cock, he showed her what he liked. How hard to grip, how fast to stroke it.

Madison loved stroking their cocks. Seeing the euphoria on Xavier's face, sent her heart soaring. Another was sucking the per-cum that seeped from their slits. Moving her thumb up spreading it on the head of his dick. She brought her thumb to her mouth. Sucking it clean, she moaned as the taste exploded on her tongue.

Xavier growled rolling carefully off the hammock. "Your time is up. Let's go, my lovely. Dimitri, bring our little tease to bed." Tilting his head back, his eyes scanned the sky. "This view is impressive. But, I'm looking forward to the amazing view from our bed. To watch you wrap those silky lips around my dick." Xavier crawled up the bed laying on his back.

Dimitri set Madison on the end of the bed. She kissed her way up his legs, till she reached Xavier's aching shaft. Dragging her tongue around his balls, she sucked one then the other into her mouth. Licking her way to the base of his cock, she then pushed her tongue flat against it, sliding it up as if it were her favorite ice cream. Getting to the top, she engulfed his cock between her lips. Her tongue wrapped around it as she took him to the back of her throat.

Xavier could not close his eyes. Watching Madison suck his cock was an ultimately delicious sight. Leaving her injured leg stretched out on the bed, she pulled her other knee up. With her hair still in the braid, nothing blocked Xavier's view as her mouth launched into sucking his cock. Her head bobbing up and down was almost his undoing.

As much as he wanted to unload down her throat, he needed to be joined with her, and, in turn, Dimitri. He put his hand on her head. When those desired filled green eyes looked at him, he pulled free from her mouth with a popping sound. "I've wanted to be buried deep within you ever since our collar locked on your neck. Now, slowly lower your incredibly stunning body down your prize."

Madison didn't hesitate. She did exactly what Xavier wanted. With Dimitri's help she slowly lowered herself. Gliding down his shaft, Madison was biting her lip, loving the feeling of him deep inside her. When she was seated on his cock, he gave her time to adjust. Making sure she had no pain in her leg. "You have no idea how magnificent you looked tonight. Your skin the perfect shade of red. It took all my control not to come when the flogger hit your soaking wet lips."

Madison felt her juices flow around his cock with Xavier's words. Knowing she had pleased them as well as herself, had Madison feeling free. She was safe and loved and it felt so damn good. She could finally let go and knew they would be there to catch her. She felt Dimitri behind her.

"Lay those gorgeous breasts on Xavier," Dimitri told her. In this position it placed her ass up and open. The warm lube Dimitri drizzled on her ass slid down causing her nipples to harden on Xavier's chest.

Anticipation was driving Madison crazy. But then she felt Dimitri slide his finger through the lube. Dimitri pushed it in her entrance, past her rim. Madison pressed her hands to Xavier's chest, adjusting her position as he added two more fingers.

Xavier watched as the ecstasy flowed over Madison's face. He reached his hand between her legs. His fingers slid through her lips separating around his cock. Pulling them back, he latched onto her clit, causing her to grind her body down on his fingers, locking them between their bodies.

Watching in the mirror, Xavier was prepared when Dimitri removed his fingers. Positioning his cock, he pushed into her. "Push back, Madison." Xavier felt Dimitri slide home, completing their joining. "You were absolutely right about this mirror. Holy shit, this is the most erotic thing I've ever seen in my life." When all eyes turned to the mirror, that's when Xavier had had enough. "I need to move now, and it's going to be fast." Placing his hands on Madison's hips holding her in place, he surged his hips up from the bed. Loving the feel of Madison's tight walls around him, and feeling Dimitri's shaft through her perineal, Xavier knew this is how he wanted to spend eternity.

Xavier was surging up and Dimitri was pushing from behind setting a see saw rhythm. Madison's orgasm built quickly. When it washed over her, blinding stars flashed before her eyes.

Xavier pumped faster and harder. The feel of her walls pulsing and milking his cock brought on the most explosive orgasm he had ever had.

Dimitri followed Xavier. Madison's tight muscles convulsing around his dick sent Dimitri reeling. He groaned with his release. The three of them collapsed on the bed. Careful of Madison's leg, they laid there catching their breath.

Madison broke the silence. "Can we celebrate every day?" A grin fixed on her face. "Because I want all my memories from now on to be filled with moments like these."

"I believe that can be arranged," Dimitri answered kissing her. "We are going to make so many new memories. You'll have a hard time choosing from them."

When they were cleaned up and were lying in bed, Madison asked them, "Would it be all right if we stopped in Colorado on our way home? I'd like to see my brother and sister. They may not want to see me, but I feel I owe them the chance. They were never part of my mother's schemes as far as I know. I wouldn't put it past my mother to have had something to do with Sarah being with Boxwood. But I won't know that till I talk with them." Snuggled between her men, she looked back and forth.

"If you think this will make you happy, then yes, of course we can stop and see your family," Xavier told her, playing with her hair he had brushed out.

"No. Not my family, just my siblings. I could give two shits about my mother. And as far as my father goes, he chose not to protect his children. He could have ended all the terrible things that happened. But he left his balls in a jar for his wife to control. He can rot with her in the next jail cell for all I care."

"I'll have Jasmine make all the arrangements. You will be Colorado tomorrow night. I have a few days before I need to be back in New York. Adding a detour to Colorado sounds like fun. I'm looking forward to meeting your brother," Xavier said smiling. "He at least got to punch that son of a bitch."

"Your dad doesn't live too far from your brother if you change your mind," Dimitri commented, playing with the engagement ring on her finger.

"I won't," she replied, then yawned. "I'm tired, but I don't want this day to ever end. I never knew a person could be this happy, my cheeks hurt from smiling," she teased them. "It's all because you both refused to give up on me." She said looking at Dimitri then to Xavier, "I love you both very much." Madison fell asleep in the warmth and security of her Masters' arms.

Epilogue

Three Months Later

Madison sat nestled between Xavier and Dimitri in the back of the black Bentley Curtis, Xavier's driver, had arranged for them. The tint of the glass hid the occupants inside.

"Are you ready?" Xavier asked. The car had stopped at the beginning of the long driveway, giving Madison the chance to change her mind.

"No. Not really, but have Curtis drive. I have to do this." Looking at Xavier, she said, "I'm sorry your dad broke his leg, but I was kind of glad." Bowing her head, a small smile played on her face. "It gave me a little more time to get my courage together. Plus, Sarah was released last week. Now, I can shock the hell out of both of them at the same time," she teased.

They were quiet the rest of the drive up. The mansion that came into view as they rounded the corner had all of them gasping. The log cabin mansion rose forty feet high.

The logs holding the front entrance to the house, looked more like full grown trees rather than logs. Glass covered from floor to ceiling in between the log beams. Opening the view to both inside and out. The heated driveway continued on to the far right side, under a stone bridge walkway, ending at the five bay garage. The bridge walkway led to the three-bedroom guest house. In the diminishing daylight, they could see the grounds were manicured. Frozen water falls and ice covered fountains accented different areas. All were covered with a fresh coat of snow.

Dimitri got out of the car first, helping Madison. Xavier came around the back of the car. The three of them stood in stunned awe looking at the huge house before them. Taking a deep breath, Madison approached the double glass front door. The portrait of a bear head was etched on the glass door. Everything was real quiet, peaceful, and serene. Madison now understood why her brother chose to live here. "Ready?" Xavier asked.

"As ready as I'll ever be."

Xavier rang the doorbell. They didn't have to wait long. When the door swung open, a little boy stood in the door way. Looking up at them, he burst out, "Mom! There are people at the door!" Shouting for her. "Who are you?" he blurted out.

"We are here to see your dad. Is he home?" Dimitri asked.

"No, he's not. Asher, go in the other room, and you know better than to open the door to strangers. Now go!" Laney Sinclair turned her full attention to her guests. "Can I help you? As I said my husband isn't home. I'm Laney can I help you?"

When Madison just stood in stunned silence, Dimitri extended his hand to Laney. "Hello, I'm Dimitri, this is

Madison, and that is Xavier. Will your husband be home soon?"

"Are you here about the rehab house Matthew is building?" she asked, looking at the three tall strangers standing on her doorstep. The woman who stood between them came up to their shoulders. The full length fur coat hid most of her body. When Madison raised her head, familiar moss green eyes looked at Laney. Turning her attention to the two men standing with her, she caught glimpses of their designer suits under their over coats.

"No, we are here on a more personal level," Xavier told her. "We can come back at another time. If you would give him my card." Handing it to her, he added, "It's very important we speak with him." Before the words were out, a blue Jaguar XF pulled in and around to the garage.

"You might as well come in. Let me take your coats," Laney said, making them feel more comfortable. "Follow me, you can wait in the great room." They followed her into the enormous room with a vaulted ceiling. Two couches rested in front of a walk in stone fireplace. A fire blazed within, warming the room. Floor to ceiling windows showed the setting sun in the distance. A table with chairs sat closer to the windows, while another two couches rested before what looked like a seventy-inch screen television. "Can I get you something to drink while you wait? I just made a pot of coffee."

"That would be nice thank you." Xavier waited till Laney left the room. "Are you all right? You're very quiet."

"My brother is going to walk through that door any minute, and I'm terrified he's going to hate me for deceiving him."

"He might be mad, but he won't hate you. Try and relax. If we thought you would be hurt, we would have never allowed you to do this." Dimitri squeezed her hand reassuringly.

The minutes passed and Madison started to pace. The waiting was killing her. Laney walked in carrying a tray laden with the coffee and some pastries. As she placed it on the table, a cry from the monitor on the end table had Laney moving to turn it down. Before she did, Matthew's voice came through talking to his daughter, "No, no, no, Amber, Daddy's here."

Madison would have dropped the cup Laney had just given her if Xavier hadn't been paying attention to her. Spilling some on both her and Xavier, she said, "I'm so sorry, I'm so clumsy." She grabbed for napkins to clean up the mess.

"No harm, are you okay? The coffee was hot."

Madison was confirming she was fine, when she heard her brother approaching.

"That's much better right, Amber? A clean dry heinie makes everything all better, right? Now, let's go see what Mommy and Asher are doing." He walked into the room with his two-year-old daughter in his arms. The little girl had a head of curly brunette hair. When she smiled, her new teeth showed. She looked over all the new people, locking her green eyes on Madison.

Realizing they weren't alone, he walked over by his wife, handing the baby to her. Laney introduced them. When Madison touched his hand, he released it as if he had been burned. Staring at her as if he was seeing a ghost. "Do I know you?"

Madison looked at her brother. He had grown a little taller, and no longer had his boyish looks. She was looking at a man. His shoulders were wider, and his hair had a touch of grey in it. He had grown into a very handsome man. A family man. "I think you might want to sit down before I tell you why we are here. You too, Laney."

They all sat and Madison told them who she was. She waited for them to take in what she had just said. Matthew stood and walked over to her. Touching her face, feeling her hair, and arms. Pulling her into his arms, all he asked was, "Why?"

"It's a long story, and the way your daughter is squirming I'm thinking it's dinner time?"

"Yes, it is. You know, she's named after you." His smile beamed with pride. "Stay, please stay and tell me everything." Matthew's pleading eyes turned to Laney.

Too shocked to give any other answer than yes, she nodded her head. "Why don't you go and get Sarah. I'll let Cook know we have three more guests for dinner." She rose with Amber in her arms, and went to the kitchen.

"How is Sarah doing?" Madison asked.

"She still has a long way to go, but she's taken the first steps. I blame her husband, that piece of shit. I did everything I could to convince her not to marry him, but she wouldn't listen. Said it had always been her dream to marry him." He inspected the two men sitting next to his sister.

"I don't think she'll have to worry about him anymore," Madison said, confirming what her brother suspected. "Matthew, these are my men, Dimitri Zilkin, and Xavier Legend." He shook hands with both men. A pleading look came over Madison's face. "I'm hoping you will walk me down the aisle when I marry Dimitri this August. Dimitri will be launching his final BDSM cruise ship in Dubai. We will be getting married before the launch."

Laney chose that moment to walk into the room. "A wedding in Dubai? How wonderful, congratulations. When?"

Matthew collected Madison. "Gentlemen, would you

please explain to my wife your plans. We will go collect Sarah for dinner." He smirked as they headed to the staircase.

"We'll be right back." Madison kissed both of them before she left.

Laney had left Amber and Asher with the nanny to eat. "So, you own a BDSM cruise line?" She was a petite woman. Her curves in all the right places. She had long blonde hair and doe like brown eyes. Dimitri confirmed her question. "After dinner if we have time, I'll have Matt show you our dungeon." Laney smiled at their shocked expressions.

Matthew knocked on Sarah's door. Opening it, he stuck his head in. "Sarah, dinner's ready. And we have some special people joining us tonight."

Matthew opened the door the rest of the way exposing Madison to her view. Madison would never had recognized her sister if she had seen her on the street. She was thinner then she remembered, and her hair was red. The eyes of green that resembled her own and Matthew's were clear.

It took Sarah a little bit to process what she was seeing. Tears filled her eyes as she ran into Madison's arms. Squeezing her so hard she was starting to hurt her. Through sobs Sarah asked her, "They said you were dead. Where have you been? What happened to you?"

"I've missed you both. Let's go eat, and we can catch up on everything after that."

The kids had been put to bed, and the adults were seated in front of the fire in the great room. During dinner the talk was light, but now came the time for truths. Sarah just started talking. "You were right about everything. I should have listened to you. After Brian got sick he was different. I was an intern." She looked at Madison. "I really fell in love with him. I really think he loved me too. The accident changed everything." Sarah put her water down. "We had a car accident. They prescribed a strong pain killer and the rest pretty much explains itself. I knew he was getting into dealing the heroin, and I didn't want anything to do with it. I had found out I was pregnant, and asked the doctor for help. I was getting sober, but not fast enough for the baby. I miscarried at twelve weeks. The depression got so bad and I knew with the drugs I wouldn't hurt anymore. At least for a little while. The day I watched a girl I had seen around overdose, was the day I went to rehab. Finally, something scared the shit out of me bad enough to really try. I didn't want to be her. I filed for divorce, and reached out to Matthew. I have a long way to go, but at least I have a chance." She faced Madison. "Now, it's your turn. How are you alive? Matthew searched for you. What happened to you after you spent the week at the Boxwoods? We all thought you were having fun."

Madison's eyes showed the heat of her anger. "He never told you what happened between us?" Sarah shook her head. "He raped and beat me repeatedly. Then threw a couple thousand dollars on the bed and left. It took me a week to even be able to get to the bathroom myself." Dimitri put a calming hand on her thigh, bringing her back. She bowed her head and composed herself.

When she picked her head up most of the anger was gone from her eyes. "There was a maid kind enough to help me. When I was able to leave, I took a bus to Los Angeles. I knew I could never go back to our house after what Mom did."

Sarah had tears in her eyes. "I'm so sorry." Looking to Matthew, then back to her. "We never knew. Mom told us the Boxwoods had you stay with them, but that one day you were just gone. They told us you ran away. That you weren't happy at home, and if you couldn't stay with them you were going to find a new home."

Matthew spoke up. "When you didn't come home after a week, Sarah called me at school. I called the police from college to put out a missing person's report. I don't think they even tried looking for you."

Hearing the sad truth, Madison needed a break. The rest of what she had to tell them could wait. "Well, the rest of my story is a long one and it's getting late. We should get back to the hotel. Can we come back tomorrow?" Madison asked.

"No you will not." Matthew stood up.

Madison had known it was too good to be true, that they would accept her. The defeated look that showed on her whole body, had her men up and moving into defensive mode. "What the fuck? You finally get your sister back, and you don't want to get to know her again. I really was wrong about you. Let's go, Madison." Dimitri took Madison's elbow leading her out.

"That's not what I meant." Matthew went to stop Madison, but Xavier and Dimitri blocked him. "I meant, we have a three-bedroom apartment attached to the house. I want you to stay. Here. Send your driver back to the hotel to get your things. Now that you're here I don't want you to leave."

Madison looked to Xavier and Dimitri; she didn't know what to do. With a nod from both of them she accepted. "Under one condition, and it's mandatory. I want both of you to promise me." Madison paused to get their promise. "Under no circumstance is Mom to know I'm alive. I never want to see that woman again. Or Dad for that matter. My name is Madison MacIntrye, soon to be Zilkin-Legend and we happily accept your invitation." Smiling she hugged her brother and sister.

The End

Enjoy this little snippet from the third and final book in the Midnight Oasis trilogy. *Dulcinea's Destiny*, *Midnight Oasis – Book Three*.

Maximillian Greco sat across the desk from Dulcinea Bedford. In her hand she held the final words from her mother. The envelope she held was already tear stained from when her mother had sealed it.

Reading the writing on the front, she recognized her mother's handwriting. 'It read, Dulcinea open this with Max, you will understand.'

"If you like I can leave the room till you're done. She asked that you remain here, but it's not necessary for me to be in the room," Maximillian asked her.

"No, it's okay, besides it's your office." A beautiful smiled appeared on her face. I know it's sad she's gone and I miss her. But she always had an angle and she could always make you smile." Max grinned back at her knowing the woman she spoke of. Dulcinea opened the envelope. The two getting comfortable in their chairs. She began to read.

Dear Sweet Girl,

If you are reading, this it means I've left this Earth. Don't cry for me, celebrate for me because you know I'm in a better place. I want you to live. Live like there's no tomorrow. I tried very hard to make our bad times as good as could be. I regret not getting to do the things we always dreamed of. I would have liked to have seen Paris and Italy, but I die happy holding onto those dreams for you.

Do you remember when you were twelve and we snuck into the movies theater? It was the first movie I took you to. Do you remember? I never laughed so hard at a sad movie. When you stood from your chair and yelled at me. "You named me after a whore? Why would you do that?" Do you remember what I said to you? "Because just like the heroine in my favorite movie, you are going to be very special to someone someday, and I hope they treasure you like Don Quixote."

You my beautiful Dulcinea are going to be able to do those things now. Max has two more envelopes for you. In one envelope are the dreams we dreamed. I might not have been able to give you much growing up, but you always knew you were loved. Now, I can give you what I couldn't when you were younger. Take what's in that envelope and live our dreams. Have fun, live for both of us.

The other envelope. Oh this is so hard. I prayed so hard on making this decision. But you have the right to know who your father really is. I pray you never meet him. **DO NOT GO LOOKING FOR HIM!** He is an evil man, and if you never meet him, he can never hurt you. Everything he touches turns to ash. If I could I would never have told you, but I don't want you to guess anymore. In the other envelope is your answer. But I beg you never open that envelope.

I will be watching over you always. Do not live your days in sorrow. I will always love you, sweet girl. God couldn't have sent a more perfect angel to me when he blessed me with you. Until we can be together again one day.

Love always and forever,

. . .

Mom

Max handed her the two envelopes. "Dulcinea, your mom was a very special woman and she loved you very much. Don't ever doubt that. She made sure you would be taken care of."

"Mr. Greco. Did you know my mother well?"

"Yes, I did. She was a good friend. Why do you ask?"

Dulcinea opened the one envelope, and looked inside. Her doe like brown eyes rounded like saucers. "How did she do this?"

"Every extra dollar she got, she invested. Right before she got sick she took out the insurance policy. Ironic right?" Max caught the comment quickly. "I'm sorry, that wasn't very sensitive of me."

"It's okay, you don't have to apologize to me." Looking back in the envelope she asked him. "What am I supposed to do with all of this money?"

"You could do the same thing and invest it. Or you could do what your mother wanted you to do! Have fun, like have an adventure. I have a friend who is launching a ship in Dubai in a few months. I could sponsor you?"

"Sponsor me for what?"

"It's a BDSM cruise. For the launch only, you need to be invited. If you're not invited, you could still go. You just need to be sponsored."

Dulcinea had heard the term BDSM, but really had never thought much about it. "What if I don't fit in?"

Maximillian looked her over from a Master's position. She was a very beautiful woman. Her breasts were big, and her waist was trim. She had great gripping hips, but what

305

drew a person to Dulcinea was her long dark hair and soulful dark brown eyes. "You'll fit in perfectly. That's why I'm suggesting it. I trust my instincts and they are telling me you need to come on this cruise. But if you don't want to participate, you can always wear the red band. It leaves Dubai in September if you're interested? You'll need to fill out paperwork, and have a medical exam."

"Do you think I should open the other envelope?" Dulcinea looked at Max.

"That's totally up to you."

Dulcinea sat in the chair holding the two envelopes, and her mother's letter. Finally, she looked at Max. A look of resolve on her face. "Okay, I'll do it. Where do I sign?" She grinned. "BDSM cruise here I come."

Jackson Blackhawk looked at his doctor and friend Peter Macalister. "You've got to be fucking kidding me? Check the results again. Somebody mixed up the results. It's not true."

"Jackson, I'm really sorry, but it's true."

"I just signed a three-year deal. What I'm I supposed to do? My life is fucking over."

"Don't be so dramatic. Your football career may be put on hold, but you're not dying. Grow a set. My suggestion is to enjoy your vacation."

"What are you talking about?"

"Dude, they still have to pay you. This was an injury on their field. Doing what they told you to do. You hit the injured reserve and you still get paid. Like I said, take a vacation. I'll give your coach my findings, so they'll have time to replace you. In the meantime, do you remember Dimitri Zilkin and Cameron Alexander from school?" Jackson shook his head yes. "They finally did what they always said they wanted to do. They have a BDSM cruise line. I happened to run into him and his fiancée. Super-hot chick. He sent me an invitation for the launch in Dubai. Why don't you come?"

"What and be the third wheel with you and Davina. I don't think so."

"No idiot. You'd have your own room. Go on line and check out the ship. It has a BDSM dungeon arena! Dude, this ship rocks. I would have to sponsor you though. So think about and let me know."

"What do you mean sponsor?"

Peter explained the terms for admission onto the *Black Diamond*. "Like I said think about it."

Jackson left the doctor's office. He got into his black Mercedes and sat there. No more football for a while? What the hell was he going to do? He started the car and pulled out. He knew he should go talk to his coach, but now wasn't the time. So, he detoured down to the docks. He parked the car, and got out. Leaning his six-foot five hard lean body on the hood, he watched the ships. Peter may have a point. He pulled out his phone and looked for the Midnight Oasis Cruise Line. The images that popped up on his phone had his dick hardening.

Jackson was a trained Master at the same BDSM dungeon as Peter and Davina. After sitting there for about a half hour he called Peter. "All right, what do I have to do?"

"Go on-line and print the contract and medical release forms. I'll do the rest. Dude, we're going on a freaking BDSM cruise. I hear there is an auction the first night, so make sure you bring your check book."

"Thanks, Peter, this really could have been a totally shitty day. I think a vacation is just what I need. Talk to you later."

He got back into his car heading back to the city. He was around the corner from his Park Avenue apartment. Sitting at the light he looked around. People were walking through the crosswalk. Couples were sitting at outdoor cafes'. He watched as a woman left a lawyer's office. Her tear stained cheeks and red nose told him she had received some bad news too.

He couldn't remember the last sub's name he had banged. That brought a whole new reality to the forefront of his brain. It had been a while since he had gotten laid. This cruise would fix that. He looked up and the light had changed. He began to roll forward, when all of the sudden she was standing right in front of his car. Her long dark hair reached her ass, and what an ass. Standing on the brakes, his car screeched to a stop.

Dulcinea was daydreaming as she left Max's office. She was going on an adventure. Even if she had no clue what she was getting into. She needed to do some research. She guessed that's what made it an adventure. When all of a sudden she realized she was in the middle of the crosswalk, and a car was coming right at her. She froze.

"Are you going to stand there all day? Or are you going to cross like everyone else." The driver yelled out the window.

She turned her face towards him. Her big brown eyes glowered at him. "In a hurry to get some place you don't want to be?" She questioned as she started walking to the other side.

She had a point. I really didn't want to go home alone. "Yeah, but I could change my plans if you're available?" He threw back at her.

She looked at the car, and the size of the man in it. "Nope, I'm good."

"I can make it worth your while?" Jackson was moving his car slowly through the intersection while cars behind him honked for him to move faster.

"You think I'm a whore?" she yelled back at him. Oh if

he ever knew my name he would think I was. She looked towards the heavens. "Thanks, Mom," she said out loud.

He got hard with the thought of those red lips wrapped around his cock. "No, that's not what I meant. I'm sorry. Would you like to get a drink?"

"Really I'm good. I have some place to be. Thanks for not running me over." She began moving down the sidewalk faster, and Jackson lost her in the crowd.

Well, I guess it's either the dungeon or my hand. He decided on the dungeon and headed that way.

The day of the launch was here. Dulcinea had flown over with Max and his friends. He had become like a surrogate dad to her. He had answered all her questions about the BDSM lifestyle. He had even taken her to his club so she could see firsthand what she could expect. And Dulcinea was very much looking forward to this new beginning.

They were standing in line to get their photos taken for their cabin keys and the computer system. "Have you ever been on a cruise?" Rayna asked her. Rayna was Max's "sub." At least that's what he called her. They had also become close. Max had Rayna take Dulcinea shopping for the cruise. Dulcinea didn't think she would wear half of what they bought, but Rayna disagreed.

"No. I've been looking forward to it since I agreed to come."

The security guard was handing her back all her credentials when she heard. "Are you going to stand there all day? Or are you going to let other people board?"

When Dulcinea heard the question, her head turned towards the familiar voice. Recognizing the voice, she asked Max to describe the man behind it. From the description, she knew it had to be the same man who had propositioned her in the street. She simply replied, "Nope, just leaving." She would not give him the satisfaction. With her shoulders held high, she turned and headed for the elevators with Max and Rayna.

The doors were closing when she heard. "You still owe me a drink."

Find out what happens to Dulcinea and Jackson in *Black Diamond, Midnight Oasis Book Three.*

Jill Shannon

Jill Shannon lives in a small town on Long Island with the love of her life and a very large dog. They've been together since high school where by the way, he received better grades on the stories she wrote for his classes. She has two professional daughters (one is an RN and the other is a Doctor of Psychology), a son-in-law, two very active granddaughters, and a beautiful grandson.

Jill has been reading romance novels since she was thirteen. The drama, suspense, and of course the love scenes all drew her in. Staying up till three in the morning just because she couldn't put the book down. Over the years Jill has expanded her genres of reading material. From historical, to paranormal, to sci-fi, and now BDSM, her dream was to write her own romance novel. She never thought it would happen with her busy life. However, Jill wanted to be able to do the same thing for others that her authors have done for her. For just a small time during your day, she would like you to be a part of the fantasy she creates.

You can email Jill at: jshannon7373@gmail.com
Follow her on Twitter: @JillCShannon
Or find her on Facebook
Visit her website.

Don't miss these exciting titles by Jill Shannon and Blushing Books!

Blushing Books

Blushing Books is the oldest eBook publisher on the web. We've been running websites that publish steamy romance and erotica since 1999, and we have been selling eBooks since 2003. We have free and promotional offerings that change weekly, so please do visit us at http://www.blushing-books.com/free.

Blushing Books Newsletter

Please join the Blushing Books newsletter
to receive updates & special promotional offers.
You can also join by using your mobile phone:
Just text BLUSHING to 22828.

Every month, one new sign up via text messaging will receive
a $25.00 Amazon gift card, so sign up today!